L'Orange Fire

Book One

Michael McLarnon

L'Orange Fire

By Michael McLarnon

For more about this author please visit http://www.lorangefire.com/

Michael McLarnon
188 Maddox Circle
Jackson, GA 30233

Ordering Information: Quantity sales. Special discounts are available on quantity purchases by corporations, associations, and others. For details, contact the publisher Seamróg Publishing at 340 S. Lemon Ave, Los Angeles, CA 91789

ISBN 978-1-942042-00-6

1. Main category—[Fiction]
2. Other category—[Mystery Thriller]

First Edition
Printed in the United States of America

Acknowledgements

This book took four years to write and countless people guided me along the way. I can't thank all of you individually, but rest assured, I do appreciate your help.

Any book is only as good as its editor, and I've been blessed to work with Debra L. Hartmann, editor nonpareil, at The Pro Book Editor. Not only did she intrepidly steer the ship that is this book, she gracefully, but forcefully, put up with my mule-headed résistance.

I would also like to thank Ann Fisher who set me on the Tao, or right path, early on, forcing me to learn to be a better writer. I'd also like to thank the dozens of people in my writing classes, especially Michael Jacobs and Angela van Schalkwyk, who have all helped me immeasurably and made the book so much better. Thanks you all.

I mustn't forget all the people who've read the early drafts and given me valuable feedback: Diane Snyder, Ellen Brewer, and Ralph Wilson, amongst them.

I'd like to thank Sherriff Gary Long of the Butts County Sherriff's Department, who opened his department to me and allowed me access to the wide range of experts in his department, including riding along with his deputies. A special thanks goes out to Sergeant Matt Garrison of the Butts County Sheriff's Department, who spent dozens of hours teaching me about all aspects of law enforcement, including what being tasered feels like (believe me, it's painful).

Andrea Baldwin, resident photography genius, for her selfless help in the photos for the book. Mary C. Simmons, graphic designer with Indie Author Publishing Services for her work with map and cover design. And the incomparable artist from Quebec City, Gilbert Plante, for the cover artwork.

Finally, I'd like to thank my wife and soul mate, Melinda McLarnon, who jogged alongside me through the marathon of writing this book.

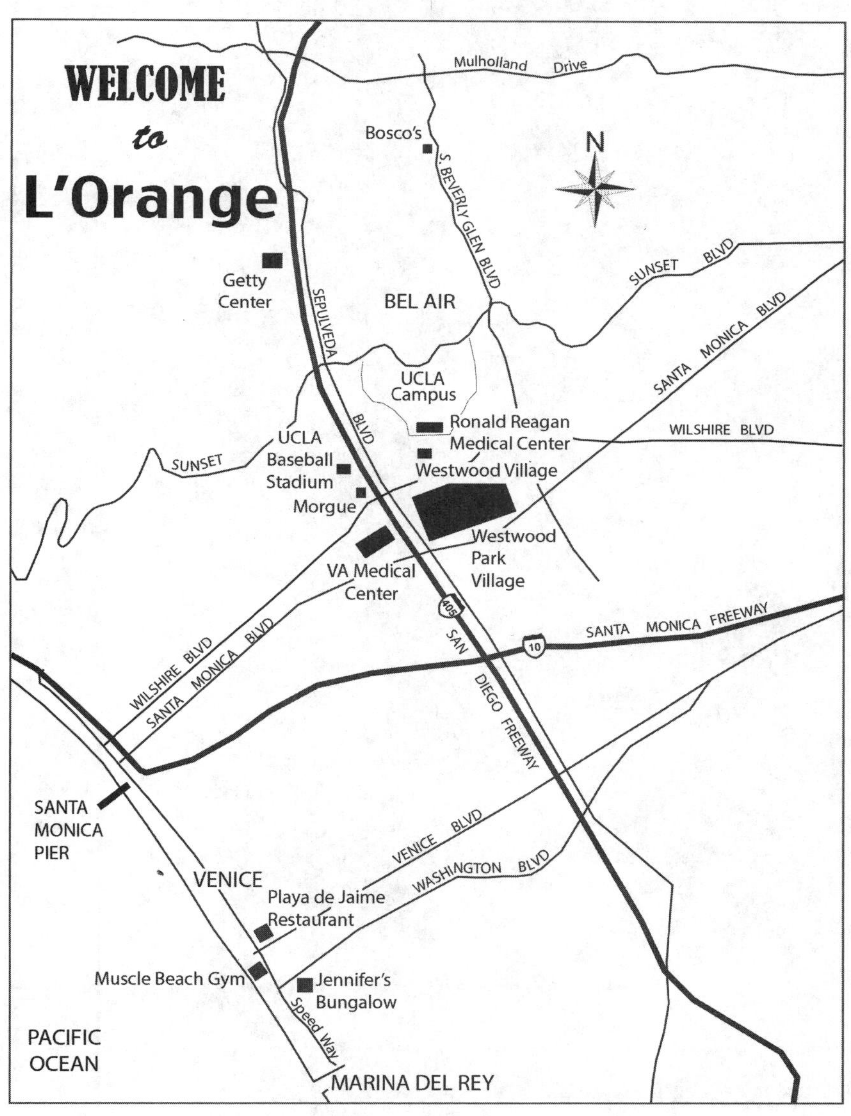
WELCOME
to
L'Orange
Mulholland Drive
Bosco's
N
S. BEVERLY GLEN BLVD
Getty Center
SEPULVEDA BLVD
BEL AIR
SUNSET BLVD
SANTA MONICA BLVD
UCLA Campus
Ronald Reagan Medical Center
WILSHIRE BLVD
UCLA Baseball Stadium
SUNSET
Westwood Village
Morgue
Westwood Park Village
VA Medical Center
405
SANTA MONICA FREEWAY
10
SAN DIEGO FREEWAY
WILSHIRE BLVD
SANTA MONICA BLVD
SANTA MONICA PIER
VENICE BLVD
WASHINGTON BLVD
VENICE
Playa de Jaime Restaurant
Muscle Beach Gym
Jennifer's Bungalow
Speed Way
PACIFIC OCEAN
MARINA DEL REY

Chapter 1

There's a story behind every dead body; Jennifer thought she'd heard them all.

She gazed down through the lens of her bio-hazard mask. Cupped in her red-gloved hands was a blood-soaked brain—the organ that makes us human—a mass of neurons that once teemed with dreams, and hopes, and fears. Like cooked cauliflower, it was fragile, so easily destroyed.

A searing bolt of pain shot down her neck, jerking her head backwards. She slid the cerebrum, which she'd removed mere moments before from the cadaver lying below her, into a basin of embalming solution. She waited for the spasm to end, then scrunched her muscles. A hot and clammy surge washed over her body, as if she were in a steam sauna. It was as though forty-five pound weights hung from her eyelids—she struggled to keep them open. It felt as if burning sand filled her eyes; the bio-hazard mask prevented her from rubbing them—a maddening feeling. Images blurred and danced and took on a dream-like quality. She became dizzy. She swayed and her legs wobbled. She felt disembodied. The overhead autopsy-room lights glinted off the observation window across the room, creating a mirror-like effect—her jaw dropped open at the surreal images reflected there.

Three ignoble creatures hunched over the dead body, each peering down with uncommon malignity from their unblinking glass eyes. Their lovely tinted azure bodies were covered in ghastly splotches of dried blood, bone speckle, and gore. Dull, coal-colored faces resembled aardvarks with metallic, matte-black snouts. Bulbous heads seemed too large for their long, blue bodies which swayed as if caught in a tidal current. Red, rubbery hands clutched honed cutting instruments. Their mechanical-sounding breathing consisted of first a metallic click, then a sudden rush of air, rasping, machine-like, and then another click closing the airway. At intervals, they emitted muffled murmurs to each other. A naked light beat down and cast a raffish pall over the waxy cadaver they encircled—an alabaster corpse, bloated and swollen, resembling a beached beluga whale.

"Doctor Singh?" The voice seemed to come from inside her head, yet at the same time somehow distant.

The largest of the three creatures looked at itself reflected in the observation window. Light glinted off its lens-like eye, making it appear opaque and white, hiding some vague, nameless horror. The dead, glass eyes were the most frightening, the most appalling, parts of the creature; if eyes are the windows to the soul, then this creature surely lacked one.

"Doctor Singh."

There was that voice again. A woman's voice. A Mexican lilt.

The voice came through her earbud again. Loud. Persistent. "Earth to Doctor Jennifer Singh!"

Jennifer broke out of her reverie with a start, skin covered in cold sweat beneath her Level B Graphene 500 Hazmat suit. The swirling mists in her mind cleared, familiar surroundings came back into focus, reflections in the window were no longer disturbing. With glove-covered hands, she moved the bio-hazard mask around on her face attempting to get the circulation going and ease her burning eyes.

Jennifer mumbled into the mask. "Sorry, Aída. I must have zoned out."

Aída Santibáñez and Carlos Gómez, Jennifer's autopsy assistants, peered up at the much taller doctor through their own masks.

"I was daydreaming myself," Carlos said. "I was surprised you agreed to stay late and do this case."

"How can you say no to the Russians?" Aída said.

"*Nyet*." Jennifer chuckled. "That's how."

Her assistants laughed; the muffling of the masks made the sound distant and sinister. Jennifer put her hands on her hips, stretched her back, and yawned and moaned at the same time.

Jennifer looked down at the corpse. Unseeing eyes with a filmy-white coating stared back. She thought it sad: a person dies a gruesome, painful death, then ends up lying on a cold slab being stared at, probed, and hacked open by strangers in alien-looking outfits. Even worse, she didn't know the name of the deceased. This cadaver—*this man*, Jennifer reminded herself—had been discovered in a desolate part of the Santa Monica Mountains without ID, his microchip gouged out of his arm, and the tips of his fingers snipped off at the joints. The only distinguishing mark was a tattoo on the right side of his neck—a Russian Orthodox cross: an upright beam intersected by three horizontal cross beams, the middle one the longest, and the bottom beam slanted downward from left to right. The dead soul's body was defunct.

She wondered who he was. He must have had a family, loved ones. They'd be worried about him. How will we ever be able to contact them? Let them know what happened? Give them closure?

She focused her mind on the present, decided to save the philosophizing for when she had a cold beer in her hand. For now, she needed this seemingly endless day to be over.

Cause of death determined—mission accomplished.

Jennifer looked back across the stainless steel autopsy table to her assistants. "That's it, guys. Let's close up shop."

Carlos and Aída breathed sighs of relief. Carlos covered the cadaver with a white sheet, then the women helped him slide the body to a gurney. Carlos wheeled the corpse out of the room and into the refrigerated storage area which took up the entire back of the morgue. Aída gathered the instruments to start the sterilization process.

Because of the bulky bio-hazard suit, Jennifer moved like an astronaut walking on the moon as she waddled to the metal desk alongside one wall. Spent, she plopped down on a metal stool and said, "Open active case file." The monitor mounted on the wall above the desk came alive, displaying the ongoing findings from the current case.

She scrolled down, using hand gestures, and reviewed the data. "Tatsu. Record," she said.

A masculine-sounding voice issued from the ceiling. "Recording."

"Cause of death: gunshot wound, right temple. Stippling pattern and lack of charring suggest use of a silencer. Tatsu. End recording."

"End recording," the mechanical voice said.

Jennifer looked around the room. "Carlos, what caliber was the bullet?"

Carlos was nowhere in sight, but his voice sounded crisp in her earbuds. "I measured nine millimeters, Doctor."

"Thanks." Jennifer reviewed data on the monitor as she dictated. "Tatsu. Record. Nine millimeter hollow-point bullet. Bilateral ligature marks on the wrists and ankles caused by piano wire. Five displaced fractures of the right metacarpals, upper extremity. Multiple cigarette burns to the thorax. Distal phalanges amputated on both upper extremities. Secondary findings: antemortem torture. Tatsu. End recording."

The digital recording signed off.

"Gruesome way to finish the day," Aida said as she placed the used autopsy instruments inside the autoclave. "Those broken fingers are going to give me nightmares."

"No shit." Jennifer stood up. "Now it's time to break the news to the Russian."

"Then the fun begins." Aida turned toward Jennifer and shuffled her feet, her red-gloved hands on her swaying hips.

Jennifer turned to watch her assistant and smiled. "What are you doing?"

"The samba." Aída's laugh rang through Jennifer's earbud. "Can't you tell?"

Jennifer laughed. "Coulda fooled me." She groaned as she began walking to the door. "After I'm done with the Russian, I'll meet you in the locker room." Her legs were so tired they seemed to have a mind of their own as she staggered out of the autopsy room and into the prep area. She pulled the Israeli-made re-breather mask off her face, grateful to take in the unfiltered air. Thanks to nanocomposite materials and graphene filters, the mask weighed less than two-hundred grams, but after ten hours it was as if she'd removed a millstone, leaving her head feeling as light as air. She rubbed her tense neck and ran her fingers through her lifeless hair.

Next, she pulled off the graphene-lined, cut-resistant, red surgical gloves, wadded them up, and threw them across the room and into the sink, saying, "She shoots, she scores." After stripping off the blue bio-hazard suit, she tossed it into a hamper with equal accuracy. She leaned back against one of the stainless steel sinks and released the air pressure of the TED hose; the compression stockings dropped to the floor. She leaned over to pick them up, but her back locked up in pain, and she left them for the clean-up crew.

She looked back into the autopsy room. Her reflection in the window stared back and grimaced, wondering who the hell that person looking back at her was. Her red hair was dull and matted down, her eyes bloodshot and lifeless, her face had red stripes where the mask sat, her cheeks were the pallor of a corpse.

Jennifer turned away and left the autopsy suite wearing the same red scrubs and scuffed tennis shoes—now sweaty and smelly—she'd donned that morning. Her legs were numb. She'd been standing hunched over all day, so she shuffled, stiff-legged, down the deserted corridor to her office. Using the last of her strength to push open the door to the wing of the building housing the medical examiner's private offices, she trudged down the hall to her private kingdom, the only office with the lights still on.

When she entered the room, a darkly handsome, middle-aged Russian man wearing a fashionable navy suit with a red tie matching the color of the Russian Federation flag stood up to greet her.

He gave a formal half-bow and extended his hand. "Thank you so much for doing this case for me." He spoke with a generic news-anchor accent. "Your administrator tells me you are...drowning."

"Perhaps he said swamped." Jennifer shook hands, then collapsed into her ergonomic office chair. "We have more work than we can handle." She gestured across her glass and steel desk. "Have a seat, Detective...?"

"Porfiry." The Russian took a seat facing her.

Jennifer pushed stacks of papers needing her attention to the side in order to see the detective. As she settled into her chair, the detective glanced around the room at the Lucite-framed photos hanging on the walls.

He gazed at her through heavily lashed eyes. "I have been admiring your photos. You take them?"

The walls of the windowless office were covered in celestial color photos and he pointed to one: a wispy, spiral-like structure of countless red and blue stars against an inky background. "That's my favorite. Isn't it the Andromeda Galaxy?"

Jennifer leaned back in her leather chair and rubbed her eyes. "It *is* a spiral galaxy, but it's known as M66." She stifled a yawn. "Sorry. It's late. You were interested in the cause of death of the Russian John Doe?"

Porfiry nodded. "He was a courier, transporting stolen goods out of Russia. I was tracking him to discover who his contact was and lost him in Las Vegas."

"He died of a gunshot wound to the head and—"

"I was aware of that. Could you be more specific, Doctor?"

"Nine millimeter. Hollow-point. Large, gaping, and irregular entrance wound. No exit wound. Point blank range to the temple. Probably used a silencer."

The Russian's eyes narrowed. "Would you mind transferring the autopsy results to my Virtual Reality contacts? I'd like to see the photos of the bullet."

Jennifer asked her computer to pull up the autopsy file of the Russian John Doe, then, using hand gestures in front of the monitor, she swiped the information to the detective's icon, which caused his brown eyes to glow blood red as his VR contact lenses lit up. A cold shiver ran down Jennifer's spine. His red eyes looked menacing—which is probably why the Russian security services chose the color.

The detective frowned, drawing his brows together as he moved his fingers on his wrist OmniPhone. Jennifer watched on her monitor as he manipulated the holographic image of the bullet.

"*Blya*!" he swore as his contacts turned transparent again. "That's the 7H21-HP."

"I thought HP made printers," Jennifer said with an impish smile.

He let out a snort. "The 7H21-HP is a Russian nine-millimeter bullet modified to be hollow point and packed to deliver subsonic muzzle velocity. It's designed for the MP-443 Grach pistol."

Jennifer shrugged. "I guess I should be impressed that you know the type of gun by looking at the discharged projectile."

"Did the entrance wound look jagged, as if from a small-bore shotgun?"

Jennifer nodded.

The Russian gave a flicker of a smile. "I've seen this particular type of bullet many times before. It mushrooms easily when it hits the skull. Any evidence of torture?"

"The wrists and ankles had been tied with thin wire, what we call piano wire. He had a number of broken fingers—"

"I was afraid of that. Were all the fingers broken?"

"All five on the right hand."

The Russian nodded, a sullen look on his face. "They got what they were looking for, the killers. They would have broken all his fingers and toes if necessary. They did this man a favor by providing a quick, painless death."

"There were also cigarette burns to the chest," Jennifer said.

The detective did a double take and leaned forward, putting his elbows on the desk. "Cigarette burns? That's unexpected." He scratched his chin with one hand as he turned his VR contacts back on and his eyes glowed red. "Would you mind sending me the photos of the burn marks, Doctor?"

Jennifer pulled the photos up on her screen and sent them to the detective's VR contacts.

The Russian nodded as he viewed the images. "Very uncharacteristic." He had a sour look on his face when he turned off his contacts.

Jennifer rubbed her eyes, then patted her cheeks trying to stay awake; she definitely was going to need a boost to make it through the night.

"You said killers." She made air quotations around the word killers. "What makes you think there was more than one?"

"They always work in teams of two."

Jennifer's mind drifted. She had solved the "how." Now it was the detective's job to find the "who." And the "why." She tried to hold it back, but gave in and yawned widely. "They? They who?"

"The Bratva."

Jennifer sat up, no longer sleepy. The Russian *Mafiya*? This spelled trouble. With the Bratva involved, there never was only *one* murder. Southern California had been lucky; it had been years since the morgue handled a case involving the Bratva. It looked like their luck had just run out. The last thing they needed now was another bloodbath.

The detective's voice snapped her out of her ruminations. "The broken fingers and the distinctive hollow-point bullet to the head, that's the signature of a branch of the Bratva from the Caucasus Mountains of Russia."

"Why would the killer, or killers, use such a characteristic method of murder? It would make them easier to catch."

"They use this signature method in order to get paid by their employers. And they kill this way as a warning to people who might cross their paths. It's quite effective." The detective paused and shook his head. "But the cigarette burns…not something you see from this group. Sloppy. Very unprofessional."

"The Caucasus Mountains. The Chechens are here in L'Orange?"

"You know your geography. Maybe Chechen. The ethnic alliances in that part of my country are in a state of constant flux. What is important is that all those groups are very dangerous and well-funded. And they are ultra-secretive; we haven't had any luck infiltrating their upper echelon."

Jennifer swiped her hands in front of the monitor, logging out of the case file, then looked over at the detective. "Last time the *Mafiya* had their turf war here, a lot of innocent bystanders were killed."

"Is anyone truly innocent, Doctor? We're all sinners, aren't we?"

"Buddhists don't believe in sin."

"I didn't know that." He paused and studied the doctor. "With your name, I should have known you'd be Buddhist. Or Hindu."

Jennifer narrowed her eyes and shot him a lopsided smile. "Names can be deceiving, Detective."

"Touché," he said, cocking his head. "To answer your earlier concern, the deceased was probably killed in Las Vegas. His body was dumped just across the state line. So there's no reason to believe the Bratva are in Los Angeles."

"I take it the Las Vegas police are handling the investigation?"

"In conjunction with the FBI and my office."

"I'll make sure the autopsy results get forwarded to the correct parties." She put her hand over her mouth to hide a yawn. "For our records, and so we can contact his next of kin, would you mind telling us the deceased's name? His microchip was gouged out of his arm after he was killed."

The detective gave a little laugh. "The name is unimportant. Even if you had his microchip, it undoubtedly would have been altered. Did you bring a tissue sample? I'll send it to the FSB lab in Moscow for DNA testing."

"Now it's my turn to say *blya*. I'll have one of my assistants get right on it."

The Russian sat back and ran his fingers through his thick, black hair. He made eye contact, his dark eyes dreamy, expressive. "You look hungry, Doctor." His voice had dropped an octave and was melodious. "Would you be available for dinner? We could go dancing afterward." He paused and arched his brows. "I'm an accomplished dancer."

The detective was handsome, but something about him made her skin crawl. Perhaps it was the image of him with the blood-red contacts. She struggled to remain cordial. "I have plans for this evening." She stood without waiting for a reply and shook his hand. "You can wait up front. I'll have the sample brought to you."

Jennifer shuffled back to the prep area and stopped in front of the entrance to the women's locker room. She stretched her sore back, shouldered the door open, and slumped against the frame. Her eyes fluttered, then closed; a kaleidoscope of dead bodies, lifeless eyes, and assorted body parts raced by in a rapid-fire montage. After an endless blur of autopsies, her energy was dim, flickering. She needed a spark to reanimate herself.

The Getty Center ball!

Donny Bosco!

Her eyes popped open and she smiled, the soreness forgotten. The anticipation of the coming evening was like throwing gasoline on an open fire, the flames of energy—and of passion—roared.

She pushed off from the door frame and strode into the locker room. Her feet slipped—the ancient tiles of the locker room floor were so slick her sneakers couldn't get good traction. She slowed, mincing her steps as if walking on ice.

She didn't want to go sprawling.

Not tonight!

Chapter 2

The adrenaline rush from thinking about the upcoming evening passed before Jennifer was halfway to her locker. Shuffling to the sinks, she splashed cold water on her face, trying both to wake herself up and wash the gritty feeling out of her eyes. Drying her face, she looked in the mirror, wondering who the haggard woman peering back at her was. The long days on her feet were taking their toll.

The locker room door creaked open. Too exhausted to turn, she let out a deep breath as the squeaking of rubber-soled shoes on worn tile moved her way.

"*¿Qué pasa*, Doc?" It was Aída. "Finished with the detective?"

"*Da*," Jennifer said with a laugh. She continued to stare at the ashen-skinned woman in the mirror. "I look like a train wreck." She shook her head at her reflected image. "Can you believe that guy had the audacity to hit on me?"

Aída let out a snort. "Just because those Russians have all the money in the world, they think they can buy anything."

Jennifer shrugged. "I didn't get that impression. He seemed...lonely."

"In that case, he should hire a Licensed Sexual Companion. Was he cute?"

Jennifer nodded. "Oh yeah! But when he asked me to dinner, all I could think of is what he looked like with those glowing-red VR contacts, like a blood-thirsty zombie rapist."

"The Russian detectives look scary in those contacts," Aída said. "Speaking of scary, wanna guess how many cases we did today?"

Jennifer watched as the stranger in the mirror shook her head. "*No me digas, chica*. It would just make me livid."

"All right, I won't tell you." Aída changed her accent and spoke with an exaggerated Mexican sing-song. "But it rhymes with dirty-sex. Which is what's on your agenda tonight." She goosed her boss. "Am I right?"

A surge of excitement flashed through Jennifer's body; her skin tingled, turned hot, ready to ignite and her face flushed. She fought a smile, then gave in. In the mirror, the glaze covering her cat-green eyes cleared and her cheeks reddened.

Aída moved into the mirror and arched her eyebrows while making suggestive movements with her hips. "It also rhymes with flirty-kicks."

"Or girthy-dicks," Jennifer said with a laugh. Then her spirits fell and she frowned. "Thirty-six?" The surge of excitement over the coming ball passed when she thought about the situation at the morgue—they were handling way more cases than they should. And cutting corners on top of that. "You've gotta be kidding me? That's three…no, four times more than we should be doing in a day. I'd raise hell with…with somebody," her shoulders slumped, "but I'm too exhausted."

Jennifer turned away from the mirror and half-perched on the edge of the counter, lowering herself to make better eye contact with her much shorter assistant.

Aída looked as exhausted as Jennifer felt. Her chocolate-colored eyes, which matched her skin, were glazed. Her rounded mestizo face sported a mischievous grin. In her early forties, feminine curves were hidden by stained red scrubs and an advancing layer of adipose tissue. Her hair was so black it looked blue.

"At least you have something to look forward to tonight," Aída said. "Me? I have to go home and work my *culo* off baking burritos and carting *cervezas* to my husband and his *primos* while *they* watch a boring basketball game."

Jennifer laughed. "That sounds like fun to me."

Aída had a puzzled look on her face. "Carting cervezas all night?"

"No. Having you cart me beers while I watch the Clippers with the guys."

"Ha, ha," Aída said with a mocking laugh. "Have you talked to *el jefe*? Any news on when the other MEs will be coming back?"

"I haven't seen Dutch all day."

Aída had a look of concern on her face. “I hate to tell you this, but bodies are stacked up in the fridge. If we don’t get help soon, I bet he’s planning to have that autopsy robot he’s been working on take our places.”

Jennifer slumped down and nodded. “You know what’s sad? I’m sure he could program a robot to have more compassion for the deceased than I have right now.” She leaned forward, put her elbows on her thighs, and propped her head up with her hands. “When I first started medical school, I had these great ambitions: find the cure for cancer, or AIDS, or obesity… maybe rid the planet of flatulence.” She laughed in spite of herself. “As things would have it, I don’t appear destined to make any great earth-shattering difference. But at least I still had some degree of empathy for the poor souls who sojourn here. Since we’ve been so dreadfully understaffed, hell, even that’s gone up in smoke, all that remains are ashes.” She looked down and shook her head. “Robots doing autopsies? That’s exactly what I feel like—working by rote, a machine devoid of feelings. I take that back, I do have emotions. I’m fed up and I’m pissed,” she let out a sarcastic laugh, “and I need a drink.” Jennifer caught Aída’s eye and sighed. “What difference does it make? The cadavers keep piling up.”

“Look on the bright side,” Aída said. “At least we’re picking up a boat-load of comp time. When we’re fully staffed, I’m taking off an entire month or two. I’m gonna lie in bed the whole time and have my hubby bring *me* cervezas.”

Jennifer rubbed her face, then held up her head—which felt like it weighed one hundred pounds—with her hands. She let out an exhausted breath. “¡*Puta madre*! I told myself I’d never let this happen. The tragicomic end of an individual’s existence has become one interminable, monotonous, and cold-blooded chore. Seeing the ignominious end to someone’s life journey; on a gelid steel table; being peered at by anonymous, overworked, and insensate strangers; being carved open as if on an assembly line—this place has become an abattoir factory.”

Aída gave Jennifer a long hug. “Mind repeating that in English?”

The physical contact of being held by Aída was reassuring. Calming. Jennifer was always amazed at the power of human touch—so underrated in the sterile medical world where the only contact a patient received was through latex-gloved hands, sharp needles, or cold stethoscopes. She put an arm around Aída’s waist and smiled, thinking about Donny and the physical contact she had to look forward to later in the evening.

The contact felt so good she forgot she hadn’t answered Aída’s question. “I’m upset because I’ve lost sight of the fact that each person we examine was an actual living person, with hopes and dreams and loved ones. I promised myself I'd never become callous and jaded. And now it seems to be happening. Like the California Maglev train, speeding along, and there's nothing I can do to stop it."

Aída stepped back but still kept one hand on Jennifer's arm and made eye contact. "We've all been feeling the same way. With just you and Doctor Tulp working, we can't keep up. Seeing those bodies lying on top of each other—"

"It's dehumanizing," Jennifer said.

Aída grimaced, her body shook. "The last few nights I've had the same nightmare. All those dead people stacked in the fridge jump up and chase me. Their eyes cloudy and white. I'm running as fast as I can to escape, but I'm not moving. It's frustrating, like being on a treadmill."

Jennifer chuckled and arched her eyebrows. "Running on a treadmill, under the right circumstances, can be quite pleasant."

"Well, I'm not as into exercising as you are, Doc." Aída turned and walked to the bathroom, talking over her shoulder. "My bladder's about to burst. After I'm done helping Carlos clean up, I'll be back to do your makeup." She opened one of the stall doors and looked back. "Just as I promised."

Jennifer raised her voice to be heard across the room. "You don't have to stay." There was no response. "I can get ready myself." Aída disappeared into the stall; Jennifer yelled after her. "I *do* know how to put on makeup. You know that? Right?"

The only reply was the sound of the metal door closing.

Jennifer sat on the counter unable to muster the energy to move. A succession of ten and twelve hour days at the morgue had drained her body. And her psyche. As tempting as going home and crashing on the sofa seemed, tonight was going to be special. She just didn't know how she was going to find the energy to make it through the night. Her shrink, the famous Dr. Gütfeldt, used cognitive/behavioral hypnotherapy on her enough she thought she could probably do it herself.

Why not give it a try?

She closed her eyes, breathed slowly and deeply, and let her muscles relax and her mind drift.

She was with Donny Bosco at the Getty Center, cuddled in his arms, wrapped in his masculine aroma. Glittering chandeliers created prisms of light off her jeweled pendant and bracelet. She saw herself lifting a flute of heavenly, bubbly, pink champagne. She sipped, the effervescence fizzing in her head. The A-listers of L'Orange streamed by, approaching and greeting Donny and her by name, effusive in complimenting the stunning couple. She turned, gazed up into Donny's blue eyes, and melted in the heat of his passion. He was tall and muscular and dashing in his white silk tuxedo and Kelly Green tartan bowtie. His air of confidence was palpable—an animal magnetism. She could feel that he was attracted to her as much as she was to him. She'd let the sexual tension build between them, which was unusual for her, but enjoyable. Tonight all that sexual tension would be blown away. Her skin tingled, her insides sizzled, she smiled—content, the decision made. It had never been in dispute.

Jennifer opened her eyes, let her body cool and mind clear while she regained her bearings. The room was empty. She'd put herself into such a deep trace that Aída walked right past her unnoticed.

Humming a waltz, Jennifer jumped off the counter and danced her way between the wooden wardrobes, stopping at the far corner—her little kingdom. A few months after joining the medical examiner's office, she sweet-talked Dutch, the morgue administrator, into knocking out the adjoining walls of three contiguous lockers to make one wide space.

She loved the feel of real wood on her fingers and the aroma of red oak as she opened the worn door of her locker, grateful the county hadn't trashed these ancient units when the morgue moved from its old site downtown to its current location on the Los Angeles VA Medical Center property. She bent slightly to peer in—the locker stood a tad under six feet tall—and pulled a bottle of Jose Cuervo Añejo and a shot glass off the top shelf. She poured a shot; the tequila sparkled in the overhead LED lights like a perfectly cut diamond. She hesitated. She'd hardly drank since the crisis at the morgue began over a month ago, but tonight was going to be a special occasion. With the shot glass in one hand, she rubbed her eyes with the other while stifling another yawn. She tossed the drink back, winced from the bitter-smoky taste, and smiled as the warm sensation moved downward from her throat to her stomach.

Just what the doctor ordered.

She was about to fall asleep and decided there was no reason not to take advantage of the wonders of modern psychopharmacology. Rustling around in the back of one of the shelves, she found a brown, unmarked medicine bottle and poured a handful of Dexedrine tablets into her palm. She put one in her mouth, paused for a second—*hopefully it would be a really long night*—then popped a second, and washed them down with another shot of tequila. She smiled, content. From a metal jar about the size of a D-sized battery, she rolled herself a flaca—a pencil-thin joint. Lolling back in one of her recliners and letting the supple leather caress her body, she put her feet up on her other recliner. She lit up and took a toke. The cares of the day drifted away in a cloud of smoke.

The night seemed even more inviting.

She tuned the Mega-Def TV installed in the back of her locker to a Zen music channel and closed her eyes. The music was unobtrusive and without form; she let her mind wander.

Donny.

Donny Bosco.

If he were a Greek god, which one would he be?

Zeus? No, too many lovers. And who wants to have sex with a swan?

Apollo? Nice physique, but unhappy in love.

Adonis? Drop-dead gorgeous. Faithful to his only true love. Why not? Donny. My Adonis.

A mellow buzz came over her as she finished the flaca. She smiled and opened her eyes. Right before her, hanging inside the locker, was the gown she'd purchased at an haute couture consignment boutique earlier in the week, just for this event. A designer gown. Luxurious crème fraiche color, the fabric a subtle stretch taffeta, provocatively cut décolletage, one shouldered, ruche, and full-length. It hugged her hips and thighs creating what the saleswoman called a mermaid silhouette. She never considered herself a "girly-girl," but she grinned as she remembered trying on the gown, and when she saw herself in the dressing room mirror—a Cinderella moment—how she felt beautiful and desirable.

Enough daydreaming. Time to get ready.

The chemical cocktail was taking effect. She forced herself up from the recliner and pulled off the red scrubs covered in splotches of dried blood and sweat. She donned her terry cloth robe, took her toiletry bag, and made her way to the shower room.

She could have used the doctor's locker room with its country club ambiance and plush showers, however, she was the only female medical examiner and didn't feel comfortable showering and dressing with the male doctors. She preferred the women's locker rooms and didn't mind sharing space with the autopsy assistants and technicians. Usually the random conversations and laughter masked the macabre reality that, mere feet away, hundreds of dead bodies lay in their refrigerated tombs. Tonight it was quiet, eerie, and spooky. The marijuana only heightened the creepy feeling. The tiny hairs on her back stood up.

Inside the shower room, she said, “Shower One. One hundred-ten degrees.” She hung her robe up and listened. She pulled the curtain back; the water hadn’t come on. She pounded the digital control panel twice with the back of her fist. “Piece of shit.” The metal face rattled, but the display remained dead. “L’Orange County,” she pounded the display once more to no effect, “more like La Limón.”

She stuck her head in the stall and manually turned on the shower. The water became scalding in seconds, causing the air in the confined space to become moist and foggy. Childhood memories of watching the nasty pea-soup fog enveloping the Golden Gate Bridge flooded back. She shivered even though the air was as hot as a sauna. Deciding it was time to forget about the past and focus on the future, she looked forward to the evening and smiled, thinking it could be the beginning of a whole new life.

She stood under the nozzle and let the steaming water run down her body. The mellow buzz from the combination of marijuana, tequila, and amphetamines, mixed with the piping hot water, unwound her sore muscles. Since the locker room was empty, she thought she might as well take advantage of the situation. She made up a silly melody with a rap beat on the fly and sang off key.

> “Double, double toil and trouble;
>
> Fiery water and soapy bubble;
>
> Wash away the day’s blood, sweat, and tears.
>
> Tonight my Prince Charming’s gonna squirm,
>
> My gown’s sure to make him good and firm.”

She stuck her head under the nozzle, laughed, and hoped nobody heard that song. Pouring a handful of aromatherapy bath salts on the shower floor, she took a deep breath, letting the complex desert scents relax her. The foul odors of the autopsy room became a distant memory.

After the shower, she dried her hair in front of one of the mirrors. She’d been tall and gangling growing up, which still affected her body image. Now, she couldn’t help but smile as she looked at herself. She was trim, toned, and muscular. Curvy in all the spots guys seemed to like, and all the spots she wished she’d had growing up. In college, she began exercising obsessively, spending countless hours lifting weights and running on the beach. Reluctantly, she’d even undergone a bit of plastic surgery—well maybe more than a bit—at the insistence of an old flame who happened to be a plastic surgeon.

She wasn't completely comfortable with her body, but as she looked at herself, she thought it wasn't too shabby for a woman in her thirties. If those snooty high school cheerleaders could see the gangling nerd now! Her face dropped, as did her high spirits as she pondered why she was concerned about what those little bitches thought? She chuckled to herself. Dr. Goodfeel would be pleased to see she hadn't made any progress on what he called her "unresolved adolescent insecurities."

Jennifer fluffed her hair—her favorite feature—bringing about the warm euphoria she'd been feeling seconds before. She'd gone to the salon earlier in the week and had it styled and dyed. She even splurged on foils, but cringed when she thought about how much she'd spent. She shook off the guilty thought and appreciated the resulting dark-copper color crackling with firehouse-red highlights. Her hair's fiery color matched her personality—at least her idealized version of her personality. She couldn't wait to see the expression on Donny's face when he caught sight of her.

The Dexedrine and tequila had kicked in and she rode the warm buzz. She leaned forward and smiled at herself in the mirror.

It was going to be a night to remember.

Chapter 3

Jennifer padded to her locker. She'd just settled into her chair and was reaching for the remote when there was an abrupt knock on the door. Almost simultaneously, the locker room door opened and a deep masculine voice boomed in.

"Jennifer?"

It was Dutch Rolstoel. Not only was he the morgue administrator, but her best friend and drinking buddy. And the only other unmarried person in the department.

Technically, Dutch wasn't her boss. The medical examiners were employed by the UCLA Medical School under contract with the county. However, Jennifer quickly learned to treat him as such, because Dutch controlled the autopsy schedule and assigned the assistants. That gave him the power to make a medical examiner's life as easy or as difficult as he chose. After butting heads with him when she first started, she decided it would be best to get Dutch on her side. They quickly became friends when she realized he was down-to-earth, nonjudgmental, didn't act like a boss, and most importantly, didn't try to seduce her. Dutch treated her like the sibling Jennifer wished she had growing up.

"What is it?" Jennifer yelled.

"I need you a second."

She sighed. "Come on back. I'm too tired to get up."

"Incoming," he yelled.

Jennifer pulled the robe closer around her body and tightened the sash as the quiet hum of an electric motor and the squishy sound of a wheelchair's rubber tires on the damp tile floor moved closer. Dutch was the victim of a random bullet that cut him down while he was waiting for his high school bus. The bullet lodged in the lumbar region of his spine causing total loss of muscle control and sensation below his navel. Stem cell therapy was moderately successful, giving him control of his bladder and bowels, but he never regained full muscle control of his legs. He didn't let that slow him down. He worked hard and become the director of the morgue. The Philosopher-King is how Jennifer thought of him, and the L'Orange County morgue is his Callipolis.

The motorized wheelchair appeared around the corner of the lockers driven by a muscular man clad all in black. Jennifer looked over and gave him a smile.

Dutch had classic Nordic features: fair skin, high cheekbones, and blue, expressive eyes. His bald head shone in the overhead lights. Sporting a trimmed salt-and-pepper goatee, he wore his standard garb for work: black military style pants which covered his atrophied legs and were tucked into black combat boots, and his tight black t-shirt sleeves barely contained his muscular shoulders. Because of all the athletic events in which he competed, his upper body was like that of a body builder's, and he wasn't shy about showing it off. Best of all—as far as Jennifer was concerned—his arms, especially his biceps, bulged with veins.

She hadn't mentioned the pull Dutch's big, veined arms had on her to Dr. Gütfeldt. She knew how he'd interpret this—it always came back to some sort of phallic reference, which was probably more his psychopathology than hers. With Gütfeldt's psychoanalytic training, he reminded Jennifer of the patient who sees sex in all the Rorschach ink blots, then blames the therapist for showing him all those dirty pictures.

"Well, well, well." Dutch smiled. "Don't we look wet and sexy?"

Jennifer gave him a weak smile. "Very funny. I thought you'd have gone home by now."

Dutch sniffed the air. "It reeks of *travka*. How many times do I have to tell you to smoke outside?"

"Changing the subject?"

"If the county inspector comes in…"

Jennifer sighed. "Relax. How many times do I have to tell you? She never comes past the lobby. She's deathly afraid of this place." Jennifer arched her eyebrows. "You want to share a flaca?"

Dutch shook his head. "Not right now. I need to ask a huge favor. Senator Schwarzenegger is here from Washington; he wants our opinion about a bill he's working on. I told him you're busy getting ready for a big date. He said he'd only take a few moments, and it would mean the world to me."

"If he's even half as good looking as his grandfather was in his prime," Jennifer puckered her lips and kissed the air, then winked at Dutch, "he can have more than just a few moments."

"He's not as big as his *opa*, but I'd say he's dashing, in a way. Polished, big smile, expensive suit." Laughing, Dutch shook his head. "You met him when we attended the Shriners Hospital banquet a few weeks back. You must remember."

Jennifer smiled mischievously. "I was just busting your chops. Of course I remember him. And I know what he looks like. He's in the news quite a bit."

Dutch rubbed his temples. "My head's about to bust trying to handle all the problems here."

"I'd be happy to prescribe something for that." Jennifer laughed. "Don't forget, I *am* a doctor."

"I just need a good stiff drink." He patted Jennifer on the knee. "Get dressed and come have a chat with the senator. I'm going to break out the good scotch."

"The single-malt Talisker?" Jennifer gave Dutch a smile and nodded. "In that case…"

Dutch turned his wheelchair to leave, then stopped. "Try to steer the conversation to how strapped we are for funding. I know you abhor begging for money, but we can use all the political allies we can get."

"*Entendido*. But you'll owe me a round of margaritas." She fluffed her hair with her fingers. "I'll be in your office in a milli. *Ya, vayate*."

"All right, I'm leaving." Dutch took hold of the joystick and wheeled away.

Jennifer waited for the door to close, then threw on a fresh set of scrubs and a clean pair of tennis shoes and left to meet the senator.

The chemical cocktail was kicking in full force and she had a nice buzz going as she waltzed into Dutch's office. Two well-dressed men sat facing the director's desk, each holding tumblers of scotch. She recognized the senator immediately. The other man she assumed was one of his aides.

"Good evening, gentlemen," Jennifer said.

Both men looked over in unison and stood. The senator placed his glass on Dutch's desk and approached Jennifer, hand extended, flashing his famous smile and luminous teeth.

"Senator," Dutch said while pouring a drink for Jennifer. "I believe you've met Doctor Jennifer Singh, a senior Medical Examiner for the Unified Los Angeles-Orange County morgue, and Associate Professor of Pathology at UCLA Medical School." Dutch handed the scotch to Jennifer. "Doctor Singh, Senator Weiss Schwarzenegger."

Schwarzenegger had his grandfather's Germanic face—strong square jaw, beetling brow, wavy blondish hair, and fair skin. He wasn't nearly as muscular and powerfully built as his grandfather, but still had an above-average physique. He wore a perfectly tailored navy suit, crisp white shirt, and a tie the same color as the red on the United States flag pin attached to his lapel.

Not too bad, Jennifer thought. *Pity he's not a tad taller.* She cringed inside as she looked at his politician's smile and realized, as phony as it was, that's probably what got him elected.

The senator shook Jennifer's hand and stood uncomfortably close, just like one of Jennifer's colleagues, a Finnish professor of nanorobotic surgery, was prone to do. She didn't back away, but held his gaze. He broke eye contact and seemed to take his time as he looked her up and down.

What chutzpah! Isn't this guy married?

She guessed she should feel flattered, Dutch told her the senator came here for her medical opinion, not to drool over her like she was a piece of meat. And she was affronted that after busting her butt for years in medical school and residency, this is what she got. Some rich guy sizing her up as if she were a Licensed Sexual Companion.

Although she supported the concept of the lyscee—after all, Jennifer believed a person should be free to do with his or her body as they pleased—it did create a whole class of men, and even a few women, who seemed to mentally rate every woman by how much they'd be willing to pay for their intimate services.

The senator continued to hold Jennifer's hand in his.

Jennifer began to pull her hand back, but he placed his other hand over hers. She reacted by pulling him closer until they were almost touching and tightening her grip until he grimaced and withdrew his hand. Jennifer laughed to herself, thankful that working out with free weights did wonders for her grip strength.

The senator acted as if nothing was amiss and cleared his throat. "Dr. Singh. I would like your expert medical opinion on a bill I am co-sponsoring in the Senate. If you would be so kind."

Jennifer took a sip of her drink and nodded for him to continue, thankful that at last, he was getting down to business.

"We would like to set up a national DNA library for every man, woman, and child in the United States. We envision collecting buccal samples when people go to renew their driver's license, are arrested, join the military, at birth, etcetera." He consulted an electronic notepad his assistant handed him. "Currently, there are a little over one-hundred-fifty million samples in the DNA library, less than one in three Americans. I would like your opinion, as a medical expert, whether expanding the database would make it easier for you to solve crimes."

Jennifer found herself lapsing into her "professor" voice. "Senator, the Medical Examiner does not solve crimes. That is the prerogative of the police department and its detectives. Our job is to establish the cause, or causes, of death. We are here to assist the police department. I think your query should be addressed to them."

The senator ran his fingers through his full hair and nodded. "Come, come, Doctor. We have the support of the Association of National Police Chiefs as well as the support of many individual police officers. Taking into consideration your disclaimer, would a national database enhance your agency's capability in assisting the police department?" He turned on his biggest politician's smile, his ivories practically aflame.

Jennifer sipped the scotch and found herself smiling dumbly, locked on his pearly whites. It must be hard for people to resist that charm, she thought. And his eyes, incredibly blue, matching his suit—he's probably wearing chameleon contacts. "My main concern, Senator, is the issue of privacy. What safeguards are there to keep the data confidential? And I'm concerned that people could be discriminated against based on their DNA."

Schwarzenegger maintained a confident, inviting smile. "The main goal of this legislation is to protect the children. If a child is kidnapped, this would better enable us to identify the abductor."

Jennifer shot him a look of disbelief and nodded. At last, the trump card. When all else fails, pull out the heavy artillery, invoke the "protect the children" argument. In her best sarcastic tone, she said, "If the law is meant to protect the children, then I'm all for trampling people's rights."

Schwarzenegger laughed. "I like your sense of humor, Doctor."

"I wasn't joking." Jennifer crossed her arms over her chest and scowled. "Really, Senator? Protect the children? That's the same lame argument that was used to pass the Mandatory Microchip Act."

"I guess that argument doesn't work on you." He picked up his drink and took a sip while studying her over the rim of the tumbler. "You'd be surprised how many people fall for it. Nevertheless, a DNA database is less intrusive than the microchips we all wear."

Dutch moved between the two and asked if anybody needed their drinks refreshed.

Jennifer had been getting herself all worked up and was grateful that Dutch came to the rescue.

Dutch craned his head and looked up at the senator. "Doctor Singh couldn't survive without her microchip." He laughed and poked Jennifer in the ribs. "She'd be too impatient to wait in a checkout line."

Jennifer nodded. "True." She finished her drink and caught the senator's eye. "But, that's not how the microchip was sold to the public. And how many abducted children have the chips saved? Two or three in California since microchipping became mandatory?"

Schwarzenegger looked at his assistant who shrugged. "I don't have the exact numbers, but I'm sure it has been higher than that. Doctor, I'm a conservative and not usually in favor of passing big sweeping laws. However, I was approached by a number of law enforcement groups who support setting up the database. I'm trying to get opinions from people that don't have so much skin in the game."

So much skin in the game? Jennifer wondered. Was that some sort of subtle come on? Probably not. Schwarzenegger was anything but subtle, at least with his eyes.

"I'm sure a DNA database would make it easier for the police," Jennifer said. "But I'm still uncomfortable. There's no way to keep that information secure from hackers."

"This bill will make the United States of America a much safer place. Perhaps a little loss of privacy would be worth it, don't you think?"

"If you want to make the US of A safer," Jennifer said, "you could push for better border screening for tuberculosis and other contagious diseases. Just here in our department, we've lost ten colleagues to TB-related disability."

Schwarzenegger moved close and placed his hand on Jennifer's shoulder. "Perhaps we can set up a time to discuss the matter privately."

Jennifer's skin crawled and she stepped back.

The senator's arm fell to his side, and he seamlessly tossed his drink down.

Dutch craned his head up at the two people towering above him. "Senator, I hate to be a pest, but if you wouldn't mind, I have a request."

Jennifer sighed and rolled her eyes; she knew what was coming. But why do we always have to beg for money? Do garbage men have to grovel to get paid?

"By all means, Director Rolstoel," Schwarzenegger said. "How can I be of help?"

"As I was explaining before Doctor Singh arrived, we have only two medical examiners presently active. Our other ten MEs were in Vancouver working with the CSIS. While—"

"CSIS is the Canadian version of the FBI, isn't it?" the senator said.

Dutch nodded. "Our medical examiners were working with a team of forensic pathologists from CSIS, trying to determine the cause of death of a group of stowaways discovered on a container ship coming from Cambodia. They asked for our help and were willing to pay. Since they were already there for a Continuing Medical Education conference, and we needed the money, I gave the okay. Unfortunately, in spite of wearing cloth masks while doing the procedures, everyone in the autopsy suites contracted..." He looked up at Jennifer. "What's it called again?"

"UXDR-TB—Ultra-Extensive Drug Resistant Tuberculosis," Jennifer said. "It's a form of TB resistant to all antibiotics and is endemic to parts of Asia and Africa. It's gaining ground among the homeless in developed countries, including ours."

The senator's face softened and he put on a practiced look of concern as he addressed Jennifer. "I'm surprised I haven't heard about that."

"We've been able to keep a lid on the news," Dutch said. "Don't want to panic the teeming masses."

"And now," Jennifer added, "we're all wearing full bio-hazard suits. It's a royal pain."

"Since there is no treatment for this strain of TB," Dutch said, "our doctors are quarantined in a sanitarium in the Canadian Rockies. They won't be allowed back into the country until they're non-infective. Their salary's coming out of the morgue's budget, since they're on work-related disability leave. Because of that, we don't have the funds to hire replacement forensic pathologists to help our beleaguered staff."

"Any idea when the other doctors will be back?" the senator asked.

Dutch shook his head and winced. "Best case scenario, nine months. More than likely, some will never recover. We don't have the funds to hire temporary examiners. Doctor Singh and Doctor Tulp are our only remaining doctors, and bless their souls, they're making a herculean effort to handle the caseload. We've just about reached our storage capacity for cadavers." Dutch put on what Jennifer recognized as his best pleading face. "If there's anything you can do to help us get a little extra funding…"

The senator reached down and put his hand on Dutch's shoulder. He lowered his voice and his face became earnest. "It's obvious you have a real emergency here." He shrugged. "To be honest," he turned one of his hands up as if begging for money, "our hands are tied in Washington. Earmarking federal funds to the morgue would be considered pork barrel, and those pesky bankruptcy trustees from the International Monetary Fund go through the federal budget line-by-line. I'm sure they'd shoot me down if I tried to appropriate funds like that."

"I don't know how you can let those foreign bankers control our budget," Dutch said, with a tone of distaste.

"They do the same thing to more than half the countries around the world." The senator put his hand on the administrator's shoulder. "I know how you feel, but you should direct your anger at our parents and grandparents. After all, they let our country's debt get so high that the United States went bankrupt. It was the greatest global financial collapse in history. At that point, what choice did we have? We were forced to give up using the dollar for the SDR in order to discharge those debts, otherwise each and every one of us would be stuck paying a million of the old U.S. Dollars in debt. It was actually a blessing in disguise."

"I understand," Dutch said, looking up at the senator. "But why are they still controlling our budget?"

"To make sure we don't get back in the same situation," Jennifer said.

"I understand your agency's problems." Schwarzenegger gave Dutch's shoulder a little shake. "But, do call my office. Perhaps my staff can think of a few creative ways to be of help."

While backing toward the door to avoid another handshake, or even something more intimate, Jennifer said, "Senator, it's been a pleasure."

"I have her out kibitzing for money," Dutch said. "Tonight she's off to a charity event benefiting the Getty Center."

The senator smiled and gave Jennifer a slight nod. "What a pleasant coincidence. I'll be attending the same event." He winked. "I look forward to seeing you there."

Jennifer turned and left the office wondering what exactly he meant by that last comment. She wished Dutch hadn't mentioned the gala so she didn't have to spend the night trying to avoid the creep. And what was his problem anyway? It was obvious from his tan that he'd just removed his wedding band. He was too slick, too polished—a politician. Although he'd tried to hide his motives, they were pretty transparent.

She told herself to re-frame the encounter—determined not to let the lecherous senator ruin her evening. She smiled with a surge of excitement. She had a spring in her step, again dreaming about the upcoming soirée.

She was about to spend the night with her own Prince Charming.

Chapter 4

Aída stood by the sinks and looked up, beaming, when Jennifer entered the locker room. "Voilà," she said. "The guest of honor has arrived. Let me present your makeup station."

Aída had placed one of Jennifer's leather swivel chairs in front of the mirrors. The shelf looked like a makeup counter in a department store.

"You really didn't have to stay," Jennifer said, amazed by the amount of beauty products on the counter. "I can get ready myself."

Aída grabbed Jennifer by the elbow and pushed her into the chair, laughing. "I've seen your work at our office Christmas parties. No offense, but believe me, you need my help." She gave Jennifer a licentious look. "Especially tonight with your big date."

Jennifer felt her face flush. She peered up at her assistant. "Just don't go overboard."

Aída rubbed her hands together and looked giddy. Her words tumbled out. "You're going to look so off the Richter, when I'm done you won't recognize yourself. Now sit back and watch the artist at work." Aída covered Jennifer with a towel, then grabbed a hair dryer and a barrel brush. "All these years we've worked together, and you've never let me fix you up. Now, three times this month. If you just took the time you could be so beautiful." Aída leaned in close and sniffed Jennifer's breath. "I knew I smelled pot in the room. And is that tequila on your breath? Or scotch? I hope you're not so wasted you can't enjoy the evening."

Jennifer sighed, thinking that this was the reason she didn't get too close to work colleagues—they feel it gives them the right to comment on your life. At least Dutch never does that.

"I just took something to take the edge off," Jennifer said. "Feel free to raid my stash if you want. *Mi* locker *es tu* locker."

Aída gave her a disapproving look. "Maybe when I'm done. But I do think you indulge way too much."

"This is a special occasion." Jennifer gave her the "boss" look and Aída dropped the subject.

Aída began blow drying and brushing. She yelled above the sound of the dryer. "When are you going to tell me who this mystery man is, Doc?"

Jennifer yelled back, trying to be heard above the whirling mechanic din. "Soon, Aída, soon. I just don't want to jinx things. Everything's going so smoothly."

Aída turned off the dryer and stepped aside so Jennifer could see herself in the mirror. Her hair was fluffed two to three times its normal size, curls straightened into alluring wisps of flames, and red hair cascading down to her shoulders and falling asymmetrically and coyly across her left eye. She saw Aída's reflection in the mirror, buoyant and nodding in approval.

Then the real toil began. Aída grabbed a radio from her locker and turned on salsa music.

Jennifer watched in amazement as Aída pulled out an endless array of beauty products: powders, blushes, creams, mascara, foundation, rouge, lipstick, lip gloss, lip liner, eyeliners, eyelash curler, eyebrow tweezers, and numerous other things she didn't recognize.

If this is what it takes to look beautiful, Jennifer thought, then count me out.

Aída powdered, sprayed, curled, painted, dabbed and sprinkled, inspected her work, then resumed more of the same. Finally, she stopped. She stepped back and turned the chair so Jennifer could see herself in the mirror.

Jennifer flushed, her heart began to race. She couldn't believe the work Aída had done and that it was really herself in the mirror.

Aída narrowed her eyes and inspected every inch of Jennifer's face. She nodded and smiled in pleasure. "You look so beautiful, Doc. Your boyfriend won't be able to resist you."

"All thanks to you," Jennifer said. "You're quite the artiste."

Aída told Jennifer she'd retrieve her boss's gown from the locker.

Jennifer pulled off her scrubs, tossed them into a hamper, and stood naked in front of the mirror. She saw her reflection and gave herself a lopsided grin and had to admit that Aída really did an incredible job. Better than she herself could ever do.

Aída returned, the gown still nestled in its plastic bag. She looked quizzically at Jennifer. "Going commando?"

"I think so. The gown is so sheer…"

"And convenient when it's time to get busy. I like it." Aída laughed. "The Dirty Doctor." She pulled the gown out of its encasement, moved behind Jennifer, and inched the tight, semi-stretch material up around her hips. "Take a big breath in and hold it," Aída said.

Jennifer held her breath while Aída pulled the gown over her breasts then closed the zipper, making sure not to tear the fabric.

"You can breathe now," Aída said.

Jennifer panted to catch her breath, thinking that's how the pearl fisher must feel after a deep dive.

Jennifer slipped on three-inch, ivory-colored satin pumps purchased especially to go with the gown, and costing more than she could really afford. Aída sprayed perfume smelling of roses, jasmine, and musk on Jennifer's exposed skin. She began dropping pinches of diamond dust over Jennifer's shoulders.

Jennifer stepped back and gave her assistant a questioning look. "Easy on the glitter. I'm not going to a *quinceañera*."

"Hush up," Aída said, moving back to the doctor's side. She resumed sprinkling Jennifer's shoulders and décolletage, then drizzled reddish glitter in her hair. She placed artificial ruby stud earrings through Jennifer's ears, clasped a tennis bracelet around her wrist, and hung a ruby pendant which reached just to the top of Jennifer's sternum.

Aída stepped back and walked with Jennifer to the full-length mirror glued to the end of one of the rows of lockers.

They both gasped.

The combination of the sparkling gems and glitter made Jennifer look ablaze in the overhead lights. The gown looked even better than when she'd tried it on at the store. It clung snugly to her chest; its daring décolletage revealed the swells of her breasts. Jennifer made a mental note not to lean over or reach out for fear of exposing herself.

Aída stood next to Jennifer, gyrating to the salsa beat coming from the radio. "Doc, you look full-out bradford cubed! ¡T-Totalamente cool-lo!"

Jennifer's heart raced and her cheeks flushed; she couldn't help smiling. She looked closer at her reflection and turned from side to side, thinking maybe she could start to like this.

Then she lost her smile, looked at Aída, and scowled. "Don't you think this is over the top?"

Aída shook her head vigorously. "This is LA. Tinsel Town. You'll fit right in. I only wish I could see you make your entrance to the ball."

Jennifer shrugged. It was too late to cut back on the makeup now, she needed to get on her way. "I'll tell you all about it first thing tomorrow," she said.

Aída smiled at her creation. "I can't wait."

Jennifer grabbed her brand-new clutch and accompanied Aída out of the locker room.

Chapter 5

Jennifer called ahead. "Slow down!"

Aída looked back over her shoulder and chuckled. "I'm usually running to keep up with *your* long legs."

Even though the gown had a slit on one side that went more than halfway up her thigh, it was so snug around the hips that she had to mince her steps and struggled to keep up with Aída. Making matters worse, her ankles were unsteady in high heels, making her walk as though she was on a bounding ship. Jennifer seldom wore heels; she found that men were intimidated when she towered over them. She could wear them tonight because Donny was at least a half-foot taller than her.

Her dress shoes echoed down the long corridor. It was late and the hall was gloomy, the building empty, and the staff long gone. Mysterious shadows seemed to lurk where the pools of light couldn't quite reach, as if the souls of the dead bodies prowled in the funereal light.

A bang echoed down the hallway.

Aída froze. She gasped and grabbed Jennifer's arm.

Her assistant's fear was contagious, sending a chill running down Jennifer's bare back.

Aída's eyes darted about. "What was that?" she whispered.

"Probably a ghost," Jennifer said, stifling a laugh.

"¡*Dios mio*!" Aída threw her arms around Jennifer's waist.

"I was just kidding." Jennifer pried herself away and looked down, holding her assistant's eyes. "It was the air ducts expanding or contracting." She laughed. "You don't really believe in ghosts, do you?"

Aída looked shaken. "You believe we have a soul, don't you? Isn't it possible dead people's souls float around here for a while until they fly up to heaven?"

Jennifer pulled Aída along toward the exit. "I only believe in things I can see."

While Jennifer had grown accustomed to being in the presence of death, and didn't believe in ghosts or anything of that sort, tonight she shivered, hair on edge, as her mind raced with images of cadavers come to life and primordial and inchoate fears welled up. She thought maybe it was the marijuana making her paranoid and that she needed to get a grip because there was nothing to fear. The macabre feeling passed.

She laughed inwardly: *ghosts and zombies don't really exist*.

As they neared the exit, a faint moaning sound—something out of a horror movie—followed by feet shuffling, came from a room off the hall, the morgue's chapel, about ten yards down the darkened passageway. A shadow moved across the corridor floor.

The two women threw their arms around each other. Jennifer's knees knocked together.

Maybe Aída was right about ghosts.

A wheezing came from the chapel. The footfalls neared. A figure emerged through the door. A balding, gray-haired man dressed in an olive uniform appeared and looked their way.

Jennifer and Aída both gasped.

The man jumped and dropped his coffee, spilling it everywhere. He grasped his chest. It was the night guard.

Jennifer let out a nervous laugh and rushed to the man's side. "Are you okay?"

"You scared the bejesus out of me," he said, catching his breath. "I thought everyone had left for the day."

Jennifer placed her fingers against the man's neck and took his carotid pulse—it was racing. "Are you having any chest pain?"

He shook his head. "I'll be fine. I was doing my evening prayers and you startled me."

The guard looked at Jennifer and his eyes widened with surprise. She passed by his station in the lobby every evening on her way home, dressed in jeans and without makeup, not looking like a Hollywood starlet. Hobbling and wheezing, the guard shambled the few paces to the end of the hall, punched the red button on the wall, and held the double doors open for the two women. Without a word, he gave a deep formal bow as Jennifer passed. For a moment, he looked young and virile.

When they were out of earshot, Aída winked at Jennifer and whispered, "You can even give an old dog a bone."

Jennifer looked over to her assistant and they both quietly laughed.

They crossed the lobby, opened the door, and stepped into an alien world.

The mountains surrounding the city were lit up in flames, tendrils of gray smoke floated miles into the air.

"Los Ángeles is on fire," Aída said. She rubbed her red eyes, which were beginning to tear.

Jennifer stifled a cough. "The angels looking down must be impressed. Their city's encircled by a fiery halo."

Aída arched her eyebrows. "I didn't think you were religious."

"I was speaking mythologically."

Jennifer's paused a moment, her senses still heightened from the marijuana and the anticipation of the coming evening. It was astronomical twilight—the full darkness of night hadn't quite fallen—a mysterious and magical time. The air was still. The cloying haze from the raging scrub fires in the mountains scattered the ambient light, as if a herd of cows passed by kicking up dust, creating a peculiar aspect; ominous and boding. The mountains surrounding the city were lit with a gloomy, coral glow from the consuming firestorms and cast the area with stark features. Sporadic spheres of crimson flames soared above the horizon. The city below was colored cerise. The western sky was liquid copper. The surrounding cars and conifers were covered with a thin coating of charcoal, cement colored cinders, and soot.

The nearby San Diego Freeway was lit up by speeding cars heading to their assignations—strings of bright white pearls rushed by at over one hundred-twenty miles per hour. Their headlights cut through the haze and the low-pitched hum of electric-powered engines sounded like thousands of distant swarming bees. Across the street from the morgue, the lights of Jackie Robinson Stadium blazed. Jennifer spent many evenings there after work with Dutch, eating fish tacos, drinking beer and smuggled-in champagne, and watching her favorite sport.

Aída jumped at what sounded like gunfire. Jennifer laughed, knowing it was the UCLA baseball team taking batting practice.

Jennifer inhaled slowly so as not to cough while trying to experience the *Tao*. The evening redolence of the desert had attracted her to Los Angeles and she searched for the aromas of desert sage and creosote bushes, the jacaranda, eucalyptus, and sycamore trees, but their scents were completely hidden by the acrid smell of soot.

Her red sedan was parked in the doctor's lot. Aída scurried ahead, unplugged the car from the recharging station, and opened the car door. The gown was so constricting that Aída had to hold Jennifer's hand as she fell backwards into the seat. She gave Aída a wave and watched as her assistant headed to the employee's parking lot.

Nestled in the plush leather seat, Jennifer collected her thoughts and felt relieved she didn't have to actually drive the vehicle. She probably couldn't anyway in the dress pumps. She logged into the Nav-Drive and instructed the device to take her to the Getty Center in Brentwood. The car backed up and pulled out of the lot, beginning the short trip up to the museum. She told the car's stereo to put on sports-talk radio. Mindless chatter came through the car's speakers.

What the hell am I doing? Here I am dressed up all sexy and…sports-talk?

She told the car to change to smooth jazz. Within seconds, the car was filled with music, down-tempo and melodic. Its mood matched her buzz.

The electric engine hummed as the car crossed under the San Diego freeway, then turned north onto Sepulveda Boulevard, flowing with the traffic for about two miles until it reached the entrance to the museum where Jennifer presented her invitation. The guard gave the Nav-Drive a code allowing it to bypass the visitor's lot and join the queue heading to the center's main entrance. Her mainstream sedan joined a stream of high-priced luxury autos as they snaked their way up the winding Getty Center Drive to the aluminum and travertine-clad museum ablaze in lights on top of the bluff. The sooty air cleared as the car ascended; at the summit, the roiling smoke had become charcoal-colored wisps.

The Nav-Drive stopped the car, waiting its turn to pull up to the brightly-lit red carpet surrounded by attendants in formal wear. As Jennifer waited to disembark, she received a text. Donny was caught in traffic coming over the mountains from Las Vegas—the fire and smoke were wreaking havoc—he'd be arriving about a half-hour late, she should wait for him inside.

Jennifer looked out to the east from where he would be coming. Black smoke rose up miles into the sky creating soot-colored clouds over the pink-colored San Gabriel Mountains. Below, the city was dotted with white and black puffs of smoke as if the angels, for which the city was named, had dropped makeup-smeared cotton balls all over the valley.

Maybe the gods are punishing us L'Orangalinos, she thought. Burn everything down, and like the Phoenix, start anew. Not a bad idea.

Her car moved forward.

But who cares? My car is next!

Her car pulled to the front of the valet line and came to a stop. A man in a black tuxedo and white cotton gloves opened the door. Jennifer swung her legs to the ground, then held her hands up letting the attendant pull her out. The attendant gave the Nav-Drive parking instructions and the car pulled away.

Elegantly dressed invitees climbed the red carpeted stairs to the brightly-lit gallery. The women were dressed in luxurious designer gowns and glittering jewels and a few had furs draped over their shoulders. The men wore tuxedos and bow ties, a few wore silk top hats, others carried opulent walking sticks.

Jennifer made it to the top of the stairs where she was intercepted by a woman in a tuxedo wearing a name tag that read: Facilitator. The woman had a broad smile and a manic energy that Jennifer found contagious.

"You look dazzling," she told Jennifer.

Without breaking eye contact, she gestured to the right. "Please step this way. We must get pictures of you in that stunning gown."

Jennifer made a feeble effort to break away, but the facilitator took her arm and pulled her along to where the paparazzi were situated. A growing sense of anxiety welled up within her and she looked for a way to escape. Anything to get out of having her picture taken. Before she could come up with an excuse to leave, they arrived at an area just off to the side of the building's entrance where a bank of blinding lights had been set to shine on a square of red carpet and a backdrop that had the museum's name and logo.

The publicity backdrop.

The facilitator positioned Jennifer on the middle of the carpet, told her to look out into the lights, to place one foot slightly in front of the other, and let her arms hang freely at her side. The tuxedo-clad lady stepped out of camera range.

Jennifer looked out into the dazzling lights, unable to shake the thought that this is what a deer must feel when staring into the headlights of an oncoming semi. She squinted and could make out the silhouettes of a horde of photographers holding their cameras, and they were all directed at her. Over the sounds of the arriving guests was the rapid-fire staccato of camera clicks. Jennifer thanked the goddesses that Aída insisted on doing her hair and makeup. Suddenly, in her low-cut gown with its bare back, she felt naked and tried to make herself smaller. She closed her eyes and frowned. She couldn't block out the clicking sound; it was as if gnats were trapped inside her skull, frantically buzzing about looking for freedom.

"Open your eyes and smile," the facilitator called over. "Enjoy yourself. You look bradford."

Jennifer squinted into the bright lights and her eyes started to adjust to the glare. She told herself to block out the negative thoughts, this should be fun.

Pleasant thoughts. Nothing but pleasant thoughts.

The munchies kicked in and she envisioned a giant slice of pepperoni pizza, a frosty mug of beer, a hot pretzel in the hot sun. She smiled broadly, holding back laughter.

"That's great," the voice yelled over. "Keep smiling. You're a supernova."

Supernova. She couldn't hold the laughter in, her muscles relaxed, her mind went blank. She became one with the moment. Time flew by.

The facilitator returned to her side. She gave Jennifer a hug. "You're my *estrella*."

She moved Jennifer around as if she were a mannequin while firing instructions with practiced confidence. "First we turn slightly to the left; perfect. Let that slit in your gown face the cameras; beautiful. Bend your leg slightly, let it peep out provocatively. *¡Así!* Don't be shy, legs are in this year, *cariña*, and yours are exquisite. Put your hand on your hip, like so. Turn your head just a touch and look toward the cameras. You're not used to this, I can tell. Just relax, have fun, think of something pleasant. Give us a big, natural smile. Voilà! You were born for this!"

The woman retreated. The rapid-fire clicking of the cameras resumed. *Status photographicus*. Jennifer figured that in the time it took her to shoot one photo of a deep-sky object, these guys could take tens of thousands of her. She was surprised, however, that she was feeling warm inside, was becoming one with the moment. She looked out over the swarm of photographers and beamed.

The facilitator yelled over, "Excellent! You're doing great."

Jennifer's eyes adjusted to the blinding light of thousands of flashes accompanying the clicking cameras. She let her mind wander. The flashes became fireflies on a hot summer night. The camera clicks turned into the cicada's song. In the distance, the mountain flames licked the sky and seemed to heat her skin, which began to tingle. In her imagination, Donny appeared, his eyes widened and his jaw dropped as he first caught sight of her.

She asked herself why she spent some of the best years of her life absorbed in books and hunched over cold, dead bodies. This is it. Things are about to change. *Blya!* This is what she really needed, not more years of therapy.

Say good-bye to shy, self-conscious Jennifer and hello to Jennifer version 2.0!

The facilitator came back. She gave Jennifer a big smile and led her off the carpet and back to the main entrance. Before parting, she input Jennifer's name and occupation into her wrist-tablet. She wished Jennifer a pleasant evening and was gone, back to the top of the stairs, before Jennifer could say "thank you."

Jennifer passed through the colossal open doors carried by the crush of debonair men and chic women coursing into the vaulted entrance hall. She broke from the current of people and found a quiet spot to wait for Donny, next to a side table holding an assortment of light hors d'oeuvres. Numerous tuxedoed young men and women walked around the lobby carrying silver trays of bubbling champagne.

Champagne! I'm in heaven.

As a tray came by, she took one of the flutes and sipped the sparkling wine.

Oh yes! I should start moonlighting, so I can afford this heavenly nectar.

She looked around the room; most of the men's eyes were drawn to her. When she looked their way, they smiled and nodded. Their female companions' reactions were mixed. Some appeared pleased and inviting, others snobby and bitter with envy.

The trays kept passing by. Two champagnes later, Jennifer felt a familiar masculine touch on her shoulder and heard Donny's deep resonant voice. The embers of passion burst into flashover. Her body shivered as her blood rushed to the surface.

She turned to greet her date.

Chapter 6

Donny resembled the sculpture of Alexander the Great sitting inside the entrance to the building: strong aquiline nose, short curling hair, and commanding forehead. Even in his silk tuxedo, it was obvious he was more muscular and defined than the partially clad statue. His purple cummerbund, amethyst cufflinks, and royal purple orchid pinned to his lapel complimented his strong, expressive lips.

Jennifer looked up, gazed into his eyes—warm, azure, penetrating—and had to smile. Even though Donny usually had a self-assured look that said he was emperor of all he saw, he appeared flummoxed, unsure of where to kiss her for fear of messing up her makeup. She pulled him close, enjoying his sensual, woodsy smell, the undertone of aged Kentucky bourbon, and a haunting hint of neroli. She turned her head.

He kissed her neck; the coarse stubble of his facial hair brushing her cheeks as his lips lingered on her skin, light as a drifting feather.

He held her hands in his. His eyes twinkled as he drank her in. "You look absolutely stunning." His deep voice rumbled like a waterfall, sending chills down her spine. "I hope no one tried to steal you before I arrived."

"Thanks. You look fantastic, Donny." She squeezed his hands and moved against him, adjusting his bow tie.

He passed his lips over her bare shoulder; her skin burned beneath them. Something tingled inside. She wished he'd sweep her up and take her right there. Wished the moment could last forever. The spell was broken when a waiter came up with a tray of champagne. She watched with dreamy eyes as Donny took two and handed one to her. They clinked glasses and tasted the magic.

"Sorry I was late," he said after taking a sip. "Going over the pass was like driving through hell. The road was so covered with smoke and flames and ashes that the Nav-Drive had to slow to a crawl. When I finally got here, that pesky facilitator dragged me to the publicity backdrop for photos."

"She did the same to me," Jennifer said. "She's very pushy."

"That's her job and she's good at it." He met her eyes. "Cameras aren't allowed inside. If you want, we could go back out and have photos taken."

Jennifer smiled at him.

Photos as a couple? He must be serious about us.

"I'll pass," she said. "I'm not keen on having my photo taken."

Donny winked and gave her a playful smile. "Don't tell me you're Amish."

She found him charming and laughed with him. "Hardly. But the paparazzi took way too many pictures already."

"Look around." He waved his hand over the crowd. "Most of the people who attend these events are gray-haired—" he leaned in close, whispering in her ear, sending another round of shivers down her exposed spine, "geezers. The paparazzi don't have many opportunities to photograph someone as beautiful as you." He raised his glass to her.

She looked around. Donny was right. Except for a handful of twenty-something blondes hanging on the arms of men old enough to be their fathers—or grandfathers—there were few people her age in the crowd.

He placed his hand around her waist. "The program's going to start in a bit, let's head to the main ballroom."

Jennifer snuggled at Donny's side and gasped when they entered the grand hall.

Glittering chandeliers hung from the lofty ceiling. A swan ice sculpture spouted champagne, surrounded by vases of snow white lilies. Scattered around the space were dining tables, each with crystal vases bursting full of long-stem white roses. Silver and white confetti drizzled from the ceiling, giving the appearance of snowfall. A string quartet played Mozart in a far corner. Women glided around the ballroom dressed in shimmering evening gowns, sparkling jewels draped around their necks, polished men hanging on their arms.

Donny pulled her against him and whispered in her ear. "You hungry?"

"Starving."

Nestled next to Donny, ensconced in his protective cocoon, she broke out in chill bumps. Leaning against him took weight off her tired legs.

Exotic aromas filled the air as they approached the food tables lining one side of the room. Jennifer filled her plate from chafing dishes filled with hot hors d'oeuvres. The food smelled enticing and her stomach was empty; she hadn't eaten since she downed a protein shake around noon. She and Donny found an empty table as a server came by with a tray of champagne to freshen their drinks.

Donny held his flute up, gazing into her eyes. "To you, Jennifer. You look voluptuous."

Jennifer smiled. She hoped he meant sumptuous.

She nodded, her cheeks felt flushed.

The food was delicious and despite the Dexedrine earlier, she finished her plate before Donny did and thought about going back for more. A waiter came by with a platter of sushi and bite-sized samosas and she grabbed a plateful.

As Jennifer nibbled on the raw fish, she leaned forward, whispering into Donny's ear, "This ball must cost a fortune. Why spend so much, when the goal is to *raise* money for the museum?"

Donny's eyes widened as he looked down on the curves spilling out of her bodice.

She gave him a smile that he didn't seem to notice because his eyes remained focused downward.

He laughed, breaking the hold her cleavage held over him, and looked into her eyes. "This crowd is used to being wined and dined. The more lavish and expensive the event, the more money you pull in. You have to spend money to make money. Same is true in my business."

Donny's attention was diverted when an elderly couple approached and he stood to greet them. The woman, gray-haired, in a sequin A-line gown, pulled Donny to her and kissed him on the cheek.

"Who is your lovely companion?" she said. "Everyone's dying to know."

Donny made the introductions and invited them to have a seat.

Donny explained to Jennifer that the woman served with him on the board of the Getty Center. Jennifer recognized the name. In her youth, she co-starred in a string of mindless romantic comedies. Her husband made a fortune developing strains of algae able to produce umami—meat flavored—proteins and transforming vertical, hydroponic-grown algae into what all but the wealthiest people now ate as meat.

When Donny told the couple that Jennifer was a medical examiner, the conversation turned to the numerous holovision crime scene shows. Like finches drawn to thistle, other couples flocked to them; a few talked as if they were experts in forensic pathology. Jennifer tried to eat between comments, explaining to the group the unreal aspects of those "reality" medical shows.

Jennifer finished her plate and the conversation turned tiresome. After an entire day performing autopsies, that was the last thing she wanted to think or talk about. She took Donny's hand to get his attention. He looked over and she rolled her eyes—a subtle gesture it was time to move on.

"If you would excuse us," he told the assembled group. "I'm going to show the beautiful doctor around before the program starts."

After a series of handshakes, cheek kisses, pats on the shoulder, and one bear hug, she was alone with her man again. She kept her hand in his as Donny worked the room, looking like the consummate politician, nodding and smiling to the other guests.

"It's amazing how popular murder mystery shows are," Jennifer said. "I should get a part-time gig advising those schlock-fests."

Donny winked at her. "I know a lot of people in the biz."

"You'll have to make the introductions for me." She paused a second, then laughed. "But then again, I don't know why they would need a *real* doctor as a consultant; it doesn't seem they're overly concerned about *real* autopsy procedures. Those shows are so fake. I can't watch them."

They stopped to look at the gelid ice swan towering above them, spouting champagne from its beak into a pool underneath. Donny refilled their flutes, while Jennifer, glancing back and forth between him and the swan and thought about the story of Zeus and Leda.

Donny turned to hand her one of the drinks.

"You better not turn into a swan," she told him.

He looked at her with a puzzled expression. Before he could respond, someone called his name.

Jennifer turned to see Senator Schwarzenegger approach, accompanied by two shorter men. One was Hispanic looking and dressed in a well-fitted black tuxedo and a red, white, and blue tie with a single white star. The other was Slavic looking, in an ill-fitting navy suit and brown loafers.

Schwarzenegger patted Donny on the back and said to his Slavic companion, "Here's the financial genius we were telling you about. He's done wonders with our portfolios." He looked toward the Hispanic man. "Isn't that right, Carlos?" The man in the tuxedo nodded. The senator turned to Jennifer and bowed. "Dr. Singh, so nice to see you again." He looked her up and down, beamed his patented smile, and his eyes came to rest on her décolletage.

Although annoying, Jennifer could see the evolutionary reason why men's eyes were irresistibly drawn to women's breasts, but couldn't understand the primordial reason why some women had the same uncontrollable reaction to a shoe store sale. This distracting thought helped her to maintain a friendly smile in the presence of this man who made her skin crawl.

Donny turned to Jennifer, a surprised look on his face. "You two have met?"

"I was chatting with Dr. Singh a few hours ago at her office," Schwarzenegger said. "She was kind enough to give me her expert advice on establishing a national DNA library, which I am proud to say I am co-sponsoring."

Donny looked at Jennifer, he bowed his head with a look of respect.

Schwarzenegger turned to his companion in the tuxedo. "Doctor, allow me to introduce you to my colleague. Senator Taíno, from the great state of Puerto Rico."

Taíno took Jennifer's hand and lightly kissed it. "*Encantado*," he said with a flourish.

A shiver went through her body. "*Eres un verdadero caballero*."

"What did she say?" Schwarzenegger asked Taíno.

"She called me a true gentleman." Taíno stepped back a pace. His head came up to Jennifer's shoulders and he craned his neck to look at her face. "My esteemed colleague mentioned the DNA database. I have concerns both about the price of this proposal and the lack of safeguards to protect people's privacy. Perhaps I could get your point of view on the subject… sometime in the future, of course."

Jennifer nodded and smiled. "It would be my pleasure, Senator."

Schwarzenegger's smile diminished, his ego probably deflated by her acceptance of Taíno's proposal, and her chilly reception to his earlier invitation.

Taíno turned to the third man in their coterie, Russian-looking with a swarthy complexion, bristle-like black hair, and deep-set, penetrating eyes.

"Allow me to introduce Inspector Porphyry Petrovich from the FSB—the Russian Secret Service."

Jennifer's eyes widened. She couldn't believe the similarity in his name with the detective she'd met earlier at the office.

The inspector bowed formally to the couple, took Jennifer's hand and kissed it saying, "*Ty krasotka*."

Jennifer replied without hesitation. "*Bahl'shoe yeh spasiba*."

The inspector arched his eyebrows, then spoke broken English with a Russian accent. "I am sorry to be dressed so poorly. I did not bring tuxedo to wear to such wonderful event." He turned to Donny and bowed. "I am in Los Angeles investigating robbery in my home country. I am following lead. Lead has brought me here, to your wonderful city. I am working with your Federal Bureau of Investigations and Customs Departments." He gestured to the senator from Puerto Rico. "Senator Taíno most helpful in arranging your government's help in this matter." He moved closer to Donny, his prominent brow furrowed as he spoke directly to him. "Very valuable merchandise stolen. We very close to catching thief. We offer substantial reward if material is returned first. As you say, 'no questions asked.'"

"What a coincidence," Jennifer said. "I was working with a member of the *Federal'naya sluzhba bezopasnosti* earlier this evening."

The inspector's eyes widened and he looked back and forth to the senators.

A cold-blooded look flashed through Schwarzenegger's eyes and his lips thinned. In the blink of an eye, his practiced smile returned and his eyes softened. "The FSB? Is that so?"

Jennifer nodded. "You probably just missed him at the morgue. I spoke with him a short time before you and I met. He's working a case of a Russian courier found murdered on the California-Nevada border."

The senator's companions remained silent, their brows wrinkled.

Schwarzenegger's smile thinned and his eyes widened. "How do you know this 'detective' was really from the FSB?" He nodded to the inspector. "You don't know of anyone else from your department working this case, do you?" The inspector gave a slight shake of his head. "You might want to check and see if that man you talked to really works for the FSB," Schwarzenegger told Jennifer.

Jennifer gave him a slight nod. "I didn't actually see his credentials. I assume he showed them to Dutch, our administrator. The detective was quite secretive about the case." She turned to the inspector. "Care to share what this is all about?"

He hesitated, looking to his two colleagues, as if expecting them to answer. After a pause, he said, "The matter is confidential. I do not have permission to discuss."

"Indeed," Jennifer said, used to the halo of secrecy the national intelligence services—both the FBI and the FSB—maintained on their active cases. They insisted the local authorities provide them with information, but it was always a one-way street. "I'll have my office check on the credentials of the FSB detective in the morning," she said.

Senator Taíno seemed to relax. He looked around the room, nodding to a few of the guests. The Russian inspector was hyper-alert and looked intently at Donny, as if sizing him up. Schwarzenegger's eyes moved downward and remained firmly focused on Jennifer's chest; she felt naked and took Donny's arm.

"Let's walk around the room," she said to him. "The dessert table beckons."

Donny let out a breath. "Please excuse us. It's been a pleasure."

He led her away. When they were out of earshot, he asked, "What was it that the Russian said to you? I've tried to learn the language, but no luck. I know you said 'thank you' to him."

"He said I look beautiful, something to that effect."

Donny chuckled. "At least he has good taste in women. He should only be half as good with fashion."

By the time they got to the dessert table, Jennifer had lost her appetite. She waved over a champagne-carrying attendant and they each took new glasses. The attractive couple stood sipping champagne until the string quartet stopped playing.

"I'm wanted on stage," Donny said. "I need to make a few comments." He gave Jennifer a hug, then said with a roguish smile. "Wait here, *mayah daragaya*."

Jennifer gave him a surprised look. *Calling me "my dear," he must be more serious about me than I thought*. "I didn't think you knew any Russian," she said.

Donny shrugged and gave her a wry smile. "Only a word or two." He turned and bounded up the stage stairs, joining the small group of museum officials already on the dais. He shook hands all around.

While one of the women made a short speech thanking the crowd for its generosity, Jennifer saw in her peripheral vision that Senator Schwarzenegger had sidled up next to her, his two sidekicks in tow. She didn't look his way and kept her focus on the stage.

"You look radiant tonight, Doctor," the senator whispered. "Easily the most beautiful woman here."

Jennifer turned to him. "It's a pity your wife couldn't attend."

He appeared at a loss for words as his eyes were inexorably drawn downward again. Jennifer imagined having the senator's naked cadaver on her autopsy table, slowly dissecting his shriveled testicles and tossing them into a specimen jar. She turned away to hide her smile and flagged down a waiter for a fresh champagne.

From over her shoulder, the senator said, "I was going to drop you a line, but I wasn't able to find your social network page."

She took a new drink and didn't turn his way. "I don't have one. I'm not that social."

The senator chuckled. "I hope you wouldn't mind if I call you in the future…"

Jennifer turned to the senator and gave him a scathing look.

He cleared his throat. "To get your expert opinion on pending legislation."

"I hope you'd make any such arrangements through my office, Senator."

She turned her attention back to the dais. There was a brief slide show of the acquisitions the museum made in the last year. The floral centerpieces were raffled off, donated items were sold in auction, and in closing, Donny said a few words of appreciation on behalf of the Board of Trustees. After the closing remarks, Senator Taíno and the Russian inspector departed without a word, heading to the stage.

Jennifer was uncomfortable being alone with the senator. She thought he was too unctuous. She looked for Donny and saw he was in close conversation with Schwarzenegger's two guests.

"You and Donny make a handsome couple," Schwarzenegger said. "I've known him for years. We've sat together on the boards of a number of philanthropic organizations. He also handles a good portion of my portfolio."

Jennifer remained silent, her eyes on Donny.

"How long have you two been together?"

"Not long." Jennifer's attention remained riveted on her man.

She flicked a glance at Schwarzenegger. "The Russian inspector seems interested in talking to Donny. Any idea of what's going on?"

"Only what he told us earlier, that he's investigating some sort of theft back home. I wouldn't worry. Donny has a number of wealthy Russian investors as clients. The inspector is probably just covering all his bases."

The powwow between Donny and the other two men broke up and they rejoined Jennifer and the senator. The lights dimmed, the band struck up a waltz, and several couples took to the dance floor.

Donny bowed to the group. "If you would excuse us again." He bent his arm toward Jennifer. "I would like to ask the doctor for this dance."

Jennifer slid her arm inside Donny's, surprised but happy to make her way to the dance floor. Donny pulled her firmly against him, his desire palpable. Jennifer wrapped her arms around his neck and swayed to the music along with the other smiling couples. The quartet played a mixture of ballroom pieces. Jennifer's feet moved of their own volition.

Too soon, the music ended. Donny asked if she would like to see the newest pieces the museum purchased over the last year, on display in a side room. She agreed even though her feet and legs were hurting and her energy was flagging. And she ached to be alone with him. They left the dance floor and entered the exhibition.

About a dozen oil paintings of varying styles adorned the walls. A blown glass sculpture hung from the ceiling. A handful of sculptures graced the floor. Right in the middle of the room was the museum's prize acquisition: an ancient Greek vase from the black-figure period. The piece, about twelve inches high, was in a lit glass case.

They walked over to the display case, stooped down, and peered in. The black colored vase contained a sylvan picture in faded red paint that girdled the vessel. Jennifer read the accompanying label aloud. "Grecian *psykter*, or wine vessel, 500 BCE, signed by the artist, Douris, as painter, purchased from the British Museum."

Donny admitted that he really didn't know much about art. "My connection to the museum is to help collect money to keep the museum operational."

Jennifer held up her champagne and toasted him. "Well, you're doing a fine job of that."

Donny walked around the piece and seemed absorbed but puzzled. "You're a crossword expert, I bet you know something about mythology. What is the significance of the...depicted scene?"

Jennifer took on the didactic tone she used when teaching at UCLA. "The painting is a classic Greek subject: a satyr chasing a group of nubile nymphs through the woods, inviting them to a Dionysian party. The satyr is a mythological figure, half-man and half-horse. They were known for pipe-playing, wine drinking, and dancing with the nymphs." She looked at Donny and mused: the satyrs also had an insatiable sexual appetite, is that why he's so interested in the vase?

This evening could turn out even better than I thought.

Donny winked. "You know a lot about mythology—those nymphs, is that where the term 'nymphomania' comes from?"

"That's right. But the satyr isn't named after the god Saturn, the Roman god of wealth and money."

"Saturn sounds like my type of god." Donny chuckled.

Jennifer's legs turned to jelly and she blinked to keep her eyes open. She'd been on her feet all day at work, now a few more hours in heels, plus the excitement of being at the gala—exhaustion was catching up with her. And the Dexedrine—once keeping her fatigue at bay—was wearing off. She grabbed Donny's hand and leaned against him, letting him take some of the weight off her feet.

He smiled and wrapped his arm around her. He looked down into her eyes. "Ready to leave?"

She melted against his rock-hard body. "It's been a long day."

They walked arm-in-arm through a side entrance and back into the main lobby. Jennifer snuggled close, enjoying the primal feeling of being safe, protected, and desired. Donny flagged down one of the champagne carrying youths and exchanged their empty flutes for two full ones. Once outside the building, Jennifer glanced over where her photos had been taken earlier. The paparazzi were gone, the klieg lights extinguished. Despite the strong shell she showed to others, she had to admit that she enjoyed the experience.

Donny took her hand and helped her down the stairs. His black Bentley was parked against the sidewalk. "A perk of being on the board of trustees," he said. He opened the passenger side door. "Would you like to come to my place for a nightcap?"

She gave him a grimace. "I'd love to, but let me follow you. Unfortunately, I have to work tomorrow. You know how short-handed we've been."

Jennifer gave the valet her parking ticket, and he sent a signal to her car's Nav-Drive. Donny held her hand and they sipped their champagne while they waited. When Jennifer's car pulled up, Donny helped her in. She was pleased to see Donny's eyes widen as she swung her bare legs into the vehicle.

"Pull ahead," she said. "I'll have my Nav-Drive follow you."

Before closing the door, Donny leaned in, kissed Jennifer on the lips, and whispered, "I'd like to cash in that rain-check tonight."

A wave of passion surged through her body.

She pulled Donny down and kissed him again, then whispered in his ear, "That's just what the doctor ordered."

Chapter 7

Saturday

Sounds of a Marina del Rey morning poured through the open bedroom window: the hollow noise of plastic garbage cans being manhandled, the whirr of a sanitation truck, a sailboat's clanging bell, seagulls cawing, dogs barking, cats meowing. Jennifer burrowed under the bedspread and pulled a pillow over her head to drown out the din. Her head pounded as if a team of masons were hammering their way out of her skull. She moaned and drifted off, caught in that twilight area—the hypnopompic state—between sleeping and waking, where reality blurs and dreams become real.

Trapped! She struggled to move, the scuba gear strangling. Caught in an underwater cave, the walls and ceiling closing in, locked in a life-and-death battle with a slithering, man-sized moray eel, its razor-sharp teeth menacingly close to severing the tubing bringing oxygen to her regulator. The monster's tail wrapped around her thigh, its vise-like muscles taut. Constricting. Crushing. Her air supply was dropping. She looked to check her dive watch; it had disappeared into the depths. The serpent's mouth gaped open. Its eyes rolled back revealing the white sclera as its rows of needlelike teeth bit through the rubber tubing.

She thrashed about the bed. Her eyes flew open and she gasped for breath.

Deep breaths. In through the nose, out through the mouth. It was just a nightmare.

Her heart rate slowed. The feeling of panic and impending doom passed. She laughed inwardly, thinking that Freud would have a field day with her dreams. Through the awakening fog, pain emerged; her entire body ached as if she really had fought that marine monster. Her head throbbed, stomach did back-flips, her mouth felt as if it was stuffed full of cotton.

Sunlight streamed into the room, warming her face. She was reluctant to open her eyes, knowing from years of experience that the bright light would only exacerbate her hangover. She rolled onto her stomach and nestled into the bed, tossing and turning, unable to drift back to sleep. Her skin, clammy and wet, stuck to the sheets. Pushing aside an empty pizza box and a pile of medical journals from the nightstand, she found the alarm clock and squinted into the bright sunshine. The digital display said: 9:35 AM. She had time to sleep off the hangover since she'd told Dutch not to expect her in until the afternoon, with the promise that she'd work late to make up for the delayed start.

The garbage truck moved on, its mechanical sounds replaced by distant crashing waves, the pit-a-pat of a jogger running by on their way to the beach, and the chatter of neighbors greeting each other. A breeze rustled the sheer curtains and brought cool, briny air through the bedroom's open window.

Goddesses, I love living here.

Something primeval had always drawn her to the sea.

After hunting around on the nightstand, she grabbed a bottle of Ibuprofen, swallowed four, and washed them down with a warm, half-empty bottle of water. She sat up and willed her eyelids fully open, relieved to see the familiar sights of her home. The nightstand was covered in mountains of crossword puzzles and unread medical journals. The ornate wooden dresser she inherited when one of her neighbors upgraded their furniture was now covered in balled-up piles of clothes. She could still see hints of the dark cherry finish that matched her bed, with its orthopedic mattress—her gift to herself since she spent her days bent over exam tables. A vanity table heaping with a hodgepodge of makeup items sat next to the dresser. The walls were covered with Lucite-framed photos of nebulae, galaxies, and star clusters she'd taken using the telescope observatory on the roof of her bungalow.

Through foggy eyes, her gaze landed on the evening gown. Draped over the easy chair in the corner, it seemed to shimmer in the early morning sunlight. Memories of the previous evening came flooding back: dancing, champagne, Donny's body. Her heart pounded, her skin prickled, red-hot feelings of desire flared up from within. She relived the end of the night—nestled against Donny while dancing in the Getty ballroom, heading back to his house, sipping champagne on his balcony overlooking the lights of the city, followed by a beautiful night of lovemaking.

She bolted up.

She didn't have time to go back to sleep.

She threw the covers off and crawled out of bed. She rifled through a pile of clothes on the dresser, found a clean set of scrubs, and threw them on. Kicking last night's high heels out of the way, she stumbled down the hallway to the kitchen at the back of the bungalow. She started a kettle of water to boil. In the refrigerator, scattered among Styrofoam takeout containers and sealed plastic bowls containing Vietnamese food, she found a bag of blueberries. She grabbed a quart of milk, gave it a quick sniff, it was okay. The kettle screamed, and she made herself a pot of gyokuro tea. She fished a cup and plastic bowl out of the sink and poured the unidentifiable dregs into the potted plants on the windowsill overlooking her detached one-car garage. She gobbled down a breakfast of granola and tea in the breakfast nook, while flipping between SportsNexxus, a national sports news holoprogram, and ¡Despierta América!, a morning news holoprogram in Spanish, on her paper-thin Mega-Definition ProjectionWall television monitor.

Ten minutes later, she was backing out of her garage into the alleyway where the garbage cans jutting into the narrow passage stopped her progress. She turned the Nav-Drive off and drove the car manually, stopping to move the obstacles out of the way. Reaching the main street, she re-engaged the Nav-Drive and told it to take her to the UCLA Medical Center Professional Building.

When the Nav-Drive took over, she decided to get in touch with Donny. He was sound asleep hours earlier when she wiggled out from under his beefy arm. She'd made the excuse to herself that she needed to go home and change before going to work.

She wondered what he must be thinking. Would he suspect she had intimacy issues?

She tried to decide on the best way to reach him. Text? No, too impersonal, especially after last night. They needed to talk. And how should she refer to him? Sweetheart? No, too early for that. Darling? No, too dated. Donny? Too impersonal? Best to play it by ear, avoid using any references until she saw how he referred to her.

Jennifer told her OmniPhone—a device resembling a wrist dive computer—to dial Donny's number. His phone rang a number of times before going to voicemail.

Shit! Not voicemail.

The phone beeped, ready to record a message.

"Hey, it's me," she said. "Listen, I had a fabulous time last night. Sorry I had to leave early, you were sleeping so soundly I hated to wake you." She crossed her fingers and her voice went up a notch. "Hope you're okay with that. Wish I could go sailing with you, but I can't take three days off in a row, not when we're so short-handed at work. You're probably on the water already, but call when you get cell service. Look forward to seeing you when you get back. Ciao."

She breathed a sigh of relief.

Well, that went about as well as could be expected.

She turned on sports-talk radio and sat back with eyes closed. After a few minutes of the mindless chatter, she nodded off.

The car slowed as it exited onto Wilshire Boulevard, waking her up. She rubbed her eyes, not believing what she saw. Smoke swirled about in the gusting Santa Ana winds; black fumes were so thick that visibility was reduced to a few car lengths. Unidentifiable fiery objects floated aloft in the wind currents. The wail of fire engines came from the south where billowing smoke rose from a nearby building, probably ignited by the floating balls of fire. She looked out in that direction onto the mixed residential area called Westwood Park Village.

The buildings, each a city block in size, were joined together from their fifth floors up, creating a self-contained virtual city housing sixty thousand people. The buildings for housing and shopping were like a single edifice several square miles in size and encompassing about one hundred city blocks. The streets were like tunnels that wound their way through the edifice. This residential area, all the way down to Santa Monica Boulevard and east to South Beverly Glen Boulevard, made it possible for people to live cradle to grave without ever going outside, and many did just that. How else to cram the population of L'Orange, over fifty million people, into the Los Angeles Basin, an area no larger than the state of Rhode Island? Jennifer was relieved not to have to live in those maze-like complexes, thinking they were more suited for rats than humans. Now she was doubly grateful—her house was close to the beach and as far from the mountain fires as possible.

The car's LED headlights struggled to cut through the haze as they wove around Westwood Village and into the doctors' parking lot for the Ronald Reagan UCLA Medical Center. Jennifer entered the lobby and jogged up seven flights of stairs, thinking that's about all the exercise she'd get today. The smoke wasn't as bad inside the building, however, she was coughing and wheezing when she exited the stairwell. By the time she reached the end of the hall, her breathing and heart rate returned to normal.

She opened a wooden office door and entered a basketball court-sized reception area jam-packed with women. Women patiently reading celebrity magazines. Women patiently listening as a total stranger sitting next to them told them their life story. Women patiently waiting to be called into the inner sanctum of the doctor's office to finally become a patient. Dozens of eyes followed her and women whispered to each other as she walked to the front desk. She pretended not to notice, but her skin prickled and an uneasy sensation descended.

The reception desk was a beehive of activity. The staff were dressed in identical cherry soda scrub tops with matching bottoms. Jennifer waved the bubbliest of the lot over—a woman who'd missed her calling as a Disneyland greeter—and flashed her UCLA ID badge. While the huddled masses looked on in disbelief, she was buzzed in to the Promised Land in the back. The effervescent receptionist ushered her to a private corner office and told Jennifer she could wait there.

Jennifer took a seat facing the utilitarian desk covered in mounds of magazines and drug samples. She gazed out the window over the main UCLA campus swarming with students. In the distance, the seemingly ever-present pillars of black and gray smoke emanated from the National Forests to the north and climbed skyward, merging with the wispy white clouds.

After a brief wait, a short, thin, patrician-looking woman with hair pulled back in a bun walked in. She wore blue UCLA Bruins scrubs and a white doctor's jacket bulging with a stethoscope, penlights, prescription pads, and other paraphernalia. Above the jacket's breast pocket was embroidered the name: Johanna Whitridge Williams, M.D. She beamed when she caught site of Jennifer.

Johanna and Jennifer had been medical school classmates at UC-Irvine. Johanna remained at Irvine to do an OB-GYN residency. Jennifer started a psychiatric residency at the same school, then worked a year as an ER doctor before transferring to UCLA where she completed a forensic pathology residency. The two women stayed in touch, and when Johanna set up her practice at UCLA, she became Jennifer's gynecologist.

"Jennifer, what a nice surprise," Johanna said.

Jennifer stood up, leaned down, and gave her a hug. "Sorry to barge in on you. The waiting room's packed, I know you're busy."

Johanna made a dismissive gesture with her hands. "It's always that way. They can wait a bit, that's why they call them patients."

"I don't have that kind of patience. Where I work, when we have a backlog of cases we tell them to chill out."

Johanna chuckled. "You missed your calling as a standup comedian. What brings you in? It isn't time for your routine exam?"

"I stopped by," Jennifer cleared her throat, "to see if you could give me a quick checkup."

Johanna sat behind her desk. "What's up?" When Jennifer didn't answer, Johanna waited a few seconds, then said, "I saw your picture in the entertainment section of this morning's Times."

Jennifer shot her a puzzled look. "What are you talking about?"

"You didn't know?"

Johanna turned the monitor so that they could both see the screen. She pulled up the LA Times WebSpace and navigated to the entertainment section. On the front page was coverage of the Getty ball. Dominating the screen was a color picture of Jennifer posing in her evening gown. The photo caption said: Doctor Jennifer Sing; Senior Coroner, L'Orange County; Adjunct Professor of Pathology, UCLA Medical School.

Jennifer leaned forward and looked at the photo wide-eyed and speechless. Excitement rushed to her head. She scrunched her eyes and scrutinized the picture, marveling at how the photographers and Aída had worked magic. She didn't believe she could possibly look that good in real life. She rationalized that everybody looks better with photographic tricks. Then her spirits sunk—the reality that all kinds of kooks were going to emerge from the woodwork hit home. The privacy she so cherished was as good as over.

Done with looking at the monitor, she sat back. "It would have been nice if they'd spelled my name correctly. And I'm an associate professor, not adjunct."

Johanna clicked on the links to the photos and paged through the attached slide show. What followed was photo after photo of Jennifer. Jennifer facing the camera; turned right and left; close-ups of her face, shoulders, and cleavage; even a shot from behind showing the plunging open back of her gown.

When the slides moved on to other guests, Johanna clicked back to Jennifer's photo on the front page. "You know, there are similar pictures of you in the Daily News, the Register, and on the Los Angeles Magazine WebSpace."

Jennifer scowled. "I hate publicity."

"I wish I could be sympathetic, but I'm kinda envious."

Jennifer rubbed one of her temples and grimaced. "Back in the reception area, I was getting strange looks from the women. I wonder if those photos are why."

Johanna gave her a look as if to say "you gotta be kidding me" but it lacked sincere surprise. "Before I even left for work, I received texts from a bunch of our former classmates texting me with the 411." She looked back at the monitor. "I must say, Jennifer, you looked fabulous. I don't remember seeing you with makeup the whole time we were in med school. Now here you are, having your picture taking by the paparazzi. Mega-bradford."

"It was bradford. I never expected they would put those photos in the paper."

"What did you think they were going to do with them?" Johanna let out a short laugh. "Put them in their family album?"

Jennifer shrugged. She hadn't thought about it, but realized that did make sense.

"How could they not put them in?" Johanna said. "You looked gorgeous."

"That's not really me." Jennifer shook her head and pointed to herself. "This is what I really look like." She gestured to the monitor. "That makeup. The hairdo. One of my assistants did that. I'll let her know you liked her work."

Johanna enlarged the front page photo.

Jennifer leaned forward in the "thinkers" pose, studied the image, and cracked a smile. "I hate to say it, but I'm actually enjoying this."

"You're a beautiful woman, Jennifer. Embrace your femininity."

"Sounds like the kind of pop psychology you'd hear on a daytime holovision show."

"However you want to phrase it," Johanna pulled up another photo of Jennifer, "it's the truth."

Jennifer gazed at the photo and thought maybe her friend was right. Although she belittled women whose entire life revolved around looking beautiful, she knew there was no reason she couldn't enjoy dressing up and turning heads on occasion.

"The photos *do* make me look good," she told Johanna. "I wonder if Donny's seen them."

"Donny?" Johanna raised an eyebrow and gave Jennifer a sly smile.

"A guy I've been seeing."

"How come he's not in any of the photos?"

"He was running late and met me in the lobby."

Johanna leaned forward and rested her elbows on the desk. "In med school you were sooo serious. Is this the new Jennifer?"

"Honestly?" Jennifer shrugged. "I'd rather wear sweats and a baseball cap and lounge around the house with a tough crossword puzzle."

Johanna chuckled. "That's not what your body language right now is telling me."

Jennifer sighed. "If things work out with Donny, I might have to change. He attends celebrity events on a weekly basis, it seems."

"I bet you make it on the LA Society A-list now, you'll be getting *beaucoup* invites." Johanna magnified the front page picture of Jennifer until it took up the entire screen. She looked at the monitor, chin in hand. "That was one beautiful gown you were wearing."

"It was so tight, it took me forever to get it on." Jennifer laughed. "And Donny spent the other half of the evening trying to take it off."

"And…was he successful?" Johanna asked with a salacious grin.

Jennifer smiled and nodded. "As a matter of fact, that gown came off a lot easier than it went on." She paused. "And that's the reason I'm here."

Johanna smiled knowingly. "Let me guess: you and your beau got hot and heavy and you didn't use any protection."

Jennifer put her head down, like a dog caught eating off the kitchen counter. "I feel like such a fool," she mumbled. "Here I am, a doctor…a medical professor…and I let my hormones take control of my common sense."

Johanna's features softened as she looked at her friend. "It's happened to nearly everyone, even me. Just shows you're human." Her face took on a business look. "What do you know about this guy's sexual history?"

Jennifer was chagrined and felt her face flush with embarrassment. "I really never got around to asking him."

Johanna let out a dismissive snort. "Don't feel guilty, that's a difficult discussion to have. And he probably wouldn't have told you the truth anyway. You *are* taking your birth control pills?"

Jennifer slunk down even more and shook her head. "I stopped taking them awhile back. I haven't been sexually active…and I'm on my feet all day long—I'm afraid of blood clots. And…I hate to admit it, all week long I knew I was going to sleep with Donny and never got around to starting back on the pill." She gazed at the floor. "To top it off, I'm in the middle of my cycle."

"Don't panic, here's what we're going to do." Johanna rummaged around on her desk and handed Jennifer a blue-colored box. "The drug rep dropped off samples of a new morning-after pill. Take them, and you'll start your period within twenty-four hours. Since we don't know your boyfriend's sexual history, I'll like to take a few blood and vaginal samples and send them to the lab."

Jennifer relaxed, relieved Johanna didn't judge her and that her friend had taken control of the situation. "Thanks. Thanks so much." Jennifer thought a moment, then cringed. "You don't have to use a speculum, do you? You know I hate that thing."

Johanna came around the desk and put a hand on Jennifer's shoulder. She spoke in a soothing voice. "Don't worry, I'll use long cotton-tipped swabs—you'll hardly feel a thing."

Jennifer breathed a sigh of relief, stood up, and hugged Johanna. "You're a gift from heaven."

"Go to Exam Room 17, put on a gown, and assume the position. I'll be there in just a second."

"After you get the samples, think you might be free for lunch?"

"Only if you promise to give me all the juicy details about last night," Johanna said and made a lip-smacking sound. The two women laughed.

"You sure you can break away? Your waiting room's jammed."

"I almost never take a break for lunch, and the reception area is always like that. I'm so busy I feel like I'm always running on a treadmill."

Jennifer grinned slyly, thinking that was the second time in two days someone mentioned being on a treadmill.

She told Johanna, "Never underestimate the pleasures of running on a treadmill."

Chapter 8

The two women walked to a restaurant called the Bruin Deli in Westwood Village. Jennifer ordered a high-protein smoothie and a roti chicken wrap. Johanna had a drink called an Island Delight and a watercress salad with tuna tartare and pomegranate dressing.

Jennifer held her forearm out to scan her microchip to pay for the meals. Johanna pulled it back. “This is my treat. Payment for the upcoming story.”

Johanna placed her own arm before the payment scanner and the device beeped.

When their meals came, they went outside, found a table with an umbrella, and watched the shoppers and students pass by on the tree-lined sidewalk as they ate.

Jennifer’s skin prickled. The uneasy sensation returned. She was getting long stares from many of the passing women.

“Am I paranoid?” she asked Johanna. “Are people staring at me?”

“You’re not paranoid, you *are* getting lots of looks. Remember, your photo is plastered all over the society pages.” Johanna laughed. “Now you know how it must feel to be a celebrity.”

“Can’t say I like being the center of attention.”

“Try wearing a big floppy hat and sunglasses.”

Jennifer laughed. “That would make me even *more* conspicuous.” She took a bite of her wrap, then chuckled to herself. “By the way, thanks for paying for the meal. Usually guys buy me lunch *before* I take my clothes off for them.”

Johanna grimaced. “If I had a nickel for every time you’ve used a variation on that joke, well…I’d have a shit-load of nickels.”

They both laughed.

Jennifer took a bite of her sandwich, then wiped her mouth. "Speaking of nickels, I saw a story recently about a woman in Miami. She'd found bags of old American coins—nickels, quarters, and such—in her basement. They were so heavy she had to hire someone to help her take them to the bank to be converted into SDR. You know how much they gave her?"

Johanna shrugged.

"One hundred-twenty SDR. For hundreds of pounds of change. That got me thinking, and I did the math. You want to guess how much a nickel would be worth in SDR?"

Johanna had her mouth full. She shook her head and mumbled, "Tell me."

"Get this: Twenty thousand nickels would equal one SDR."

"Which just about buys you a soda nowadays."

Jennifer sighed. She couldn't remember ever using the old US currency, even though the switch-over occurred when she was in grade school. The old currency—pennies, dimes, quarters, dollars—was lost somewhere in the fogs of her memory.

Johanna glanced at her Omni then poked Jennifer in the arm. "C'mon, I've haven't got all day. Make like a Russian and quit Stalin, you've gotta tell me about last night, girl."

Jennifer took the last few bites of her chicken wrap, then wiped her mouth. "The gala at the Getty was fabulous. Donny, my date, helps to raise money for the museum so they can keep purchasing new art. He introduced me to a bunch of celebrities, politicians, wealthy people; the A-list. He seems to know just about everybody. He even surprised me by asking me to dance in this magnificent ballroom."

"He's not a dancer?"

"Last weekend he took me to the Mount Sinai Hospital Ball and left me stranded on the dance floor while he talked business. But last night… we danced until my legs were about to fall off."

Johanna groaned. "I wish I'd been there, I love to dance. I've never been to one of those high-society events."

"Neither had I, until recently. Let me tell you, dancing with Donny was like a dream."

"What sort of business is he in?"

"Big time investments. Runs a hedge fund, and has been very successful. He's quite wealthy." Jennifer took a sip of her drink. "It was an enchanting evening. All the beautiful people, dancing, amazing champagne…and Donny." She sighed. "At the end of the night I was exhausted. Donny asked me if I wanted to come back to his house. Hell, I was dying to."

They both laughed.

Johanna rubbed her hands together. "This is getting interesting."

"I had my Nav-Drive follow Donny's car. He drives a Bentley, no less. You should see his place. It's in Woodland Hills. Or Beverly Glen. I don't know why, but I get the two mixed up. Anyway, his house is like a museum, all white marble and Greek columns. I parked my car in his gargantuan garage—it's bigger than my entire house—and went into the mansion. The garage led to something called the keeping room, and it led to the kitchen, something right out of Architectural Digest."

Johanna grinned and arched her eyebrows. "Wow, I'm loving this."

"Donny pulled a bottle of really expensive champagne from the wine refrigerator, and we walked into his living room. I kicked off my shoes and sank so deep into the thick carpet, I could hardly see my feet!"

Johanna laughed just a bit too hard, and a piece of watercress popped out of her mouth.

Jennifer smiled, reliving the moment.

"The living room had all sorts of expensive pieces of art hanging on the wall. Jumbles of colors, shapes, textures—he seems to prefer abstract art. The back wall was all glass, from floor to ceiling. You could see the twinkling lights of the city and the distant flames glowing in the mountains. Donny put on music: Ravel's Boléro." Jennifer winked at her friend and laughed. "I don't think any woman can keep her clothes on with that playing in the background."

Johanna chuckled silently.

"The music playing, we went out onto the balcony. An outdoor pool with a Jacuzzi sat on one side. Sliding glass doors leading to the master bedroom on the other. We sipped champagne and made small talk. The air was clear and I could smell the eucalyptus and cedar trees, sage, jasmine, and rosemary. He had a woody, musky smell. I snuggled next to him. Without a word, he turned me toward him and slid my gown off. Right there! I was completely naked. Speakers were scattered around the patio, the music was reaching its crescendo with an insistent, throbbing beat. He pulled me to him, picked me up, and carried me to his bedroom. He called me his mountain flower, I opened my petals, and we did it."

Johanna shook her head. "Mmmm."

"It was fabulous."

Johanna continued to make mumbling sounds.

"It was still dark outside when I woke up; spent and sore. Passion's embers from the night before were still smoldering. I wanted to stay, but I had work today. I decided to leave before Donny woke and had a chance to stoke my flames."

"If I was in your high heels," Johanna arched her brows, "I would have snuggled back in."

"I didn't want to leave. Donny was lying at my side, his big, muscular arm draped possessively over me. He looked so peaceful and content. But duty called…or maybe things were just moving too fast. I managed to extricate myself without waking him. I kissed him on the cheek, he smiled in his sleep and snuggled down into the covers. I gathered my things and stole out of the house."

Jennifer sipped her smoothie and looked to see if there was anything left of her chicken wrap. There wasn't.

Johanna shook her head and slurped the last of her Island Delight. "I'm so envious. I wish I could get my Kutu fired up like that."

Jennifer laughed. "You call your hoo-haw Kutu?"

"Not my hoo-haw." Johanna was also laughing. "Kutu's my husband."

"Isn't his name Kenny?"

"Kutu's my pet name for him—it's his Samoan name. Anyway, here you and Prince Charming are shooting off fireworks when Kutu and I only set off a few firecrackers every now and then."

Jennifer used her compassionate voice, the one she used when she had to tell family members a loved one was dead. "It's hard to maintain the fire. You've been married, what, five years?"

"Six. And you're right. I shouldn't expect the kind of experience you had last night. But sometimes…it seems like Kenny and I are just going through the motions—it's gotten routine. I think we should just keep the television on while we make love so we don't miss any breaking news."

"Maybe you could try something to spice up the bedroom once in awhile. To use a phrase, which I abhor, step outside the box."

"Actually, I want Kutu inside the box more often," Johanna said with a laugh and pushed Jennifer's arm. "You're probably right about spicing up the bedroom. I've got a cheerleader skirt that gets him hot and bothered. Maybe I'll wear it tonight. We might set off our own fireworks."

"Hell, yeah," Jennifer said.

"Have you talked to Donny this morning?"

"I tried calling him, but he's out on the ocean, sailing. Probably out of cell range." Jennifer smiled broadly and poked Johanna. "But we have plans to get together this coming week."

The bells from the campus began to ring—noon.

Johanna consulted her Omni. "I'd better get back to work."

"I meant to ask you, I thought UCLA hired you to handle tertiary care."

Johanna let out a laugh. "I thought I was hired to handle complex referrals from the local OB/GYNs. We get plenty of referrals for the tertiary care clinic. But when I explain what the treatment's going to cost and the chances of long-term survival, most women decline treatment. They'd rather leave the money in their Medical Savings Accounts and let their children inherit it than deplete their funds on a long shot."

"That happen a lot?"

"If the patient has children or grandchildren, you bet. So I'm stuck doing routine GYN exams most of the week. I could train a chimp to do my job.

"Gross." Jennifer shivered. "Chimps have such hairy hands."

Chapter 9

Jennifer used her wrist OmniPhone to page her vehicle, then made small talk with Johanna while they waited. Her car pulled up to the curb a few minutes later.

"I'll call you when I get those lab results," Johanna said. "We need to do this more often." Then she left on foot, heading back to her office.

Jennifer climbed in for the trip to the morgue. "To the salt mines," she told the Nav-Drive.

The car pulled out, crossed under the same expressway, and passed the same UCLA baseball fields as the night before, except then she was in a state of heightened anticipation of an exciting evening ahead. Now she felt apathetic and blasé.

She pulled into the lot and parked in her favorite spot, in the shade of a sycamore tree. The front lobby—where people waited to be called back to identify the body of a loved one—was devoid of visitors. On the counter sat a bouquet bursting with dozens of cream-colored roses in a cut-crystal vase. Her heart began to race. Donny sent her flowers the last time they went out and she hoped this arrangement was from him, too.

The clerk sitting behind the desk craned his neck to see around the blooms. He caught Jennifer's eye and waved her over. "Doctor, these flowers arrived a few minutes ago for you."

Jennifer blushed, legs atremble, as she plucked the attached card with shaking hands. She turned away to hide her excitement while she read the message:

Thank you for the wonderful evening.

These flowers cannot compare to your beauty.

DB.

Jennifer beamed, relieved Donny wasn't annoyed that she'd left without waking him. She brought her wrist up to her face and used her Omni to send Donny a text thanking him for the flowers and closed it by telling him to please be safe.

Please be safe?

She chuckled to herself realizing how possessive that made her sound.

She picked up the arrangement to put it in her office for safe-keeping.

The clerk shot up from his post. "I'll get that for you, Doctor."

He held the vase with both hands and looked through the rose stems to see where he was walking. Jennifer held the swinging door to the morgue open. When the clerk nearly walked into the door jamb, Jennifer led him by the elbow down the hallway.

"Thanks, Doctor." He smiled at her. "I saw your picture in this morning's Times." He blushed. "You looked very pretty."

That's weird. This is probably the first time I've said more than two words to this guy.

"Thanks…" She couldn't remember the clerk's name. "You're too kind."

She took in a deep breath. The aroma of rose attar was intoxicating. Lightheaded, she passed the administrator's office arm in arm with the clerk.

Dutch looked up from behind his desk. "Dr. Singh! Come in. I want to hear about the ball."

Jennifer sighed. She wanted to get the autopsies out of the way. It was a Saturday, after all, and she didn't want to spend the entire day cooped up in the morgue. She turned and entered the office, accompanied by her flower bearer.

Dutch cleared a place on his desk and the clerk set the vase down. He bowed to Jennifer and left without a word.

Jennifer slipped into a chair facing Dutch's desk.

Doctor Nicolas Tulp, clad in a bio-hazard suit, minus the mask, poked his head in the office, nodded, and took a seat next to Jennifer.

Tulp was the only other medical examiner not out on disability. Dark-complexioned and a head taller than Jennifer, he was a Sikh with a full beard and the traditional turban—making fitting him with a bio-hazard suit a nightmare.

"I'm surprised you came in after your big date," Dutch said, trying to stifle a laugh. "I thought you'd be jetting off to Nigeria."

Jennifer shook her head. "Nigeria? Why the hell would I—" It dawned on her. "Don't tell me."

Dutch consulted his computer monitor and read. "King Yoruba, of Nigeria, wants to make you his queen. He'd like you to charter a jet and fly out to his kingdom. All you have to do is send him your banking information so he can wire money to your account."

Tulp turned to Jennifer and said with his clipped BBC accent, "You are a lucky woman, Jennifer. Queen of Nigeria."

"Queen of the Interweb scammers is more like it," she said to the turbaned one.

"I saw your photos on the LA Times WebSpace," Dutch said. "You looked fantastic. No wonder our email is inundated with people requesting your hand in marriage."

"That's why I don't have a social media page, and my Omni blocks all calls from unknown numbers."

"Otherwise your Omni would be ringing off the hook," Dutch said. "And great job mentioning you work here. Excellent publicity for the morgue."

"They said I'm a coroner, not a medical examiner."

"What the hell," Dutch said. "Most people don't know the difference." He addressed the doctors. "I wanted to thank you both for jumping in and picking up the slack while our colleagues aren't available."

"Don't mention it," Jennifer said.

"I don't know where we would have stored the bodies if you two hadn't sped up the procedures. I know we're cutting corners, but there's really no alternative. If there's anything you can think of, anything to expedite the process even more, please let me know. When we get back to full staff, you're both due a ton of time off."

"We are all deluding ourselves," Jennifer said. "They're never coming back. They'll die the slow death of consumption up in the Canadian Cascades."

Tulp rubbed his thick black beard and addressed Jennifer. "Don't be so pessimistic. You're Hindu, learn to accept the *hukam*."

"*Hukam* is a Sikh concept," Jennifer said, amused that Tulp couldn't get it through his turbaned head she was neither Indian nor Hindu.

"Indeed," Tulp said. "Then you'd be wise to get in touch with your *dharma*."

Jennifer looked at Dutch, who shrugged and gave her a thin smile back. They had often joked between themselves about Tulp's stubbornness on the subject.

Tulp turned to Dutch. "Any progress on getting us help with the autopsies? I haven't taken a day off in weeks."

Dutch's expression turned serious. "We're making progress, Dr. Tulp. Many academic pathologists are willing to volunteer their time, but the county is worried about liability in the event one of them should get injured or contract an incurable infection. The county's gun shy after what happened in New York following 9-11."

"That was ages ago," Jennifer said. "Can't the doctors who volunteer sign hold harmless agreements?"

"The county attorney's working out a hold-harmless contract with various medical schools around the country, allowing their pathology professors to lend us a hand. The documents are being passed around amongst the law firms, and as soon as the lawyers feel they've racked up enough billable hours on the case, we should be good to go. My guess is, we'll have this wrapped up within a couple weeks."

Tulp gave Dutch a nod and stood up. "I'm getting back to work." He bowed to Jennifer. "I saw your photos from last night. You looked beautiful. My wife can set you up with a nice Indian man." He shot Jennifer a serious look. "You're not getting any younger." With that, Tulp turned and left the room.

Jennifer turned her gaze to Dutch; her friend had leaned back in his chair, his hands were over his head, and he was laughing silently.

Jennifer shook her head and laughed with him. "Why does he keep trying to set me up with Indian men?"

Dutch shrugged.

"I keep telling him that Singh is a Nepali name," Jennifer added. "And I'm only one-sixteenth Nepali at that."

"Tulp's so serious he's funny." Dutch gave Jennifer a look that she always imagined a brother would give his favorite younger sister. "Tell me, how was the ball?"

"Totally bradford." Jennifer became serious. There were dozens of autopsies to do, and they wouldn't get done by sitting around and chitchatting. "I'll tell you all about it tonight over a couple beers." She stood up to leave, then settled back in the chair. "There's something I need to discuss with you, before I forget."

Dutch nodded.

"The Russian detective that came over late yesterday afternoon. Detective Porphyria, something like that."

Dutch nodded while he looked at his monitor. "Detective Porfiry. What about him?"

"He may not be legit. I ran into Senator Schwarzenegger at the ball. He was with a senator from Puerto Rico and a Russian inspector from the FSB. None of them knew anything about this guy."

"You can't expect them to be aware of all Russians here in LA. The city's overrun by them."

"Get this." Jennifer arched an eyebrow conspiratorially at Dutch. "The Russian inspector at the ball. His name was Porfiry, or something like that, also."

"Isn't that a common Russian name?"

"That would be too coincidental."

Dutch shrugged. "I'll check with the Russian embassy. See what I can find out."

Jennifer drummed her fingers on Dutch's desk. "It wouldn't be the first time someone's gotten in here on false pretenses."

"If he isn't FSB, what was he doing here?"

"He said the method by which our Russian John Doe was killed was the trademark of the Chechen mafia. Perhaps he was here to verify that the killing took place." Jennifer shivered when she thought about the Russian asking her out for dinner and dancing. "We gave him a tissue sample of the deceased. He could take that back to confirm the kill."

"Russian Kafkaesque intrigue." Dutch clucked his tongue. "I'll make a few inquiries. And I'll notify the detective from Vegas PD handling the case about the matter."

Jennifer stood and moved toward the door.

"We still on for the baseball game tonight?" Dutch asked.

Jennifer broke out into a big smile. "Wouldn't miss it for the world, buddy."

When Jennifer entered the dressing room, Aída was sitting before her own locker, in the process of changing. She ran over in bra and panties and squeezed her boss. Aída's words poured out in a torrent. "I saw your pictures in the paper. You looked so beautiful! Did you have fun last night? Are the flowers out front from your mystery date? I bet he couldn't keep his eyes off of you, could he? Did he like the hair and makeup? *¿Dormiste con tu chavo?*" She finally took a breath.

"*¡Que metiche eres!* Thank the goddesses, Carlos isn't such a gossip." Jennifer fell back in her leather recliner and her assistant settled on the bench next to her. "To answer your questions in order: yes, things went great last night and I had a lot of fun; the flowers are from him; it wasn't just his eyes he couldn't keep off me; he did like your makeup work; and no comment to the final question."

Aída arched her eyebrows, jumped up, and hugged Jennifer again. "I'll take that last one as a yes." She studied Jennifer's face. "You did sleep with him!" Jennifer lifted a shoulder and gave a lopsided smile. "When are you going to see *Señor Misterioso* again?"

Jennifer tried to fight it, but she ended up smiling broadly. "*Señor Misterioso* is sailing with another couple on their private yacht and will be back in three or four days. We're going out next Friday, attending a black tie benefit at City Hall."

"Sounds like you two are getting serious." Aída turned and walked to her locker, saying over her shoulder, "I've gotta get dressed, but you'll have to tell me all about the ball."

Jennifer donned the bio-hazard suit and walked to the autopsy suite.

Before she knew it, the day was over and she was back in street clothes, walking alongside Dutch's wheelchair across the street to the UCLA baseball field. They were going to watch a bunch of young guys swing their lumber and run around the diamond in tight-fitting baseball pants.

◇◇◇◇◇◇◇

It was dark by the time she returned to her house and was relieved to finally be alone. She went to the refrigerator, pulled out a half-full bottle of champagne, and popped the cork. She should have been tired, but the excitement of the game was still with her. The Bruins won in extra innings. She matched Dutch in beer drinking, but not in hotdog eating. She planned on running a couple extra miles in the morning to burn off the extra calories, then back to the daily grind despite it being Sunday.

She poured the champagne into a wine glass, went to the living room, and curled up in her favorite chair—a cloth loveseat-ottoman combination, off-white with sea-green stripes. She tried to work on the New York Times Friday crossword puzzle, but was restless. Her mind kept ruminating obsessively about why Donny hadn't called back. She looked over to the lovely roses he had sent, now sitting on an end table on the other side of the room. She thought he must have had a wonderful night or he wouldn't have sent them. She rued begging out of the cruise; she could have worked double shifts when she returned. Were her intimacy issues were coming out? Was she was using her job as an excuse to avoid getting emotionally involved? It was Saturday and she was sitting by herself working crossword puzzles, lamenting because the rest of the world was home with their families.

Jennifer drained her champagne glass in one big swig and stood up. She intended to return to the kitchen to get another glass. Instead, she found herself seated before her vanity mirror applying makeup and wearing a hip-hugging, green leopard skin miniskirt.

A familiar feeling came over her—a feline urge to hunt.

She stood and adjusted the skirt so it was snug over her hips. It felt good. She padded back to the kitchen barefoot, popped open a fresh bottle of champagne, and rolled a flaca.

She lit the flaca and headed to the closet where she fished out her favorite top—an onyx-black faux wrap, with a daring and revealing V-cut front to lure her prey. She pulled on black Italian designer leather boots with half-inch kitten heels.

Back at her vanity, she put on dark eye makeup and red lip gloss. After a quick and satisfied once-over in the mirror, she headed out to her car and rode up the coast.

A cool breeze blew off the ocean as she walked north along the Santa Monica promenade. On a side alley, she strutted toward the basement of a luxury hotel to one of her favorite clubs, the Tavern on the Beach. She knew most of the bartenders. They had live music and an active singles scene.

Laughter poured out of the club as an attendant opened the door for her. She dug in her purse and found a red-colored bill—five SDR—and tipped him as she entered. The air was warm and smelled of marijuana, perfume, and sex pheromones. Her body moved of its own volition, keeping time to the down tempo music coming from a jazz trio in the corner. Through the haze of smoke, she searched the brick-walled club for anyone she knew.

People stood shoulder-to-shoulder around the bar; it was always packed on weekends. Although there was a fairly even number of both sexes, she noticed only the men; some in sport coats, others smart casual. The majority were in their twenties and early thirties.

Jennifer wove her way through the crowd to the far end of the bar, opposite the band. One of the bartenders recognized her and motioned that he'd be right over. Jennifer surveyed the scene, imagining herself as a baseball manager looking over the roster and deciding the batting lineup.

A thirty-something-year-old man in dress jeans and a cotton top stood next to her. He glanced her way and gave a weak smile.

She decided not to put him in the lineup, he'd probably swing too early and dribble a weak grounder—wouldn't even get to first base.

Farther down the bar, two men were talking to each other, the shorter one kept looking her way surreptitiously.

Jennifer laughed to herself. No, he looks like a Yankee. Probably a pull hitter.

She looked farther afield and saw that she'd lured her first prize—a film industry type, early thirties, and smartly dressed in black slacks, dark blazer, and a dark purple shirt. He walked her way with a confident look in his eye and moved with athletic grace. He was above average height with a broad, swimmer's build.

Now we're talking. A power hitter. I'll put him in the middle of the lineup. He's sure to make it 'round the bases.

Out of the corner of her eye, she watched as he looked her up and down.

Inside of her, flames of desire rose, followed by a pang of doubt. *What am I doing here? Am I cheating on Donny?*

Her suitor shot her a smile as he neared. As rapidly as they came, the doubts washed away. She and Donny hadn't made any promises to each other.

The young film exec sidled up. He smelled fresh and was even bigger close up.

He put an elbow on the bar and leaned close, his breath tickling her ear.

"What would you like to drink, my lady?" He winced, probably realizing how silly that must have sounded.

She enjoyed his discomfort while she sized him up and flashed him a coy smile. "Would you like to play a little game?"

Chapter 10

Sunday

In desperation she battled, squashed against slime-covered walls of the dank pit.

Trapped! In complete darkness!

A crushing weight bore down. Her feet slid out from under her on the slick stone floor. She crashed down, her back slammed on the rock surface. Her head hit the floor, she saw stars. She writhed about, wrestling something long, thick, and rock-hard. Hands gripped just below its swollen head, she gritted her teeth, muscles taut, and squeezed with all she had. A flicker from a burning torch, and she saw it. A green-mottled snake. An anaconda. The serpent's tail wrapped around her body, squeezing the breath out of her. Its black tongue flicked in and out tasting her fear. Its cold, reptilian eyes, inches from her face, bore into her soul and paralyzed her.

She jerked awake.

The raucous cawing of seagulls outside her window roused Jennifer from the recurring, angst-ridden dream. She thrashed about and the covers fell to the ground. A cold sweat covered her body. Her heart pounded. Her mind raced. She rolled on her stomach, buried her head in the pillows, and let out a muffled groan. The nightmares had all but disappeared, and now, two nights in a row. As the drowsiness cleared, panic was replaced by a throbbing headache, cotton mouth, and queasy stomach.

The night before was a blur. She didn't know when she got home, or how.

This is it—time to go on the wagon.

Outside, the air was hazy, not the usual morning ocean fog, rather a sinister and foul miasma—cloying and foreboding—roiling mists of thick, gray, opaque murk. A charred, fetid smell of fire drifted in from the open window. She hoped the smoke was brought down from the mountains by a shift in the wind direction, and not their wooden claptrap neighborhood up in flames.

Jennifer groped around on the nightstand and came up with a bottle of ibuprofen. There were only three soft-gel capsules left. She grabbed her water bottle—empty. A wine glass stood next to the lamp. Putting it to her lips, she used what was left of the warm, flat champagne to wash down the little red pills.

Well, that was a short wagon trip!

The digital clock said 8:45. It was Sunday morning. She lay back to let the pills take effect while she slept a little longer, thinking then she'd get in a long run before heading to work. She wrapped a pillow around her aching head, then bolted up.

Mrs. Ng!

She couldn't sleep if she was going to exercise before meeting Ng for their weekly trip to the Asian market.

Her muscles ached as if she had really wrestled that serpent and the throbbing in her head felt like the pounding of jackhammers inside her skull. She kicked aside the boots she'd worn the night before and shuffled into the bathroom. Standing before the grimy mirror above the sink, she cringed. She looked as bad as she felt—hair tangled and matted down, eyeliner smudged, lipstick smeared, skin dehydrated, and cheeks ashen. Jennifer splashed her face with cold water, still laden with now-streaked foundation—the stuff she'd splurged 50 SDR for when she started dating Donny.

She trudged into her kitchen. The sink was full of dirty dishes that she pushed aside in order to fill the tea kettle. She placed the kettle on the gas-burning stove to make tea—green tea; the panacea, in the gospel according to Ng. She wiped off the sleek granite counter with a paper towel while she waited for the water to boil. Her eyes stole to the breakfast nook. The roses Donny sent sat in the middle of the inlaid table. A few petals were beginning to wilt and a solitary petal sat atop a pile of crossword puzzles next to the vase. A pang of remorse shattered her nerves when she flashed back to hitting the bars last night and what she only vaguely remembered doing.

Not for the first time in her life, Jennifer tried to analyze herself. Was she an alcoholic? Sure, she liked to drink, but so did Dutch, and most of the other people she knew. And sure, she had the occasional blackout. But she wasn't obsessed with drinking. It doesn't affect her ability to work, or her social interactions. She laughed to herself. Or did it?

She'd never had unsuccessful attempts at stopping, mainly because she'd never tried to stop. She could say with certainty that her drinking wasn't out of control. People at AA would probably say it was, but they have a hair-trigger attitude toward drinking anyway. She certainly didn't drink more than many people; especially after the financial tsunami wiped out people's savings, alcohol consumption had skyrocketed. And with people's confidence in the future shaken, attitudes toward drinking, and casual drug use, had loosened up since the early parts of the century.

What had gone on last night?

She was almost grateful for blackouts. She wondered why she had this…compulsion to go out and have pickup-bar-sex. It was as if she was like a different person at times. She could only conclude that it was her behavior that was out of her own control, not her drinking.

And whatever happened last night, she rationalized that she really didn't cheat on Donny because oral sex isn't really cheating. Then she laughed, thinking, who was she trying to kid? She knew they didn't have any agreement—Donny could be lying in bed with another woman right now. Now that was a disturbing thought though.

Donny sailing the ocean with a nubile, bikini-clad bimbo.

A hollow feeling settled in the pit of her stomach—she knew she should have said screw the morgue, let the bodies pile up, and just gone sailing with Donny. The excuse that she had to work, might have been just that. An excuse. A fear of intimacy. The loss of her freedom. She couldn't decide if any man was worth giving that up for.

She'd been staying home and not been clubbing or drinking. It had been months. Now, sleeping with Donny must have triggered a primitive, subconscious fear and that had to be the reason for the vivid dreams.

Fear of what? What was there to be afraid of? And why did she have such a fear in the first place? And those snake dreams, so transparent. Dr. Feelgood interprets all dreams the same way—you can't blame him—the dreams are very Freudian. Even though the dreams are chilling on the surface, she wondered if they could be hiding something even more appalling from her subconscious. Some deep, veiled fear.

Not for the first time, she thought that maybe she should switch psychiatrists, or just stop going altogether.

The kettle whistled breaking her reverie. She made an over-sized mug of Vietnamese lotus tea, added a dollop of honey, and then sat at her table sipping the green liquid. Almost immediately she felt better. She decided not to underestimate the power of suggestion and the placebo effect. The discomfort dissipated and her energy returned. A long run was in order, then out to the ocean on the surfboard—Jennifer believed there wasn't a healthier form of yoga.

As she sipped the tepid tea, she was still plagued with gnawing uncertainties. Why hadn't Donny gotten in touch with her? What did the other night mean to him? Does he have similar intimacy problems? Or, is this typical guy behavior, thoughtful and solicitous, until they get you in bed. She decided to chalk it up to sometimes men are like that. For now.

Jennifer finished the tea and downed an energy bar, primed for a vigorous workout. She changed into spandex running shorts and a sports bra, laced her running shoes, threw on a baseball cap, and walked out into daylight that seemed to paint the neighborhood's brightly-colored bungalows in muted pastel colors resembling a Monet landscape. Clouds of acrid smoke swirled about in the ocean breeze cutting visibility to the point that she couldn't see more than a couple houses away. She hurdled the wooden gate separating her bungalow from the pedestrian walkway and jogged toward the ocean. Through the smoky haze, she made out her next-door neighbor, Mrs. Ng, wearing a UCLA Bruins baseball hat—a present from Jennifer—and a loose-fitting cotton *gi*. She was performing the balance and flexibility exercises of Wing Chun—a type of martial arts Jennifer sometimes practiced with her Vietnamese neighbor.

Jennifer slowed down and yelled over. "Mrs. Ng, I'll be back in a bit. We still on for the Asian market?"

Ng looked up and bowed formally. "Take your time, daughter. I'm not going anywhere."

A warm tingle went through Jennifer's body every time Ng called her "daughter."

Jennifer waved, then trotted down the walkway. She turned right and picked up speed as she ran north along the glorified alleyway named Speed Way.

As her muscles and tendons warmed and loosened, she gradually increased her pace. Hitting the promenade at Washington Boulevard, she took the running/bike path, joining the small crowd of mid-morning exercisers and running north past the familiar sights. The waking Venice Beach stores and cafes and the sleeping homeless people looking like survivors in a post-apocalyptic movie were the typical morning display among the constant decor of scattered palm trees. The growing tent city of people that had sprung up on the beach itself, an encampment as far as the eye could see, was new. Row after row of army-type tents set up by various rescue groups covered the area. Surrounding them were thousands of camping tents ranging in size from single person tents to family shelters. This fearful army of people had fled as far west as they could go, carrying all the worldly possessions they could take, their homes likely incinerated by the relentless flames.

Synchronizing her breathing and stride, she reached her cruising speed. She recognized a few familiar faces in the passing runners and inline skaters—familiar, yet foreign and unknown—and nodded to them. At times, she felt like a comet wandering out in the Oort cloud, barely affected by the gravitational pull of other bodies. She looked at her watch and decided to run thirty minutes out, then turn back, figuring that at her usual pace she'd cover six to eight miles. Because of the overwhelming workload at the morgue, she hadn't run in almost a week and her legs felt fresh and springy. She passed Muscle Beach Gym, bustling with lifters in spite of the early hour and a dog park equally brimming with barking and yapping canines, then a number of other parks, houses, and shops. There was little breeze and the running was easy. The smoke wasn't so bad close to the shore, but was still present and made her cough at times.

Jennifer made it past the Santa Monica pier, then turned around. She finished her run at the Muscle Beach gym, where she was a member. She broke into a controlled sprint until she was even with the gym, then stopped, bent to stretch, and braced her hands on her legs as she caught her breath and recovered. She walked over to the fenced-in weight area and looked in. A few men and women were lifting, but no one she knew, so she walked back home.

She changed into her wetsuit and water sandals, took her surfboard, and walked out to the beach. She paddled out far past the surf and beyond the hazy air. She lay on the board and rode the low swells, enjoying the cold Pacific and the fresh air, approaching a form of what her father, a Buddhist, called "*bodhi*," or enlightenment.

Back home, she made herself a light breakfast and walked down the hallway toward the front of the house. On the left was the door leading to the master bedroom. The guest bathroom was on her right, as well as two other doors, the first leading to an extra bedroom that she used for storage. She entered the second door leading to her home office and the entrance to the rooftop observatory via a pull-down ladder. Leaning over the desk, she turned on the laptop and logged into the program controlling the telescope that she'd programmed to photograph the Dumbbell Nebula. Checking the progress, she found that the CCD sensor, or camera, still needed twelve more hours of exposure. With the forest fires wreaking havoc with visibility, that could take a month or more to accomplish.

She left the office and repaired to the living room, which took up the entire front third of the bungalow. Two of the walls were covered in celestial photos she took and had framed in clear Lucite, similar to those in her office. The back wall consisted of floor to ceiling book shelves crammed medical text books and religious tomes. The furnishings consisted of two "comfy chairs," a worn couch, and a few coffee tables.

She plunked down in one of the comfy chairs, munching down breakfast as she paged through professional journals on the small television and watched SportsNexxus on the wall-sized, paper-thin ProjectionWall monitor.

Her OmniPhone rang.

Donny!

She jumped out of the chair and rummaged around the house for the device. She ended up finding it hidden under a stack of papers on the bed stand. She looked at the screen, crestfallen. It was Johanna Williams, her gynecologist.

"Hope I didn't wake you," Johanna said without preamble. "I stopped by the office to catch up on paperwork and have the results of those swabs we did the other day."

Jennifer had forgotten all about the tests. She braced herself for the worst. "What's the damages?"

"You can rest easy. The results for STDs were negative."

Jennifer let out a sigh of relief. She'd dodged a bullet. "That's excellent news."

"There is one thing, however, that is a little strange. The PAP test came back negative as well."

Jennifer scratched her head. "Negative PAP. What does that mean?"

"It's a test for semen."

"I understand that. Prostatic acid phosphatase." Jennifer said a bit too loudly. "I meant, how could that be? Our lab can detect semen using PAP for a minimum of forty-eight hours after unprotected intercourse."

"There are a number of possibilities—"

"Johanna, you mind if we go to VCC?"

She agreed.

Jennifer returned to the living room and switched her phone to Video Calling and Conferencing, telling the OmniPhone to use the ProjectionWall monitor. She faced the wall-sized screen where Johanna's head appeared as large as an Easter Island statue. Johanna's hair was pulled back, she was devoid of makeup and wore a casual floral blouse.

"I'm really confused," Jennifer said. "How is it possible that there was no semen?"

Johanna looked straight out from the screen. "What happened to you isn't unheard of. It's called a 'dry hump'—"

"You mean to tell me I was dry humped?"

"It looks that way. There are a number of possible causes—the first is that your boyfriend, Donny, could be suffering from retrograde ejaculation."

Jennifer pulled up memories from her days in med school. Retrograde ejaculation was a medical condition where sperm and semen, instead of being expelled through the urethra, are pushed back into the bladder. "I thought that only affected old men," she said.

"Not necessarily," Johanna said. "The most common cause of retrograde ejaculation is from previous prostate or urethral surgery, which, true, is much more common in older men. In younger men, medications can induce the condition. Alcohol is the most common cause. The use of certain blood pressure medications or antidepressants can also bring it about."

"We were drinking a lot that night."

"That could explain it. The other cause of the dry hump is the...," Johanna hesitated.

"C'mon. Spit it out. I can take it."

"The male faked orgasm," Johanna said quickly. "Lord knows women fake orgasms all the time, but men can do it too, and for a number of reasons. Alcohol and the SSRI-type antidepressants are frequent culprits. They cause delayed or inhibited orgasm. When that occurs, a man may fake an orgasm because he gets too tired to continue, or he doesn't want to disappoint his partner, leaving her with the idea that she can't satisfy him. To use a non-medical term, he doesn't want to 'wear out his welcome.'"

Jennifer's eyes widened. "I haven't heard from Donny since the ball. That may explain everything. Maybe his experience was not as earth shattering as mine." Jennifer was crushed, the euphoria from the morning workout gone.

"You could write whole books on why men don't call women back after sex, Jennifer." Johanna looked at her watch. "I know the valet at the Bel-Air Country Club, she's a patient of mine. She can get us in there. I could meet you at noon for lunch. The bartender makes the best kumquat mimosas. That would cheer you up."

Jennifer frowned and shook her head. "Thanks for the invite, but I promised my neighbor I'd take her shopping. Then I've got to be at work later."

"Some other time then. Try not to worry. I bet you'll hear from Mr. Wonderful any minute." Johanna cut the connection.

Jennifer sat back in her comfy chair wracked with conflicting emotions and unanswered questions. She wondered if Donny could be on some type of medication and if he had faked an orgasm. Thinking about the fact that they were both drinking a lot, she wondered if it was better for her than it was for him. If he was too embarrassed to call.

Who the hell knows!

◇◇◇◇◇◇◇

An hour later, Jennifer unlocked Mrs. Ng's door with a key the elderly lady had given her years ago. Ng came out of her kitchen wiping her hands on a paper towel. She smiled when she saw Jennifer. Ng was in her late eighties, short, and bent over with age. Her skin was clear and unwrinkled, hair so black it seemed blue. She wore loose-fitting cotton pants, open-toed sandals, and a casual cinch top.

Ng and her husband fled Vietnam during one of their country's endless civil wars and settled in Southern California. Her children had become adults years ago and lived with their own families. Ng's maternal urges were now focused on Jennifer, whom she treated as a daughter. After her husband died, she was determined to spend her last days in the house she loved and that contained so many memories.

They walked out the back door to the detached garage where Ng parked her bright red sedan. Ng refused to go anywhere in the car by herself, saying she didn't trust the Nav-Drive; Jennifer believed Ng's actual motivation was that she was starved for companionship.

Jennifer sat behind the steering wheel as the car took them to the Asian Market located east of downtown, a few blocks from the main train station. Jennifer pushed the shopping cart as she followed Ng up and down the aisles, buying exotic-smelling oriental foods. Ng spent a great deal of time at the fish counter, speaking in Vietnamese and ordering strange looking fish Jennifer never saw anywhere else. When Ng got home, she'd spend the rest of the day making a week's worth of fish sauce and broth for her Vietnamese dishes.

Ng asked if Jennifer was hungry. Although she wasn't, she didn't want to miss out on the savory food served at the market. They went to one of the booths and each ordered a bowl of Vietnamese soup called Phở, an aromatic broth filled with sliced beef, rice noodles, and green vegetables. Jennifer always found the soup so delicious she could never resist ordering a large bowl.

They found an open table in the food court, threw fresh bean sprouts and fish sauce in the soup, and dug in.

"I saw you with your new boyfriend last weekend." Ng said as she slurped up the soup. "He is handsome. Are you still seeing him?"

That was the million SDR question. Was she still seeing him or not?

Jennifer nodded. "Yes. At least I think so. His name is Donny."

"I'm happy to see you with someone, Jennifer. I know that astronomy professor hurt you, but you've been alone too long. It's not natural. A woman your age should have steady boyfriend, get married while still young...and so beautiful. Men like you, I can see. You shouldn't be alone."

Jennifer thought about Donny and the uncertainty she had about their relationship and became choked up. She put her plastic spoon down. "I do want a steady boyfriend. But marriage..."

Ng said, "When I was a young girl, I had big dreams. I dreamt of becoming an actress, or curing cancer, traveling the world, being the first president of Vietnam. Dozens of dreams. When I first met Mo, I didn't want to get married; I thought it would steal my freedom to do all the things I had been dreaming of. I kept him at distance. He thought I was playing hard to get, he pursued me even more." Ng took a sip of her green tea. "I finally said yes to him. At the time, I know not why. But I'm glad I did. As they say: the Tao is not unvarying. Listen to an old woman, Jennifer. I found out that I had fulfilled my true dream, the real and only dream. To marry, to have children, to live to see cycle repeat itself." She paused, lost in her thoughts. "I may have given up some freedom, but the joy I got from my husband and children…I cannot describe to you."

Jennifer remained silent with her head down. Her eyes welled up and she dabbed them with a napkin as she pondered what Ng said. If only it were that simple: trade freedom for happiness. Maybe she was right. Is there something inside her trying to protect her from herself? Picking the wrong guys? Keeping her from getting close to another person? From falling in love, only to be hurt? And what about those damn snake dreams? Was it intimacy issues she wrestled with in the dreams? Was she trying to keep from getting too close for fear of being disappointed and hurt? By wrapping herself in a sort of emotional cocoon, she may be paradoxically hurting herself even more.

Mrs. Ng stood up and hugged Jennifer. "Daughter, we were born to love and be loved. It's just that simple. To love and be loved, that's the answer. There is no doubt in my mind."

Jennifer stared at her soup, appreciating its complex and conflicting mixture. Ng's presence was reassuring and comforting.

Jennifer didn't say a word but her head swirled with questions she wanted to ask her:

What is this love you are talking about? How do you find it? How do you give it?

Chapter 11

After helping Ng unload the groceries, Jennifer fought the temptation to climb back in bed; but duty called. Corpses were piling up and the refrigerators couldn't handle many more bodies. She changed into scrubs then hopped into her car. When her car pulled up to the morgue, the visitor's lot was full, which was surprising because they didn't get many visitors, and when they did, it was only one or two people dreading what was to come next. Now, people spilled out of the lobby and loitered around the entrance. And they didn't appear somber. They seemed to be having a party.

Jennifer drove through the doctor's lot and parked behind an ambulance in the loading area, out of sight from the hordes out front. She pushed through the double doors of the loading dock and entered the administrative area.

The hallway was dark but light spilled out from Dutch's office. The administrator looked up from his desk when she peeked in and a look of relief rushed across his face. Grabbing the wheelchair's joystick, he maneuvered around the desk and hugged Jennifer around the waist, his head pressed against her chest. Jennifer wasn't sure what to do; Dutch rarely was shaken up. And just as rarely did he have physical contact with her, which was one of the reasons she got along so well with him. When he squeezed her tight, she put her hands on his bald pate and stroked it, trying to be soothing.

He spoke with a shaky voice. "I had the scare of my life this morning."

"What, you wake up with an erection?" Jennifer said with a straight face.

Dutch released her and turned red with laughter. "That might be your best comeback of all time." He pulled away and continued laughing as he maneuvered the wheelchair around to his desk. "I need a drink." He pulled a bottle of scotch from the credenza, poured a couple fingers each into two tumblers, and held one out to Jennifer.

Jennifer reached out, then pulled her hand back. It was tempting. But she knew one drink usually led to the next, and she had a full shift ahead of her. She wondered about drinking in the afternoon and if that might be a sure sign of alcoholism. She didn't drink as much as Dutch, but he had more body volume. She rationalized that he also had reasons she didn't have to justify his drinking.

Jennifer rubbed his shoulder. "What's going on, Dutch? Looks like you saw a ghost."

"Just about." He downed one of the glasses, but still looked shaken. "Just before you walked in, I was going through the recent deliveries, and I almost shit my colostomy bag."

Jennifer gave a short laugh. "That's funny, but you don't wear a colostomy bag."

"I used to before I had stem cell therapy." He sipped from the other tumbler. "Anyway, LOPD sent us a body this morning. The victim's name is none other than," he paused dramatically, "Doctor Jennifer Sing."

Jennifer's jaw dropped. "Holy shit! Same as mine?"

Dutch arched his bushy right eyebrow. "This Dr. Sing spelled her name the right way, without the 'h' at the end." He tossed back the other drink. "Thank God you're okay."

Jennifer had a seat. "No wonder you look frazzled. Who is she? The deceased?"

Dutch opened the file on his computer. "She was a part-time professor at UCLA. Did you know her?"

Jennifer paused in thought for a second, then shook her head. "I don't think so. What kind of doctor was she?"

Dutch scrolled down the file. "She is…or was…a psychiatrist. Owned a place called the Diamond Rehabilitation and Sports Medicine Clinic."

Jennifer stood up, took the tumblers from Dutch, and refilled them. She added just a finger in one, which she kept, and two fingers in the other, which she passed to Dutch. "Sports Medicine? You mean she was a *physiatrist*. A doctor of rehabilitative medicine."

Dutch consulted the file. "That's right."

Jennifer raised her drink to Dutch and they clinked glasses.

"*Proust*," they both cheered.

She sat down, facing her friend. "So, LOPD's on the case. I take it she's a homicide?"

"Looks that way. One of the homicide detectives called, said she's on her way to observe the autopsy."

Jennifer sighed. When a homicide detective came to observe a case, the autopsy always took longer—just what she needed now. At least it was a female detective, she wouldn't have to fend off unwanted advances and unpleasant stares.

"Who would that be?" she asked.

"Beela White."

Jennifer nodded. White was a competent detective.

"I'm not usually superstitious," Dutch said, "but I don't want you doing the autopsy. Tulp is across the highway. He can come back after he's done teaching and handle the case."

"He needs the time off. I'm going to do the case. The only superstitions I have involve golf."

Dutch laughed. "And baseball. Don't forget baseball."

Jennifer took a small sip of the scotch. She stood up and poured the rest into Dutch's tumbler.

Dutch looked up at her. "There's no way to keep you from doing the autopsy, is there?"

"*Nyeto*. Would you mind asking Carlos to prep the body while I get ready? And send White back when she arrives."

"Yes, boss," were the last words she heard as she left the office.

In the prep area, she slipped on the TED hose, then donned the bio-hazard suit and mask. Aída and Carlos looked up when she entered the autopsy suite; even through the bio-hazard masks, she could see they both had surprised looks in their eyes.

"Afternoon, crew. Ready to get started?" Jennifer said.

Aída made the sign of the cross. "¡*Dios mio*! I thought Dr. Tulp was going to take this case. Aren't you superstitious?"

"Not at all."

"Not only does she almost have your name, but she's almost a dead ringer for you, too. Red hair. Greenish eyes. Not quite as tall though. And…," Aída said.

"And what?" Jennifer asked.

"Take a look at this." Carlos pulled the sheet off the body with a flourish.

Jennifer bent over, took one look at the body, and yelled out, "Holy shit!"

Carlos looked at Jennifer. "I thought you'd say something like that."

"Would you look at that?" Jennifer picked up the deceased's right hand and turned it over. "Tatsu. Record."

The digital recording came on.

Jennifer dictated her findings as she examined the body. "Case: Jennifer Sing, MD. Gross examination reveals displaced fractures of the second and third metacarpals on the right hand. Antemortem. Bilateral ligature wounds on wrists and ankles; piano wire variety. Jagged bullet entrance wound, right temple. Stippling pattern suggests muzzle distance six to twelve inches. No exit wound. Stop recording."

Jennifer looked to Carlos. "That's the same kind of entrance wound as the Russian last week."

"It sure looks that way."

"What the hell's going on?" Jennifer said to no one in particular.

"This is giving me goose bumps," Aída said.

"What about time of death?" Jennifer said.

"Last night, between eight PM and midnight," Carlos said.

Jennifer examined the body closer. "No cigarette burns. Any signs of sexual assault?"

"She was found fully clothed," Aída said.

"Do a full sexual assault workup, Aída. Carlos, let's open the skull. I want to see that bullet."

Carlos used the Stryker saw to open the top of the skull, then used a scalpel to help Jennifer pry out the brain. Using long-nosed forceps, Jennifer removed a hollow-point bullet lodged in the left parietal lobe.

Carlos measured the projectile using digital calipers. "Nine millimeters, Doc. Similar type mushrooming as we saw in the Russian case."

Using forceps, Jennifer held the bullet and brought it to the wall monitor where she opened up the file on the prior week's unknown Russian. She examined the projectile using a magnifying glass, then compared it to the images of the bullet they'd recovered on Friday. They were almost identical.

She handed the bullet to Carlos. "Send it to the lab. Make sure they compare the two."

Carlos placed the bullet in an evidence container and labeled it.

Jennifer dictated. "Cause of death, nine millimeter hollow-point bullet wound, right temple. Massive brain trauma bilaterally."

Aída finished up with the sexual assault samples. "PSA and Acid Phosphatase tests were negative. No vaginal hemorrhages or petechiae."

Jennifer dictated. "No presence of semen or vaginal trauma."

She continued to dictate the findings as they completed the autopsy. They were about to close the abdominal cavity when the door swung open. A bio-hazard clad individual hesitated by the door.

"Detective White?" Jennifer said into her mask.

The new arrival looked around at the trio. "Which one of you said that?"

Jennifer raised her hand. "Right here. Come join us. I'll fill you in."

"Sure thing, Doc," came through Jennifer's earbud.

The new arrival trundled to the exam table. "Hard to recognize people in these space suits."

"I'm Doctor Singh." Jennifer gave a small nod. She pointed to her assistants with her red-gloved hands. "And that's Aída and Carlos." They each made a slight bow. "We're just finishing up. Death caused by close range hollow-point bullet to the right temple. But you already knew that."

"That was our crime scene assessment," the detective said. "There were two things that really interested me. One was the unusual bullet entrance wound. It looked like a close-range shotgun blast."

"It was actually caused by a special Russian-made nine millimeter bullet." Jennifer said.

"Really?"

"I'll explain in a minute. What was the second thing? The broken fingers?"

"Right. Did they occur before death?"

Jennifer nodded. “She was tortured.”

“The couple was estranged. Her family’s trying to pin the murder on her husband,” the detective said. “I don’t think that’s the case. Husbands don’t usually torture their spouses before killing them.”

“What you’re apparently not aware of is that we had a case just two days ago with the exact same cause of death. Las Vegas PD and the FBI are on that case and— ”

“Las Vegas and the FBI? What the hell’s going on?”

“Let me show you what we found. Then I’d like to talk to you in my office.”

Jennifer showed the detective the bullet. She went over the findings that indicated the fractures of the fingers occurred prior to death. Next, Jennifer showed the detective the damaged brain.

“Anything else you want to see?” Jennifer asked.

“That will do it. Thank you.”

“Follow me. I’d like to go over both cases with you.”

They went to the prep area where they removed their bio-hazard suits.

“Where’s your partner, Detective?” Jennifer said. “The Bowling Ball.”

Beela laughed. “He retired. Had a stroke— ”

“Not surprising,” Jennifer said.

The detective smiled. “My new partner’s in orientation. He’ll be joining me later in the week.”

Jennifer raised her eyebrows. “A new detective? I’m sure it’ll be gratifying to teach someone the trade.”

“I don’t know about *gratifying*,” the detective said, “we’re so overwhelmed with cases, I don’t know how much time I’ll have for hand-holding.”

Jennifer laughed. “I know all about being swamped.”

They left the autopsy wing and entered Jennifer’s office. Jennifer gestured to the chairs facing her desk. “Have a seat, Detective.”

“Please, call me Beela.”

Jennifer sat behind her desk and turned the computer monitor so they both could see the screen. “We had a case last week that you should find interesting.” Jennifer pulled up autopsy photos of a dead body lying on the morgue table. “This is the Russian, Vladimir Doe.”

Beela looked puzzled. "Vladimir Doe?"

"That's what I call a John Doe when he's Russian."

"Then what do you call an unidentified Russian woman?"

"Unlucky."

"That's clever."

"He was found in the desert just this side of the California-Nevada border. The similarities with your case are eerie." Jennifer showed a series of autopsy photos to Beela as she explained the case. "He was shot close range in the temple with a nine millimeter hollow-point, just like the case you're working. Same jagged entrance wound. Both had their wrists and ankles bound with wire and were tortured by breaking their fingers. A Detective Porfiry was here, said he was FSB."

"*Said* he was FSB? Do you have reason to believe he wasn't?"

"We're checking into it. Porfiry told us that Vladimir was a courier, transporting stolen goods."

"That explains why Doctor Sing's home was ransacked. The killer was definitely looking for something."

"Killers," Jennifer said. "According to Porfiry, these guys work in pairs."

Beela nodded. "Interesting."

"I'll port the information we have on the FSB agent to your Omni."

"The FSB is like the FBI, they don't like to share information. Who's working the case for Vegas PD?"

Jennifer consulted her monitor. "Detective Mazzetta." She sat back and took a breath. "One thing doesn't sync in this case. The FSB detective told me this gang breaks the victim's fingers until they get the information they want. However, they only broke two of Doctor Sing's fingers. So why ransack the house?"

"Maybe they ransacked it before she got home. They didn't find what they were looking for, then lay in wait for the doctor to return, and she told them where the loot was."

"That's a possibility." Jennifer thought for a second, then cringed. "If the Russian mafia is involved, I don't think we've seen the last of the killings."

Chapter 12

Dutch wheeled into the room. "Sorry to interrupt, Dr. Singh. The Sing family's creating a ruckus in the lobby. Would you mind going out there with me to calm them down?"

Jennifer rolled her eyes. "What a way to start the day." She stood up and went to shake hands with the detective. "Beela, let me show you out."

Beela patted Jennifer on the shoulder. "I'll go with you. This will give me the opportunity to interview the family members I didn't get the chance to talk to yesterday."

"Be my guest."

They followed Dutch to the lobby. As they neared the swinging metal doors, chanting and wailing came from the other side. Jennifer looked through the door's window; men and women dressed from head to toe in eggplant colored Bedouin-type clothing chanted and moved frenetically about. "The Vin Marianistas," Jennifer announced. "Just what we need."

"I like those people," Beela said. "They're harmless."

Dutch tooled his wheelchair around and looked up at the two women. "I have problems accepting a religion based around chewing cocaine leaves."

"I once worked in a clinic serving the Huichol Indians in Mexico," Jennifer said. "They believe peyote is one of the gods. It's not that I have a problem with the Marianistas and cocaine, it's that they're always so jacked you can't talk sense to them."

"If anybody can do it, you can." Dutch said, then pounded the red button on the wall with the back of his fist, unlocking the doors.

Jennifer swung the doors open to a cacophony of jungle sounds. The bongos sounded like war drums, the sitar like a giant mosquito buzzing her head, and the chanting like warriors ready to go into combat. The distinct smell of marijuana wafted in the air. A wicker basket filled with cocaine leaves sat by the door.

Dutch wheeled over to the counter and talked to the lobby attendant. Jennifer moved aside as a gray-haired, wild-eyed woman grabbed Beela by the waist and danced around the room with her. Beela managed to extricate herself and came back sweaty but laughing.

"Looks like a fun crowd," Jennifer yelled above the noise. "But it's time to break up the party." She walked over to the bongo player. He took the joint out of his mouth and offered it to her. Jennifer shook her head and yelled to him, "Stop the music for a minute. I need to talk to the group."

When the bongo player stopped, the other instruments fell silent. The people who had been dancing and chanting stopped, looking befuddled.

Jennifer stood on a chair and said in a loud voice, "Can I have your attention? I'm Doctor Singh." She waited while the surprised murmur from the crowd died down. "No relation to the deceased. I'm the medical examiner, and I just finished examining your beloved one."

A hush fell over the room. All eyes were fixed on her.

"Dr. Sing died from a single gunshot to the head. Death was quick and painless."

A woman's voice yelled out, "It was that no good ex-husband of hers."

There were jeers of agreement.

Jennifer spoke in the direction where the voice came from. "We aren't sure—"

Another voice, female and frantic, yelled, "I have to see my baby!"

Jennifer spoke with her calm voice, loud enough, she hoped, to be heard above the crowd. "You can view the body later today at the funeral home."

The same voice yelled out louder, "I need to see my baby. Now!" An older woman with a manic look in her eyes rushed to the double doors leading to the autopsy suites and began banging on them with her fists. The doors didn't budge. She threw her body against the unyielding metal, calling for the rest of the crowd to help. Another woman joined the fray, then another. Pandemonium broke out: wailing, screaming, pounding. The drumming and high-pitched string music resumed, this time at a faster tempo.

Beela rushed to Jennifer's side. She hollered to be heard above the din. "Need any help?"

Jennifer gave a short laugh. "We've got this under control. That door's solid as a rock. They'd have better luck trying to break through the concrete-block walls." She jumped off the chair. "C'mon. Let's see if we can calm those ladies down."

They pushed their way through the crush to the besieged door. One of the women let out a scream, her eyes rolled back into her head, and she fell to the ground.

Jennifer knelt next to the prone body—it was the woman who had stormed the door first, presumably the mother of the deceased.

"Just what we needed." Jennifer checked the woman's carotid pulse. She yelled to the lobby attendant, "Bring over the crash cart."

The mourners gathered around, pressing in from all sides.

Jennifer looked up and found Beela. "Detective. Clear the lobby."

Beela pushed the crowd back, barking out in an authoritative voice, "You heard the doctor. Everyone out. Now!"

Many in the crowd muttered and craned their necks trying to see what was going on. Dutch helped Beela push the stragglers out of the building, then he bolted the front door. The mourners peered in through the windows while they chanted.

The attendant wheeled the crash cart over to Jennifer. Beela came back and watched over Jennifer's shoulder.

Jennifer tore the unconscious woman's shirt open, grabbed the paddles from the defibrillator, squirted them with blue gel, and placed them on the woman's chest. The defibrillator screen showed a green tracing which looked like the chaotic, choppy whitecaps during a whale of a storm. The machine gave off a steady, high-pitched tone.

"V-fib," Jennifer muttered over her shoulder to Beela and Dutch.

Having lost control of her bladder, the woman lay in a puddle of urine. Jennifer stood up and dragged the unconscious body to a dry part of the floor.

She knelt back down. "Call an ambulance, one of you."

"There's probably one in the loading dock," Dutch said to the attendant. "Run on back there."

Jennifer positioned the paddles on the woman's chest. The random pattern persisted.

"Everyone back."

She pressed the button on the paddle. The woman's body jerked as a jolt of electricity passed through her.

Beela squeezed Jennifer's shoulder and let out, "Sweet Jesus."

The pattern on the screen changed. It looked like the storm had passed. Waves broke steadily on the shore. The machine gave off a rhythmic beep-beep sound. Jennifer relaxed.

Two paramedics, pushing a stretcher piled with bags of medical gear, burst through the doors. Jennifer began to stand up when the reassuring rhythmic sound of the machine changed to a high-pitched, continuous whine.

Jennifer glanced at the screen. The choppy pattern had returned. "Son of a bitch."

The paramedics hurried over and began pulling out their equipment.

"Turn the defibrillator up to two-forty," Jennifer said to one of the EMTs.

The tech adjusted the machine.

Jennifer yelled. "Clear."

She pressed the paddle button and the body under her jerked again. This time the high-pitched sound remained.

One of the paramedics started an IV. The other pricked the woman's finger, blotted a drop of blood on a credit card-sized hand-held electronic device, and scanned the woman's microchip with the same device.

He read off the screen. "She's got a history of MIs and hypertension. She's on beta-blockers and HCTZ." His eyes darted around as he scrolled around on his display. "Electrolytes look okay, except slight hyperkalemia." He turned to Jennifer. "You want us to give her an amp of epi and Dronedarone?"

"Give her an amp of bicarb and Dronedarone." Jennifer spoke in a tone that demanded respect. "But skip the epi. She's been chewing cocaine leaves all day and has more than enough catecholamines on board."

The medic injected two amps into the IV and nodded.

Jennifer reached over to the defibrillator and turned the switch to 360J.

"Clear," she said and pushed the button on the paddle.

The woman's body jerked.

The machine began emitting a rhythmic beeping sound.

The medics took vital signs and slapped gel-coated electrodes on both of the woman's shoulders. "Thanks, Doc. We'll take it from here. We're wired into CardioCentral."

Jennifer looked up and almost bumped into both Dutch and Beela's heads; they were inches away, peering over her shoulder. She reached her hand up to Dutch. "Give me a hand." Back on her feet, she patted the closer EMT on the shoulder. "I'll stick around until you get her in the ambulance."

"I'd better go interview the family," Beela told Jennifer. "And, Doctor, impressive work there."

Jennifer gave her a small grin. "In my business, Detective, you better be ready for anything."

Chapter 13

Wednesday

After leaving a voicemail for Donny on Saturday morning, Jennifer resolved to wait for him to call her back. Monday was an uneventful grind of autopsy after autopsy—nothing like the adrenaline rush from handling the heart attack the day before. By Tuesday, the resolve not to call Donny weakened, then broke. She pulled out Donny's business card and dialed his office. She rationalized that talking to his receptionist would be less awkward than talking to Donny himself.

A female voice answered and informed Jennifer she had reached Nor-Kor Investments.

"I'm trying to get in touch with Mr. Bosco," Jennifer said.

"Whom may I say is calling?"

Whom indeed?

She didn't want to sound like a clingy girlfriend. But she did sleep with the man, and they did have plans for the weekend. She decided that sometimes you just have to suck up your pride and take it on the chin.

"Dr. Jennifer Singh," she said. "I'm a friend of Mr. Bosco's"

"Doctor Singh!"

The receptionist seemed happy to hear from her. She thought that was a good sign.

"Mr. Bosco hasn't returned from the weekend. But don't worry, he's frequently out of contact when he goes sailing."

Jennifer breathed a sigh of relief. She thought it was refreshing, in a way, that Donny could get away from the constant interruptions of OmniPhones, social messaging, and the like.

"Mr. Bosco will surely be back tomorrow," the receptionist said. "He has an important meeting scheduled in the morning."

Jennifer furrowed her brow. Odd. Donny's running a high-powered business. How could he be out of touch for such long periods of time? Then again, she didn't know much about how he ran his business—maybe he has trusted assistants who handle the day-to-day stuff. She frowned. Something in the back of her mind bothered her. The receptionist seemed too glib. Maybe this isn't the first time she's had to cover for Donny jilting a girlfriend.

Maybe I'm just being paranoid.

"Let Mr. Bosco know that I called," Jennifer said.

"Will do. And I look forward to meeting you."

Jennifer hung up and looked around the kitchen. The bouquet Donny sent her still sat on the table, but the blossoms were beginning to wilt and a few petals littered the table. She changed the water, then headed off to work. The day was an uneventful ten hours of nonstop autopsies. When she went to her locker to change, she checked her OmniPhone and her spirits dropped, still no word from Donny

By the time she made it home, the sun was down. She thought about lacing up her basketball shoes and playing hoops on the Venice Beach courts, but ended up collapsing in bed. She fell asleep doing a crossword puzzle.

Wednesday morning, Jennifer awoke at sunrise and ran four miles on the packed sand, skirting the breaking waves. Back home, she sat down for breakfast and watched SportsNexxus, but couldn't rid her mind of the fact that Donny should have been back from his cruise.

Had something happened to him? A shipwreck? Hijacked by Mexican pirates?

He still hadn't called and Jennifer was beginning to feel certain that could only mean one thing: he was no longer interested. She wondered what that meant for their plans to get together later in the week. She reflected on how his receptionist hadn't seemed concerned that he was out of touch. And she still could figure out what was the significance of the 'dry hump.' Did that have anything to do with Donny's behavior?

She hated herself for being so paranoid. That was the reason she was hesitant to get emotionally involved with men. It could only lead to hurt and disappointment.

She finished breakfast then joined the rush hour traffic. Her UCLA-blue AvtoVAZ electric car pulled into the doctor's parking lot before eight in the morning. When she passed the administrative offices, she was surprised to see the light on in Dutch's office. She peeked her head in. Dutch sat behind his desk and a young woman dressed in scrubs stood looking over his shoulder at his monitor.

Hallelujah, Jennifer thought, another pathologist to help us out. Pretty and young looking, too. She hoped that maybe now the homicide dicks will focus on the new girl on the block and leave her alone.

Dutch looked up. He had a surprised look on his face when Jennifer walked in. The woman smiled. She was in her mid-twenties with light-brown hair pulled into a bun and cocoa-colored skin and eyes.

"Didn't expect you in so early," Dutch said. He put his hand on the younger woman's arm and smiled up at her. "Doctor Singh, I got married over the weekend. I'd like to introduce you to my new bride, Mary Seacole."

The woman stopped smiling and a look of confusion spread over her face. She took a step away from Dutch.

"You two must have met at dance lessons," Jennifer said.

Dutch starting laughing. Mary looked even more confused.

Jennifer chuckled. They were expecting a new pathology resident, and Dutch always liked to play pranks. "You're probably wondering right now whether you're in the morgue or an insane asylum," she told the befuddled woman. "Dutch is quite the joker. You must be our new resident."

Mary nodded and appeared to relax a bit.

Jennifer reached out to shake hands. "I'm Jennifer."

Mary's arms were skinny and her handshake weak. Jennifer resolved to talk to her about exercising, because doing autopsies all day long required a considerable degree of stamina and strength.

Dutch grinned, looking pleased with his prank. "I hope we haven't made such a bad first impression on you that we scare you away."

"We?" Jennifer said.

Dutch chuckled and turned to Jennifer. "Doctor Seacole will be spending the next three months with us. She's a second year pathology resident at Loma Linda."

"I've been thinking about sub-specializing in forensic pathology," Seacole said to Jennifer. "I've heard great things about you, and I'm really looking forward to working here."

"I love your accent," Jennifer said. "Where are you from?"

Mary replied in an exaggerated Island accent, "Mon. I be from Jamaica."

Jennifer laughed. "Thank the goddesses you have a sense of humor! You won't survive here without one."

"Doctor Tulp does somehow," Dutch said.

Jennifer ignored him. "Los Angeles is a long way from home for you, Mary."

"I've moved around a lot. I went to medical school in Manchester, England. *Pip pip*. But I didn't like the cold, rainy weather. And the people 'der didn't like my warm, sunny personality. After med school, I wanted to go somewhere warm and friendly. So, here I am."

"And it's a pleasure to have you," Dutch said. "I'm happy to hear about your interest in forensic pathology. We're always short on pathologists."

"Have you ever done a forensic autopsy before?" Jennifer asked. Seacole shook her head. "By the end of the day, you're going to be an expert. Both Doctor Tulp and I are each pounding out over thirty a day, and we still seem to be falling behind."

Dutch asked the two women to have a seat and adjusted his wheelchair behind the desk. "Allow me to briefly explain how this department operates—or doesn't operate." He chuckled to himself. "We cover the entire L'Orange county area. That's over fifty million people. On average, we get between two to three thousand cases a month, depending on the phases of the moon and a few other technical factors. With the recent fires, those numbers have gone up a bit."

"You have a busy department," Mary said. "Are there that many murders in L'Orange?"

Both Jennifer and Dutch broke out laughing. "Not at all," Dutch said. "Homicide is only a small fraction of the procedures we do, making up about fifteen hundred cases a year. Most of our cases are relatively mundane. We're required by law to do an autopsy on all suspected suicides, that's about five thousand a year. However, the largest number of are unwitnessed deaths, around twenty thousand a year."

"I guess my view of your work's been influenced by holovision shows. I thought all you did was homicides."

"And just because a case is sent to us by the homicide detectives," Jennifer said, "doesn't mean the person was murdered. We play a big role in determining whether a person's death was caused by homicide or not."

"We're funded for twelve pathologists," Dutch said, "but could really use fourteen. We usually schedule about an hour per autopsy. However, we have a situation that our police friends like to refer to as FUBAR. If you're not familiar with the term, Doctor Singh can explain it to you later."

Mary blushed. "I know what it means."

"Sorry to offend you," Dutch said. "Recently, ten of our illustrious colleagues went to Vancouver to attend a weekend continuing education program. They were doing a group autopsy, and lo and behold, they all contracted tuberculosis. Not just any tuberculosis, but," he looked towards Jennifer, "what was it called again?"

"UXDR-TB," Jennifer said. "Which stands for—"

"Which stands for a microscopic rod of fat that has completely FUBARed my little operation here," Dutch said.

"It actually stands for Ultra-extensive Drug-Resistant TB," Jennifer told Seacole. "But who's keeping score?"

"Thank you, Doc," Dutch said. "As if that isn't enough, the geniuses in the county manager's office decided that we didn't need disability policies on our employees, something about the risk-benefit ratio. The State Labor Board declared that my doctors were infected as part of their employment, so they're entitled to worker's comp. Now, we're paying them to vacation up in the Canadian mountains, while I have two doctors to cover the entire county."

"Do you have any idea when they'll be able to return to work?" Mary asked.

Dutch grimaced. "The tuberculosis sanitarium does weekly sputum cultures. In order to re-enter the country, a doctor has to have three consecutive negative results—in other words, not be actively contagious. So far, none of them has even one negative culture result."

Jennifer shook her head. "It doesn't look good. She looked at her Omni then said to Seacole, "We better get to work."

"Detective White called," Dutch said. "She's on her way here. Your first case is a homicide she's working."

"I'll orient Mary," Jennifer said. "Send the detective back when she gets here."

"Welcome to the county morgue," Dutch added with morbid humor. "Try not to get sick."

The two women left Dutch's office and walked to the lockers. When they passed the break room, Jennifer asked, "You want a coffee?" Mary shook her head. "Good. It's a pain trying to go to the bathroom wearing a bio-hazard suit."

Jennifer paused outside the dressing room door and began explaining how the morgue worked. "The dieners, or autopsy assistants, do the prep work. They'll have the bodies lined up like an assembly line—quite a dehumanizing way to go 'gentle into that good night.' They'll have taken the appropriate X-rays, which we can view digitally on the monitors, taken any necessary fluid, skin and fiber samples, scraped under the fingernails, and so on, and so on. I won't kid you, the autopsies we're doing right now aren't always of the highest quality. We're cutting corners. It's embarrassing, but we're doing the best we can. Dutch has me out begging for funds, but so far that doesn't seem to be going anywhere. We're a hidden and forgotten branch of county services, so we just have to make do."

"Can't you hire temporary pathologists to help out?"

"We don't grow on trees; there's less than a thousand board-certified forensic pathologists in the entire country. It would take months to recruit and credential replacements." Jennifer frowned grimly. "Right now, we're all we've got." Jennifer opened the locker room door and pointed to the area around her locker. "Take any unoccupied locker you wish for the duration of your rotation."

Aída was at her locker slipping protective covers over her shoes.

"Doctor Seacole," Jennifer said. "Allow me to introduce you to Aída Santibáñez."

They shook hands.

Jennifer showed Seacole where the clean scrubs were housed. "Grab your size and change." Jennifer reached up to the top shelf marked TALL, took a pair, and went to her locker. Mary took an unoccupied locker next to Jennifer's. Aída grabbed one of Jennifer's chairs, took a seat, and put her feet up on the bench.

“Aída,” Jennifer said. “Wanna guess how Dutch introduced our new doctor to me?”

“That she was his long, lost daughter?”

“Close. As his new bride.” Jennifer turned to Seacole. “Dutch is quite the kidder, but he’s harmless. You should join us after work. We’re going across the street to see the UCLA baseball game. They’re playing our arch-rivals: USC.”

Seacole spoke with a hesitant voice. “I really don’t understand baseball. In Jamaica, we play cricket.”

“Here’s what you need to know about baseball,” Jennifer said. “Muscular, athletic men running about in tight-fitting pants, swinging big bats, while you suck down plump, juicy hot dogs—it doesn’t get any more Freudian than that.”

“Sounds like fun,” Seacole said. “Do they have foot longs?”

Jennifer started chuckling salaciously. “Oh, so you like them long, do you? Personally, I like them short and thick, like a bratwurst. Something you can really wrap your hands around.”

Aída arched her eyebrows and chimed in. “If you’re talking about what I think you’re talking about, I like the chorizo. It’s not too big, but it sure is hot and spicy.”

Seacole looked confused. “We’re not talking about food anymore, are we?”

Jennifer and Aída both laughed, saying in unison, “Nope.”

“In that case, I like bangers and mash, *Gov’ner*.” Seacole joined in the laughter.

Jennifer patted her on the back. “You’ll fit in just fine here.”

Aída swung her legs to the ground and stood up. “I better go help Carlos.”

“Detective White will be observing our first case,” Jennifer told her. “Notify me when she arrives.”

Aída said she would and left the locker room.

While Jennifer slipped on clean scrubs, she was silent, brooding, trying to come to grips with the reality that her colleagues would probably die of tuberculosis and never return. She swiveled to face Seacole, who sat waiting for her. “Dutch didn’t tell you, this Laos strain of tuberculosis that our other medical examiners contracted is extremely virulent and antibiotic resistant. We're back to treating TB like the days before World War One. Isolation at high altitudes, where the air is thin and dry. Like something out of a Thomas Mann novel. So while Nicolas—Doctor Tulp—and I are working our asses off here, our colleagues are living it up at a ski resort, hiking the mountains in their *lederhosen* during the day, and dancing the oompha with *dirndl*-clad *fräulein* at night."

"Can't you use nanobots to treat TB?" Seacole asked. "You can program 'bots to attack just about any type of bacteria. They work wonders on multidrug-resistant gram-negative sepsis."

"TB bacilli are clever, Mary. They don't leave their tuber-home very often, and the bots can't penetrate the tuber-walls. A typical dose of nanobots costs over twenty-thousand SDR and has a half-life of three days. My colleagues would burn through their MSAs in no time."

"MSAs are what, again?"

"Medical Savings Accounts. Money we each have to put aside to cover our future medical expenses."

"And why don't these doctors tap their accounts to pay for the nanobots?"

"They'd rather leave that money to their family than waste it on a futile cause."

"I'm still trying to figure out the US healthcare system. Wouldn't National Healthcare kick in after they drained their MSAs?"

"It would, however, the utilization panels wouldn't authorize paying for hopeless treatments."

"I've heard a few of my professors call those 'death panels'. They say they don't seem to approve any costly treatments, except for the well-connected."

"That's not true. Our system's similar to the National Health Service in the UK. And utilization panels have been around in the US since the 1960s. Back then, before organ cloning, there were a limited amount of organs available for transplant, so panels were formed to steer the available organs to the recipients with the greatest chance of long-term survival. The utilization panels are the logical extension of that concept, using financial funds in place of organs as the limiting factor."

"Logically, I agree with you, Doctor Singh—"

"Call me Jennifer."

"Sorry," Seacole said. "Jennifer. But emotionally, I couldn't disagree more. While I've been working at Loma Linda, I've seen people who we have the technological prowess to cure, but are denied treatment because of cost savings." She paused, looking for words with which to continue. "It's really hard to stomach."

"Basing financial decisions on emotion is what caused our country's problems in the past," Jennifer said. "I served a two-year term on a utilization panel, and perhaps that's why I have a different perspective from yours. You're new to our system. Let me explain how the panels work. People on the panel are volunteers—experts from the medical community, like ourselves, as well as those from various walks of life. If a patient disagrees with the computer algorithm determination not to fund treatment, the case is reviewed by a panel of eleven committee members. You might be surprised, Mary, but in the two years I served, we didn't vote to overturn a single initial determination. My criteria was: if that were me in that situation, would I be willing to spend my own hard-earned money on the treatment, or would I rather pass that money on to my heirs," Jennifer shook her head, "if I ever have some."

"It just seems so unfair that people are denied care by the bean counters."

"We're all going to die someday of something. But look at the bright side, even with utilization panels, life expectancy is more than twenty years longer now than it was at the turn of the century. Living to be one hundred now is commonplace. Tens of thousands of people no longer die in traffic accidents every year. With preventive medicine, we live healthier and longer than ever before. And don't forget that before the utilization panels, the skyrocketing costs of medical care helped to throw our country into bankruptcy."

Seacole frowned. "All the rosy statistics in the world don't help when you have to tell an individual patient that a potential life-saving treatment has been denied."

Jennifer patted Seacole on the back and said with a sad laugh, "That's something you won't have to worry about here at the morgue."

Carlos's voice came over the intercom informing them that Detective White had arrived and was waiting in the suite.

Jennifer stood up and turned to Seacole. "Let's get all sexy for our clients."

In the sink-lined prep room, Jennifer helped Mary put on her biohazard suit and mask. Then, they each slid on red graphene-lined, cut-resistant gloves.

Jennifer talked to Seacole to test the communication. "Let me warn you, the first time you see an autopsy you might get uncomfortable, lightheaded, dizzy, maybe even pass out. It's normal. Take a seat until the feeling passes. You'll get used to this in no time."

Jennifer pushed open the doors to the autopsy salon and ushered the new resident in. Detective White stood near the body, clad in full morgue regalia. Aída was completing the preparation of the instrument trays. Carlos stood at the sink, filling specimen jars with formalin, which would be used to preserve tissue samples.

"Good morning, Detective," Jennifer said and introduced Mary.

"I have a partner working this case with me," Detective White said. "A newbie. He's running late, had to get some papers signed. Go ahead and start, I'll fill him in later."

In the center of the room was the corpse, covered with a clean white sheet. Only the tips of his toes were exposed. Attached to one of the big toes was a toe tag. Two surgical lamps hung over the body, bathing it in stark light.

Jennifer and the detective waddled over to the autopsy table. Seacole followed close behind and was silent. Jennifer sympathized with the resident, flashing back to her first time observing an autopsy and how her knees shook and her stomach was full of butterflies.

Gathered around the dissecting table, Jennifer turned to her assistant. "Aída, what do we have here?"

"Victim was found yesterday morning in his home," her assistant said. "Time of death was over twenty-four hours before the body was discovered. Significant contusions to the cranium were noted at the scene. We did a complete set of cranial X-rays."

Jennifer addressed her comments to Seacole and the detective. "First, we'll do a careful external examination looking for anything unusual. Then, we'll review the digital X-rays before opening up the body."

Carlos reached forward and pulled the sheet off the body.

Jennifer froze.

No! No. No, it can't be true!

Her body swayed, then shook. She reeled. Her head swam. She lurched forward, violently. A flood of dizziness overwhelmed her. A tsunami-sized wave of nausea rose in her throat. She fought for breath. Her legs became weak, rubbery. Everything turned dark. She grasped for the table.

She saw stars, then complete blackness.

Chapter 14

Tendrils of consciousness slithered to the surface, tickling Jennifer awake from a deep, dreamless sleep.

Mierda, my head is killing me. Not another hangover.

Bright light beat against her closed eyelids. She decided it was best to keep them shut—a good strategy for a throbbing headache. But this headache was different, not the generalized type, but localized on her forehead, above her left eye. She wasn't sure what happened. Had she gotten so drunk she had a blackout?

I'm definitely going on the wagon.

She remained still, lying on her back, listening to the nearby susurration of people in conversation. It was weird because they seemed so close, as if they were in her bedroom.

Something icy cold and wet plopped on her forehead, exactly where the pulsating pain arose. Jennifer was confused because it didn't feel like a normal hangover headache.

Have I suffered another fugue episode? How many hours, or days, did I lose this time?

Through the inchoate buzz, she made out a woman's familiar voice gently calling her name.

Aída? What's she doing here?

Jennifer opened her eyes a crack, wincing, expecting an exacerbation of the headache. Instead, pairs of eyes looked down at her from various angles, all nervous with looks of worry. Directly above her and just inches away were the familiar dark-brown eyes of Aída. Directly behind were the chocolate-colored eyes of Carlos, the bright-blue eyes of Dutch, and the slate-colored eyes of the new resident.

Mary Seacoast. Something like that.

A dribble of cold water ran down Jennifer's face. Aída mopped it up, then put the cold pack back on her forehead, right where it hurt. The throbbing pain dissipated.

Across the room, Detective White talked quietly to a man standing next to her; they were both looking her way. It was hard to make out the color of the unknown man's eyes with the overhead lights casting them in shadows—but they were unusually intense and hyper-vigilant. Hawk-like. The man himself seemed avian in some strange way. Perhaps it was the angular shoulders, the peregrine profile, the thin neck; perhaps it was just the way he comported himself. Dressed all in brown, he could be mistaken for a UPS delivery man.

Aída continued dabbing the cold cloth on Jennifer's forehead and made eye contact with her. "Doctor Singh's awake," she said to the assembled group.

Everyone sighed and appeared to relax.

Beela separated herself from the bird-man and perched next to Jennifer. She held Jennifer's hand, which felt comforting and soothing.

Jennifer looked around the room trying to orient herself. She wasn't in her bedroom. She was lying on a light brown polyester couch, across the room were are a pair of vending machines. *The employee break room?*

Aída seemed to sense Jennifer's confusion. "You suffered a concussion, Doc."

"How do you feel?" Dutch asked.

Jennifer felt groggy, her words came out as through molasses. "I have a terrible headache."

Dutch's face turned red, his nostrils flared, and he clenched his fists. "I was afraid something like this might happen. You and Doctor Tulp have been on your feet way too much. That's it! We're limiting everyone's hours. When bodies start piling up in the street, the county will be forced to help us out."

"You hit your head on the side of the autopsy table and were knocked out cold," Aída added.

Autopsy table?

Memories began coming back. She was prepped, ready to start the first case of the day. Carlos removed the sheet and…

A chill colder than the freezing towel on her head wracked her body. Bile surged up her throat. She fought to keep from vomiting. Her thoughts scrambled and blood rushed to her head. She felt on the verge of passing out again. "Aida, who was that we were about to work on?" she asked in a small voice filled with trepidation. She prayed she was wrong.

Aida shrugged her shoulders.

Beela spoke up. "The deceased is a case I've been assigned to out of Beverly Glen. A male by the name of Donny Bosco."

A tidal wave of nausea washed over her. She pushed the wet cloth off her face, rolled to her side, and threw up on the tile floor. Gasping for breath, she let out a wail and her eyes filled with tears.

Aída pulled Jennifer tightly against her chest.

Detective White rubbed Jennifer's back. "Let it all out."

"That name is familiar," Dutch said. "Donny Bosco. Jennifer, isn't he the man we met two weeks ago at the Opera charity event?"

Aída was the first to put two and two together. "*¡Ay! Dios mío*. Doc, is that who you've been dating?"

Sobs shook Jennifer's body as she clung to Aida's scrub top.

"Carlos," Dutch said in a weary voice. "In my desk is a bottle of Talisker; please bring it here. I think we're all going to need it."

Carlos shrugged. "What's a Talisker?"

"Do you live under a rock, man? Talisker is the finest single malt scotch whiskey ever made."

Carlos nodded and left the break-room as Aída continued rocking Jennifer.

Carlos returned with a bottle, grabbed a stack of plastic cups from the water cooler, and held them out to Dutch. Seacole took the cups and said she'd help. She placed the bottle on one of the tables and began filling the cups with a couple fingers of the amber nectar.

She passed the cups of whiskey to Dutch who chugged the first one. He handed the next to Aída. "Get the doctor to drink this."

Tears flowing down Jennifer's cheeks, she cried silently, her breathing no longer erratic.

Aída held the cup to Jennifer's lips and got her to drink it down in one swallow. Jennifer shivered. She wiped her face with the back of her hand and sniffled.

Dutch passed around shots to each of the group.

The bird-man looked at Beela. When she tossed hers back in one chug, he followed suit. Seacole poured herself a double and nursed it.

Dutch motioned to Seacole. "Pour the doctor another." When Seacole passed the drink to him, he handed the drink to Jennifer and spoke softly, in a tone Jennifer had never heard before. "Doc, we all feel so bad for you. Let me know if there's anything I can do."

"Thanks, Dutch." Jennifer tossed the whiskey back and handed the glass back to Dutch who had Seacole pour a refill which he tossed back.

"I'm a little better now." Jennifer paused and blew her nose in a tissue Aída handed her. "We do countless autopsies every day, but you never expect to see someone you know lying on the table!"

"Okay, everybody out," Dutch said. "The doctor needs a little privacy. Carlos, reschedule all today's cases to Doctor Tulp. He's in the locker room getting changed. Doctor Seacole, you can work with him today."

Dutch leaned toward Jennifer. "Take as much time as you need." He turned his wheelchair and started for the door.

As Carlos and Mary Seacole followed him, Beela asked, "Mr. Rolstoel, would you mind if my partner observes the Bosco autopsy? I'd like to ask Doctor Singh a few questions."

Dutch nodded. "That would be fine."

The bird-man joined the rest of the group at the door.

"Do you need anything else, Doctor?" Dutch asked.

Jennifer shook her head slowly and sniffled. "I'll be okay,"

Dutch nodded.

He left the bottle of Talisker.

◇◇◇◇◇◇◇

Beela and Jennifer sat quietly next to each other on the couch. The detective reached for the scotch, poured two shots, and handed one to Jennifer. The two women looked at each other and Jennifer gave Beela a thin smile, then they touched their plastic cups together and downed their drinks in unison.

Beela sat quietly for a few moments, feeling for Jennifer. "Doctor, I know Mr. Bosco's death is very painful for you, so I'll try to keep my questions brief." Jennifer looked down and nodded. "Could you tell me how long you knew Mr. Bosco?"

Jennifer spoke in a monotone. "We'd been dating for three weeks."

"When was the last time you saw him?"

"Last Saturday morning."

"Tell me about that last time."

Jennifer regained control over her emotions. Her voice become stronger. "Friday evening, Donny and I attended a charity fundraiser at the Getty Center. He was returning from Las Vegas, so we planned to meet at the museum. After I finished here for the day, I changed in the locker room and Aída helped me with my makeup and hair—" She choked up, but quickly regained her composure. "I met up with Donny in the lobby of the museum. We stayed at the event for about two or three hours, then I followed him back to his house." Her thoughts rushed back to that night, and the fact that she'd never see Donny again.

Beela waited silently a few moments. "You followed Mr. Bosco to his house. What happened next?"

Jennifer's blood boiled. She shot the detective an angry look and her voice rose. "What do you think happened next? We fucked our brains out."

Beela put a hand on Jennifer's shoulder and spoke softly. "Sorry, Doctor. I had to ask."

Jennifer took a deep breath. Tears ran down her face. "I'm sorry for flying off the handle. You're just doing your job." She wiped her face with the collar of her scrub top. "My nerves are just on end."

Beela rubbed Jennifer's shoulder. "I know this is hard for you." She waited while Jennifer regained her composure. "So, you spent the night with Mr. Bosco?"

"That's right. I woke up sometime before dawn and headed home. I had to work that day."

"Was his house locked up?"

Jennifer thought about her question for a second; the events of that morning seemed a distant blur. "I sort of tiptoed out without waking him up. When I left…I'm not sure…I think the patio doors were open…when I pulled my car out, I didn't have the garage door controller…I must have left the garage open."

"Did you have any further contact with Mr. Bosco after you left him Saturday morning?"

Jennifer's eyes misted over. "That was the last time I saw him, sleeping soundly on his bed. When I arrived to work around noon that morning, there was a vase of roses sitting on the front counter that he'd sent me. I left him a text message thanking him for the flowers and a wonderful evening. I never heard from him. I assumed he didn't want to see me again. Now…I feel so bad. He didn't call me because he was…" Tears slowly ran down her face.

"Do you know what time the flowers were delivered?"

Jennifer shook her head. "They were here when I got in…around noon. The clerk at the front desk signed for them."

Beela jotted down a note to herself. "Was it unusual that Mr. Bosco didn't return your text?"

"I'm not sure. As I said, I only knew him for a couple of weeks. He had plans to go sailing with friends. I thought maybe he didn't get cell service out on the water."

"Do you know where they were heading?"

"Their plans weren't set in stone. Donny said they liked to sail by Zen, going wherever the winds took them. He mentioned Baja. Ensenada. Maybe SCUBA in the kelp forests off San Diego."

"Do you know who these people were he was going to sail with?"

"Some friends of his…I'm blocking on their names. I never met them, but from what Donny told me, they have a boat docked in Marina del Rey. A deep-water sailboat."

"When you were with Mr. Bosco, did he seem nervous or worried? Did he act different than he usually did?"

Jennifer paused. She thought Donny had acted strangely at the ball and maybe the reason Donny wanted to dance was to get away from the Russian inspector. She still didn't know for sure if that's who that guy really was. She also wondered if she was just being paranoid because she smoked a lot of pot that night. She decided leaving those details out would prevent the detective from thinking she was crazy.

"No, he seemed quite happy," Jennifer said. "We had a lovely time at the gala. He was very proud of the money he helped to raise for the new art acquisitions. He showed me a whole room full of them." Jennifer yawned and her eyelids became heavy. Her head nodded forward.

Beela held Jennifer by the shoulders and helped her lie down. "You look tired. Why don't you take a nap? I'll see if I can wrestle up a blanket."

Beela returned to find Jennifer curled up on the couch, sound asleep. She pulled a cotton blanket over the doctor, then sat at one of the tables. She capped the whiskey bottle, then waited for her partner to return from the autopsy.

Chapter 15

Once outside the break room, Dutch introduced the bird-like man in brown to Carlos Gómez and Doctor Seacole. "This is Detective Horace Griffin, LOPD Homicide."

The detective extended his hand. "Call me Race."

"Detective Griffin is working the Bosco case with Detective White," Dutch said, then wheeled away.

Race followed Carlos and Mary Seacole down the hallway and through a set of double doors which read: Autopsy Suites, Authorized Personnel Only. Above the doors was a sign which read: *De mortuis nil nisi bonum*. Race looked closer, someone had crossed through the word "nisi." In the prep area, Carlos pointed out an observation window looking onto one of the autopsy suites where a body was laid out, covered by a white sheet.

"That's Donny Bosco," Carlos said to Race. He turned to Seacole. "Doctor, go ahead and put on a bio-hazard suit. I'll help the detective get changed." Carlos led Race to the men's locker room and handed him a set of scrubs. "Change into these. Don't want to get those nice clothes dirty."

Race hung his coat up in the locker and began to undress.

Carlos paced behind the bench, breathing fast and loud, nostrils flared, face reddened, and veins popping out of his neck. Race glanced over, not sure if Carlos was in medical distress.

"¡*Puta madre*!" Carlos swore. "When you nail the *cabrón* who killed Doctor Singh's boyfriend, I'm gonna smash his skull in."

"Wouldn't blame you if you did," Race said as he slid out of his pants.

Carlos plopped down on the bench, took a few deep breaths, and rubbed his temples. "Doctor Singh's the best. I pulled strings to get assigned to her."

Race glanced Carlos's way. "That so?"

"Some people say she's aloof and overly cerebral. But get her talking about sports—especially college sports—you wouldn't think a beautiful woman like that would be into that sort of thing. But she is. Says it's the ultimate reality TV." Carlos smiled, his face no longer beet red. "She treats Aída and me as equals," he looked around and spoke conspiratorially, "not like some of the other doctors who seem to feel superior." He arched an eyebrow and gestured toward the locker room door. "We're all equals when we reach that exam table across the hall."

Race slid on a pair of scrub bottoms. "Sounds like you're lucky to be working with her."

Carlos gave a nod. "And Dr. Singh's sense of humor is off the Richter. Dry as fancy champagne."

"That right?"

"Yeah. She's funny…although, I don't always understand her jokes. But be careful, she doesn't like anyone to make fun of the cadavers. Says it's disrespectful."

Race finished changing and sat down facing Carlos. "It's not as if they can hear."

"Says it's karma, kismet…something like that."

Race mulled that over. That seemed to make sense, why evoke evil spirits? "What about Dr. Tulip? What's he like?"

Carlos chuckled. His angry outburst seemed to have passed. "You mean Dr. Tulp? He's nice enough, but serious. I don't think anyone's ever seen him laugh."

"You do work in the ultimate deathly serious business."

Carlos laughed. "You get used to death. For most of us, laughter is how we cope."

Race stood and leaned against the locker, fidgeting, looking for pockets to rest his hands. He found none. He thought about the fact that in minutes he'd be observing his first autopsy, seeing intestines and brains pulled from Bosco's dead body. He felt his anxiety level begin to skyrocket, so he put his hands behind his back and snapped his anxiety band, hoping Carlos didn't notice. "Dr. Singh had been dating the deceased?"

"Apparently so." Carlos let out a big breath. "Listen, I'm sorry about losing my temper a minute ago, but we really love Doctor Singh. She's had a rough time…with men. She seemed so happy the last few weeks, since she had been dating Mister…I forgot his name. The deceased."

"Bosco. His name is, was, Donny Bosco. Did Doctor Singh ever talk about him?"

Carlos paused, lips pursed, eyes far away. "By name, no." He made eye contact with Race. "But we knew she was dating someone special. It's weird, she never did tell us his name, said she didn't want to jinx the relationship. I guess in the end it didn't make any difference, though, did it?"

Race nodded. "So that's how Bosco ended up on Doctor Singh's table. None of you knew that she was dating him?"

Carlos looked downcast. "I wish we'd known. We could've saved her that horrible scene." Carlos caught Race's eye. "How come *you* guys didn't know Dr. Singh was dating the deceased?"

"We spent all yesterday at the crime scene. There was tons of evidence to process. And it took longer than normal. This is my first case and my partner was teaching me how to handle a crime scene. We probably would have found out about Dr. Singh's relationship to the deceased later today."

"That's really bad timing," Carlos said.

Race nodded and hesitated, not sure if he should ask about Dr. Singh's history—he didn't want to snoop or be nosy. But, then he thought: hell, I'm a detective now, investigating a homicide, any information I find could prove to be valuable. "You mentioned Dr. Singh's had poor luck with men?"

Carlos nodded. "When she first started here, she was dating a plastic surgeon. He ended up leaving her for one of his patients. It hit her really hard. Then, for three or four years, she dated an astrophysicist from the California Institute of Technology. We all thought they were going to get married, until one day he runs off with his lyscee. She'd sworn off men until she met Mr. Bosco. And now look what's happened."

"What bad luck," Race said.

Carlos slapped his knee and stood up. "We better not keep Dr. Tulp waiting. He's liable to start without us."

They left the locker room and Carlos helped Race don a bio-hazard suit. "Through those windows you can look into the actual autopsy suites," he said.

The prep area was lined with sinks. A row of window panes looked onto a dozen identical rooms, each with its central stainless steel table, surgical lighting, cabinets for storing instruments, and a stainless sink on the far wall. All the rooms but one were dark. In that room, two people in bio-hazard suits were busy at work. The shorter of the two was preparing instruments. The other, tall and thin with a giant swollen blue head resembling a Portuguese man o' war, was looking at a computer monitor.

"The tall one in there is Doctor Tulp," Carlos explained. "You're probably wondering why his head looks so big. Under the hood, he wears a turban, for religious reasons."

"Is he a Sikh?"

Carlos nodded. "The other person is Aída, you met her in the break room."

"This is my first autopsy," Race said. "What's it smell like in there?"

"The cadavers are chilled to thirty-five degrees, so it's not too bad, mainly a chemical smell. Formaldehyde. The only time it might get bad is when we open the stomach—but we'll be wearing re-breather devices. Not only do they filter out pathogens, they really cut the odor. I'll put a masking agent inside yours to help conceal the smell." Carlos placed a piece of blotter paper, which smelled strongly of peppermint and cloves, inside Race's mask. "That should do the trick," Carlos said. "If you get lightheaded, just let me know." He looked inside the suite. "We better get in there, they're ready to get started."

Doctor Tulp turned as the door opened and gestured them over. Tulp towered over Race. He introduced himself, then pointed to the monitor. His clipped English accent crackled and hissed in Race's earbud. "The technicians have taken X-rays of the deceased. Let us take a look at them before we get to the body, shall we?" Tulp displayed a series of X-ray views of Bosco's head and moved the cursor over two irregular cracks. "This is the right temporal bone. You can see two distinct fractures, jagged in appearance, that radiate from a central point and spread out like a spider web. This one here," Tulp moved the cursor again and zoomed in on the larger of the fractures, "radiates into the parietal bone." He zoomed back out. "These are called stellate fractures and are usually caused by blunt trauma to the head. They are new fractures, no signs of healing, so they would have occurred within the last few weeks."

Tulp pulled up other set of skull X-rays on the monitor and zoomed in. There were similar web-like cracks, but much fainter. "Here I can just make out another fracture," Tulp said. "This one well healed, on the left parietal bone. Probably occurred months or years ago. Perhaps a sports injury when he was in high school, or a fight that occurred a year ago." He shrugged. "Who knows, not germane."

Tulp pulled up another series of shots and moved the cursor around. "These are the posterior right ribs. Notice that ribs six through ten have multiple fractures. From their appearance, I would say they were caused by blunt trauma—just like the ones on the skull—and they occurred around the time of death. They are not old. There are two older healed fractures, here and here, on the left ribs on about the same level as those on the right."

"What does that mean?" Race asked, his voice sounding muted and distant.

"The fractures of the left ribs are fully healed and would have occurred more than six weeks ago. The fractures on the right side occurred around the same time as the skull fractures. On those, we do not see any evidence of healing." Tulp turned off the monitor. "Follow me."

Race followed the giant-headed doctor to the body. Tulp pulled off the white sheet.

Bosco's eyes were white and cloudy. His mouth was open, the inside coal-black, and his skin was mottled white, black, and purple. Even in death, Race could tell that Bosco had been a handsome man with chiseled features and thick hair. His body took up the entire table and was covered in slabs of muscle. Everything about him was huge. Race looked down between Bosco's legs, happy that the mask covered his self-satisfied smile as he thought: well, almost everything.

Tulp bent over, his head a foot or so away, as he examined the body with a magnifying glass the size of a hardcover novel. "First, we will do a gross examination of the body, looking for anything out of the ordinary." He held each of Bosco's hands in turn and examined the fingernails. Then, he examined the wrists and forearms. "No evidence of defensive wounds," he told Race.

"That confirms what we thought," Race said. "There was no signs of a struggle at the crime scene."

"Turn on the UV lights," Tulp said.

Aída turned and flipped a wall switch. Another bank of lights came on.

"Sometimes we can pick up skin alterations under ultraviolet light that we can't see under normal conditions," Tulp said as he examined the body from head to toe. Tulp shook his head and said, "didn't see anything new," then told Aída to cut the UV lights.

Race found his attention drawn to Bosco's milky, unseeing eyes. He snapped back as Tulp began to explain. "Notice the purple discoloration on the chest, abdomen, and fronts of the legs, arms, and face. This is called livor mortis, a condition wherein the blood collects in the dependent areas—"

"Dr. Tulp, excuse me," Race said. "Does that mean the lower areas?"

"Yes, indeed. Blood collects in the lower areas of the body by simple gravity. From the appearance of the livor, I would say this man died face down and the body had not been moved from the time of death."

Tulp held the magnifying glass over Bosco's right temple and leaned in closer. "Notice here, this area of purple swelling. This is called a hematoma. It is located over the area where we saw the newer skull fractures on the X-rays, so that is consistent. Notice the black and blue coloration and the shiny appearance."

Race nodded.

Tulp gestured for Race to move closer and had him look through the magnifying glass. "Look closely at the wound. See the crushing of the epidermis but absence of skin breakage? The instrument that caused this wound is something round, like a metal pipe, roughly one to three inches in diameter." He made a clucking sound. "Or a baseball bat. A smaller diameter object, like a billy club, would not create the width of the contusion we see here. A larger object would probably cause a crushing fracture in the skull, not the stellate fracture we saw in the X-rays."

Carlos took photographs of the area, then Tulp picked up a scalpel and made an incision into the hematoma. As he pressed down with his gloved hand, thick black clotted liquid oozed out.

"Classic antemortem wound." Tulp explained. "What we are seeing is clotted blood. That means the victim's heart was still beating, at least for a while, after the injury occurred."

"This wasn't the cause of death then?" Race said.

"People's hearts don't usually stop beating immediately on receiving a mortal blow. We need to dig a little further to determine the cause of death."

Tulp asked the assistants to turn Bosco's corpse over. When the body was face down, Tulp examined the skin, paying particular attention to the right side of the head. He directed Race's attention to the right posterior skull and repeated the same procedure: photographs, opening the wound with the scalpel, and squeezing out the black clotted fluid.

"Here on the posterior skull," Tulp said, "over the area where we saw the second fracture on the X-rays, is another contusion, again antemortem and consistent with the first contusion."

Tulp then used the magnifying glass to examine the right side of Bosco's torso. He explained what he saw as more photos of the area were taken. "We have discoloration in the areas where we saw the fractured ribs. Notice that this area appears different from the wounds on the head." He had Race look at the wounds with the magnifying glass. "Remember, the head wounds had swelling, a deep purple-black coloration, and were somewhat shiny. These wounds are different—they are whitish, there is no swelling, and instead of being shiny, they are dull, almost parchment-like."

"I'm guessing these are postmortem wounds," Race said.

"Possibly," Tulp said. "We need to open them up to be sure before we can make any definitive conclusions."

Tulp cut into the area and pressed down. This time there was no leakage of fluid. "Notice there is no blood pooling, so what we have here is a classic case of a postmortem injury. From the appearance of the wounds, I would say they were caused by a blunt object, about the same size as that used to make the skull wounds. A one- to three-inch diameter pipe, or something similar."

Race was perplexed. "Doctor Tulp, are you saying that Mr. Bosco was killed by two blows to the head? Then after he was dead, someone beat him in the back? Why would they do that?"

"First of all, just because he was hit on the head before he died doesn't necessarily mean that's what killed him. We have to complete the autopsy before we can make a definitive statement on cause of death." Tulp turned and looked at Race, his eyes appearing larger through the lenses of the mask. "Second, answering the 'why' is your job. I answer the 'how.'" Tulp examined the wound closely. "When you find the killer, you can ask him."

Race smiled to himself. *Very true*.

Tulp said, "Considering the significant postmortem trauma, the killer might be very mentally unstable. And, I've occasionally seen this as part of some occult religious rituals."

"Satanic cults," Carlos said.

"Whatever the cause, this finding should have a significant impact on your investigation." Tulp looked at the body intently for a moment. "Since the relevant wounds are to the head, we will open the cranium first."

Tulp took the scalpel and cut into the skin all around the top of Bosco's head, then pulled the skin free.

Race thought he was going to cringe and took a deep breath, but he found himself strangely dispassionate as if he were looking at fish at the seafood market, minus the odor. All he smelled was the peppermint/clove masking agent.

He leaned forward to get a close view of what Tulp was doing as the doctor continued to explain. "Let's look at the two fractures of the skull. Indeed they are stellate fractures as we suspected from the X-rays. It doesn't appear that the bone has been pressed into the brain. This would rule out the use of an object such as a hammer or axe. And a bigger object, such as a sledgehammer, would have led to bone spicules being crushed down into the brain."

Carlos picked up a dull silver device with a circular-toothed saw blade at one end. He flicked a switch and the saw emitted a buzzing sound.

"This is called a Stryker saw. It's a vibrating saw, similar to the type used to remove casts," Carlos explained. "It'll cut through bone, but leave soft tissues intact. We'll make a transverse cut all around the top of the skull, then we can remove it—just like taking off a hat."

The high-pitched sound and the smell of burning bone caused Race to tense up, as if he were sitting in a dental chair. Carlos cut around the skull. When he turned off the saw, Race relaxed and shook his head to dislodge a bead of sweat that had formed on his nose.

With Aída's help, Carlos pried the skull cap off exposing the cauliflower-like cerebrum.

Tulp used the magnifying glass to exam the brain and gestured for Race to come closer. Tulp pointed inside the cranium. "We see a large amount of black, clotted blood—the medical term is a subdural hematoma—quite massive. Notice how it has pushed the brain off to the side as well as downward."

The assistants removed the brain from the cranial cavity by severing it from the spinal cord. Race leaned in close, amazed that he wasn't at all uncomfortable with the autopsy.

Tulp held the brain in his hands, turned it over, and pointed to a tail-like appendage. "This area is the brain stem. I can see ischemic damage—damage caused by lack of blood flow. Pressure from the subdural hematoma pushed the brain stem against the foramen magnum, which is the bony opening where the brain joins with the spinal cord, causing the victim to suffer respiratory and cardiac arrest. In other words, it would have caused both his breathing and heart to stop."

Tulp handed the brain to Race and pointed out where the brain stem had been compressed. Race was dumbfounded—he held in his hands not just a brain, but what was once Donny Bosco. All his hopes, desires, and memories, that which made him a unique individual. Race handed the brain to Carlos who placed it in a liquid-filled jar.

"Here is what most likely happened," Tulp said. "Our victim was hit once on the right side of the head causing one of the skull fractures. From the severity of the blow, it probably knocked him unconscious. He would have fallen forward, face down. Then, around the same time, another blow to the back of the head. At this point, he would have been unconscious, but not dead. You with me?"

Race nodded his understanding.

"As our victim lie unconscious, the fractures caused tearing of the blood vessels in the area between the brain and the dura covering the skull. The growing clot led to increased intracranial pressure, pushing the brain down and to the side. Eventually, the pressure pushed the brain stem against the foramen magnum. The brain stem gets pinched, stops functioning—remember, the brain stem controls our vital processes: breathing and heart rate. Our victim stopped breathing, his heart stopped, all before he could regain consciousness. Do you follow?"

Race nodded. "Yes, sir."

"Later, after he's dead, someone hits him again, repeatedly, this time in the back. Violent blows. Enough to cause multiple rib fractures."

"By the same weapon?" Race asked.

"By the same *type* of weapon," Tulp said.

Race moved the mask about with his gloved hands, trying to scratch a nagging itch on his nose. "How long would you say between the blows to the head and his actual death?"

"With this kind of trauma, between ten minutes and one hour."

"What about actual time of death?"

Doctor Tulp looked up from the body. The overhead lights glinted off his mask hiding his eyes. "The victim had been dead more than twenty-four hours before the body was discovered. Rigor mortis, or muscle rigidity, had already passed. We took nasal and buccal swabs. One of the things we look for is blow-fly larvae."

"What's that? A blow-fly?"

"The blow-fly, scientific term calliphoridae, are very tiny flies that are attracted to dead tissue. They are highly specialized. Supposedly they can detect the smell of a dead body from ten miles away. Adult flies will appear on the body within an hour or so of death. A few hours later, they will begin laying eggs, and twenty-four hours after that, the eggs will have hatched into larvae, or maggots. In this case, we found immature larvae in the nasal samples. That means the body had been dead at least twenty-four hours. The absence of more mature forms of the fly means the body had been dead less than a week."

"Let me get this straight," Race said. "The time of death was anywhere from twenty-four hours up to one week before the body was found?"

"Exactly, Detective. Sorry we can't pin the time frame down more for you. If you find it necessary, we could send the nasal and buccal swabs to the forensic entomologist we use in Baltimore."

"I'm sure the department would never pay for that," Race said. "We'll just have to pin down a time of death by old-fashioned police work."

"That's the spirit," Tulp said. "Now, I am going to examine the abdomen and thorax. We might get an idea about time of death based on the state of the internal organs. I'll open the stomach and intestines. That should give us an idea of how much time passed between the victim's last meal and death. However, you would need to know when he ate last in order to make sense of the information."

"I'm sure we can find that out," Race said.

"Feel free to leave now, Detective. This is the part when people witnessing their first autopsy have the most problems. The smell is intense, even with these high-tech masks. If we find any other pertinent information, I'll let you know."

"When will the final report be ready, Doctor?"

"The preliminary report will be ready by the end of the day. The final report will be out when we receive the toxicology findings. Barring any unusual delays, within seven days."

Race thanked Doctor Tulp and made his way out of the room. Carlos followed Race into the anteroom to help him take off the bio-hazard suit. As the door to the autopsy suite was closing, Race could hear the buzzing sound of an electric saw as it cut into Bosco's rib cage.

He didn't look back.

◇◇◇◇◇◇◇

Jennifer woke to the sound of the break room door opening. Her next thought was of being thankful her head no longer pounded.

The bird-like man walked into the room and she had a chance to get a better look at him. She couldn't help but think that he even walked birdlike, not walking per se, kind of hopping on the balls of his feet, barely touching the ground. She'd had a few whiskeys and thought maybe that was the reason he looked peculiar. He was short, about five foot five, maybe less. Thin, probably around one-fifty. From his wool blazer, dress shirt, and striped tie down to his wool pants and matching leather shoes, he was a study in brown. Although his clothes were banal, they seemed well-tailored and made of higher-quality fabric. His complexion was a light chocolate, about the same as men who tan heavily for bodybuilding contests or people of Arabic descent. His black hair was cut short, but was thick with a slight curl. He had no facial hair.

Detective White made the introductions. "Doctor Singh, allow me to introduce my partner in crime, Detective Horace Griffin. He'll be working with me to find the person who murdered Mr. Bosco."

Race walked over to Jennifer and extended his hand.

Jennifer took the detective's hand, it was small and delicate. Her analytical tendencies kicked in with no forethought and she assessed him almost clinically. Close up, he looked youthful. His skin was smooth with little beard growth. He could have passed for a college student, hardly old enough to be a homicide detective. His face was gaunt and angular, with an aquiline nose that was sharp like a beak. He was hyper-alert, as if ready to jump at the slightest stimulus and his eyes were constantly scanning the area as if for some hidden, lurking danger.

A rara avis.

"You can call me Race," the detective said. "Everyone does."

Beela handed one of her cards to Jennifer. "We've taken enough of the good doctor's time." She put her hand on Jennifer's shoulder. "I'll be in touch in a few days to see how you're doing. And again, my condolences."

The detectives left.

Jennifer downed another shot of scotch and sat back on the couch. Feelings of guilt plagued her. She'd assumed Donny hadn't called because he was no longer interested after getting her in bed when in fact, the whole time, he was dead. Brutally murdered.

Chapter 16

Only two cars were parked in the visitor's parking lot: Beela's battered sedan and Race's crimson Marussia B2-H sports coupe.

Beela walked up to Race's car and whistled. "This yours?" Race nodded. She walked around the vehicle and peered in the windows. "Hybrid?" He nodded again. She ran her fingers over the metallic paint and shook her head. "How do you even get into this thing?"

"The doors open upwards," Race said. "Stand back and I'll show you."

Beela took a few steps backward, Race pressed a button on his key fob, and the driver's side door swung up.

"Wow!" Beela shook her head. "How can you afford this baby on a detective's salary?"

"Working Vice paid well." Race chuckled. "Really well."

Beela looked over at Race and gave him a half-smile. "Homicide, not so much." She looked inside the car. "Well, slick, you might want to sell the Batmobile and get yourself a beat-up four-door sedan like I have. First time you have a suspect pee in the back seat of your car, you'll know what I'm talking about."

"We have to use our own vehicles for transporting criminals?"

Beela nodded and laughed. "The department's strapped for cash." She gestured for Race to follow as she clicked her fob and unlocked her car. "I know a little place nearby where we can have lunch."

Race arched his eyebrows. "At ten in the morning?"

"You can tell me about the autopsy before we meet with our boss, Major Primus." She winked at him. "Plus, I'm buying."

Race rubbed his stomach and hopped into Beela's car. "I'm suddenly famished."

Beela gave instructions to the Nav-Drive and turned to Race as the car pulled out of the lot. "I rushed out of the house without eating. I don't function well without breakfast. Had a meeting with one of my kid's teachers."

"How did it go?"

She shrugged. "Not as fast as I'd hoped it would. I almost missed all the excitement here."

Race cringed inside. "I can't imagine how Doctor Singh must have felt when she saw her boyfriend on the autopsy table." He shook his head. "What are the chances of that happening?"

Beela let out a short laugh. "Actually, fifty-fifty. Get this, the county only has two coroners active right now, out of their usual dozen."

"What?"

Beela explained the situation with the treatment-resistant TB. "Here's something you might be interested in." She gave him a little wink. "Before the administrator—the guy in the wheelchair—required the medical examiners to wear bio-hazard suits, Doctor Singh had a pretty good following of young male detectives. If she was assigned to do an autopsy, the detectives on the case made sure they were present for the procedure."

Race tried to hide his interest and looked away. "Is that right?"

Beela nodded. "You didn't see her at her best back there. She is *very* attractive. Fiery red hair, and those killer green eyes. And I'd die for a body like hers. She's quite the belle of the abattoir ball."

Race smiled but didn't make eye contact. "I'll be sure to keep that in mind."

"Don't play coy." Beela poked him in the ribs. "And don't get your hopes up. As far as I know, she'd never as much as gone out for drinks with anyone from the LOPD."

Race met her eyes. "You seem pretty impressed by her."

Beela nodded. "The other day, I saw her save a woman's life without batting an eye or breaking a sweat. It was impressive."

Dr. Singh indeed was impressive, Race thought. Despite her rumpled scrubs and smeared makeup, he had to admit he was aroused in her presence. *But what difference does that really make? She's way out of my league*. He momentarily fantasized about getting down and dirty with the doctor as the car came to a stop in front of a restaurant called the Bruin Deli.

Beela opened her door and looked over at Race. "Stop daydreaming." She laughed. "You'll get to see Dr. Singh again in a day or two, and you don't want to embarrass yourself by drooling."

Race smiled back sheepishly. "We have to interview her again?"

"It's a good idea to interview people twice, they often remember things more clearly the second time around." Beela gave him a little smile. "And she passed out before I could finish getting her statement."

Beela stepped out of the car and glanced back at Race, who hesitated. "We're in a no parking zone."

Beela placed a sign that said "Police Vehicle" on the inside of her windshield, and winked. "One of the perks of being a cop."

Race stepped out of the car and held the door for Beela as they went inside the air conditioned deli. The joint was empty. Beela walked up to the counter, and without looking at the menu posted on the wall, ordered a Tandoori chicken wrap and a watercress salad. Race scanned the menu and hesitated. There must be over a hundred different items, he thought.

The woman behind the counter stared at Race and tapped her fingernails on the metal counter.

Too many choices! Race reached inside the sleeve of his jacket and snapped his rubber stress bracelet twice. The jolt of pain focused his mind.

"I'll have what she's having," he said.

Beela smiled at him. "Good choice."

Beela scanned her microchip to pay. They reached the end of the deli counter just as their food was set out. After picking up their meals, they found an empty table outside on the sidewalk. Race explained the results of Bosco's autopsy while Beela dug into her belated breakfast.

When he finished describing the autopsy, Beela said between bites, "Look, Race, this is your first week working homicide. You'll get to see the saddest, goriest, and most tragic sights in this business."

He gave Beela a wink. "I've watched tons of cop shows."

"Not the same thing. This is real life. I've seen things on this job that they'd never show on the holovision because they're too unbelievable. Or too sad. Or too gross. Usually all of the above. And our show doesn't end at the top of the hour. You can't change the channel." She paused and gave him a wry smile. "And don't forget the smell—"

Race wrinkled his nose, remembering the stench of the crime scene. "That's something I wasn't prepared for yesterday."

"You won't get used to it, not really, but you learn to cope." She pointed her fork at him. "There is a good part, like when a crime is solved and you get to tell the victim's family that the murderer is headed for prison. You'll feel a sense of having helped them deal with their tragedy. I know it doesn't bring their loved one back, but it creates a sense of closure and they can start healing. And you will have played a role in justice being done." She paused a second and picked at her meal.

Race said, "The thing that really attracted me to homicide, is the challenge of solving puzzles. Some people like to do crossword puzzles or Sudoku, but for me solving murders is the ultimate puzzle."

Beela was scarfing down her salad, but stopped to say, "That's part of the reason I went into homicide as well. Do you know what the most important tool we have in solving homicides?"

Race shook his head.

She pointed to her temple. "Our brains. That's your first lesson. Granted, there are the occasional murders are tough to solve. True mind benders. But you won't believe how amazingly stupid most criminals are, almost like they want to be caught." Beela moved her salad around the plate. "Sadly, we get lots of cases where we just run out of time. We have too many cases and a limited number of detectives. Those cases get shunted to the cold case files. Once they get sent there, there's barely a chance that they'll get solved. In a few months, you'll be handling so many cases you'll look forward to sending the older ones there."

Race frowned. Is that the way things work? What a difference between Vice, where, thanks to confiscated drug money, funding was rarely an issue.

"Don't look so glum," Beela said. "We can only do our best. For instance, I know we'll solve the Bosco case."

Race's spirits picked up. "You think so?"

"Guaranteed."

"I was going over the Sing homicide, and I wanted to run something by you."

Beela waved him off with her fork. "You don't have to get involved in that case. I picked it up before you joined the team."

"Technically, I was on your team as of Saturday. I had the weekend off and started orientation Monday."

"What'd they cover?"

Race had just started in on his wrap and finished his bite. "Health insurance, workers' comp, pensions, sexual harassment policy, and vacation and sick days. At the end of the day, I was notified to report to the precinct the next morning, so I didn't get a chance to complete the rest of the week."

"You'll just have to learn on the job, that's where I picked up most of what I know. I had the same partner the whole time I was in homicide—the Bowling Ball."

Race chuckled. "I've heard about him. Didn't he take offense to being called that?"

"He actually liked it, said it gave him the motivation to try to lose weight. Not that he ever did. His idea of a diet was to cut back to six donuts a day from the usual dozen. Which leads directly to why they pulled you from orientation."

Race gave her a puzzled look. "Donuts?"

Beela laughed. "The Bowling Ball wasn't supposed to retire until the end of the month, which would have given you time to finish orientation and allow two more weeks where the three of us could have worked cases together. Monday, hard to believe it was only two days ago, we were sitting in the car doing a stake out. He had a vanilla crème doughnut in his mouth. He suddenly stopped chewing. Right then, I knew something was wrong. He usually wolfed those things down. I rushed him to LA County Medical. They said he was in the middle of a stroke."

Race stopped chewing and put his food down. "I'm sorry to hear that."

"He'll be okay. They gave him a blood clot busting drug and he went home yesterday morning. That's why you're here with me today, instead of at the academy."

Race put on his earnest face. "I'd like to help out on the Sing homicide, especially now that you've lost your old partner. I think Bosco's death is related to the murders of Dr. Sing and the unknown Russian."

Beela stopped chewing and stared at Race. "Let me get this straight. You're working two homicide cases, randomly selected, and you think they're related?"

"I reviewed the cases last night, after we left Bosco's place, and I think I see a thread."

"A thread?"

Race set his fork down and leaned toward Beela. "Look at the timeline. The Russian was executed in Vegas last Thursday. Bosco left Vegas the next day and was beaten to death here sometime Saturday. Dr. Sing was killed later that day. In all three cases, the murderer seems to have been looking for something."

"Murderers," Beela said. "Plural. The Russian detective handling the case told Dr. Singh he believes the murderers worked in pairs."

Race nodded.

"I grant you the Russian and the Sing cases are related," Beela said as she chewed her salad. "But I don't see how Bosco fits in. He wasn't tortured. He wasn't killed with the distinctive hollow-point bullet."

"Does a murderer always have to use the same method?"

"No." She gave him a slight nod. "But if they do, it certainly connects the murders. What connection do you think Bosco has with the other two vics?"

"Let's say the courier passed merchandise along to Bosco and—"

Beela stopped eating and shot Race a hard look. "Hold on a nanosec. Before you start implicating Bosco in a smuggling ring, remember he was well respected. A pillar of the community. The Bowling Ball taught me to be careful casting aspersions on murder victims."

Race glared back at her. "Sorry, but we're trying to solve his murder. Don't you think we owe it to Bosco to have an open mind?"

"What I mean is, we have to tread carefully." Her face softened, and she patted Race on the hand. "Keep in mind that a person spends a lifetime building their reputation, and when they're dead, they're in no position to defend it."

"Understood." Race leaned forward and spoke quietly. "But just between us, let's say the courier passed the merchandise, whatever it was, on to Bosco. And Bosco passed it on to Sing."

"That's a stretch."

"Would you mind if I pursue that angle? On the QT."

Beela nodded a few times and swallowed her food. "Go for it. Just don't become obsessed with the idea. Another thing my mentor taught me was to keep an open mind."

They ate in silence. Beela took the last bites of her wrap and wiped her face.

"While you were in Vice, Race, you ever work with Helena?"

Race looked over and saw that Beela had finished eating. "Not that I can remember. Who is she?" He shoved the rest of his sandwich in his mouth.

"You'd remember her. She's the department's Cyber sapiens. She assists on all homicide cases."

"Cyber sapiens, huh," he mumbled with a mouth half full. He took a sip of his drink and swallowed the rest of his meal. "An artificial intelligence? Like the Nav-Drive? Or the OmniPhone concierge?"

"She's not like that. There's nothing artificial about her. Spend time with her and you forget she's not human."

Race wiped his mouth. "The Nav-Drive is amazing, but it's still just a very sophisticated computer program."

"You're about to meet Helena, then you can decide." Beela pulled up the sleeve of her jacket and checked the time on her LOPD OmniPhone. She chuckled and showed it to Race. "Don't you just love the color the department chose for our Omnis?"

The OmniPhone was neon orange.

Race pulled up the sleeve of his blazer and showed Beela his bright orange wrist device. "There's one good thing about having an ugly Omni," he said.

"What's that, partner?"

"You don't have to worry about somebody trying to steal it."

Chapter 17

Beela dropped Race off back at the morgue parking lot. She rolled down her window and yelled, "Race you to the station, Race!"

Race slid into the deep bucket seat of his car, which molded itself around his body. He used the right-side joystick to back out of the parking lot, then programmed the Nav-Drive to follow Beela's car to the station. He told the radio to play one of his programmed channels, sat back, enjoying the luxury leather smell while he watched holographic Egyptian pop music videos, and tried to put the pieces together linking Bosco's murder with Dr. Sing's and the Russian courier. The car's gas engine kicked in, accelerated up to 120 mph effortlessly, and merged with the southbound traffic on the freeway.

He knew that Beela could be right about Bosco's murder not being related to the other two. But there was something about the three murders, something he couldn't put his finger on, which seemed to link them in his subconscious. He knew the key was to find a connection between Bosco and Dr. Sing. Perhaps the reason the doctor's marriage was falling apart was her husband found out she was involved with Bosco. Race planned to have a talk with her estranged husband. Bosco had been dating Dr. Singh, the medical examiner, and it struck Race that it would be quite a coincidence if he'd also been seeing Dr. Sing.

He was puzzling through the connections between the murders when his car exited the freeway and began maneuvering through the mile-long mazes in the residential cities. To conserve space, from the fifth floor up, tunnel-like structures extending over the roadways connected individual buildings into something more like one large building several square miles in size, but with roads through it. Virtual cities unto themselves, the larger ones housed hundreds of thousands—in the case of the mega-residence called Anaheim, a million—people. Many residents were content to live their entire lives without venturing into the unfiltered air of outdoors.

Race couldn't imagine living with that self-imposed limitation and not experiencing the outside world, which is why he lived in a stand-alone high rise condo building.

The car pulled up at the station, located in a bleak neighborhood surrounded by a low-income, high-rise housing complex. This particular structure appeared to be a monster, menacing and eerie, because of its cloak of swirling, sooty smoke from the raging fires surrounding the city. The only greenery in sight were a pair of stunted cedar trees with their sparse leaves brown and wilting.

Race disengaged the Nav-Drive and steered the car to follow his partner to the back of the police station. He swiped his police badge and pulled into the detective's parking lot. Beela parked in a spot with an electric charging station. She plugged her car in to be recharged and met Race by the door.

The wind had shifted since they left the morgue and was blowing in from the east, bringing with it a light gray smoke and the distinctive smell of the fires. Race began coughing. "People call Southern California paradise," he said to Beela. "I'd hate to see what hell is like!"

Beela let out a laugh. "Come on upstairs and find out."

Race tried to stifle his coughing as he accompanied Beela to the rear entrance of the precinct. He frowned as he took in the battered, nondescript, two-story brick building. The rear of the building had few windows and all were covered by metal bars the thickness of a man's wrist. A microchip had to be presented to open the biometric lock-controlled steel-plated back door; they held their left forearms against the device and were buzzed in. They climbed one flight, the tread all but worn off the metal stairs, to the detective's squad room.

Race shook his head. The room was grim, something out of a Dickens novel. A dozen or so industrial-style, gunmetal gray metal desks were arranged in rows, each with worn swivel office chairs. The desks themselves were spartan, containing only a computer monitor and a goose-neck lamp. A row of printer-scanners sat on a metal folding table in the corner next to a battered copy machine. The room was windowless. The walls were a faded hospital green, vaguely luminescent in the sallow light thrown off by the banks of grime-coated LED lights. Along the back wall were two sturdy-looking doors, each labeled DATAPORT. A sink and a cabinet with a line of coffee makers sat on the other wall. The smells of brewed coffee and cheap cologne permeated the air. And there was something else, a faint undertone of fear and desperation, like that from a trapped animal.

The right wall consisted of two interrogation rooms and one private office marked Major Primus. The major's office had glass windows looking over the squad room. Its shutters were closed and a dagger of light slashed out from the open door.

The squad room was empty. Race assumed the other detectives were out working their cases or having lunch. "Is this place always this dead?"

"Dead?" Beela groaned. "Bad choice of words, slick. How about a cup of coffee before we meet the COD?"

"COD?" Race chuckled. "Sounds fishy."

Bella smiled thinly, as if she'd heard that joke far too many times. "The Chief of Detectives, you numbskull. Major Marius Primus. By the way, *he* doesn't have a sense of humor."

Race surveyed the room. "Where's my desk? I'd like to be near the back wall."

"We use what's called the 'open office' system. When you need to use a desk, avail yourself of any one that's free. The efficiency experts felt it would be more economical than giving each officer their own desk, since most of our time is spent out in the field." Beela looked over toward the private offices. "The major's door is open. Let's grab that coffee, and I'll introduce you."

They filled Styrofoam cups that were stacked on the counter, then Race followed Beela to the major's office. The door stood ajar. Beela made a courtesy knock, peeked in, and then entered, Race at her heels.

A silver haired man wearing a navy sports coat sat facing an antique-looking oak desk. He looked up and smiled when they entered. "Just waiting on the major," he said. He pushed against the armrests of the padded wooden chair and, little-by-little, stood and straightened his back. He extended his weathered hand. "Captain Graham Beane," he said. "HQ assigned me to help you with the Bosco murder."

"Glad to have the help," Beela said.

Race and Beela took turns shaking his hand.

Beane had a youthful appearance for his age, with a full head of hair, a firm handshake, and a mischievous glint in his eye. He looked like the kind old uncle Race always wished he'd had. Beane motioned for Beela and Race to take the unoccupied chairs.

Race looked around the major's windowless office. The walls were covered with photos of a middle-aged man posing with a variety of well-known political and entertainment figures, along with framed diplomas from two colleges and a number of commendation plaques from LOPD. The major was nowhere in sight.

Beela settled into her chair. "Have you seen the chief?" she asked Beane.

"Good morning everyone." A voice called Race's attention to the desktop where a man's 3-D image emerged above the holoprojector—the same man in the photos scattered around the office. The holoimage looked back at the group, making eye contact with each of them. His voice came through a pair of speakers situated on either side of the room.

"Major," Beela said to the image. "Good morning."

The holoimage looked in Race's direction. "I am Major Marius Primus, Chief of Detectives for this district." The major's voice had a slightly hesitant quality, reminding Race of how Neil Armstrong sounded when he walked on the moon. "Let me apologize for not being with you in person. I am going to be caught up in meetings all day, so we will do this as a video conference."

"Pleased to meet you, sir," Race said.

The major nodded to him, then addressed Beela and the captain. "I would like to formally welcome Detective Horace Bannon Griffin to our team. He comes to us highly commended, with seven years' experience working in Vice." He caught Race's eye. "Detective Griffin, my apologies for snatching you from your orientation program, but our department is very short-staffed." The major looked at Beela. "Detective White, I am sure, will do a great job breaking you in."

"I'll try my best," Beela said.

"Second," the major said, "I am sure you have had a chance to meet Captain Graham Beane. Captain Beane is a retired LOPD homicide detective."

Race looked over, nodded, and smiled at the captain.

Primus addressed the group. "Let us discuss the Bosco homicide. HQ has designated this case level A. Bosco was well-known in the upper-crust circles in the county. Race, an A rating means that your team will not be taking any new cases until you close this one. That is also why I have assigned Captain Beane to help your group. The department has allocated fourteen days to work the investigation. Hopefully, it will not take that long to solve. I will be monitoring your progress daily, you can contact me anytime. Detective Griffin, since this is your first homicide, you should not have any prior obligations and can devote yourself full-time to this case. Detective White, what is your status for the next week?"

"I'm due to testify tomorrow in State Court on the Cabezas case." Beela turned to Race and explained that Cabezas had been shot in the head and killed by his girlfriend, who was claiming temporary insanity. "I'll probably be out all day."

Primus nodded. "Fine. Detective Griffin, work with Captain Beane tomorrow. Anything else?"

Beela mentioned that she had a couple of depositions scheduled for later in the week.

"Work the Bosco case around them." The major turned to Beela. "You are the lead detective, bring the team up to speed on the case."

Beela turned on her VR contacts and moved her fingers around the wrist controller of her OmniPhone as she spoke. "Yesterday, at 9:23 AM, we received notice of a one-eighty-seven in Beverly Glen, near the reservoir. When we arrived at the scene, the patrol officers had secured the area. Typical ultra-wealthy neighborhood, no crowd hanging around outside the tape—the very rich, it seems, are different from you and me."

Beane laughed. "Anywhere else, yellow police tape draws a crowd as easily as the Hollywood red carpet."

Beela smiled. "The house itself is a museum-sized mansion with an oversized garage, two-story entrance-way, marble walls, and fluted Ionic columns. Think Grecian temple."

"Plenty of parking for Apollo's chariots," Beane interjected.

Primus scowled at Beane and told Beela to continue.

"The murder was called in by the cleaning people, Mr. and Mrs. da Silva, a Brazilian couple. The patrol unit told us that when they arrived, the couple was sitting on the front stairs, shaky and pale. The responding officers checked the master bedroom, verified that there was a dead male, and posted the one-eighty-seven. We brought Mr. da Silva into the house to identify the body, then took their statements."

The major looked down as if he was jotting notes, then nodded for Beela to continue.

"The da Silvas reported that they've been cleaning Bosco's house for five years. They come every Tuesday morning and spend the day. They arrived at the residence around nine AM. They have a key and were accustomed to letting themselves in. The front door was unlocked, which they said was not unusual. The couple separated. Mr. da Silva started mopping the floors in the entrance foyer and kitchen area. The missus went around the house planning to strip the beds and collect the towels from the bathrooms, then get a load of laundry started. She went to the master bedroom last. When she walked into the room, she noticed blood spattered on the walls near the bed, and the bed itself was covered in blood. She reports noticing a putrid smell and what looked like a body, covered by a sheet, lying on the bed. She began to scream hysterically. Her husband came running, peeked under the sheet, and verified that it was their employer. They dropped what they were doing, ran out the front entrance, and immediately called 911. Other than slightly lifting the sheet to make sure it was indeed Bosco, they maintain they didn't touch anything in the master bedroom. We scanned their fingerprints into the system, then let them leave."

"Signs of forced entry?" Primus asked.

"That's the weird thing," Race said. "There was no reason for someone to force their way in. The cleaners stated that the front door was unlocked. I walked around the house and found the gate to the backyard, the rear patio doors, and the French doors leading from the balcony to the master bedroom were all wide-open. Anyone could have strolled right in."

"Dr. Singh told me that the garage and the patio doors were open when she left the house Saturday morning," Beela added. "The garage door was closed when we arrived to the scene."

"You think it was a robbery gone bad?" Primus asked.

"That's a strong possibility," Beela said. "There were no signs of vandalism, but items were strewn about. The killer was searching for something. In the closets, clothes were piled everywhere. Bosco's home office was ransacked, the shelves were empty, and the drawers of the desk and credenza were open. Papers littered the floor. Packets of what appeared to be drugs in sealed plastic bags lie on the desk. Some contained marijuana, field tests on the others were positive for pharmaceutical grade cocaine. In addition, there were bottles of pills and plastic containers with various powders. All were placed into evidence and sent to the crime lab."

"Do we know what, if anything, was stolen?" the major asked.

Beela shook her head. "The deceased's watch might be missing. I'll let Race tell you about that later."

The major nodded. "What about the crime scene?"

"The master bedroom had blood on the wall above the headboard," Beela said. "A spatter pattern consistent with blunt trauma. The sheets under the deceased's head were bloodstained. No apparent signs of a struggle in the bedroom, or on the corpse. Bosco's wallet was on the nightstand, it had no money but was filled with business cards. We scanned the contents of the wallet into evidence. Bosco apparently didn't use a wrist OmniPhone. We found an OmniPhone minitablet registered in his name in a pair of tuxedo pants lying on the patio, just off his bedroom door. Helena is analyzing his contacts. Wadded up dress socks and men's boxer shorts lay next to the bed. The forensic team took photos of the room, then we uncovered the body. Bosco lay on his stomach, completely naked. He had a swollen and bloody area on his right temple, about the size of a golf ball. Forensics noted that the body was at room temperature and he'd been dead for over twenty-four hours."

"Must have smelled ripe," Beane said.

"It was rank, thanks for reminding me." Beela grimaced. "The house was a treasure trove of fingerprints. The fingerprint tech reported at least twenty distinct sets of prints. Again, Helena is working on a list."

Primus interrupted. "I have seen the preliminary identification. You can go over them later in detail."

Beela nodded. "We didn't find the murder weapon. An obvious implement would have been one of the two metal lamps on either side of the bed, however, forensics didn't find blood or tissue on either of them. Bosco had a number of baseball or softball bats in his garage, they also tested negative for blood. Hard to tell if any were missing."

Beela used her Omni to pull up information on her VR contacts. "The master bath had towels thrown haphazardly over the towel rack right outside the door-less shower, others were wadded up on the floor. Two of the towels were stained and tested positive for blood—they were sent to the lab for DNA. The techs found traces of blood in the shower, same blood type as Bosco's."

Primus asked. "You think Bosco tried to clean himself up after he was hit?"

Race shook his head. "The medical examiner, Doctor Tulp, believes that Bosco was knocked unconscious by the blows and died without coming to."

"The killer may have used the towels to clean himself off," Primus said. "If we are lucky, he may have left something the lab can work with."

"I wouldn't hold my breath," Beela said. "The lab's really backed up. Said it would be at least a week before—"

"I will call the lab myself," Primus said. "Get them to move it to the front of the line. This is a high priority case. What else?"

"During the autopsy," Race said, "the medical examiner found that Bosco had actually taken two blows to the head."

"They were so close together that they looked like one," Beela added.

"Dr. Tulp discovered postmortem wounds on the right side of Bosco's back," Race told the major.

Primus's eyes widened. "Postmortem? Someone was wailing on Bosco after he was already dead?"

"That's what the ME concluded," Race said. "The blows were severe enough to cause multiple rib fractures. Actual death would have occurred ten minutes to an hour or so after the initial blunt head trauma."

Primus simply nodded.

Beela said, "Spatter pattern was consistent with medium velocity impact, consistent with the autopsy results."

"Let me recap the circumstances," Primus said. "Bosco takes two blows to the head, which were the cause of death. Then, someone hits him in the back, probably with the same weapon, after he is already dead. Ten minutes or more after the head blows." He paused. "That is strange. What do you think it means?"

"I haven't had time to process the information yet," Beela said. "We just became aware of the postmortem wounds about an hour ago."

The major nodded for them to go on.

Race said, "Where a person would usually wear an OmniPhone, Bosco had an untanned area on his left wrist, which was quite unusual. The pattern resembled that made by a leather watch band. Maybe alligator."

Primus narrowed his eyes and looked at Race. "You can tell that from looking at his wrist?"

"Race has hawk-like eyesight," Beela said to Primus. "To me, the pattern looked like it was made by a typical Omni. But then again, Bosco used a minitablet Omni."

"We didn't find a watch anywhere in the house," Race said. "Given Bosco's lifestyle, I would imagine it was very expensive. A Rolex, or something like that."

Primus nodded. "Go through Bosco's credit card statements, maybe he paid for the watch that way. Check the high-end jewelry stores, find out who sold it to him." He nodded to Race. "Detective, I want you to follow up on this."

"Yes, sir"

"What about time of death?" Primus asked.

"Doctor Tulp confirmed that Bosco was dead at least twenty-four hours before the body was discovered," Race said. "And he had been killed no more than seven days before that."

"That is a long window of time."

"We can narrow that window down a little," Beela said. "Bosco attended a charity event at the Getty Center last Friday night with Doctor Jennifer Singh."

The major raised his eyebrows. "Doctor Singh? The medical examiner? How does she fit into the case?"

"I took the doctor's statement this morning. She'd been dating Bosco for three weeks. After they left the Getty, the doctor went to Bosco's and spent the night. She left early Saturday morning, before dawn."

Beane laughed. "She have intimacy problems?"

Beela glared at Beane. "What's so funny about that? Maybe she had to go to work the next morning."

Primus shot Beane a look and mused. "So we know that Bosco was alive early Saturday morning. Can you narrow the time frame down any further?"

"We spoke to an elderly neighbor of Bosco's," Beela said. "Mrs. Billings-Li. She reported seeing him Saturday, around nine AM, picking up his newspaper from the driveway. She was on her way to the senior center in Hollywood, in one of those elderly vans. In addition, Doctor Singh received a vase of flowers from Bosco later that same morning. There was a pile of newspapers in the driveway, starting with Sunday's LA Times. So the time of death would be after Saturday mid-morning and before Monday afternoon."

Primus looked at Beela. "Still a long period of time, but better."

"I'm sure we can narrow it down once we get the investigation going. We canvassed the neighborhood with little luck. Most people were either away, or refused to answer the intercoms on the gates guarding their driveways."

Beane raised his eyebrows. "Gated driveways? Was Bosco's gate open when the housekeepers came on Tuesday?"

Beela nodded. "We ran across Bosco's landscaping service, they were coming to do the yard. They service Bosco's place every Tuesday. They have the code to open the front gate, and a key for the gate leading to the back yard. They state that when they pulled into the neighborhood around seven, to do another yard on the street, Bosco's front gate was open."

"Anything else I need to know?" Primus said.

"The other person that we were able to contact lives in the house between Bosco and Billings-Li, one Dona Godgifu. She's in her late thirties, early forties."

"By the way," Race said. "Billings-Li is ninety-five, but doesn't look a day over ninety."

Beane chuckled. Primus remained serious.

"Godgifu told us that she barely knew Bosco," Beela said with a serious face. "She'd been to his house a few times, the first time about five years ago when he threw a house warming party, and a few other parties since. She told us she takes her dog for a walk up the street once or twice a day. When she walked past Bosco's Saturday afternoon, she saw a car with Nevada plates parked in his driveway next to the garage." Beela looked at Beane. "The gate was open at the time. She doesn't remember seeing the car the next day." Beela looked at Primus and arched her eyebrows. "And Dr. Singh told me that Bosco had just returned from Vegas."

Primus looked at the group, frowning. "That could be useful info. What was Bosco doing in Vegas?"

"He goes there regularly on business," Beela said. "We're trying to track down where he stayed this last time and with whom he does business."

"What about surveillance cameras?" the major said. "A house like that must have a sophisticated system."

Beela frowned and shook her head. "He had one, but the service had been turned off. He fell behind on the monthly monitoring fee. We're analyzing traffic cameras from both Mulholland and Sunset. There was heavy smoke from the fires that night and some of the photos are blurred beyond recognition. We're trying to find out if the neighborhood association has a system in place."

Primus looked off camera, distracted. "I need to be off in a few minutes, but good work so far." He made eye contact with each of the detectives. "I know we usually work closely with the Medical Examiner's office, but since Doctor Singh was dating the deceased, we need to be careful sharing information with them."

They all nodded.

"You have a number of good leads. The brass is keeping close tabs, so keep me apprised." The major's image faded away.

Beela stood up. "Race, time you met Helena. The fourth member of our team."

Chapter 18

Race followed his fellow detectives across the squad room, still dark and empty, to a door marked DATAPORT 1. Beane bent down and held his face a foot or so away from the electronic scanner at the side of the door. The device scanned his retina, then the light changed from red to green, and the door clicked open. They entered and the lights inside came on.

The room was windowless, the walls and ceiling covered in acoustic tiles, and the door had metal mesh on its inner surface. They each took seats in leather swivel office chairs around the oblong wooden conference table which dominated the room.

Beane sat down. "Helena."

Race squinted as the lights dimmed slightly, taking on a red tinge, and watched as an image appeared over one of the hologram projectors sitting on either side of the table. Hovering inches above the flat, black pad was a life-sized holographic image of a woman's face and neck down to the beginning of her shoulders. Dressed in a neutral colored, high-necked shirt, she seemed to be in her mid-twenties. Her pleasant face revealed a slight smile and two dimples. Slate-blue eyes beneath long, dark lashes took turns making eye contact with each of the three people seated in the room. There was an airbrushed quality to her tanned skin, subtle freckles dotted the sides of her nose. Blond hair styled in a simple flip reached down to her shoulders. A hint of coral lipstick covered her full lips, blue eye shadow complimented her eyes, and best of all, in Race's opinion, she had a cute button nose.

From the speakers located around the room came a woman's voice, friendly with a hint of a Valley girl accent.

"Good afternoon, Detectives Beane, White, and Griffin."

Race said hello reflexively.

"Race, let me introduce you to Helena," Beane said. "Helena is the department's AI detective—"

"Cyber sapiens," Helena cut in, a hurt look on her face. She shot Beane an icy glare. "And I work for more than just the LOPD homicide department."

Beane nodded. "I stand corrected. She'll be assisting us in this case."

"And in all our cases," Beela added.

"Nice to meet you, Detective," Helena said.

Race couldn't help but smile at the holographic image when she nodded and smiled back at him. "Same here," he said.

"Helena," Beane said, "short for 'Human Electronic something or other,' started as a low-level Artificial Intelligence to assist us detectives with many of our routine tasks. Over time, programmers added various logic protocols so that Helena could analyze data and function independently. The program became more and more complex to the point where Helena eventually became self-aware."

Helena said, "Captain Beane, that occurred when my program was ported to a quantum computing platform."

Beane rubbed his temples and laughed. "All that quantum gobbledygook makes me giddy." He nodded to Beela and Helena. "Maybe one of you two should take over."

"Be happy to," Helena said with a nod to the captain. "The programmers developed me to have certain female traits. There are two schools of thought on why they did that. The official story is that they wanted to incorporate a certain amount of intuition into my analysis. They felt that this is more of a feminine trait. The other theory is that because all the programmers working on the project were males, many of them with limited female relationships in their own lives—the stereotypical 30-year-old nerd living in his mother's basement—they projected their idealized view of a woman into the program. Probably a little of both is true."

"I'm going with the nerd theory," Beela said.

Beane nodded in agreement.

Helena looked directly at Race and said, "While you and Detective White were on the Bosco crime scene, I was analyzing the data as you collected it. I compiled telephone records and all of Bosco's bank activity. I completed an initial analysis before you left the scene."

"How is that possible?" Race said. "You'd need a warrant to get that information."

"There is a judge on duty 24-7. I emailed the warrants and received a virtual signature from him in minutes."

Race slapped the table. "I wish we had access to you when I was working Vice."

"That would not be advisable. Hackers are continually trying to break into my programming code. And communication between detectives in the field and myself can be easily compromised with equipment that can be bought on the Interweb."

"That's why we have to meet in secure locations like this DataPort," Beela said, "when we want to discuss sensitive matters."

"This room is essentially a Faraday cage," Helena told Race, "blocking electromagnetic radiation from passing through the walls. Captain Beane will be your liaison with me when you're out in the field. Or, of course, you can use the DataPorts at any of the police stations around the county. Just log-in and access me on your own there."

Race sat back. "Your avatar, Helena…is that how the programmers envisioned you looking?"

Beane said, "The image Helena is displaying can be modified to each person's taste. Since I was the first person to log into the system for this session, the image and voice she's displaying are the ones I created for her. It's a rough approximation of my daughter right after she finished graduate school. She lives in Barcelona now, and I don't get to see her often. When you get a chance, ask Helena to open the system control panel and create your own avatar."

"As long as that avatar is an attractive female," Beela said with feigned annoyance. "Helena won't allow anyone to create a male image."

"There are certain parameters," Helena said with a sly nod. "I will take care of most of the tedious and data intensive work detectives used to handle. Also, I will be pursuing lines of inquiry on my own, based on lessons I have learned on previous cases. I also use what humans term 'hunches,' which are actually statistical probability calculations."

"I think a hunch is more than just a mathematical calculation," Race said.

"I disagree with you there, Detective. But right now we are working an active case, so why not table that discussion for a later date."

Race was impressed with how she did seem to have a mind of her own. "There is a hunch I have." Race glimpsed Beela rolling her eyes. "I'd like to run it by you." He turned to Beela, gave her a pleading look, and waited.

"Go ahead," she said with a shrug. "Get it off your chest."

Race leaned forward and addressed Helena. "I believe the Bosco murder is related to two other recent murders. That of Dr. Jennifer Sing, a Physical Therapy doctor murdered here in Los Angeles on Saturday, and a Russian John Doe believed to have been a courier, killed last week in Las Vegas."

Helena pursed her lips and paused a second. She scrunched her eyes as if in deep thought.

Race imagined she was pulling up those cases and analyzing them. And he was becoming more and more impressed by Helena's human-like behavior.

"What makes you think they are related?" Helena finally said.

"Both the doctor and Bosco had their houses ransacked. Their killers were looking for something. The Russian and Bosco were both in Las Vegas, contemporaneously. Bosco was living large. Maybe he ran into financial difficulty and became involved in smuggling."

Beela said to Race with a stern voice, "Do *not* make those kinds of statements about Bosco outside our circle without proof. Bosco was an upstanding citizen, and if word got out that we're trying to tie him to illegal international trafficking, our asses would be on the line. And I don't want to go back to working patrol."

"But between us, anything goes," Beane said. "There's an unspoken code that binds homicide detectives called 'in car talk.'"

"It means this doesn't leak outside," Beela said.

Race gave Beela a slight nod. "Understood."

"My virtual lips are sealed," Helena said. She turned to Race. "I have done a preliminary analysis of your hypothesis, Detective. I classify the odds of Mr. Bosco's murder being related to the other two as highly unlikely, less than ten percent. As Detective White pointed out, there is nothing to suggest he was involved in a Russian smuggling ring."

Race sighed. "I still have this gut feeling the killings are related."

Helena caught his eye and gave him an encouraging look. "Don't discount your intuitions. There may be something there, something that you are not conscious of, that is causing you to link the murders together. I have observed that a human's gut feeling is correct more often than statistical probability would suggest."

Beela tapped her foot. She shot both Helena and Race a look. "Guys, let's focus on the Bosco case. The clock's ticking. What have you learned, Captain?"

"Young people," Beane clucked his tongue, "so impatient." He pulled an eTablet and reading glasses out of his blazer pocket. He slipped on the glasses and consulted his tablet as he spoke. "I have a list of all the calls made and received by Bosco over the last three years, as well as his voice mail and text messages. We've pulled up all financial papers and bank records for both Bosco the individual and the professional, and all the businesses associated with him. Helena's obtained Bosco's last seven federal and state personal income tax filings."

Beela was still tapping her foot. "And?"

"Let's start with Bosco's neighbor, Mrs. Dona Godgifu. She told you she 'barely' knew him. However, there have been dozens of calls between her and Bosco in the last couple years, and they happen in spurts. Her husband, Leo, is in the import-export business and frequently travels out of the country. The calls between Bosco and Godgifu coincide with the times when her husband is out of town, and they occur on either Thursdays or Fridays. There was one text message from Godgifu to Bosco that is the 'smoking gun' if you will." He furrowed his brow and made a few swipes with his fingers on his eTablet. A ProjectionWall monitor on one of the walls came to life and a text message appeared. "The text from Godgifu reads: 'lg just left cu 2nite meow.' My money says the little lady was having an affair with Bosco, taking advantage of the times when her husband was out of town."

Beela raised her eyebrows. "She may know more than she let on yesterday. We'll use this information as leverage to get her to talk; otherwise, we share it with her husband. Did we find any of her prints around Bosco's house?"

Beane nodded. "On the sliding glass door leading into the master bedroom, on the lamp sitting to the left of the bed, and on the headboard."

"So Godgifu wasn't upfront about her relationship with Bosco." Bella's tone was sarcastic. "Can't say I blame her. The shock of her lover's death, the fear of her affair being made public…but it does move her way up on the usual suspects list."

Beane consulted his eTablet. "Bosco's name comes up in a number of companies. One of them lists Leo Godgifu and Bosco as partners. NOR-KOR Enterprises. It seems our victim had dealings with *both* the husband and the wife. Bosco might have been screwing both Godgifus."

Beela gave him a snide look.

"Think about it. He's sleeping with the wife and taking advantage of the husband financially. A couple of time-tested motives for murder."

"Infidelity and money *are* two of the three most common motives for murder," Helena said.

"You think Leo was aware of his wife's infidelity?" Beela said.

"There is no way to tell from the data I have compiled," Helena said.

"Bosco runs a hedge fund and invests money for the über-wealthy," Beane said. "Some of the biggest names in L'Orange. Bosco's luxurious standard of living doesn't match his reported income. I suggest we have a forensic accountant look over his business dealings. He may have been running a scam, or a Ponzi scheme. One of his investors gets wind of it and cashes Bosco out."

Beela nodded to the hologram. "Get authorization from Major Primus. Let's conduct a forensic evaluation of Bosco's businesses and income stream."

"Will do, boss," Helena said. "I will forward Bosco's financials on to our forensic accountant."

Beela turned to Beane. "What other fingerprints showed up?"

Beane projected a floor plan of Bosco's house on the wall monitor that showed where each fingerprint was found. They were all labeled with two letters—the initials of the people who matched the prints. Ones that couldn't be matched were listed as UKI, UK2, etc. A legend matched the initials to the person's names.

Beane pulled a laser pointer from a drawer under the table and pointed at the map as he spoke. "The house is riddled with good quality fingerprints. I already mentioned Dona Godgifu's prints, they're labeled as DG. Mr. Bosco's, labeled DB, are all over the first floor—no surprise there. Doctor Jennifer Singh's prints, seen on the screen as JS, were found on the balcony railing outside the master bedroom, in the bedroom and master bath, as well as on one of the doorknobs leading to the garage."

"That's consistent with what the doctor told us this morning," Beela said.

"On the drugs found on and in the desk are prints of Klaas Bruin, a high-end drug dealer."

Race's head popped up. "I know Bruin. Had dealings with him when I worked Vice. He doesn't seem the type to knock off one of his clients. His clientele was always the rich and famous, and Klaas dresses the part. Besides, he's a part-time preacher or minister."

Beane nodded. "Helena doesn't think he's the likely killer either. He has no priors. But we shouldn't leave any stone unturned."

Beela said, "Race, you're the logical person to talk to Bruin. Track him down, find out what he knows." She nodded to the captain. "What else can you tell us?"

"The da Silva's prints were found all over the house," Beane said. "On the front doorknob was a print of a woman named Brigit Kojacy. Lots of calls back and forth between the two love birds. She called Bosco twice Saturday afternoon, the second time she left a text that said: 'need 2cu ASAP BK.'"

"We'll need to talk to her," Beela said.

"This is Ms. Kojacy." Beane projected a picture of a young, attractive woman with dark hair and haunting eyes on the wall monitor. "According to her Social Interweb page, she's an aspiring actress from the Midwest. She lives in Hollywood and has been seen with Bosco at a few functions. And she's young and attractive. She's probably paying her expenses the old-fashioned way, by dating the wealthier members of our society. We know Bosco was sleeping with Doctor Singh, this Brigit woman, and the neighbor. I'm sure there are lots more. I'll try to track down Bosco's other squeezes." Beane licked his lips. "That might be a fun way to pass an afternoon."

Beela groaned.

Beane looked down and consulted his eTablet. "There are lots of smeared prints and others we can't identify. They're listed on the floor plan as UK."

"What are the chances of identifying any of them?"

Helena answered. "Very slight. They do not match anything in either the FBI's IAFIS or Interpol's MetaMorpho databases, or any of the other international databases I have access to. If those prints are in the system, they are locked away pretty tight."

"Were you able to access the Russian AFIS?" Race asked.

Beane looked up from his tablet. "Why are you interested in that?"

"We're working up the assumption that Dr. Sing and the Russian courier were killed by Chechens. If any of those unknown fingerprints found in Bosco's house match ones for those other murders, well..." Race looked Beela in the eyes.

Beela simply shrugged her shoulders. "Let's not get ahead of ourselves."

"I did access PahLits, the Russian's general AFIS database," Helena said. "Similar to many other country's systems, they have a separate and more secure system for sensitive information. To access that, you would have to get permission from their State Department or the FSB."

Beela said, "I'll get in touch with the FSB detective working the Russian courier case and see if he'd run our prints through his system." She turned to Beane. "Any idea what Bosco was doing in Vegas?"

Beane scrolled around on his eTablet, then shook his head. "There are recurring charges on his microchip at a strip club called the Puce Palomino. The most recent charge we have been able to find from him was at a gas station in West Vegas on Friday evening. Bosco was driving a gas powered Bentley and he must have filled up for the trip back to LA."

Beela had a confused look on her face. "How could Bosco be in Las Vegas and not run up any room or food charges?"

"He may have used an account that Helena couldn't link to him," Beane said.

Helena had a hurt look on her face. "Do not forget, you can pay for everything in Las Vegas with cocaine. And you did find a stash in Bosco's home office."

Beane nodded to her. "That's a possibility. Also, Bosco may have been a 'whale,' a big spender, and gotten his room and meals comped. I'll call my contacts in Vegas and see what they can come up with on the QT."

"Either theory would explain how Bosco was able to fly under the radar," Beela said. She turned to Helena. "See if you can find any other accounts that Bosco may have been using."

Helena gave her a nod.

"Any luck tracking down Bosco's watch?" Race asked.

Helena shook her virtual head. "Not yet. He did not use any bank accounts I can link to him to buy one." She looked Race in the eye. "Ask people who knew Bosco to describe the watch. If they know the name brand, that will help."

"Will do."

"I took the liberty of contacting Bosco's homeowner's association," Helena said. "They have surveillance cameras at either entrance to the neighborhood. Unfortunately, their landscapers planted seasonal flowers a few months ago and now foliage blocks the cameras. I reviewed data from cameras on Mulholland Drive and Sunset Boulevard, concentrating on people relevant to this case. Here are my findings: Bosco passed the intersection of Mulholland and North Beverly Drive at 11:11 pm, Friday, in a black Bentley registered in his name. In addition, a blue convertible, registered to Brigit Kojacy, passed through the intersection of West Sunset and North Beverly Glen twice on Saturday, heading northbound at 5:51 pm, and southbound fifteen minutes later."

"What about Dr. Singh's vehicle?" Beela said. "If we knew when she left Bosco's, we'd have an outside limit on his time of death."

"There is no record of her vehicle passing either intersection. Remember, it was very smoky that night and the cameras around the city do have a tendency to malfunction. Additionally, hackers routinely break into the police computer systems and corrupt the data."

Beela turned to Race. "Race, I'm going to be in court all day tomorrow. Get with Helena first thing in the morning and she'll give you a plan of action. We need to re-interview Mrs. Godgifu, and get statements from Klaas Bruin and Brigit Kojacy." Beela turned to Beane. "Captain, see what you can pull on the Godgifu family. I'd like to know more about their import-export business."

Beane saluted. "Will do, boss."

"Race, let's head back to Bosco's to conduct a further search. I'd like to canvass the neighborhood again to hit the houses we missed the first time. Time permitting, we'll swing by Bosco's office and interview his staff."

"How about some kick-ass sushi first?" Beane said.

Beela frowned. "We just had a late breakfast in Westwood Village."

"Too bad," Beane said with a raised eyebrow. "It was going to be my treat."

"In that case," Beela said with a smile. "I'm starving."

Chapter 19

Dome Oh was a traditional Japanese, country restaurant. Its wooden structure was made of upright, roughhewn logs and supported a deep-eaved, pagoda-style roof made of black curved ceramic tiles.

Race and his partners crossed the wooden bridge that spanned the koi pond guarding the entrance, with its bubbling brooks, cascading cataracts, and lush lily pads. They entered through the shōji style sliding door made of bamboo frame and translucent paper, into the high ceiling restaurant with its enticing aromatic smells of spices and teas.

A waiter wearing loose black pants and a traditional Japanese short-sleeve happi coat with an embroidered kanji symbol 道 greeted them at the door. He bowed and said to them, "This way."

As they passed the open kitchen, the staff yelled out. "*Konnichiwa*."

Beane waved and yelled, "Back at 'cha, bitches."

Both Race and Beela gave Beane dirty looks, but the kitchen staff laughed and waved back to the captain as if they were good friends.

The waiter seated them at a table fashioned out of a tree trunk about three feet in diameter and cut horizontally. The seats were made of smaller trunks of cedar covered with a thick pad. He handed out menus, bowed, and left.

A waitress in a red floral kimono with a shimmering design of bamboo plants and sage leaves came by and set a pot of tea on the table. Beane poured the green tea for each of them, then carefully picked up the handle-less cup and blew across the lip.

"Life isn't fair," he said, sipping the steaming hot drink. "My doctor has me on one pill to get my cholesterol down, another to get my triglycerides down, a third to get my blood pressure down, and a fourth pill to get Mr. Winkie up."

Race laughed while Beela rolled her eyes. "Why do you men always have to have a name for your penis?" she said.

Beane chuckled. "How the hell are you going to have a conversation with it if you don't know its name?" Race's face turned red as he and Beane burst out laughing. Bella gave them both a scolding look as a few of the nearby customers looked over.

Beane stopped laughing and wiped his eyes. "My doctor tells me that if I don't take those pills and follow his diet, I'm going to die soon. The only reason I follow his advice is I want to stay alive as long as possible to spite my wife and make her life a living hell."

Now Beela laughed.

Beane sat forward, he had the look of a comedian on a roll.

"Race, let me tell you something. Working homicide can be a depressing affair. Your entire job is to deal with dead people, work with the grieving families, and track down killers. The only way to survive is to have a sense of humor."

"So, what you're saying, is that if I have a good sense of humor, homicide won't drive me insane?" Race knew he was probably being set up,

"No, Race," Beane tried to hold back laughter. "But at least you'll be laughing when they put you in a straitjacket and cart you off to the funny farm."

Beela groaned.

A different waitress, dressed in similar kimono to the other waitress and with an "I Voted" button pinned to the left side of her gown, came over with a look of concern on her face. She bowed slightly. "Is everything okay here?"

"We're ready to order, my dear," Beane said. He explained to Beela and Race that the restaurant specialized in sushi bowls. "It's the same thing as traditional sushi, except the ingredients aren't rolled, but served in a deep bowl." He told the waitress, "I'll have the spicy eel bowl."

Beela ordered the spicy tuna bowl.

Race looked over the menu, most of it in Japanese. He looked up and nodded toward Beela while he told the waitress, "I'll have what she's having."

The waitress took their menus, gave Beane a scolding look, and left toward the kitchen.

"I saw that voting sticker on the waitress's kimono," Beane said while he pulled orange VR glasses out of his blazer pocket. "Don't tell me there's another election going on."

"It's a special election to fill the vacant central L'Orange congressional seat," Beela said. "Our congressman was promoted to a Cabinet-Level position."

"Hell's bells," Beane said, while turning on his glasses. "There's an election just about every damn week. Who's running?" He scrolled around using his OmniPhone. "In one corner, we have the Republican. A small businessman who promises limited government, lower taxes, and fewer regulations. In the other corner, the Democrat. An independent businessman, who believes in smaller government, fewer taxes, and limited regulations. Hard choice."

"All the candidates say the same thing," Race said. "What's the point of even voting?"

"Just a second," Beane said. He chose his candidate using the "eeny, meeny, miny, moe" method, then turned his glasses off. "When I was a kid, Race, you didn't have to be a taxpayer to vote. Candidates outdid each other making pie-in-the-sky promises. We lived in fiscal fantasy land—living large on the backs of our yet-to-be-born grandchildren. Since more than half the people who voted back then didn't pay taxes, they had no compunction in voting for candidates who promised to raise rates on those who did. That's how the old US of A went bankrupt. People lost the incentive to work."

Race flashed back to high school civics classes. How the IMF, based on Puviani's theory of financial illusion, created the current system where voting became a privilege based on being a taxpayer in good standing, rather than an inherent right. But he became angry thinking about how the department was so underfunded that they had to ration how much time they'd spend on a case. The taxpayers didn't know how their frugality affected the day-to-day running of the people sworn to protect them. Then again, they probably did. The über-wealthy could hide behind gated communities and bodyguards, knowing that *they* wouldn't have to face the consequences. His face felt flushed and he clenched his fists at his side. He took a few deep breaths and snapped his wrist band, trying to control his anger before he spoke. "It hardly seems fair. Taxpayers are always going to vote to reduce taxes, leaving the LOPD high and dry."

"I disagree." Beane smiled sympathetically to Race. "They just want us to be better stewards of the money they entrust us with." He gave Race an encouraging look. "I saw the expression on your face when the COD explained the rating system for investigating cases. None of us really like the system, Race, but resources are finite. To put things in perspective, let me give you a little history of how our country got to this terrible point."

Race took a sip of tea, amazed how the green tea seemed to calm him. "Go ahead. I'm a big fan of ancient history."

"Now, now, remember who's paying for the meal." Beane let out a little sigh of reminiscence. "When I was young, I hated when the gray-hairs talked about the good old days. According to them, everything was so much better when they were young. 'Young people nowadays' was their mantra. Now that I've joined their club, I look back, and things are so much better now than back then."

"Hardly seems that way," Beela said.

"Well it is," Beane said emphatically. "When I joined the force, dinosaurs were still roaming the Earth and the police force was called LAPD, the *Los Angeles* Police Department. Figured I'd put in my thirty years, draw a decent retirement, and pass my golden years living in a golf-course condo in Mexico. Well, I put in my time and now I'm retired. And I only have to work twenty hours a week to receive my retirement, which, by the way, is exactly half the salary I earned when I was working full time." He laughed. "But I'm not complaining. At least I have an excuse to get out of the house. And I never was that good a golfer."

Beela sipped her tea and smiled. "That's not the real reason you're still working. You're just like my dad. You have the fever, you love working homicide."

Beane held his hands up. "Busted. Homicide's the only hobby I have. Don't tell the guys in the Crystal Palace, but I'd probably be doing this even if I didn't get paid."

"I'm sure they're aware of that," Beela said with a laugh.

Beane finished his tea and poured another round for everybody. "There's been big changes in the department since I joined, Race. Big changes. Many of them for the best. It all began during the period known as the Great Tsunami. You've studied it ad nauseam in school."

Race thought back to his days in high school history class and the lessons his teachers drilled into the students' heads every year about the global financial collapse. Since the collapse started in Japan, it became known as The Great Financial Tsunami. Japan, with a federal deficit closing in on ten times their GDP, and confronting a demographic crisis where retirees outnumbered full-time workers, was the first to declare bankruptcy. The Japanese youth were no longer willing to work from dawn to dusk to pay debts incurred by their parents and grandparents. Some simply gave up trying, moved back with their parents, and went on welfare. Others, en masse, refused to pay the seventy-five percent of their taxes that was being used to cover past debts. Japan's collapse set off a domino effect. One after another, countries defaulted. When the European Union went under, it was a matter of weeks before the tsunami washed over the United States. Since the beginning of the twenty-first century, the federal debt had grown to amounts that were beyond human comprehension—close to one hundred trillion of the old US Dollars, not including the unfunded liabilities of the so called entitlement programs of Social Security and Medicare. Creditors lost faith in our economy and called in their debts. Like a mafia enforcer, the International Monetary Fund took over. When the dust settled, the IMF, at the behest of creditor nations and to the chagrin of the debtor nations, imposed the new global currency, the Special Drawing Rights, known as SDR. People's life savings were all but wiped out, receiving one SDR for every thousand US Dollars. Creditor countries—China, Russia, and Norway, amongst others--came out in an even stronger position than before. Democracy was shaken to the core and voting became a privilege. Social Security and Medicare collapsed, forcing people to save up for their own retirement and healthcare costs. Birth rates plummeted, alcohol consumption and suicide rates soared. People's confidence in the future was shaken.

"You were talking about The Great Financial Tsunami," Race said to Beane. "What about it?"

"For one thing, that's when Los Angeles and Orange Counties merged to save money. Everything *seemed* to be going along fine. Then, bang! The tidal wave hit. The federal government went bankrupt, setting off a domino effect. Governments all down the line went bust—state, county, cities—they'd grown so dependent on subsidies from Washington. Over half of California's budget was being paid by the feds, and they were either borrowing or printing three out of every four dollars they spent. Other countries wouldn't accept our currency, and that's when the IMF stepped in and imposed the SDR."

"The rainbow currency." Beela turned to Beane. "Do you still translate SDR into the old US dollars in your head?"

"My body might be old, but my mind's not." Beane shook his head. "Besides, trying to convert SDR into dollars would be too depressing." He gestured at their meal. "This lunch, with tip, will come out to thirty SDR. That would have been, what, thirty thousand dollars?"

"I see your point." Beela nodded. "The thought's disturbing."

"Goodbye greenbacks," Beane said. "And good riddance. Here's the funny part: bankruptcy was actually a blessing in disguise. Even though our country is no longer *numero uno*, we have a lot more individual freedom now than when I was growing up. Just like steel that gets stronger when put to the fire, our country is much stronger, and certainly freer, after coming through the financial flames. That's why I'm not fazed by the doom-and-gloomers who are worried about the fires currently encircling our City of Angels. We're being tempered and we'll come back even stronger. And it causes people to think and fend for themselves. When I was in school, we spent most of our time on silly stuff, which is why so many people had grown dependent on the government. For example, in high school we had to take Sex-Ed every year, which involved sitting at tables and practicing putting condoms on bananas. My senior year, a girl in my class had gotten pregnant for the third time. Her guidance counselor brought her into the office and asked how it was that she kept getting pregnant. Didn't she learn anything from the classes? The girl said she couldn't understand either, because every time she was about to have sex with her boyfriend, she put a condom on a banana."

Race burst out laughing. Beela rolled her eyes. "My father told me that story. It's an urban legend."

Beane simply laughed. "It's not far from the truth, Race."

For Race, high school wasn't a pleasant time, he wasn't in the "in" crowd and felt like an outsider. But he was grateful for the education. Starting in first grade, and continuing through college, using a token economy, the importance of saving money and investing it safely was taught on a daily basis.

The waitress returned to the table carrying a tray. She placed ceramic bowls filled with raw seafood, julienne vegetables, bean sprouts and wasabi on a bed of rice before each of them. From a chilled ceramic pitcher, she poured honey-colored liquid into three flat saucer-like cups. "Sake," she explained. "Complements of the *bitches* in the kitchen." She smiled, and arched an eyebrow as if to say "touché," then bowed formally.

Beane stood and bowed back. "*Domo*."

Race picked up the shallow saucer and sipped the cool rice wine. He never drank sake before and was surprised. It was semi-sweet with a hint of apples.

Beane tossed his drink back and shook his head. "Hard to believe. When I joined the force, you could get fired for drinking on the job."

The waitress asked if anyone needed forks. They all shook their heads. She bowed deeply and left.

Beane grabbed his chopsticks and nodded to his tablemates. "*Itadakimasu,*" he said, then plunged in.

Race imitated Beane, picking up the bowl and using chopsticks to push food into his mouth.

"Before the waitress came," Beane said between bites, "we were talking about freedom, weren't we?"

Both Race and Beela shrugged and kept eating.

"Before the global collapse, I didn't feel very free. There were rules about almost everything. The politicians and bureaucrats in Washington even wanted to regulate how you took a crap—I shit you not."

Beela scowled at Beane. "You *do* know we're eating, don't you?"

"Sorry." Beane looked like a dog that was caught eating off the table. "The point I'm making is that the politicians in Washington had too much time on their hands, they meddled in everything. Everything was a crisis. They passed bills as a solution to problems that didn't even exist. Those meddlesome geniuses in Washington, they thought that if it took six gallons to flush a toilet, if they mandated that each flush would only use four gallons, we'd use thirty-three percent less water. But you couldn't flush down shit," he looked over to Beela, who glanced at him sideways, "your own excrement, with so little water. You had to have a plunger and flush two or three times, using more water than before."

Beela put her bowl down and shook her head. "Could you please talk about something else?"

Beane shrugged and shot Race a smile. "Our founding fathers set up a 'checks and balances' system to prevent overreaching government. It turns out that the only real check on government control of our lives is to take away the checkbook altogether."

Race laughed. "I like that line, Captain."

"Thanks," Beane said. "The real damage of our bankruptcy was to the communal psyche. People felt insecure, they distrusted the financial system, they distrusted one another, and most importantly, they distrusted the future—at least a better future. People's entire life savings all but disappeared. The *mordita*, or bribery, became accepted just about everywhere. People couldn't survive on what they were being paid. Same thing happened at LOPD. Over time, these behaviors have become ingrained, accepted, commonplace, even expected."

"The Post-Tsunami Anomie," Beela said. She caught Race's eye. "Let me make this clear: we don't accept bribes."

"Bribe is the wrong word for it," Beane said. "We do the job we're paid to do. And if people are willing to pay us extra to go above and beyond…"

"Then we go above and beyond," Beela said.

"To be honest, Race," Beane said. "The system runs more smoothly this way than it used to. If you don't trust the future, you live for the moment. Used to be, we were really anal," he looked at Beela, who gave him a warning look, "tight as a drum. Everything you did was some calculation based on whether or not it would help you live longer. Now it's: *laissez les bon temps rouler.*" Race gave Beane a questioning look. "Let the good times roll," Beane explained.

They all finished their bowls and waited on the Captain. "What a coincidence," Beane said. "I've finished my meal just as I was finishing my point. This brings us to the system the department's set up to handle homicide investigations. It's a triage system. To be honest, it still grinds my gears, but *c'est la vie*. We detectives used to work cases until we solved them, working nights, weekends, whatever it took. Beela, I'm sure your father has told you this before."

Beela nodded. "Every time I see him."

"Race, things aren't that bad. They say there's a silver lining behind every dark cloud. Murder rates have dropped sixty percent from when I joined the force—LA used to be a veritable war zone. Before drugs were legalized, people were being mowed down in the streets in broad daylight, in front of dozens of witnesses. The homicide rate in LA back then was ten per hundred-thousand. Now it's less than three. To make matters worse, no one would testify. They didn't trust the police, bystanders claimed they saw nothing. Now that we're no longer at war with our own citizens, people are happy to cooperate with us. Makes solving crimes so much easier."

Beela looked to Race and said, "Even with this triage system, we solve a higher percentage of cases than before the Tsunami. We're clearing over eighty percent of our homicides inside one year. Back when Beane was starting out, it was around sixty percent. Wasn't it, Captain?"

Beane was divvying up the rest of the sake and nodded. "A lot of that improvement is we now have the help of Helena. I'd buy her a beer, but I don't think she drinks."

Race laughed. "So how does a homicide get ranked in this 'triage' system?"

"HQ—the Crystal Palace—uses a branch of economics called Penalnomics," Beela said. "It allocates how much time and effort we devote to each homicide, based on a computer algorithm which factors in things like a person's net worth, social standing, physical looks, the Q score—how famous a person is—and other components."

"The adorable, blond haired girl gets rated much higher than a homely old man like me," Beane said.

"As well she should." Beela gave Beane a playful wink.

Beane laughed. "The higher the score a victim rates, the more time we're allowed to spend investigating a case. The computer rated Donny Bosco as a level A because he was very wealthy, had a high Q score, was an attractive man, etc. For Bosco, that means a number of things. One, I've been assigned to help you two out. Two, our group won't be assigned any new homicide cases during this time. Three, we've been given an entire two weeks to work the case. In the unlikely event that we haven't closed the case in two weeks, the major will evaluate to see if we can be given more time."

Race was troubled. "What about people who don't get classified as an A?"

"You and I, Race, we would rate a level C. We are the worker bees; neither wealthy, famous, or, at least in my case, good-looking. But don't worry, as Beela pointed out, the percentage of cases we solve is higher than before this system was put in place. The worst cases are the people who merit an F: the homeless and Skid-Row Alkies. In those cases, we simply file a report, and unless someone comes in to confess, we make minimal effort."

Race shook his head in disgust. "That's rather cold and calculating. How does the public put up with this system?"

"Mainly by denial. The police deny having such a system, the press doesn't investigate, and the public doesn't care as long as their taxes don't get raised." He put his hand on Race's shoulder and gave him a slight shake. "Cheer up. There are still quite a few good guys out there, officers trying to do things the right way, like we used to do. But they get trampled by the stampede of slackers heading to the exit."

"Gentlemen," Beela stood up, "time for *us* to stampede to the exit. Time's a wastin'."

Chapter 20

Wednesday Afternoon

The sea was in his DNA.

Doctor Seymour Gütfeldt swiveled his ergonomic chair and looked out the window, which made up most of the outside wall of his office. The ocean loomed in the distance through the mid-afternoon haze. When he was finishing his psychiatric residency at UC San Diego, his main criteria when renting an office space was that he had to have a view of the Pacific, if only a sliver. He felt like Ishmael in a Herman Melville novel—inexplicably drawn to the sea. His eyes fixed on photos of two masted sailboats in action hanging on the walls and his mind drifted. He stood at the helm of the boat of his dreams—a forty-seven foot Catalina sailboat—the wind blowing in his peppered hair, brine in his black, trimmed beard, the sun beating on his cheeks, his wife and young son manning the sails as they cruised 'round the world.

His father and grandfather were both psychiatrists in Manhattan. Psychoanalysts. He'd planned to follow in their footsteps. However, through a quirk of fate, he became somewhat of an expert on repressed memories, which is what the bulk of his practice consisted.

A few months after completing his residency, he was called to the emergency room to evaluate a woman who'd been picked up confused and wandering the streets in the Gaslamp Quarter of San Diego. The woman had no idea who she was and carried no identification. He diagnosed her as suffering from a fugue state—a type of amnesia of personal identity usually brought on by a severe trauma. He admitted the patient to his service at the psychiatric unit of UC San Diego Medical Center. The next morning, the woman's identity was discovered. Her husband had reported her missing the previous day and her name was Jody Williams. Seymour hypnotized her and discovered the traumatic event that triggered the fugue state. An unsuccessful rape attempt the night before she disappeared. She'd gone for a walk after dinner, was assaulted and dragged into nearby bushes. Although she was able to escape, the emotional shock caused her to suffer temporary amnesia.

When she came out of the hypnotic state, the patient regained her memory, recognized her husband, and Seymour released her from the hospital. He continued seeing her in therapy twice a week. He found his patient had other memory gaps and periods of time for which she couldn't account. After a series of hypnosis sessions, it turned out his patient was really not Jody Williams, but a woman named Jane D. Roberts, who'd disappeared twelve years previously from her home in Alaska. After the death of her mother, when Roberts was twelve, her father and uncle began sexually molesting her. At age sixteen, she escaped from their remote cabin and hiked for days through the woods accompanied only by her Siberian Husky. She ended up in Sitka where she took a job at the local newspaper and married a commercial fisherman.

For their honeymoon, the newlywed couple flew to a beach resort in Mexico and rented a seaside cottage for a week. They consummated their marriage that first evening. Unfortunately for the new bride, the remote cottage, which was described as a romantic hideaway, triggered memories of the Alaskan shanty and the horrors she suffered there. When her husband awoke the next morning, his wife had disappeared. He reported her missing to the Mexican authorities, but she was never found.

Seymour discovered through the hypnosis sessions that the isolated beach cabin and her new husband's sexuality triggered memories of the unwanted sexual advances in the Alaskan wilderness. The emotions were overwhelming. She fled the cabin and completely lost any memory of her true identity. She assumed the identity of Jody Williams, a woman who had disappeared while hiking in the Sierra Madre Mountains in Mexico. Roberts didn't remember how she came into possession of the missing woman's passport and driver's license, but she had assumed that Jodie was her real name. She lived the next dozen years under that name, married, and lived in Tacoma.

When first the local media, then later the national media, caught wind of the case of a woman taking on another identity for twelve years, there was a frenzy of news coverage and Seymour became a media celebrity. He appeared on national television, giving interviews and explaining to the general public the concept of a fugue state. The issue the media became fixated on was the fact that Ms. Williams/Roberts was legally married to two different men—as Jody Williams to a husband in Washington; and as Jane D. Roberts to a commercial fisherman in Alaska. There was rampant speculation as to whether the woman would divide time between her two husbands. A television miniseries even came out in which the fictional woman did just that—Seymour declined to be a consultant for that show. After a few weeks, interest in the case waned. Seymour's patient had her marriage in Alaska annulled, and they both went back to living a quiet life: Seymour in San Diego, and the patient in Tacoma.

Seymour found that the case had made him relatively well-known and he began receiving referrals from local practitioners, even from other parts of the country, to treat patients who suffered from repressed memories and other symptoms of childhood trauma.

He had what would be considered a successful practice. He had a full caseload and was doing what he loved. What he hadn't anticipated was how difficult it was to stay afloat financially, to support his wife and son solely on treating patients as his father and grandfather did before him. He was resigned to the sad fact that he would never be able to afford his dream: that deep-sea sailboat; he could hardly afford to keep his beat-up car running. Recently, the Nav-Drive went on the fritz, and he spent most of his meager savings to get it repaired.

With patients responsible for their own medical expenses through their Medical Savings Accounts, it was hard to compete against other lower-cost therapists: the psychologists, licensed clinical social workers, hypnotherapists, and the assortment of other so-called therapists. Even the lyscees took business from him; they were usually cheaper and you were guaranteed to leave their sessions with a smile on your face. Worst of all, computerized psychotherapy programs were making inroads into his patient base. A patient could buy almost any type of therapy module, from brief psychotherapy, such as cognitive behavioral therapy or neuro-linguistic programming, to long-term intensive therapy such as psychoanalysis, and receive treatment in the comfort of their own home and at a fraction of the cost of seeing a real therapist. The only saving grace for Seymour was that the other therapists and computerized programs weren't allowed to prescribe medications.

To make ends meet, he tried a number of different jobs to supplement his income. He was able to make extra money testifying as an expert witness. Even though the pay was lucrative, the cases were so few and far between that what he earned after taxes was barely enough to take his family to Baja for a week every year, and not by sailboat. He briefly appeared on the talk show circuit as a television psychiatrist. He was photogenic and articulate, but he never became completely comfortable in front of the cameras. And once the repressed memory case faded from the headlines, the media requests dwindled, then stopped.

So he found himself sitting in his office this Wednesday, a day he usually didn't schedule patients. He had been at home playing Interweb poker, trying to make a little extra money, when his office notified him that a patient had an emergency and needed to see him urgently. He tried to see patients *during* a crisis, as he found that was the time when a breakthrough was more likely to occur.

Seymour was still in his reverie, skimming across the waves in his dream boat, when the phone on his desk buzzed—his appointment had arrived. He picked up the receiver and told the receptionist to send the patient back. He swiveled his chair back in position behind his desk—a modern piece of furniture made of matte black metal rods supporting a thick green glass top.

When his door opened and his emergency patient came into the room, he did a double take. The first thing he noticed—it was impossible to notice anything else—was:

The red miniskirt.

An impossibly short, tight miniskirt.

Red leather.

Something began to stir in his trousers.

His eyes were drawn downward, gazing on the long, muscular, perfectly shaped legs that ended in fashionable black ankle boots.

Seymour forced himself to tear his eyes from her legs. He scanned the black, tight-fitting, sleeveless V-neck Henley Tee emphasizing the swell of breasts, a leopard skin patterned silk scarf thrown provocatively over one bare shoulder, and hair that seemed to be especially red—almost on fire. His eyes finally settled on her face; a coy, seductive smile was on her lips. He sensed a challenging look in her eyes. And there was something new—she wore heavy, exotic eye makeup.

He was unsure of what to say as she sauntered in, accentuating the sway of her hips by putting one foot almost directly in front of the other. Seymour continued to watch in silence as she put her dimpled knees together and eased herself into one of the leather consultation chairs facing him. She sat back and crossed her bare legs. As they sat there looking at each other, Seymour's thoughts flashed to Sharon Stone in the film

Basic Instinct, defiantly sexual as she stared down a team of trained police investigators.

Although he felt sexually aroused, he needed to take control of the session. And his emotions. "Have a seat, Jenn," he said.

Damn! She's already sitting.

He knew his patient could sense his unease, and that she seemed to enjoy it.

He thought it best to address the elephant in the room first, before getting to the reason for the emergency consultation.

"Jenn, I have been seeing you in therapy, on and off, for quite a while. This is the first time you have dressed in less than what one could call," he cleared his throat, "conservative fashion. Would you care to discuss this?"

Jennifer's expression was surprised and defiant. "Seymour, I did *not* wear my green leopard-skin miniskirt. And I'm not on the prowl. I decided to get dressed up today, that's all. Does this bother you, Seymour? The way I'm dressed, does that make you uncomfortable?"

He rubbed his beard and cocked his head in thought. True, she wasn't wearing the leopard skirt she wears when out chasing men. But, those last questions were asked in a very aggressive manner. She's definitely challenging me. But this behavior is completely new for her. She's always been so sexually repressed. However…this might be a good sign. She may finally be making a therapeutic breakthrough. Then again, she's had hypomanic symptoms in the past. Is she in the midst of a full-blown manic episode? If so, she may require hospitalization. And he needed to acknowledge his own reactions; he was certainly ill at ease…and sexually excited. She had the upper hand here…which was probably what she needed right now. She was in some sort of crisis, feeling vulnerable, and needing to be in charge. The best thing is to be totally honest.

"The way you're dressed does make me feel uncomfortable. I think you knew it would."

She looked taken aback. "I had a terrible shock earlier this morning, and wanted to feel pretty. I'm sorry if that makes you uncomfortable."

Seymour nodded and remained silent, thinking. From the way she said that, he doubted she was remorseful. Her body language screamed that she was enjoying his unease. He decided it was best to leave this issue alone and change the subject to the reason for the emergency visit. He was hopeful that the explanation for her provocative appearance might become obvious.

"Jenn, tell me what brought you in here today? You told my receptionist that you were having an emergency."

He watched as she uncrossed her legs and recrossed them before answering.

"I've had the biggest shock of my life. Since our last session, I've been dating a wonderful man. This morning, as I was getting ready to do the day's autopsies, I pulled off the sheets of the first case, and voilà, there was my boyfriend...," she began to tremble and her voice quivered, "... my lover! I was in such a shock that I passed out right on the spot. As I fell, I hit my head on the exam table. You can see the swelling on my forehead. I'm still shaky. I took two Xanax when I got home, but they're just barely taking the edge off."

Seymour felt more comfortable now, dealing with therapeutic issues. He felt he was highly capable at helping people dealing with crisis, and less adroit dealing with his own sexual issues. Now that she mentioned the Xanax, he did detect mildly slurred speech and thought she probably took more than just Xanax based on the unmistakable smell of alcohol over her floral perfume.

"That had to be an incredible shock. Tell me what's going through your head right now, whatever comes to mind."

Jennifer leaned forward, put her elbows on her knees, and her chin in her hands; the swells of her breasts now even more exposed.

Seymour swallowed and tried not to stare.

"Guilt," she said. "I mainly feel guilt. Friday night, Donny—that's his name—Donny and I went out and had a wonderful time at a charity gala for the Getty Center. You may have seen my picture in the LA Times, it seems everyone else has."

Seymour shook his head.

"No matter. After the event was over, I went to Donny's house, more like a mansion, up in the hills. I had been drinking quite a bit, and we had sex that night."

Jennifer stopped talking. Seymour waited. He thought it was best to let the patient decide what was important.

"I feel guilty about...about a lot of things," Jennifer said. "When I woke up early the next morning, I left while Donny was still sleeping. I didn't wake him up." She closed her eyes, holding back tears. "I didn't say goodbye. Maybe I needed my space. Instead of talking to him in the morning, I left a voicemail telling him what a wonderful evening I had. I should have at least woke him up that morning instead of sneaking off and leaving him wondering why I left. When he didn't call me back the next few days, I assumed he was dumping me. I was angry at him, when all the time, he was probably lying dead, brutally murdered. I feel horrible about doubting him."

Jennifer looked out to the ocean, a pensive look on her face.

Seymour stroked his beard and waited.

She continued to gaze out of the window while she spoke. "I found out that when we had sex that night, the night of the ball, I got what would be called a 'dry hump.'" She turned to Seymour. "Do you know what that means?" He nodded. She looked back out of the window. "While I was having an awesome experience, it appears that it wasn't quite so good for Donny, which is also the reason why I thought he hadn't called me back."

Seymour waited.

Jennifer remained silent, studying the sea. Her eyes batted closed a few times.

Seymour could tell that Jennifer was adrift and broke the silence.

"You know that dry ejaculation—the 'dry hump' as you put it—is not an uncommon event, especially for men taking certain antidepressants. Those men say they still enjoy sex just as much, so it shouldn't have affected Donny's enjoyment of the encounter. But your assumption was a natural one, under the circumstances."

Jennifer looked down, shaking her head. "It's what I did next that is weighing on me. When Donny didn't call me back, I put on that leopard-skin skirt," she locked eyes with Seymour, "you know what one I'm talking about, and I went out to some of my favorite bars on the beach and was looking to pick up men. I got stone-cold drunk and had a number, more than I care to admit...really more than I can remember...of casual sexual encounters." Jennifer put her face into her hands and began crying.

Seymour offered her a box of tissues, which he always kept handy on his desk, and quietly waited for her to regain her composure. He needed to stop her from focusing on guilt and toward the positive aspects of her relationship with her boyfriend. It would help her cope better with the unexpected loss. And he was relieved, now that she was crying and vulnerable, she didn't seem so sexy. Now he could see why she needed to feel in control of the situation—everything else in her life was falling apart, out of her control.

He sensed that the crying jag was running its course.

"Those are all legitimate reasons to suffer guilt," he told her. "But what were your feelings for Donny? Tell me about the relationship you two had."

Jennifer dried her eyes, still not raising her head or making eye contact, but her lips lifted into the beginnings of a smile. She seemed lost in her thoughts and Seymour allowed her time to process them. He had learned to be comfortable with silence and found that these interludes were sometimes the most productive parts of a therapy session.

Jennifer finally looked his way and spoke. "I know I had been drinking quite a bit that night, both at the gala and later at Donny's house, which may account for this, but I seem to have had a blackout...a memory loss. I remember making love to Donny, then waking up in the morning in bed at my house. I don't remember getting in the car or the ride home."

Seymour nodded. The heavy drinking probably caused her to suffer alcohol-related amnesia. Blackouts. She'd had them in the past. "I think it might be a good idea if I hypnotized you, perhaps you can relive the last night with Donny. That might help you deal with the loss."

Jennifer agreed. She uncrossed her legs, stood up from the chair, and walked over to the therapy couch—the type made famous by none other than Freud himself—which sat against the wall under the window. She sat down, swung her legs up onto the couch, and lay back.

Seymour rolled his own chair behind Jennifer, out of her sight. As he sat behind his patient, her long, exposed legs and the swell of her breasts were a distraction. Seymour couldn't help but think that this would have been a good time to have those cheesy disposable sheets with which to cover his patient.

Get a grip, he told himself.

Chapter 21

Seymour ran his hands though his beard and collected his thoughts. Jennifer's head was elevated by the natural rise of the therapy couch. He looked on as she gazed out at the ocean shimmering in the afternoon sun. She began to breathe slowly. Deeply. He had hypnotized Jennifer many times, noticing that she often became mesmerized even before the induction began. She once told him that she felt so relaxed after the sessions that she'd pay the extra fee and use the High-Speed lane to be back in Marina del Rey in less than an hour and out bobbing on her surfboard.

Seymour readied himself for the induction. He wouldn't use any technique that involved touching Jennifer. Her current state of dress (or undress) would make any such physical contact potentially sexually provocative. He opted for a basic relaxation method that he used in patients who were easy to induce.

He moved his chair all the way behind her so he would be out of her line of vision. He talked in his hypnosis voice; deeper, slower, atonal, and rhythmic.

"Let loose now, allow a good pleasant feeling come across your body…

"Let every muscle and nerve go limp and relaxed…

"Feel your body relaxing and sinking pleasantly into the couch…

"Let that feeling of relaxation deepen with each breath you take…

"In…

"And out…

"Feeling more and more relaxed…

"Each time you breathe in and out you can double your relaxation…

"Until you have reached the deepest state of peace and calm…

"With each easy beat of your heart you let yourself sink further and further…

"Let yourself drift along…

"Detached…

"Nothing seems to be important…

"Everything is peaceful…"

Seymour continued the induction for a minute or two longer. Jennifer's breathing slowed down to less than ten breaths per minute. Her eyes were closed, her eyeballs stopped moving, and her muscles relaxed, then went limp.

When he felt that she was sufficiently under, he moved to the therapeutic part of the session. Speaking in a slow, serene, soothing voice, he continued, "Now let your mind go to that night at the Getty Center… you are relaxed and peaceful…let your mind drift…when you are ready, tell me what you see."

He waited—one had to be patient—while Jennifer's mind drifted to the scene he wanted her to re-experience. When she began, her voice was no longer defiant and challenging as it had been minutes before, nor did she speak in her usual edgy and wary voice. Now Jennifer's voice was softer, younger, more laid-back, ethereal. She spoke slowly, matching the cadence that Seymour had been using. She seemed to be savoring each word as she painted the picture.

She began hesitantly. "I'm standing on the patio of a beautiful house. It's nighttime. I'm overlooking the twinkling lights of Los Angeles. The air is warm, a light breeze blows against my shoulders and arms. I can see, almost feel, the fires in the mountains nearby. It's as if the warm flames are licking against my skin…

"I see my reflection in the sliding glass doors. I'm wearing a full-length evening gown. I feel beautiful. I look at Donny, his eyes are filled with desire for me. The light from the fires outside and the lights from the house seem to reflect off my skin, like thousands of little stars blinking in and out. The gown is tight around my body. I breathe deeper than normal as the fabric presses against my ribs, and each breath, in and out, I feel warmer, my skin atingle…

"Donny's presence seems to shake me…his masculine odor, woody and amber, intoxicates me. I'm holding a champagne glass in my hand…I raise the glass to my lips and the effervescent liquid pours into my mouth, bubbles down my throat, the dry grape flavor warming me inside. I'm relaxed and pleasantly detached…

"His hand touches my bare shoulder, my legs become like Jell-O… he turns me to him. He's like a Greek god, like Zeus, towering over me, enveloping me in his embrace, placing soft, hot kisses on my shoulders and neck. As I look into his eyes I feel my body melting from his heat, the gown feels constricting and hot. I need it off. Donny puts his arms around me and unzips the gown and it falls to my feet…

"I unbutton his tuxedo shirt and pants. We leave our clothes lying on the floor. He picks me up and carries me through the open glass doors into his bedroom…

"I pull him with me as he lays me down on the bed. I look up into his eyes. He sets my skin on fire with his hot, hungry kisses…

"I tell Daddy how much I want him, he tells me he wants me too. As I pull him onto me, I can feel my longing ready to burst. I can feel his urgent desire pressed against me. There's a hot breeze coming in from the open patio doors, and I open myself to him. We reach a beautiful rhythm, bobbing on a choppy sea, we become one…"

Jennifer screamed. "No!"

Seymour jumped. His heart skipped a beat.

Jennifer jerked up and gasped for air, hands covering her face. Her shoulders heaved, she hyperventilated, and her face was pale and sweaty.

Seymour rubbed his chin, wondering what caused her to snap out of the trance. She was in the middle of a panic attack and it was time for him to take charge.

"Everything's okay," he said, still using his hypnosis voice. "Listen to my voice. Breathe in deeply through the mouth."

"What happened?" Jennifer asked between breaths.

Seymour grabbed his white lab coat, which was hanging by the door, and draped it over Jennifer's shoulders.

"Deep breaths, Jenn."

Jennifer shivered, then sighed. Her breathing slowed and became deeper.

Seymour took a moment to process the session.

Daddy?" That was not a slip up. Was she getting ready to reveal a deeply hidden and sordid secret from her childhood when she snapped out of the trance? It certainly added to his belief that she might have been molested as a child. Was it premature to have her relive that intimate moment so soon after Donny's death? Could his haste for a therapeutic breakthrough have influenced his treatment?

Jennifer looked around and asked again, this time with less panic, "What happened? I was feeling so relaxed, floating along, and suddenly I felt as if I were drowning."

"You were reliving events from the night of the gala. You had reached an emotionally charged moment and woke yourself up. It's not uncommon."

Not uncommon, Seymour thought, but certainly highly significant. From what she'd told him, she seemed to be having symptoms of a hypomanic episode. Difficulty concentrating, drinking heavily and in binges, having trouble controlling her risky sexual behaviors, provocative dress. She'd never had a full blown manic episode, but the symptoms of the hypomania could be just as dangerous.

"You need to start back on your mood stabilizing medication, Jenn."

"I stopped taking Valproate months ago," Jennifer said. "I don't like the side effects. Besides, I like the way I feel. I'm energetic and I have more than enough energy to make it through the ten-hour shifts at work."

"The problem is that once you slip over the edge into full-blown mania…"

"I'm not going to take medication. But I promise to monitor my symptoms and I'll come in weekly."

"You know that your binge drinking can trigger a full-blown manic episode, as well as exacerbate your memory gaps. I would ask you again to consider AA."

"I'm not going to give up good champagne and tequila," she said adamantly. "So I've blown the first step. I went to an AA meeting once. I don't believe in an exterior higher power. Only we have power over our own lives, so I'd never be able to get past their first three steps."

"Yes, you've told me before you're a Buddhist…or Taoist, and AA could present a problem for you. There are plenty of groups that don't use the higher power template, such as Pagans in Recovery or SMART recovery. I'd be happy to give you a referral to one of those groups. I also could refer you to an addiction recovery therapist."

"I don't think so, Seymour. I don't think I have a problem. And don't give me that cop-out statement that I'm in denial."

Seymour did think she was in denial, but knew pushing the issue wouldn't be productive. She seemed to be coping with her boyfriend's death as well as could be expected, but the guilt was still an issue. He thought a Cognitive Therapy approach would work well in this case. He worked with her so that when she became mired in negative guilt feelings, she should let her mind move to the pleasurable memories of her times with Donny.

"I'd like to see you in one week for a follow-up session."

Jennifer crossed her heart. "And I promise not to wear the leopard mini-skirt to our next assignation."

Seymour stood and opened the office door for her—something he rarely did for patients.

He followed her with his eyes as her red mini-skirted hips passed through the doorway.

Chapter 22

Jennifer sashayed down the hallway, disappeared around the corner, and Seymour's trance was broken. He shook his head and grinned.

My wife is going to be in for a pleasant surprise tonight.

He returned to his desk and wrote up his notes for the session. His mind was reeling. So much new material came up—and the psychic jolt when Jennifer called her boyfriend "Daddy" topped it all off. He needed to keep an open mind about the underlying cause of her illness, but it was hard to discount the theory that her problems arose from childhood trauma—probably sexual abuse. First, her inability to remember her childhood. Then, the dissociative episodes. Now, referring to her boyfriend as "Daddy."

He tapped his pen against his temple and decided he would get feedback from a colleague on the course of his treatment of Jennifer.

Seymour shared a suite with four other psychiatrists. Alexandra Tralles was the senior member of the group and had been one of his mentors during residency. Over the years, they often bounced difficult cases off each other. Their earlier teacher-student relationship had evolved into a relationship of equals.

Alexandra had the last office down the hallway—the coveted corner office and a mark of seniority. Seymour reached her doorway in a few strides and peered in. Alexandra was at her antique teak desk reading. She was an eclectic psychiatrist, noted for her work on the psychosocial aspects of the treatment of schizophrenia. She'd also served as the former president of the False Memory Syndrome Foundation until five years ago when she went into semi-retirement.

"Alexandra, have a minute?"

She looked up from her work, smiled, and waved him in. "Ready for the big bocce tournament tonight, Ziggy?"

Alexandra and Seymour were teammates in informal bocce tournaments. They played in a league on Wednesdays at Balboa Park in San Diego, and on Friday evenings played pick-up games on the beach in Little Italy, near the airport. Occasionally, on weekends, they brought their spouses along and played on the beach, afterward sharing a relaxing dinner together.

"Wouldn't miss it for the world. Those arrogant surgeons are going down," he said with a laugh.

"Arrogant surgeons?" Alexandra smiled. "Something bothering you?"

He took a seat facing her desk. "In a way. I was wondering if you had time to discuss a complicated case."

"Of course. Let me make us a pot of tea."

Alexandra did a year-long sabbatical in Tokyo, and now was into everything Japanese. He sometimes thought happily that at least she didn't make him take off his shoes.

She went to a side table and brewed a pot of Japanese green tea, gyokuro. As the water heated, she lit a wedge of incense and placed it in a palm-sized ceramic container shaped like a duck as part of a ritual she called *kōyō*. She poured them each a cup of green tea, added a dollop of yellow sugar, then sat down opposite Seymour.

Seymour sipped his tea and collected his thoughts. "Where to begin. We've talked about this patient before, she's a medical examiner from Los Angeles."

Alexandra nodded for him to go on.

"I've been seeing her on and off for five years. She was referred to me because she had suffered a fugue state. While she was doing her internship—ironically enough during her psychiatric rotation—she disappeared. The school contacted the police and filed a missing person report. One week later, she was found in Tijuana. An elderly taco vendor noticed a *gringa* in trouble, so she took her in. One of her professors was shopping in the Mercado, stopped to buy tacos, and recognized her working behind the counter. They brought her back to Los Angeles and the next morning she was back to normal. She finished her internship a month later than the rest of her classmates, then moonlighted in the emergency room for a year, after which she began a pathology residency. While I was basking in my fifteen minutes of fame from the Williams/Roberts case, she made an appointment to see me. And I've been seeing her in therapy, sporadically, ever since."

Alexandra crossed her legs into a modified lotus position—a sign to Seymour that she was fully invested in the case. "You ever find out what triggered the fugue state?"

"Not as of yet. Based on her sexual neuroses, perhaps she was assaulted by a patient." Seymour paused to sip his tea. "Then again, she was doing a psychiatric rotation at the time. The trigger might have been something as innocuous as identifying with one of her patient's psychopathology."

Alexandra nodded for him to go on.

"She hasn't had any further fugue states since that time. Her main symptoms now involve problems with sexual intimacy, self-destructive behavior manifesting itself as binge drinking and risky sexual behavior. In addition, she complains of headaches and memory lapses. She has obsessional behaviors, especially as relates to excessive exercise. And she suffers from vaginismus, so her sexual relations tend to be oral gratification."

"Does she have dyspareunia as well?"

Seymour shook his head. "She's able to insert a vibrator without pain. And she reports having pain-free intercourse both when she's in a long-term relationship, and as recently as last week with her," Seymour coughed, "with her, I guess you'd call him, her ex-boyfriend."

Alexandra tossed back her tea and rolled the cup between her palms. She had a puzzled look on her face. "Where are you now with her therapy?

"She called me this morning for an emergency session. It turns out, the man she had just begun to date, and with whom she had become sexually intimate, had been killed. He was found murdered in his mansion yesterday." Seymour leaned forward and narrowed his eyes. "The kicker, she found out about the murder in the most macabre way. Remember, she's one of the medical examiners for L'Orange County."

Alexandra cringed. "No!"

Seymour gave a slight nod. "As she entered the morgue to do an autopsy, she pulled off the sheet covering the body. Lo and behold, there was her new lover."

She put her tea cup down. "Ouch!"

"She fainted right on the spot. She called from the morgue, frantic."

"Poor girl."

"Today's session may be an important point in her treatment, that's why I wanted to go over it with you."

"Certainly." Alexandra looked off and sighed. "This is the thing I miss most about not teaching."

"I wish I had more time to discuss cases, as well." Seymour began stroking his beard, which he found helped him focus his attention. "The first thing I need to tell you is that she was dressed provocatively. She was wearing a short red leather skirt, a revealing low-cut blouse, and had on heavy makeup. For her, this is very unusual. She has always been conservatively dressed in the past, wearing scrubs or blue jeans. And she seldom wears makeup."

Alexandra arched her eyebrows. "I was looking out the window earlier while I was on the phone and I saw the woman you're referring to. I couldn't miss that red miniskirt. Oh la la!" She laughed, then gave Seymour a sympathetic smile. "I can see what you mean, she is quite attractive. And I'm sure she'd realize the reaction she'd cause dressed that way."

Seymour felt chagrined and was sure his expression showed it. "She was aggressive and challenging about the matter of her attire. She seemed to take pleasure in the fact that she was making me uncomfortable. This is the first time she has been seductive like that."

Alexandra smiled wryly. "Seymour, this was just the first time you *noticed* she was manipulating you. I'm sure she's done that in the past, but more subtly. She probably wanted you to know this time."

"That could be. I told her the way she was dressed made me uncomfortable."

"Excellent! Dealing with the seductive patient is always difficult. By the way, Ziggy, you've always been a bit sexually repressed. It's cute actually."

Seymour shrugged. "And I take it you're not?"

Alexandra laughed. "What chutzpah—deflecting the conversation with a board-certified psychiatrist. Well, if you must know, we're in the same boat there. I'll let you in on a little secret. When I get in the mood and want my husband to be intimate with me, I serve him a slice of banana crème pie. That's my signal for him to get ready."

Seymour laughed. "Banana cream pie. How deliciously symbolic. Freud would have eaten that up." He paused. "When my wife's in the mood, she just grabs the bull by the horn, metaphorically speaking."

"We're from different generations."

Seymour finished off his tea and put the cup down. "Getting back to the session. Considering that the patient was in a state of shock over the terrible events, I moved the session on to her present problem. She's had problems maintaining a long-term romantic relationship. Her modus operandi is to have a number of brief, anonymous sexual relations, with the focus on oral gratification."

"You're amongst friends, Ziggy. The word is 'blowjob.' She likes to give them, receive them, or both?"

"Mainly give them. She has this game." Seymour sat forward and tapped his forehead with his hand. "Oh my God! It's like a lightning bolt. I just now understand the meaning." Alexandra's eyes widened. "She's very competitive in everything," Seymour said. "She likes to play a betting game. She bets a round of drinks. She gives the 'contestant' a blowjob. If he has a…"

"Orgasm?" Alexandra said.

"Right. If she can get him to have an orgasm in less than five minutes, she wins and he pays for the next round. Otherwise, the next round's on her."

The corners of Alexandra's lips upturned. "I take it she doesn't lose that bet often."

"I believe she's undefeated. But now I can see the psychodynamics. She needs to be in charge."

Alexandra rested her forearms on the arms of her chair and recrossed her legs. "Most women have that same need, they're just good at disguising it, making their partner think the opposite. And don't forget, you believe she was molested as a child. She may be playing out a role from her childhood. Having a time limit may be her way of terminating the unwanted advances when she was young."

"How so?"

"Let's say someone was molesting her when she was a child. She had no way to make it stop. Now she is an adult and by putting a five minute time limit, she now controls both when things start and when they stop."

"Makes sense. Sadly, it seems she had made a breakthrough and was opening herself up to her new lover. She spoke rather clinically about their relationship, as would be expected for someone in the early stages of shock. I ended with a hypnosis session. I had her regress back to the night she was last with her now deceased boyfriend. She related having a very pleasurable sexual encounter with him, culminating in vaginal intercourse, without vaginismus. She snapped out of the trance very abruptly, seemed to be actually re-experiencing the sexual encounter physically. Breathing heavy, sweaty, etcetera."

"What do you make of that?"

"The intense emotions aroused by reliving the sexual act may have triggered her underlying neurosis. Even under hypnosis, the affect was too intense for her defense mechanisms to handle."

Alexandra nodded. "Or, it simply could have been that she was re-experiencing the intense climax. That has been known to snap a person out of their trance state."

"True. She seems to have a memory lapse from the time she left her lover's house before dawn to the time she woke up later the next morning at her own place."

"Dissociative amnesia?"

"Perhaps. However, she'd been drinking heavily that night, so an alcoholic blackout is certainly in the differential diagnosis," he said. "She self-prescribes Xanax and Valium, which also causes anterograde amnesia."

"You're thinking drug-induced amnesia."

"That, and perhaps the sexual encounter that evening triggered the memory lapse."

"So, we're back to dissociative amnesia."

"It's possible. She's had a fugue state in the past. So she'd be susceptible to lapse back into one again."

"What about Multiple Personality Disorder?"

Seymour gave a smile and played coy.

"You're holding something back," Alexandra said rubbing her hands together. "I can't wait to hear this."

Seymour nodded and scooted to the edge of his chair. "She referred to herself at least on one occasion in the first person plural, referring to herself as *we* instead of *I*. She's occasionally done this before during a stressful point in therapy."

"Interesting. Go on."

"I've saved the bombshell for last. While she was hypnotized, she called her lover, whose name by the way is Donny, she referred to him as Daddy."

Alexandra's attention focused like a laser beam. "Now *that* is very interesting!"

"She referred to her new boyfriend in an overly idealized manner, calling him a Greek god, Zeus I believe it was, consistent with borderline personality disorder."

"You should study Harry Stack Sullivan, Ziggy. He wrote that over-idealization is a common and normal occurrence when one falls in love. He called it 'parataxic distortion'."

Seymour nodded. "Point well taken."

"So," Alexandra said, "she referred to herself in the first person plural, which is a clue she might have MPD. Anything else?"

"She does have problems recalling personal information, which fluctuates. But, to date I haven't found any evidence that she has a distinct, separate personality or behavior state."

"Not even under hypnosis?"

Seymour shook his head.

Alexandra uncoiled her legs. As she went to refresh the tea, she said, "When I was a resident, we used to refer to Multiple Personality as Dissociative Identity Disorder. I thought the terminology hid the real nature of the illness. Psychiatry had gotten too politically correct." Alexandra picked up the teapot and refilled the cups. "I'm glad the powers that be changed the terminology back to MPD. I think it's much more elegant." Alexandra handed Seymour his cup, then took her seat and crossed her legs over each other. "With your patient's symptoms consistent with a dissociative disorder, it begs the question: was she a victim of sexual or physical abuse as a child?"

"That's the million SDR question, isn't it?" Seymour stroked his beard. "She has no memory of being abused as a child."

"It's not unheard of for adults to have repressed those events from childhood. The brain can wall those memories off."

"True," Seymour said. "But you have to remember, although over eighty percent of patients suffering from a dissociative disorder report being abused, that leaves twenty percent whose illness is caused by something else."

Alexandra had a twinkle in her eye. "You're the expert on this sort of thing. What else could cause her symptoms?"

"The next most common cause is severe trauma, either living through a war experience or surviving a natural disaster. When she was ten, or there about, she lived through the big San Francisco earthquake. Her house was right on the fault line. It was destroyed and she suffered a significant head injury."

Alexandra rubbed her chin. "That could account for her symptoms, don't you think?"

Seymour gave her a noncommittal look. "Possibly. However, I don't want to rush to any premature conclusions. I find it important to keep an open mind."

"Has she undergone a complete neurological workup?"

"Right after she came out of the fugue state. I did a complete neuropsych workup including magnetoencelpholography and MRI. Other than a few soft neurological signs and nonspecific changes to the hippocampal-amygdala system, it was negative."

"What was her childhood like?"

"She has few memories from before the quake, likely caused by post-traumatic retrograde amnesia. She reports being socially inept in high school. She remembers being tall, gangly, and geeky-looking and felt excluded from the 'in' cliques."

"She sure has changed," Alexandra said. "But those high school experiences can leave permanent emotional marks."

"She dealt with the negative high school emotions through sublimation, turning to obsessive studying in order to cope."

"At least that's a mature defense mechanism," Alexandra said. "If she looked like she does now when she was in high school, I'm sure her career path would have been different." Alexandra checked the time. "She'd have ended up being a model, or a lyscee."

Seymour laughed. "There're usually one in the same."

Alexandra nodded in agreement. "I've got a patient coming in soon, Ziggy. Let's put everything together and see what we can come up with."

"My diagnosis is Dissociative Disorder. I plan to continue to probe to see if she has MPD or can remember any sort of childhood abuse."

"Have you interviewed her parents?"

Seymour shook his head. "They died shortly after she graduated from high school."

"Another trauma," Alexandra said. "Does she have any other family?"

"She hasn't mentioned any. I've been very careful not to plant any thoughts in her mind of early trauma."

"So where do you go from here?" Alexandra sat back and steepled her fingers, allowing Seymour time to think about the case.

Seymour rested his chin in his hand. "I've tried to be very careful about not putting false memories in her mind. What, if anything, happened to her in the past is unclear. I know that there's disagreement about the validity of hypnosis-related memories. My own belief, and I think it's yours as well, is that memories dredged up in hypnosis may or may not be true, and need to have corroborating evidence."

Alexandra nodded. "I always bought into the idea that hypnosis is useful in dislodging memories that are stuck. I subscribe to the school that says normal memories are laid down in the hippocampus, but memories from very traumatic events are laid down in the limbic system and the amygdala, and as such, may need an altered state of consciousness to access them, as they can be too affect laden to tolerate in the normal state. But the actual content that comes up during hypnosis isn't any more reliable than what they tell us in a non-trance state. And you're right to be careful not to put false memories in her mind, the so called, False Memory Syndrome."

"It's hard to have patience waiting for the client to reach an emotional point where she's able to bring those memories to the surface."

"I've had patients where it took years before they were at the point to confront those memories head on," Alexandra said.

Seymour sighed. "She doesn't make that much as a medical examiner. Even though I charge her a discounted rate, finances may be part of the reason she doesn't come in as regularly as she should."

"I hear you, Seymour. These days only the wealthy can afford long-term psychotherapy."

"Speaking of which, I'm just treading water financially. My caseload's made up of patients who I have to charge a reduced rate. I need to find another way of making money." Seymour let out a sarcastic laugh.

Alexandra nodded knowingly. "Our success as psychiatrists cannot be measured in money. I measure mine in the number of people I've been able to help live happy, productive lives."

Seymour frowned. "When I first moved to San Diego, I saw those sailboats out on the ocean and I said to myself that's what I want to work for. To be able to buy a Catalina and spend the weekends sailing with my family. Now, it looks like it's just a dream."

Alexandra let out a long breath. "When I was doing my residency, I had this idea that I would one day buy a fancy fur coat. Silly, I know, living here in San Diego. But that's what I set on. I was like you, working hard but never able to afford the coat of my dreams. Then one day, the parents of a patient of mine were so happy with the work I'd done with their daughter that they surprised me with a fur coat. A Russian sable stole! I guess I must have told their daughter about my dream. I'll tell you what I did. I tried that stole on for the family that day and we were all happy. And that's the last time I've worn it. It's hanging in the back of my closet. I'm no happier now than I was before." She sat forward and met Seymour's eyes. "But when I get sanguine and full of doubts, like you are now, I pull my fur coat of the closet, and as I stroke the soft fur, I think about all the patients I've helped over the years. And that's what really makes me happy."

A light began to flash on Alexandra's desk.

"Well, Ziggy. It looks like my appointment is here. *Sayonara*."

Chapter 23

Thursday

Race opened his eyes and was instantly wide awake. Familiar objects in his bedroom were indistinct in the tenuous light coming from the alarm clock. All night, he'd tossed and turned, buffeted by disturbing dreams of murder and death. Bosco's milky, dead eyes staring back at him, the feel of Bosco's squishy brain in his hands, the smell of death and embalming fluid. He propped himself up on an elbow and peered through the blinds. It was pitch-black outside and too early to get up for work. Beela, his partner, was going to be in court all day. Captain Beane wouldn't be in until the afternoon. Today was going to be his first day working on his own as a homicide detective, and there was so much he needed to accomplish. He didn't bother to pull the covers over his head; he was too amped to fall back asleep.

He'd waited years for this opportunity—to investigate murder and mayhem—yet now he questioned if he had the *cojones* for the job. He didn't understand how he could be qualified to work cases on his own so soon after joining Homicide. He'd spent his whole career working in the drug underworld with people who made a conscious decision to break the law. Now, he'd need to learn how to deal with law abiding citizens thrust unwillingly into horrible situations.

If the department weren't so woefully underfunded, he'd still be attending orientation sessions at police headquarters—the Crystal Palace. The orientation he did receive involved topics unlikely to help him investigate murders—sexual harassment training, followed by diversity training, stress in the workplace and improving community relations. After a break for lunch, the inanity continued with presentations on how to document and get reimbursed for work-related expenses, a motivational talk about self-affirmation, ending with a yogi teaching transcendental meditation to each of the participants. Nice skills to have, but he couldn't see how they'd help him solve Bosco's murder.

Tuesday had been his first day on Homicide. No sooner had he arrived at the station and met his new partner, Detective Beela White, when they were called out to the murder scene and he was thrust right into the soup. He observed his partner as she and the CSI team went about the task of investigating the case. And Beela went out of her way to explain what she was doing—from explaining the meaning of spatter patterns and how to look for signs of forced entry, to how to conduct a witness interview. The work was slow and tedious. And they didn't solve the case after an hour, like on TV.

Without thinking, he swung his feet onto the floor, ran his toes through the shag carpet, and sprung out of bed. He took a steamy shower, then looked at himself in the fog-coated mirror above the sink. He didn't need to shave—he could go days without touching a razor and still look clean. Instead, he splashed himself with musky-smelling cologne.

He went back to his bedroom, strapped the orange-colored LOPD OmniPhone to his wrist, removed the VR contacts from the saline solution and placed one in each eye, and planted the earbud in his ear, then checked the Bluetooth connections.

For the last seven years he'd been assigned to Vice, where his work attire consisted of blue jeans and college-logo tee shirts—clothes not fitting for a homicide detective. With that in mind, over the weekend he'd made a trip to Rodeo Drive and splurged on a "Detective Wardrobe." At an upscale men's store, he purchased an entire wardrobe—everything in shades of brown and matching everything else interchangeably, to make dressing easy in the morning.

He randomly threw on a pair of slacks, sport coat, and tie and went into the kitchen. The counters were spotless, the sinks empty and shiny, as if Architectural Digest were coming to photograph his condo. He reached inside his refrigerator—everything neatly in its place—and poured a glass of grapefruit juice. He toasted a buttery-smelling croissant, and downed his breakfast while he watched an early-morning news program. Bosco's death was one of the headline stories. The newscaster was a surfer-type who seemed overly energetic for the early hour and had few details to share with the viewers. His toothy smile and breezy tone when speaking of the murder was grating, as if he was revealing a salacious tidbit about a movie starlet. At least there were no on-scene reporters to over-dramatize the situation, and no pictures of Bosco's mansion; the security team Bosco's neighborhood association hired saw to that. Race was excited to see his case on holovision, however. His leg began shaking, he couldn't sit still—time to head to the police station and start the day.

Before he left the condo, he paged his car and it was waiting for him at the curb when he exited the elevator. Despite snapping his anxiety bracelet, his mind obsessed about how he was going to handle the day on his own. He jumped into the coupe but didn't engage the Nav-Drive—he needed something to occupy his mind on the drive in. He took the joystick control in one hand, and the accelerator/brake control in the other, and nosed out of the underground garage.

The sky was copper colored, but it should have been black at this early hour. Smoke from the mountain fires filled the valley with a black, sooty presence. The acrid smell burned his nose. Visibility was only a couple car-lengths, causing him to drive slowly. The few cars on the freeway at this early hour zipped by him. The headlights cast an eerie glow that he found sinister and frightening. After a few tense minutes straining his eyes to see through the miasma, he engaged the Nav-Drive and was pushed backwards as the gas-powered engine kicked in and roared. Within seconds, he joined the rest of the traffic speeding along at 120 mph.

The car cut through the billowing smoke and within fifteen minutes pulled into the detective's empty lot. Even at this early hour, people milled around the front entrance to the precinct, so he buzzed himself through the back and ran up the flight of stairs to the second floor detective's squad room. The aroma of coffee wafted from across the room. Red emergency lights cast mysterious shadows over the unoccupied desks. In the ethereal gloom, he imagined the ghosts of detectives past—the hundreds or thousands of investigators who'd come before him.

I'm one of them now.

His previous doubts faded away. He raised his hands above his head and shuffled his feet, feeling like a boxer who'd just knocked out his opponent. He'd finally done it. Reached the pinnacle. He laughed to himself, *I'm the mayor of Detectiveville*.

"I'm a homicide detective," he announced to the unoccupied chairs. His voice echoed off the bare walls.

It felt good to say the words out loud.

A homicide detective.

A duty to right the wrongs of those who could no longer speak for themselves.

The euphoria shattered when he remembered the LOPD homicide triage system. He was on his first case, and already he was being pushed from the right path. He put his arms down, flopped into the nearest chair, and gritted his teeth. Regardless of the rating some computer designated for his cases, he resolved to treat them all as A+. Just because someone was more successful in life, Race couldn't see why they should get more resources expended on them. He felt that humans are all the same in death and all deserve to rest in peace. Letting a computer calculate a person's worth, boil it down to a mathematical formula, apply some kind of algorithm seemed ludicrous to him.

What was even more unsettling was that everyone—from headquarters on down—seemed to accept this wretched state of affairs. He could understand how Helena accepted this system. After all, she was just a very sophisticated computer program, wasn't she? Beela and Captain Beane, even the Chief of Detectives, seemed to have no problem with this cold, impersonal system. He couldn't understand that analytic attitude from other human beings.

Was this to be my fate?

Over time, with the crush of an overwhelming workload, does death becomes routine? Would he look forward to shunting cases off to an impersonal, cold case file? It was depressing to think that, in time, this is how he would probably become. The only question was how long would that take? All new detectives were probably like he was right now—filled with lofty ideals. Did the daily crush of cases and familiarity with death breed the seeming indifference they now had?

When he'd started working Vice, he had lofty ambitions, morals, and values; how quickly they were subverted. How quickly he picked up the ethos of that department. Vice, it seemed, was aptly named. You can't buck the system. And if you try, the system will buck you off.

He stood up and paced the room, straightening the chairs as he went, thinking about the ghosts of detectives who preceded him. He wondered what changed them and if it was inevitable.

Can one fight the tide? Is this the way the world works?

He wondered if, after a while, a detective just stopped asking himself those questions. Maybe there was a point when you just woke up, went to work, went through the motions, mindlessly followed the rules, counted down the days to retirement, counted down the days until death. Don't ask any questions. Deciding maybe there really was no right answer, he resolved to do his best today. Tomorrow he'd leave for tomorrow.

He ran his hands through his hair and shook his head, discouraged. Perhaps to the dead it didn't matter if they were avenged, maybe the dead don't care what we do here on Earth. They're in a better, loftier place. Did it really made any difference to Bosco if they found his killer, or killers? He's still dead either way. His ashes are still going to be buried or scattered. Perhaps it's better to remember the good about a person; what made them a special and unique individual. Investigating their death meant dredging up secrets they may have tried all their lives to hide, exposing those secrets for the world to see. And the deceased wouldn't be able to protect themselves from that final invasion of privacy.

Would Bosco rather rest in peace with his secrets intact?

He shook his head and wondered what the hell he was thinking. This wasn't just about Bosco. Bringing Bosco's killer to justice wasn't just about avenging his death. It was about taking a murderer off the streets, someone who might murder other innocent people. His blood started flowing, he was amped as if he drank too much coffee, or too much Coke-Point Five.

Hell yes, he was going to find Bosco's killer! To serve and protect, baby.

He searched around, found the light switches, and turned on all the banks. The room came into focus, the ghosts of detectives past disappeared into the gloom. He was now *The Man*. Now he was the one who'd add to the history of the room. He poured himself a cup of coffee while he decided on his course of action for the day. Beela's rule about striking while the iron was hot, or don't wait until the trail has gone cold, popped into his mind. Whatever it was, it meant that he should try to get some serious work done today, and not wait until she returned to resume the investigation.

He walked over to one of the DataPorts, scanned his microchip, and opened the door. Red-tinted lights came on as he stepped inside and took a seat.

"Helena?" he said to the empty room.

An avatar materialized over the table—the face of Captain Beane's daughter. She had a hint of a smile showing a single dimple and a look on her face that said "business." Her melodious female voice filled the room. "Good morning, Detective Griffin. You are in rather early."

Race put his coffee down and made eye contact with the hologram image. "Good morning, Helena."

It seemed strange to be addressing a computer. He didn't wish the Nav-Drive a good morning. And what did good morning even mean to Helena? That the electricity bill had been paid? That no one was hacking her code? Was it really even morning inside her electrical circuits? He looked at the avatar as the projected image smiled back and decided she looked cute, someone he could go out and have a drink with.

A drink. That's it!

First thing on the agenda was to change the avatar. It didn't feel right lusting after Captain Beane's daughter, even if she was just a computer-generated hologram.

"Pull up the application to change avatar images," Race said.

Helena gave him a disapproving look. "Detective, your time would be better spent on investigating your open case. You can change avatars later. The clock on Bosco's case is ticking."

What the hell! When did a computer contradict an order?

He knew she was right, the clock was indeed ticking. On the other hand, he questioned if he should let a computer push him around. Did she outrank him? He decided it was best not to argue.

Can you even argue with a computer?

He could always change the avatar later, something really sexy.

"Helena, what do you suggest would be the best use of my time?"

His attention was drawn to the wall monitor as Helena pulled up the homepage for the Bosco case.

"The preliminary toxicology results are in from the lab," she said. "There were traces of cocaine, amphetamines, alcohol, MDMA or ecstasy, and THC in Bosco's samples. There is a note from the lab that these are only preliminary results, there were a number of other compounds that they are trying to identify."

Race nodded and waited while Helena pulled up other information.

"I would advise you to start this morning by interviewing a woman named Brigit Kojacy."

Race cleared his throat. "You think that's a good idea? I've never done a witness interview before."

"There's a first time for everything." Helena smiled sweetly at him. "I will be listening in on your OmniPhone. If you run into any problems, I will be right there in your ear."

Hardly relieving, Race thought, but it would have to do.

Helena projected the SocialMedia page of an attractive, dark-haired woman in her early twenties on the wall monitor. "I have downloaded Brigit Kojacy's information to your OmniPhone. According to her SocialMedia page, she has an audition later this morning. I have located her microchip and she is currently at her home in West Hollywood. Go see her first and find out what she was doing at the Bosco residence Saturday afternoon. Also, see if she can give you a description of the type of watch Bosco wore so we can track it down."

Race thought that sounded like a good idea.

"I have confirmed the time the studio van came by last Saturday to pick up Mrs. Billings-Li," Helena said. "Indeed, she passed Bosco's house around nine AM. You should re-interview her, see if she remembers anything else. That is standard operating procedure, Detective."

He thought that was another good idea. You never know what someone might remember the second time around. Plus, Billings-Li was such a nice lady, to boot.

"Remember, Detective, there were a number of calls from Bosco's neighbor, Mrs. Godgifu, to Mr. Bosco. I would infer that the two were having an affair. Go back and talk to her, confront her with this information. See what she has to say."

Godgifu seemed so prim and proper, Race was concerned that bringing up such embarrassing information would be unpleasant.

"Helena, how would you suggest I handle Mrs. Godgifu?"

Helena smiled. "Excellent question. Tell her you know that she had been having an affair with Mr. Bosco and divulge a little of the evidence we have. She will initially deny it. Be firm and do not let her squirm out. Reassure her that if she cooperates, you will see to it personally that this information remains private. You understand?"

Race nodded, impressed by the fact that someone did a good job of programming. Helena seemed to understand humans better than we understand ourselves. Race asked Helena if she had any other suggestions.

"Spend the rest of the morning canvassing Bosco's neighborhood. Get statements from anyone else that might be home. And follow up on any leads you uncover during the course of the morning. Captain Beane will be in this afternoon. Check in with him after lunch."

Race thanked Helena for her help.

The squad room was still empty when he left the DataPort. The door to Major Primus's office was closed and the lights out. The smell of coffee was still enticing. He poured black coffee into a to-go cup, then took the stairs two at a time and exited through the back entrance. He squirmed into his car, programmed the Nav-Drive with the address to Brigit Kojacy's residence—Melrose Avenue in West Hollywood—then sat back and sipped his coffee. He was nervous. He'd never interviewed anyone on his own before.

The day is about to get interesting.

Chapter 24

Early morning traffic was light until he turned onto Western Avenue and everything came to a complete stop. All three northbound lanes were at a standstill with people laying on their horns. Race snapped the rubber band on his wrist twice to calm himself, then sat back, ready to wait out the delay.

Hell, I'm a cop. Serve and Protect.

Race told the Nav-Drive to wait for him, then stepped out of his coupe and walked past the stopped vehicles. A city bus blocked the right hand lane, the uniformed driver yelling and flinging his hands about. Race walked through what was now a parking lot of scattered cars and trucks to where the bus driver was gesticulating. And there in front of him was the problem: a disheveled man dressed in a parka and army surplus clothing stood in the middle of the road, yelling to all who could hear that the government was reading his mind.

Race nodded to himself. Paranoid schizophrenia. Had to be.

The bus driver told Race the mental health crisis unit had been called. Race's parents suffered from schizophrenia, and from experience, he knew the crisis unit could take a half hour to arrive, then even longer to get the situation under control. He didn't want to wait that long and decided it was time to take action.

Race walked up to the hallucinating man. The stench of body odor and urine was overwhelming. When the man turned toward him to yell at an imaginary voice, Race pulled out his canister of paralyzing gas and sprayed him in the face. The man instantly lost muscle control and a look of surprise filled his eyes as he fell. Race caught him under the shoulders and eased him to the ground. People in the first rows of cars broke into applause. The bus driver and two other drivers helped Race carry the limp man to the sidewalk. He used plastic zip tie handcuffs to secure the psychotic man to a street sign pole so he wouldn't be able to get into traffic when he regained muscle control. Mental health could cut him loose when they arrived.

Race turned toward his car, stopped, and looked back. He cursed under his breath, thinking that if his brother didn't take his meds, he could end up in that man's situation. He looked in his wallet, all he had was a fifty SDR note. He folded it up and slipped it in the limp man's shirt pocket.

Race walked back to his car, receiving another round of applause from the stalled drivers. All he felt was empathy for the poor deluded man.

The Nav-Drive took Race to Melrose Heights Condominiums—the residence of Brigit Kojacy. His car pulled to a stop at the high-rise building landscaped with flowering hedges and seasonal colors. An imposing sign with gold lettering read:

Melrose Heights

Luxury high-rise abodes for people of discerning taste.

The building was a tower of white steel and tinted green glass at least sixty stories tall. He parked near the entrance, in a spot labeled: Prospective Residents. He stuck his police sticker on the dashboard and walked into the marbled lobby.

A pasty-skinned and overweight security guard with a bald head and the silhouette of a pistol plainly visible under his navy blazer sat between Race and the elevator banks. The man put his eMagazine down and eyed Race from behind the security counter as he approached.

"Can I help you, sir?"

Race pulled out his police badge.

The modern day Charon looked it over with what Race thought was a degree of suspicion.

"I'm here to see Miss Brigit Kojacy." Race spoke with what he hoped was an authoritative voice. "Police business."

The guard held the badge inches from his face and turned it over in his hands while studying Race, then returned the badge. "Sign in here. Miss Kojacy is on the thirty-third floor."

Race stepped in the wood-paneled elevator. "Thirty-third floor," he said. His knees buckled as the elevator whisked him quickly and quietly upwards. When he exited the car, he faced a cherrywood table with a vase of fresh-cut flowers. Race used the gold leaf framed mirror hanging above the flowers to adjust his tie. There were only two doors, both solid wood, located on either side of the carpeted hallway from the elevator.

He walked up to Brigit Kojacy's apartment and rang the doorbell. It gave off a short series of musical notes—a haunting classical melody of some type. In lieu of a peephole, security cameras were located just above the door on either side.

He stepped back so the cameras could get a good view of him, and he waited…and waited…

He rang the bell again, stepped back, and waited…and waited.

As he rang the bell for the third time, the elevator pinged. A police officer, dressed in the full dark-blue LOPD uniform, exited and walked his way. He appeared to be in his mid-fifties and very fit, with short gray hair peeking out from under his police hat. He wore a police duty belt with handcuffs, pistol, tactical baton, paralyzing spray, flashlight, and ElectroLaser. On his right shoulder, a communicator was attached to the epaulet, and he wore an ear bud.

He walked directly up to Race and spoke in an authoritative, practiced voice. "Sir. May I see your ID?"

The officer's voice and steely look seemed to brook no resistance, something Race was determined he would have to practice.

Race reached inside his blazer, pulled out his leather badge wallet, flipped it open, and showed the officer his shiny-new detective's badge. "Detective Horace Griffin. LOPD Homicide. Is there a problem, Officer?"

The officer studied the badge, then scanned it into the OmniPhone on his wrist. He scanned Race's microchip with the same device. He looked off into the distance for a moment listening to his ear bud, nodded, then smiled at Race. "Sorry about that, Detective. Can't be too careful these days."

"No problem. Just doing your job."

"New to the area?" Race nodded. The officer reached out to shake hands. "Marcel Campos."

"You can call me Race."

"Race," Marcel laughed. "I like that name. The rent-a-cop downstairs gave me a call to check you out, thought you looked too young to be a detective."

Race smiled. "A lot of people make that mistake. I still get carded when I buy beer, even though I'm closing in on thirty."

Campos laughed. He had a disarming and friendly way about him. "So what brings a homicide detective to Melrose Heights? There hasn't been a murder here, has there?"

Race hesitated, unsure of how much to confide in the officer. "We're investigating a homicide. The lady in this unit," he nodded to the door, "may be able to help."

Campos called the security officer and told him to ring Miss Kojacy and tell her it was okay to open the door.

The two men waited silently in the hall. After a minute or two, the door swung open.

And there she stood.

Miss Kojacy.

Barefoot.

Wearing a short, silk chemise with spaghetti straps, provocatively low-cut. A diamond pendant hung down to the hollow of her café au lait-colored throat. A diamond and ruby tennis bracelet draped her delicate wrist.

Race fought to keep his jaw from dropping. *Now* she *is definitely a person of discerning taste*.

She was shorter than Race, no more than 5'1" or 5'2". Her black wavy hair cascaded down to her shoulders, her dark eyes were warm, and her skin was remarkably smooth and youthful. Light streaming from the windows behind seemed to make her shimmer as if she were an angel. Or a goddess.

Race stared at her as if shell-shocked, unable to say a word. He slipped his fingers under the sleeve of his blazer and snapped his stress bracelet quietly.

Campos piped in. "Excuse us for interrupting. Are you Brigit Kojacy?"

"Yes." Her voice was sultry with a hint of a mid-western accent. "What can I do for you?" She held the door open with one hand, which raised the hem of the lingerie dangerously high.

"Detective Griffin needs to ask you a few questions about a homicide he's investigating. Would you mind if we stepped inside, ma'am?"

Race regained his composure. "Actually, I have to take you down to the station for questioning. Please get dressed, Miss Kojacy."

She stepped back and shot Race a vulnerable look. "What's going on? Am I under arrest?"

Campos looked puzzled.

"You're not under arrest," Race said. "But you need to come down to the police station to answer some questions."

"Do you have a warrant?" She looked back and forth at the two men. "This is…unheard of. I'm not a criminal. I've never broken the law in my life."

"Please get dressed and come with me, ma'am." Race tried to use a calm voice, but the timbre of his voice went up an octave.

Kojacy crossed her arms over her chest and furrowed her brow. "What are you here for anyway? I'm really busy. I have an audition later this morning, then I'm meeting a client for lunch." She blocked the doorway with her body and set her jaw. "You can ask any questions you want right here."

Race pulled handcuffs out of his jacket pocket.

Campos's eyes widened and he grabbed Race's arm, pulling him back toward the elevator. "What are you doing, Detective?" He spoke quietly, but his words stung.

Race confessed to Campos that he had never done an interview on his own and was planning to transport Kojacy to the precinct and enlist the help of his partner, Captain Beane. "I don't want to screw this up and get sent back to Vice."

Campos spoke sotto voce, but now with an understanding empathy. "Do you really need to take her to the station? She seems cooperative."

"She was present at the scene of the crime. I have cause to bring her in."

Campos smiled. "I'm not a detective, but I interview people all the time. I'll give you a hand. Besides, I don't think you're safe alone with the little lady."

Race shot a glance Kojacy's way. She was still standing in the doorway, arms crossed and glaring back at him. "Why? Is she armed?"

Campos laughed and patted Race on the shoulder. "Not only is she armed, she's legged, boobed, assed, and apparently she also has your tongue."

Heat flooded Race's face and he looked away.

Campos gave Race a push toward Kojacy's apartment. "C'mon, Detective."

Race turned to the apartment. Brigit arched her eyebrows and smiled at him. She must have heard every word of that conversation. His face flushed even more and he chided himself, he was going to have to remember he wasn't dealing with drug dealers anymore.

Campos explained to Brigit that they would conduct the interview in her apartment.

She stepped back from the door and motioned for the men to follow her.

Race's hawk-like eyes observed her shapely legs and practiced sway of her hips as she made her way into the condo. In the foyer, Race passed a vase of fragrant, cream-colored roses on the side table. The living room had floor to ceiling windows offering stunning views of the San Gabriel Mountains with plumes of black smoke rising sky high and the famous Hollywood sign partially shrouded in the roiling mists. She told the men to have a seat. They each took one of the plush leather chairs across from the equally ritzy white leather couch where Kojacy sat.

She crossed her legs and swung her dainty foot back and forth as she looked at the two police officers. She had an "I'm in charge" demeanor. "Now, what was it you wanted to ask me?"

"I'd like to ask you about your relationship with Donny Bosco," Race said. "I'm a homicide detective investigating his murder."

Brigit lost her impregnable look. Her lips trembled, her skin became pale. She made the sign of the cross and cried, "*O mój boże!* Donny…he's dead? He was murdered?"

Oh shit, Race thought. She must not have seen the news. What a terrible way for her to find out her lover's dead. Note to self: in the future be more tactful, never assume that the person you're talking to knows about the murder.

Kojacy's body trembled, her eyes watered, and a river of tears spilled down her face.

Campos cleared his throat and spoke softly, "Would you like a glass of water, ma'am?"

She shook her head and stared downward. "Am I a suspect? You can't think I killed Donny. Do I need a lawyer?" She looked over to Campos with a mascara-smudged face. "Would you mind going over to the wet bar and pouring me a glass of cognac? If either of you two would like something stronger than water, help yourselves."

Campos looked at Race who gestured that he didn't want anything.

Campos placed an afghan that had been hanging over the couch around the stunned woman's shoulders.

With smudges of black mascara on her cheeks, quivering lips, and wrapped in the comforter, she didn't seem quite the goddess of beauty Race first took her for. Tearful and defenseless, she was human. He relaxed, since now he could finally relate to her.

Race spotted a bathroom and retrieved a box of tissues, which he handed to her. Campos returned with a snifter of Rémy Martin. Kojacy mumbled thanks, and without looking at the drink, took a large sip. Her shoulders trembled and she pulled the afghan close around herself.

"Miss Kojacy, my deepest condolences," Race said. "I'm so sorry for the way this interview started. I shouldn't have assumed that you knew Mr. Bosco was defunct." Race cringed: why had he used that word? "That is to say, dead. It's been on the news since last evening."

She wiped her eyes. "That's okay, Detective. There's no easy way to tell someone bad news like this."

"I do have a few questions. Do you need some time to collect yourself?"

Her tears stopped flowing. She took a tissue and dried her face. "Thank you, Detective. You're most kind. How can I help you?" She sat back, holding the snifter in one hand. She pulled her legs up under her.

Race waited while she took a sip of cognac, then asked, "When was the last time you saw Mr. Bosco?"

"Do I need a lawyer?" she asked in a small voice.

Campos leaned forward, putting his elbows on his knees. "You are certainly entitled to one. However, if you want to have one present, then the detective *would* have to bring you down to the station. In my experience, if you don't have anything to hide, it wouldn't hurt to answer his questions."

Race added, "The information you provide may help us catch Mr. Bosco's killer."

Kojacy nodded, dabbing at her eyes. "Go on."

Race told her that he was going to record the interview. He instructed his OmniPhone to record audio.

Campos interrupted. "For the record, you should identify the time, place, and circumstances of the interview."

Race did so, then asked, "Miss Kojacy, what was your relationship with Donny Bosco?"

She answered with a sigh. "He was my boyfriend…," she averted her eyes, "my lover."

"How long had you known him?"

"Two, going on three years. I met him shortly after I moved here."

"How often would you see Mr. Bosco?"

"I'd go to his place on Saturday afternoons. Sometimes he would come here, but not often."

"You would go to Mr. Bosco's on Saturday afternoons?" Race thought that was a strange answer. "You didn't see him any other times?"

"Yes. No. I'm sorry, you asked two questions." She paused, her lips trembled, and her eyes welled up. "I saw him only on Saturdays. I scheduled my time so I could be available for Donny then. He had a busy schedule, and so do I. Donny wasn't my only boyfriend, and I wasn't his only girlfriend."

"So, Donny had another girlfriend?"

She let out a short laugh. "Not another girlfriend. Lots of other girlfriends." She paused and finished off the cognac, then held it out to Campos, who went to refill the snifter. She looked Race straight in the eye. His heart started to flutter. "I didn't mind that he had other girlfriends," she said. "We had our Saturday afternoons together. As long as Donny treated me nice, I couldn't complain."

Race got the picture. The barter system. "How did you two meet?"

Kojacy sighed, her eyes focused on something far away. "I moved to Los Angeles after high school. Like a moth attracted to bright lights, I was drawn to Hollywood. In Kansas City, where I grew up…well, the place is practically dead. And the climate there: freezing in the winter, sweltering in the summer."

Campos handed her the snifter.

She swirled the dark amber liquid in small practiced circles. "I wanted bigger and better things for myself than marrying a railroad worker. Those are about the only jobs there. I was young and beauty fades quickly. I moved here while I still had both. I wanted to get into modeling and acting.

A high school friend of mine had moved to LA, she told me I could move in with her."

Race nodded politely. "Go on."

"My girlfriend was dating a guy who introduced me to Donny. She said Donny had lots of connections to the movers and shakers in Hollywood. He seemed to fall for me right away and we started dating. I figured out right away that he wasn't a one-woman man, and we came to an agreement to have an open relationship." She smiled, showing a hint of her perfect teeth. "He was really generous with his money. He introduced me to his wealthy friends, and I started dating a few of them as well. He was okay with that."

Race nodded. What wouldn't any man do to spend an afternoon with this goddess? "Miss Kojacy, the rent on this apartment is almost ten thousand SDR a month. You lease an Audi for over a thousand a month. You have expensive furnishings and jewels."

She looked down and snuggled into the afghan. "I'm not a lyscee. Donny was my *boyfriend*. He gave me money out of the goodness of his heart. I don't need a Sexual Companion License for that."

"That's not what I was implying," Race said. "It's obvious you're receiving money from more than just Mr. Bosco. Perhaps one of your other boyfriends became jealous of your relationship. Didn't want to share you anymore."

"I don't think that would happen. I've always been upfront with men."

"Have you?" Race paused a second. He held her eye. "Always?"

Brigit sipped the cognac silently and looked away.

After pause, Race said, "Maybe someone you met recently isn't happy with the arrangement. Would you mind telling us who else you've been seeing?"

"Some of them are married. I don't want to ruin their lives. And I don't think any of them is capable of murder."

"Who knows what evil lurks in the hearts of men?" Race said.

"The Shadow does," Campos mumbled.

Brigit's nose crinkled, as if confused by the ancient reference. "You're right." She nodded. "You can never tell about people. I'll give you those names when I get back. Just keep that information on the down-low."

"I'll do what I can," Race said.

Brigit relaxed. "Fair enough."

"When was the last time you saw Mr. Bosco?"

"Last Saturday," she quickly answered.

"Today is Thursday. So you saw him last Saturday? Five days ago?"

Brigit stammered, "No…not this past Saturday. The Saturday before that."

"Are you sure it was over a week ago?" Campos asked.

Brigit nodded. "I'm sure. As I told you, Saturday afternoons were our special time together. When Donny was in town, I'd drop by his house and we'd spend the day, and sometimes the night, together. He was home two Saturdays ago, and I spent the night at his house."

"And you haven't been out there since?" Race asked.

She shook her head, eyes downcast.

"We have your cell phone records," Race said. "You placed a number of calls to Mr. Bosco this past Saturday morning and early afternoon."

"I called to see if he still wanted me to come over. Donny said he'd be back from Vegas on Friday night, so I kept Saturday open for him. He didn't return my calls. Probably had something come up, wouldn't have been the first time that happened. I guess I called a few times Saturday, just got his voicemail. But I didn't see him. Or even talk to him."

Race sat forward. "Just one more question, Ms. Kojacy. Would you happen to know what type of watch Mr. Bosco wore?"

Campos looked surprised at the question.

Kojacy flicked a glance at Race, then looked off into the distance. "It had some French woman's name…Valarie Constantine. Something like that. That watch was beautiful. It would hypnotize you if you looked at it too long. Its face was made of platinum and encircled with diamonds, at least a hundred of them. It was really different, you could see the whole inside of the watch, all the moving parts. Fascinating. I think I heard him refer to it as a 'skeleton watch.' He was in love with it and it was probably his most prized possession. He never wore an OmniPhone on his wrist, he had a mini-tablet Omni that he kept in his pocket."

"Did Mr. Bosco wear the watch all the time?"

"Every time I was with him. The only time he took it off was when we were in bed together." Brigit coughed, her face blushed a tad. "Although, sometimes…if the passion overwhelmed him, he'd forget to remove it."

Race stood up. "Thank you, Miss Kojacy, that's all for now. You've been very helpful, and we appreciate your taking time out of your busy schedule."

Kojacy pulled the afghan snugly around her shoulders and saw Race and Campos to the front door.

Race paused just outside the door. "Sorry for your loss." He turned and accidentally pressed the doorbell. The haunting melody began playing.

"Sorry," he said. "That tune sounds familiar, but I can't place it."

She looked away as tears began to flow down her cheeks.

"It's Chopin," she said. "*Nie ma czego trzeba*."

Chapter 25

Race returned to his car and turned his VR contacts on. Helena's holographic image appeared before his eyes.

"I was monitoring your visit with Miss Kojacy, Detective Griffin," she said.

"I thought you said you'd jump in and help me out."

"It did not appear that you needed my help. Good job back there, Detective."

"Really?" Race said into the air. "You think it went well?"

"Genius move to try to handcuff her at the start. It really got her to open up to you."

Race shrugged. It did work out well, even though that's not what he'd planned. Beginner's luck, perhaps.

"Thanks, Helena. What's our next move?"

"I suggest you to go to Bosco's house and do another walk-through. While you are there, canvass the area. A few of the residents might be home now. Also, re-interview Godgifu and Billings-Li. Mrs. Godgifu has a spa appointment this afternoon, talk to her first. Mrs. Billings-Li is at the gym, she should be home by the time you get there. At her advanced age, she may have forgotten something the first time you talked to her."

Race cut the connection and told the Nav-Drive to take him to Bosco's residence. The car pulled out of the building's driveway and waited to make a left turn onto Melrose Avenue. Race glanced across the street and spotted a strip shopping center. There was a cleaners, dress shop, pizza parlor, a French bistro—and a jewelry store called La Joya of Melrose, from the look of it, a high-end establishment. He checked the time and it wasn't even ten yet. He decided there was plenty of time to swing by the jewelers and start tracking down Bosco's watch.

Find the watch, find the killer. Occam's razor states that the simplest solution is often the correct solution.

He manually drove across the street and parked in front of the jewelers. The door chimed when he entered and the armed security guard looked his way with hooded eyes. Race presented his detective's badge and told the guard he'd like to speak to the manager. He was directed to the rear of the store.

Race skirted the square glass display in the center of the room and passed the display cases lining either side. He nodded to an elderly woman dressed in a full-length fur and carrying a tiny dog with pink bows in its ears, then nodded again to a well-dressed couple—the man in a blazer, his companion in a miniskirt and young enough to be his granddaughter. They all looked able to afford whatever expensive jewelry they chose to buy. Salespeople fawned over them.

At the rear display area, Race introduced himself to the manager, Arjay Raffles, a man with regal bearing and a somewhat haughty expression. Race showed Raffles his badge and asked if they could speak in private. Raffles wrote down the badge number. "Wait here, Detective," he said. "I will be right back."

Race waited and gave one of those uncomfortable smiles to the salesman standing across the display case from him.

Race cleared his throat and the salesman, whose badge said Philippe, looked over. "Philippe, would you mind showing me your watch display?"

Philippe gave Race a look of what he thought might be disdain. "You are interested in our collection of *chronographs*?"

He led Race to another display case where dozens of timepieces lay shining under the display lights. The price tags were all hidden under the watches.

If you had to ask the price, you probably couldn't afford them.

Philippe pointed out the various brands. "Our chronographs are all fabricated in Switzerland. Rolex is the most well-known, we have a nice selection. Here is an assortment of our Audemars Piguet, another fine Swiss watchmaker. The Royal Oak Offshore would look good on your wrist," he gave Race a thin smile, "very masculine looking. This is a Patek Philippe—" he gave Race that look that said, "Don't even try, I've heard every joke." "We have two Vacheron Constantin chronographs…"

Vacheron Constantin!

Race thought that sounded a lot like "Valery Christine" or whatever Brigit called it. He was willing to bet that was the brand Bosco wore.

Race interrupted the chronograph tour, deciding to match the self-important tone of his tour guide. "Philippe, would you be so kind as to acquaint me with the Vacheron Constantin chronograph?"

Philippe smiled. "Ah, you are a man of exquisite taste. Vacheron Constantin is the pinnacle of Swiss horology—you couldn't possibly do better. They are based in Geneva and are the oldest and most respected manufacturers of timepieces in the world. Napoleon Bonaparte and Harry Truman, as well as many popes and other world leaders have worn their products. They were founded by Monsieur Jean-Marc Vacheron and François Constantin—hence the name—in 1755. They range in price from twenty thousand to over a million SDR."

A million SDR for a watch!

He figured he could buy five Marussias with that much money and still have enough left over for an authentic steak dinner.

"You might be interested in knowing that Vacheron Constantin produced the most expensive watch ever made. It contained over eight hundred parts and sold for eleven million SDR." Philippe further explained their chronographs are made from either stainless steel and titanium or 18-carat gold. "We only keep a few in stock. However, we can help you custom design one that would be unique."

Race let out a low whistle. "These chronographs must keep really good time, considering the prices."

Philippe smiled and said conspiratorially. "That OmniPhone you're wearing, which I imagine cost you less than one hundred SDR, keeps time better than the finest Vacheron Constantin. These chronographs are more a statement of who the wearer is."

Race chuckled. "In that case, my watch is making the statement that I need to get a better paying job."

Philippe laughed politely.

"What are the straps made out of?" Race asked.

"Most are made of alligator or crocodile."

That was exactly what Race was expecting. It matched the pattern on Bosco's wrist.

Race glanced around the store and for the first time noticed at least a dozen miniature, closed circuit cameras that were focused on each of the display cases, as well as two that were focused on the front door. The prosaic chime of the door opening drew his attention to the front of the store and in walked his new friend, Officer Marcel Campos.

Campos greeted the security guard buddy-buddy, then looked his way, tipped his hat, and smiled. The officer came to the back of the store and patted Race on the shoulder. "Well, well, Detective. Creating more trouble here? I didn't expect to see you again so soon."

The manager came out from the back of the store and approached the trio.

"I'll vouch for the detective," Campos said to Raffles. "He and I go way back."

Race turned to the manager. "Mr. Raffles, I'm investigating a homicide—"

Raffles held his index finger up to his lips and looked around to see if any of his customers had overheard. "Please," he spoke so quietly that Race had to strain to hear him, "come back to my office and we can speak in private."

Raffles opened the half-door separating him from the officers, and invited them to follow him down a short hallway where two steel doors with heavy, impact-resistant glass cutouts lined either side of the passage. Behind the door on the left sat an elderly man with wispy white hair—almost a spitting image of Albert Einstein—using a magnifying glass to examine a small pile of gems. Behind the other, two security guards were seated in the room. One was looking at a bank of monitors that showed images coming from the security cameras out front, the other reading a girly magazine.

Raffles brought the two men into his windowless office located at the end of the hallway and asked them to take a seat. Race sat in one of the leather chairs facing Raffle's metal desk. Atop the faux wood top sat a computer monitor and stacks of magazines. Behind Raffles, the back wall contained shelves with worn reference books on watches and jewelry, and a few framed photos of Raffles and his family.

Race explained he was investigating a homicide and that the deceased had a watch missing. "I'm hoping you might help us track down the watch. I'm pretty sure it was a Vacheron Constantin. Do you sell used watches? I mean chronographs?"

Raffles laughed. "Back here you can call them watches, if you like. To answer your question, we only sell new timepieces. The only pre-owned watches we see are people bringing their timepieces in for an appraisal, either for insurance purposes, or in preparation for selling."

"Is that right?"

"I'm one of the few certified watch appraisers in the county."

"Then how would one go about selling a high-end timepiece?"

Raffles leaned forward. "Selling a Vacheron Constantin isn't easy. You can't go to a traditional pawn shop. You'd only get a few hundred SDR, even for a watch worth hundreds of thousands. The most common way to sell luxury timepieces is to use one of the reputable on-line brokers. In order to list with one of them, you would have to present a letter of certification for the chronograph from someone like me."

"Could you give me a list of the other brokers and appraisers?"

"With pleasure," Raffles said. "And I will notify the other certified appraisers in L'Orange to be on the lookout for a Vacheron. We're a tight knit group."

Raffles printed out a list and handed it to Race. There were five other stores listed in L'Orange County, all but one of them in either Hollywood or Beverly Hills.

Raffles said, "All luxury manufacturers, including Vacheron, keep a database on each timepiece. When one tries to sell the piece, it's a simple matter of matching the serial number on the back of the watch with the maker's database. Reputable sellers of previously owned high-end watches will not touch a watch without proof of ownership. In reality, there are no professional watch thieves—it's too easy to get caught the way the system is set up."

Race said, "The watch I'm trying to track down belonged to Donny Bosco."

A look of genuine angst rose on Raffles' face. "Oh dear. I'm so sorry to hear that. Mr. Bosco was one of our regular customers. He would come in every month or two and buy an expensive present for one of his girlfriends. He purchased a number of necklaces, earrings, bracelets, things of that sort."

"You said girlfriends? I take it he brought in more than one?"

"Oh dear." Raffles looked down and fidgeted with his tie. "I probably said too much."

"Bosco is dead," Race said firmly. "Protecting his privacy isn't as important as catching his killer. Could I see a list of the purchases that Mr. Bosco made?"

Raffles hesitated. "I would need to see a warrant before giving any specific information on a client."

Race spoke to his Omni, asking Helena to get a warrant—she told him she'd have it sent to the jewelry store. As Race turned off the device, the printer behind Raffle's desk started to hum, and it spit out a single page. Raffles pulled a sheet out of the printer, looked it over, and nodded. He then told his computer to print out the purchases made by Donny Bosco. The printer spit out two pages.

Raffles passed the papers over to Race. It was a detailed account of Donny Bosco's purchases at La Joya. While Race perused the information, Raffles consulted his monitor. "Apparently, Mr. Bosco had not purchased any chronographs at our store. Do you have any other information on the watch, Detective?"

Race spoke to his Omni and asked Helena to play back the part of the interview where Brigit Kojacy described the watch. Race listened on his ear piece, then relayed the information.

Raffles nodded and smiled. He pulled a tome from the bookshelf behind him, paged through until he found what he was looking for, and passed it to Race. Race scrutinized the information as Raffles explained. "The chronograph you're describing is either the Patrimony Traditionelle Skeleton, or the Malte Tourbillon Skeleton. Models start at 325,000 SDR. Adding diamonds, of course, increases the price—how much would depend on the quality of the stones. The Skeleton watches are unique, dazzling. I've personally only seen a few."

Race continued to study the printout. It appeared Bosco was spending between a quarter to a half million SDR a year at La Joya. The store would certainly miss one of its most loyal customers and the staff would probably go into a state of mourning.

Raffles said, "If you'd like, I can contact the manufacturer in Geneva, see if they have any record of Mr. Bosco purchasing one of their products. There aren't many Skeleton timepieces out there, so it shouldn't be too difficult."

"That would be much appreciated." Race handed Raffles one of his cards.

Campos told Race to expand the alert to all of the jewelry stores and pawn shops in both California and Nevada. Race contacted Helena and had her send out an alert.

"One final thing, Mr. Raffles," Race said. "Are you familiar with a woman named Brigit Kojacy?"

Raffles answered almost immediately. "Yes, a lovely woman. Beautiful. She comes in regularly. You know, she lives right across the street."

"She's the one who gave me the description of the watch. I take it she would come in with Mr. Bosco?"

"Oh, indeed. And she always left with a new piece of jewelry."

Race nodded. "Thanks for your time and help. When you hear from the manufacturer, give me a call. And if the watch should end up here, by all means, call me right away."

Raffles walked Race and Campos to the front of the store and let them out through the half-door. He gave Race a formal half-bow. "Pleasure meeting you, Detective. If you should ever be in the market for a nice gift for a special someone, we'd be happy to be of service."

Campos turned to Race as soon as they were out of the store and said, "I know it's early, but let's go next door and grab a slice of pizza. They make some of the best pies in Los Angeles. Besides, there's something I'd like to talk to you about."

Chapter 26

Mel n' Rose's Pizza was two doors down from the jewelers and looked out of place among the luxury residences and high-end retailers—a blue-collar watering hole in the midst of high-end splendor. The restaurant advertised Milwaukee-style pizza.

Race peered through the windows wet with condensation, then turned to Campos. "I've heard of New York thin-crust and Chicago deep-dish, but never Milwaukee-style pizza. What do they do, pour beer over it?"

"Very funny, Race." Campos chuckled. "By the way, good job with Kojacy. I liked the way you used the threat of handcuffing her and taking her to the station to get her to open up."

Race thought what the hell? He caught a lucky break with Kojacy and might as well take credit for it. He smiled and gave Campos a slight nod. "Psychology 101."

"You 'da man," Campos slapped Race on the back and opened the door for him.

Race walked into a fifties-style restaurant. It could have been the set for *Happy Days*. He closed his eyes and took a long breath in through his nose. It was heavenly. The joint smelled of yeast, garlic, and oregano. Behind the counter, a man wearing tight, black denim pants and a baker's apron over a white tee shirt rolled up to the shoulders was taking a call-in order. He looked up from the phone and smiled when Race and Campos walked up.

"Race," Campos said. "Let me introduce you to Mel, the owner of this pizza palace."

From somewhere in the back, a female's voice yelled out, "He's the co-owner."

Campos laughed. "Mel, this is Detective Race Griffin." He put his hand on Race's shoulder. "He just joined Homicide."

Mel wiped off his flour-coated hands and extended his right hand. "The meal's on the house for our men in blue." He spoke with a sing-song Nordic-type accent—regional accents were pronounced as people didn't travel around the country as often since the Financial Tsunami. "The usual, Officer Campos?"

Campos nodded. "Ten-four."

Mel looked at Race.

"I'll have the usual, too," he said.

Mel chuckled. He handed them each plastic glasses and told them to help themselves to drinks and that their Italian sausage pizza would be out in twenty minutes.

Campos and Race grabbed Cokes and sat at a table with shiny metal legs and a white Formica top. Race looked around the room. Pictures adorned the walls—scenes from the glory days of Milwaukee: sepia-colored photos of breweries, children in thick woolen jackets skating on frozen lakes, Studebakers parked in front of frozen custard stands.

Race again thanked Campos for his help at the jewelers.

Campos waved it off. "Let me explain how things work in West Hollywood. The local businesses and residents have contracted with LOPD. They pay to have a squad of us patrol cops freelance the area. We go wherever there might be a problem. We try to get to know the businesses and residents. The idea is to try to prevent trouble before it happens, instead of the usual cop role, which is to mop up afterward."

"My building does the same thing," Race said. "Part of our monthly fees."

"Lots of neighborhoods get together and pay for these community police details. I liked the idea and signed up. I miss not working with a partner, but helping to make the community safer kind of makes up for that. And there's perks, like the free pizza and drinks we're getting. LOPD doesn't pay us beat cops much, so a little extra here and there goes a long way."

Race nodded. "What brought you to the apartment building?"

"The security guard wasn't sure who you were—frankly, you look too young to be a detective—so he called me. I jump when one of the luxury buildings call—they always tip well."

"Tip?" Race wondered if he could work something similar in Homicide. It was going to be difficult to live on the salary he was going to be making. "You get tips for doing your job?"

Campos pulled out a crisp twenty from his wallet. "I'll be happy to split my part of the take with you."

"You mean the building paid forty SDR for you to come check me out?"

Campos pulled a wad out of his pocket and spread them out under Race's nose like a deck of cards. "They paid eighty SDR. I have to split that with my boss, who passes a little to his boss, and so on up the line. But go ahead, take the twenty."

Race shrugged, then plucked the blue-colored note from Campos's fingers and put it in his pocket.

"Everyone has to have a way of making a little extra," Campos said. "You know that triage system the department has that dictates how much time you can spend solving a case?" Race nodded. "Guess what happens when you run out of time on a case."

Race shrugged. "I imagine you're about to tell me."

"I like your style," Campos said. "Oftentimes, the family or friends of the deceased pay to keep you working the case on the side. The brass is okay with that…as long as they get to share in the spoils."

Race smiled and felt relieved. "I was wondering how I could make extra *dinero*. In Vice, opportunities were boundless—I became an expert on civil and criminal forfeiture laws. That's how I ended up with the B2-H sitting out front."

Campos looked out of the window and whistled. "Is that thing street legal? It looks like a racing car." He looked back to Race. "What did that baby cost you?"

"Nothing." Race hesitated, he was embarrassed to tell Campos that the car was worth more than either of their take-home pay working five years. "I ended up with it from a drug forfeiture."

"You might want to trade that in for something more practical." Campos blew on his badge and pretended to polish it with the back of his hand. "Now that you're in the big leagues."

Race nodded. "You know, I was bummed about the idea of allocating time spent investigating a homicide case based on a person's net worth, or how cute they were. I like the idea of working directly for the deceased's loved ones."

Campos gave him an impish smile and said with a wink, "It almost seems noble." He sipped his drink. "By the way, this Donny Bosco…what did the system rate him?"

"A."

Campos whistled again. "Must'a been a heavy hitter."

Race snorted. "Ironically, that's the way he was killed. Beaten over the head with some sort of pipe or baseball bat."

"What's the story with the watch?"

"I noticed Bosco had a tan line on his left wrist where a man would wear a watch. The silhouette didn't look like any Omni I've ever seen. We didn't find the watch in his house. So, we find the watch, we find the killer."

"Maybe. You don't think little Miss Kojacy's involved, do you?"

"We know she was at Bosco's house last Saturday afternoon. That's six days ago, not the thirteen she told us."

Campos raised an eyebrow. "You didn't call her on that."

"Now I have leverage on her. I'll wait for the right time to use it."

Campos smiled and nodded. "Smart thinking, Ace."

"Kojacy was at Bosco's during the time frame we calculate he was killed. She also made a number of calls to his cell earlier that day, all unanswered."

"That still leaves the question: Was she involved in Bosco's killing?"

"I doubt it. Bosco was a big, muscular man. I can't imagine her being able to beat him to death. Plus, he was her sugar daddy. What's the motive?"

"I can think of a few." Campos counted them out on his fingers. "Maybe Bosco was getting possessive and didn't want to share her anymore. Maybe she hit the jackpot and hooked the big kahuna of sugar daddies, and he didn't want to share. Maybe Bosco and Kojacy were involved in kinky sex play and things got out of control."

"That seems a reach."

Race looked up as a smiling waitress with a '50s style dress and giant teased bun hairdo came up with a pizza. The rectangular pie was steamy and just about covered the table. Race felt his stomach churn. The pie looked and smelled delicious. The sauce and cheese melted together on a paper-thin crust, Italian sausage slices cut on a diagonal and slightly charred, the garlic had a caramelized exterior and moist interior.

The two men grabbed hot slices.

Race took a bite. "*Mamma mia!* This is delicious." He finished his first piece in two bites. "So this is what people with discerning taste eat."

Campos paused a moment, then started chuckling. "That's hysterical, Race. That's what that pretentious sign across the street says."

Race finished another square of the pie. "Y'know, that jewelry store had a lot of expensive merchandise but only that one armed guard out on the sales floor."

"Don't be fooled," Campos licked his fingers. "The security there is extremely sophisticated. All those cases have impact-resistant, nano-crystal glass. Even a sledge hammer wouldn't do more than just cause a few cracks. And, if armed robbers come into the store, those two guards in the back room would activate an alarm, sealing the front door and notifying the police. A SWAT team would be on site in minutes. The robbers would be twiddling their thumbs, locked inside, waiting for the police to pick them up."

"What happens if they take hostages?"

"SWAT would release carfentanyl into the ventilation system. It's the same stuff that's in my knock-out canister. It's odorless and colorless and works within seconds. The SWAT team puts on their gas masks and waltz in; they give the sleeping beauties a shot of the antidote, naloxone; hostages wake up and go home; and the criminals wake up handcuffed and in the back of a paddy wagon."

Race was on his fifth square of pizza and mumbled, "This stuff is awesome. My life's going to be forever changed."

"I take it you'll be back for more?"

Race nodded. "Hell yeah."

Campos lowered his voice and leaned toward Race. "Don't tell anyone I told you this, but La Joya has a vault in the basement where they take their wealthiest clients. They have stuff down there in the seven and eight figure range. They even have a separate guard just for that area."

Mel came around from behind the counter, pulled a chair up to the end of their table, and joined them. "So you have a new sidekick?" He looked Race's way. "Detective, welcome on board." He called the woman over that brought the pizza to their table. "Detective Race, allow me to introduce my boss, and *co-owner* of Mel n' Rose's, my wife, Rose."

Race was going to correct Mel about his name, but thought better of it since he was eating free pizza.

Rose nodded. She pulled a napkin from off her shoulder and hit Mel with it, saying she had to get back to the ovens before the pizzas became burnt.

Mel waved to his wife, then grabbed a piece of their paper-thin pizza. "This shop's named after my wife and me, not after the street. When we moved here from Milwaukee and saw this place was available on Melrose, we couldn't pass it up."

"What's Milwaukee like?" Race asked between bites. "I've never been to the Midwest."

"Well…it's almost deserted. There's fewer people there than back in the 1860s. Like most of the middle of the country, Milwaukee's just a hub to transport raw materials to either coast." Mel snatched up another piece of pie. "Rose's family has been in the pizza business for over a century. Her grandmother, Maria, started the operation in what was then a bustling part of town. By the time we took over, Milwaukee had contracted so much that our place was out in the boonies. Almost everyone lived within a mile or two of Lake Michigan. Since we had to move the business anyway, we decided to move here. And things have been good. As far as I know, we're the only place serving Milwaukee-style pizza in all L'Orange."

Race looked down to grab another piece. They had eaten the entire thing. He leaned back in the chair and wiped his mouth. "This is the best pizza I've ever had. I'll be back for sure."

"We get all our ingredients straight from back home," Mel said. "That's what makes the pies so good. The sausage is made from real pork. The cheese, from real cow's milk." The phone rang and Mel stood up. "Business is booming. Look forward to seeing you again, Detective."

Campos rubbed his stomach. "What's next on your agenda, Race?"

"I'm heading back to Bosco's to interview his neighbors."

"Mind if I tag along? As long as his place is south of the Ventura Freeway, it's in my district."

"It's between Mulholland and Sunset."

"Then, I'd be happy to help. Besides, I love checking out those mansions up in the hills."

"Planning to buy one anytime soon?" Race laughed.

"Soon as I get my next paycheck, pal."

Chapter 27

Bosco's mansion was on a cul-de-sac of about two dozen palatial estates each protected by gated entrances. Race pulled up to the gate leading to his place; yellow police tape hung from one stone pillar to the other. He stepped out of his car, removed the tape, drove down the driveway, and parked in front of the eight-car garage. Campos pulled in next to him and they met between the cars.

Campos gazed at the Grecian palace Bosco had called home. "What a place!"

"You can put a bid on it," Race said with a grin.

Campos poked him in the ribs. "I just might do that."

"As we were pulling in," Race said, "I saw the senior center van dropping off the lady who lives two doors up the hill. Let's catch her before she takes her nap."

"You're the boss, boss." Campos gave him a half-salute. "By the way, Helena contacted me while I was driving over and assigned me to follow you around this afternoon. That okay with you?"

Race smiled. "Fantastic. You don't mind?"

"Beats driving around all day looking for trouble." He nodded to Race. "What's the story with the old lady?"

"She may be the last person to have seen Bosco alive. We're worried about the statement she gave us the other day. She's in her nineties and is probably on a bunch of meds."

They walked to the street and headed up the hill, which was so steep that Race had his hands on his thighs and fought for breath when they reached the solid-wood gate leading to the Billings-Li's estate. The house sat back from the street, surrounded by a six-foot brick wall, a row of Leyland cypress towering above the fence. Race pressed the intercom to one side of the gate. The maid buzzed them in after they presented their credentials to the built-in scanner. They walked down the cobblestone drive bordered by mature sycamore trees. Campos let out a gasp as the full house came into view. It was like the Bosco mansion, only larger. Resembling a Greek temple with a portico two stories high supported by white marble Ionic columns.

Race walked up to the door, which was twice his height, and rang the bell. The housekeeper must have been waiting for them, because the door opened almost immediately. A short woman with Quechua features, wearing a crisp white apron over a black mid-length dress, spoke to them with a Spanish accent. "Mrs. Billings-Li is out on the patio. Follow me, Officers."

The house was like an art museum with wide open spaces. Gold-framed paintings adorned the marble walls. The ceiling, which must have been twenty feet high, was painted in Italian-style frescoes. A spiral staircase led to the second floor.

They followed the housekeeper through the formal living room, then through open French doors to the covered patio where an elderly lady sat in a recliner, watching a holographic movie.

When she saw them enter the patio, Mrs. Billings-Li turned off the video. She smiled and stood up. Placing one foot gingerly on the ground before moving the next, she walked over and extended her blue-veined hands, which had a fine tremor. "I remember you from earlier this week," she said to Race. Her voice wavered slightly. "Weren't you with a female detective?"

Race took her hand and held it gently, like it was an egg, and placed his left hand on top of hers. "That's right. My partner's testifying in court. I'm working with Officer Campos this morning."

"Would you gentlemen like anything to drink?" They both nodded. She spoke to the housekeeper. "*Triaga una jarra of agua de sandía*...for our guests...*por favor*." The housekeeper nodded and disappeared into the house. Billings-Li invited the two men to sit in the easy chairs that dotted the patio.

"What a beautiful home you have here, ma'am," Campos said looking around.

"Don't call me ma'am." She gave Campos a smile that must have been very sexy when she was younger. "That makes me feel old. My name is Barbara. Please, use that."

Campos nodded.

"It is a beautiful house, Officer. But way too big for my tastes. My second husband built it for me when we married, that's why I can't sell it. He called it my Taj Mahal." She swept her hands around the patio. "I spend most of my time out here. I love the view and the fresh air. Although I have to tell you, there have been a few days recently when the wind blew so much smoke this way I couldn't sit outside."

"How long have you been living here?" Race said, trying to make small talk while they waited for their drinks.

"Oh, about forty years. My husband, Mr. Li, owned factories in China, but always wanted to live in Los Angeles. His first wife died and his children had moved out on their own. He was a fan of my movies." She paused and nodded to them. "I was once an actress, you know. We were fortunate; my husband had most of our money invested in China. When the dollar started its plunge, our stake in China actually became more valuable. I guess whenever there are losers, there are winners."

The maid returned with a glass pitcher filled with pink liquid. She poured both men a glass and gave Billings-Li a refill.

"Watermelon water," the housekeeper explained.

"You didn't come to chat." Billings-Li took a careful sip of her aqua. "What brings you back, Detective?"

Race put his drink on a coaster. He looked down the hill and could see the backyards and pools of the adjoining houses—Godgifu's and Bosco's—through the foliage. "I wanted to ask: When was the last time you saw your neighbor, Mr. Bosco?"

Billings-Li's face dropped, and she looked much older. "Poor man, so handsome and virile. I'm sure there are a lot of women who will be missing him." She shook her head. "I'm sorry, I got distracted. What did you ask, young man?"

Race repeated the question.

"You asked me that last time, and the answer is the same: Saturday morning. The studio sends a van out to take us old ladies to the Hollywood television studios where we sit in the audience while they tape shows. I saw Mr. Bosco picking up his newspaper when we went by in the van."

"You go every week?" Campos asked.

She shook her head. "Sometimes those old bats get on my nerves. But I did go last week. I remember because one of the neighbors was going to be on *Late Night*, promoting a new movie of hers."

"Do you remember where Mr. Bosco was standing when he was picking up the newspaper?" Campos asked.

"He was right by his garage, bending down. We have a real nice paperboy. He brings the paper down by our garages so we don't have to walk all the way up to the sidewalk."

"Did you happen to get a good look at his face?" Campos said.

"No…well…I really don't remember now. Let me think a minute and picture the scene in my head."

Race and Campos waited, sipping the *agua de sandía* while Billings-Li was thinking.

"Officer, the best I can tell you is I don't remember seeing his face or not. I just assumed it was Mr. Bosco. I know I saw a man picking up the paper. It was his house. So I would assume…"

"How well did you know Mr. Bosco?" Race said.

"I met him a number of times. He's…he was very friendly, very charming, and handsome. If I were younger, I probably would have gotten to know him really well."

They all shared a laugh.

"Do you know your neighbors, Leo and Dona Godgifu?" Race asked.

"Not very well. We're all isolated in our gigantic jails we call mansions. I've talked to Mrs. Godgifu a few times, bought Girl Scout cookies from her daughter, that's about it. I've seen her husband, but never met him. I understand he travels a lot, some sort of diplomat. He seems Oriental, but not Chinese like my ex-husband." She nodded to herself. "Korean, I'd say."

"Do you know if Mr. Bosco and the Godgifus were friends?"

Mrs. Billings-Li got a far-off look in her eyes and seemed to be weighing her answer. "Last time you were here, I may have been a little evasive. I'm not nosy, and what people do is their own business." Her face seemed to harden. "But there's a murder involved and social niceties go out the window. I know Mr. Bosco and Dona were more than just friends." She looked Race directly in the eye. "She was having an affair with him."

Race nodded. Just as they'd expected. "What makes you think that?"

"I have trouble sleeping and I don't like taking medication, so I sit out here at night with the lights out watching TV. I've seen Lady Godgifu running back and forth between their two houses late at night." She pointed down the hill with her shaky hand. "Look there, young man. From my patio I can see right down the hill to the backyards of both their houses."

Race looked down the hill. The backyards of the two houses were clearly visible as was the pool on the patio of Bosco's house.

Billings-Li said, "Godgifu lets herself in through his gate, climbs up the stairs to the balcony, and disappears into Bosco's house. She's there for an hour or so, then she sneaks back to her house." She pointed to Bosco's gate.

Race raised his eyebrows. "Why do you think she was having an affair?"

"You'll probably think I'm hallucinating, or some such." She shook her head, her eyes widened. "Well, I'm not a peeping Tom, but when Mrs. Godgifu sneaks to Bosco's house, she's…," Billings-Li leaned toward them and spoke in a conspiratorial tone, "she's completely naked." She paused dramatically. "I could see, right through those leaves, her beaver, clear as day."

Chapter 28

After the maid showed them out, Campos looked over at Race and chuckled. "Interesting case you've got here." He slapped Race on the back. "I *knew* the people who lived in these fabulous houses were different from you and me—but women running around the neighborhood naked! I really gotta move up here."

"I know a haunted house that will soon be on the market," Race said with a wink.

Race and Campos walked up Billings-Li's driveway to the street.

"Let me run something by you." Race told Campos about the other information they had gathered indicating Godgifu was having an affair with Bosco. "I was planning to confront Godgifu with the evidence."

Campos grimaced, as if he'd just bitten a lime after downing a shot of Tequila. "What would that get you? You can get her to confess she was having an affair, but you're trying to find out who killed Bosco, not who he was sleeping with. I suggest we go a tad slower with the little lady—"

"You haven't seen her." Race laughed "Bosco lived large in more ways than one."

"To each his own," Campos said. "How about we just hint that we know about her affair, see where that leads?"

"How exactly do we do that?"

"Let's play it by ear. Ask indirect questions, see where things go. Let her sweat a little. You ever play poker, Race?"

Race shook his head.

"You should. It would help you a better interrogator. If Mrs. Godgifu doesn't know what cards we're holding, who knows what she's liable to tell us."

Campos patted Race on the shoulder and started down the hill to the Godgifu mansion. At the wrought iron gate, they flashed their badges before the security camera and the maid buzzed them in.

As they walked down the driveway, the mansion came into view. As impressive as the Billings-Li home, it was a Richard Meier-style building with a white porcelain-panel and glass exterior, soaring roof lines, and sharp angles. Dense foliage of exotic jungle plants, ferns, and flowering vines covered the yard. The end of the driveway was circular and in the center stood an ornate fountain shooting water into the air and showering a marble sculpture of the birth of Aphrodite.

Race and Campos took the walkway to the front door. They crossed a foot bridge, which spanned an artificial stream, ending in a pond where various colored koi—the size of kindergarten children—swam lazily among the lily pads and water grasses. Bird of Paradise plants the size of mastodons grew on either side of the glass door. Race rang the bell. Chimes echoed inside the house followed by footsteps on marble, and the door opened.

It was Mrs. Godgifu.

She was a moderately attractive, thirty-something woman, a tad overweight, yet solidly built. She wore a floral silk shawl thrown over a sea-green cashmere sweater, carbon-black slacks, and low-heeled ivory loafers. A silver pendant necklace with a blood-red ruby hung down to her ample chest, a diamond and ruby tennis bracelet adorned her wrist, and ruby stud earrings nestled gleaming in each lobe.

She stood in the middle of the doorway, blocking the way. "Detective." Her voice was acidic, her eyes narrow slits. She looked Race up and down, then gestured with her chin toward Campos. "And who is this?"

"This is Officer Campos," Race said. "If you don't mind, we have a few questions to ask you, Mrs. Godgifu."

She moved her arms away from her body and the shawl spread out, making her look larger. Her floral perfume wafted their way. "Ask away."

Race paused. This wasn't the reception he received the first time he and Beela interviewed Mrs. Godgifu. He wondered if she was more comfortable talking to a female detective. Or perhaps her reticence might be caused by something he was doing. Although he wanted to ask Campos for help, he didn't think it wise; like a wolf, Godgifu would probably sense weakness and pounce.

Race craned his neck and looked over her shoulder; the uniformed maid stood with eyes downcast, wringing her hands. Before entering the house, he and Campos agreed to not open with the adultery card, but Godgifu's attitude, and the cowering maid, irked him.

"Mrs. Godgifu. We've come across evidence that you may not find pleasant. We've analyzed Mr. Bosco's OmniPhone records, and there are numerous calls between the two of you, and they occur when your husband is out of the country."

Godgifu's mouth thinned and her lips turned down. She crossed her arms protectively across her chest and glared at him.

Race didn't break eye contact.

"When Detective White and I interviewed you yesterday, you told us you…your exact words were that you 'barely know Mr. Bosco.' Yet, you called him, and he you, more than twenty times in the last year."

"What are you implying?" She looked daggers at Race. "Mr. Bosco is—was—my neighbor, nothing more. This interview is over."

She backed up a step and went to close the door.

Race leaped forward and his brand new shoes slipped on the polished marble floor. Off balance, he stumbled; his head landed on Godgifu's bosom and sank into the pillow-like softness. Her eyes softened and her hips seemed to move imperceptibly closer to his. He grabbed her arm with both hands to right himself. Beneath her velvety sweater, her arms were thick, rock hard.

Race straightened up, then pulled out a set of handcuffs. "I'm going to have to take you into the station on suspicion of murder." The gambit had worked well with Kojacy, so he thought it would work with this bird. He held the handcuffs toward her. "Please turn around and put your hands behind your back."

The momentary softness in Godgifu's eyes hardened. Her face turned red, veins bulged from her neck. She yelled, the words echoing off the stark marble walls of the foyer. "What the hell are you doing? Are you crazy? My daughter gets out of school in a couple of hours. I've got to pick her up!" She pointed a finger at Race. "I'm going to call my lawyer! You'll be sorry. You don't know who you're fucking with!"

Campos took his time, walking as if on an afternoon stroll, and stepped between the two. "Mrs. Godgifu, please calm down," he said in a tone that was at once gentle, yet authoritative. "If you just answer the detective's questions, we'll be out of your hair in a few minutes. But you need to tell the truth, otherwise we'll have to bring you in."

Godgifu glared at Race, her nostrils flared, and her breathing was shallow and rapid. "Do I need a lawyer?"

Campos put a hand on her shoulder. "Not if you didn't do anything. Although, if you want a lawyer, we can take you down to the police station and resume the questioning there when he arrives."

"Let's talk in the study." She turned brusquely on her heel and walked away, limping slightly. Not looking over her back, she gave off an air that she expected Race and Campos to follow her like servants.

They dutifully followed her through the marbled foyer and into a two-story room. One area was dominated by an ornately-carved elm and burl wood desk, the other by a fireplace and sitting arrangement. Godgifu sat on a leather couch, Race and Campos sank into a pair of burgundy-colored leather chairs facing her. The maid stood just inside the door and fidgeted with her apron strings.

Godgifu yelled to the maid. "Bring my guests something to drink." Then she muttered something unintelligible under her breath.

The maid nodded her head without taking her eyes from the floor. As she turned to leave, Godgifu yelled, "And some snacks." She caught Race's disapproving look and added in a normal tone of voice, "Please."

The maid kept her eyes averted as she disappeared from sight.

Godgifu muttered, "Jesus Christ." She looked toward Race and Campos. "You wouldn't believe how hard it is to find good help."

Race nodded. "I have the same problem."

Campos smiled. Godgifu shot him an angry look.

Race sat quietly, waiting her out.

Godgifu leaned forward and rearranged items on the marble coffee table that separated her from the officers. She sighed deeply, seeming to regain her composure.

"I'll tell you the truth," she said. "But please don't let this information out of this room. I have a young daughter and would hate for her to find out what her mother's been doing."

"We can't make any promises," Campos said. "But it's unlikely what you tell us will make its way to your daughter."

She nodded a few times while she pulled the shawl around her shoulders. "Okay, okay. I wasn't completely honest with you before. I'd been having an on-again, off-again affair with Bosco." Race nodded for her to continue. "Leo," she turned to Campos, "my husband," she looked back to Race, "he travels a lot on business. He's a very successful importer-exporter. We'd been here about five years before Bosco moved in next door. He threw a house warming-party, invited the neighbors up and down the street. Leo and I went. The houses here are pretty well separated from each other and we don't see our other neighbors very often."

Race remained silent. He knew that free association, or using open-ended questions to encourage open sharing, could be quite revealing. He'd used the trick many times while working undercover for Vice—a technique he'd learned from his own therapist, who'd often used it on him.

"At the party," Godgifu said, "we introduced ourselves to our new neighbor. When Leo told Bosco that he was in the import-export business and had high level contacts in North and South Korea, Bosco's ears seemed to prick up. He asked Leo a lot of questions and wanted to find out how high up Leo's contacts were. When Leo told Bosco that he spends over half the year overseas, Bosco glanced my way. He had a little grin and a sparkle in his eye. He looked me up and down, like he was grading a side of beef. Before he excused himself, he asked for Leo's card, said he might have a business proposition for him. We had a few glasses of wine and mingled, eventually Bosco caught me by myself. That's when he hit on me."

She looked at Race and nodded her head, as if to say, "I can still turn heads."

"He said that if I needed company when Leo was out of the country, I should call him. Or come over. When he said 'company' I knew what he was talking about. I told him Leo was all the company I needed. He said he understood, but if I should be lonely in the future, I should drop by."

The maid tiptoed into the room pushing a cart with a teapot and a platter with assorted Girl Scout cookies.

"See anything you like?" Godgifu said, staring at Race with a smile.

"I'll have a spot of tea," Race said with an impish smile.

Campos shot a look at Race while he nodded to the maid.

The maid poured three cups of tea and handed them out. She picked up the platter and offered cookies to the officers. When she turned toward her employer, she bumped her knee on the coffee table and half the cookies fell to the floor. She bent to clean up the mess.

Godgifu flew out of her seat. Her face turned beet red, and her veins looked like they were about to burst. "Damn it!" She yelled. "You— " She stopped and looked over at the officers. She took a number of deep breaths, then said through clenched teeth, "Clean up the mess. When we're done in here, come back and vacuum."

Godgifu sat down and sipped her tea in silence. The maid picked up the cookies and slunk out of the room.

Godgifu took a couple deep breaths. Her color came back and she acted as if nothing happened. "Where was I?"

"You were at Mr. Bosco's house warming party," Race said over his cup of tea. "That was five years ago, when he moved in, right?"

"Something like that. After the party, I'd see him every so often, jogging down the street, at neighborhood functions, sometimes across the back fence. He continued to let me know the offer was still on the table. He was persistent, but not obnoxious. To tell you the truth, I was flattered to have such a good looking guy interested in me."

Godgifu reached forward, picked up a Thin Mints, and popped it in her mouth. Between chews she said, "In the meantime, I had learned about Bosco. Enough for my purposes. I can see his patio and pool from our deck. He always had lots of young, pretty girls over, but he didn't seem to get attached to any one woman. I knew his type, and actually that's what interested me. Eventually, I succumbed to his advances. Leo was away for longer periods of time, and I was pretty sure that he was having affairs with girls in Korea. I thought, what the hell? I might as well have a little fun too, and there was no chance Donny would get attached to me."

Race chewed on a Caramel deLites and waited for her to continue.

She remained quiet, and Campos said, "How often did you and Mr. Bosco get together?"

Godgifu cleared her throat. "I told you, Bosco had tons of girlfriends. Occasionally, one of his girlfriends didn't spend the night, and if I saw he was free, I'd sneak over—our back yards are adjacent—and crawl in bed with him. He was amazing, even after spending the evening with another woman he was, how to put it politely, continuously aroused. I hadn't seen anything like that since high school."

Race felt his face flush and took a sip of tea. "You mentioned Mr. Bosco had a business proposition for your husband. Did they work together?"

Godgifu nodded and inhaled another Thin Mints. "My husband's from the Fu clan in Manchuria, in what is now North Korea. Leo went to school over there, he's fluent in Korean and Mandarin. Because of his Manchu heritage, he was able to forge bonds with many of the influential people in North Korea. He's close friends with the president, Kim something or other. Bosco had lots of wealthy clients here, and Leo helped him invest their money in Korea." She leaned forward and spoke in a conspiratorial voice. "Personally, I think a lot of the currency Bosco was investing was dirty, and the two of them were using Leo's diplomatic status to launder it through North Korea."

Race sat forward. "What makes you think that?"

Godgifu laughed. "Bosco talks in his sleep. Plus, I'm not stupid. Nobody makes those kinds of returns on investment."

"What would your husband do with the money he handled for Mr. Bosco?"

"Leo doesn't have to go through customs when he enters or leaves either of the Koreas, he can move suitcases across borders without any problem. He uses the money to buy Korean goods—container-loads of electronics which he ships back here using a company he and Bosco formed."

Race rubbed his chin. He thought what Godgifu was describing made sense and could be the thing that linked Bosco to the killings of the Russian courier and Dr. Sing—if he could find out what the courier was transporting.

"Did Mr. Bosco and your husband have dealings with Russians?"

"I think either of them would trade with the devil if there was money involved."

Race chuckled, thinking what she said was probably true. "Let me ask again. Did either of them talk about dealing with Russians?"

Godgifu shook her head. "They didn't. With all the trips Bosco made to Las Vegas, I'll bet he was laundering money from there."

"Do you know if Mr. Bosco and your husband had a falling out?"

"As far as I can tell, the scheme was working perfectly. Leo now had something to export—cash—to go along with his importing business."

Race stood up, ready to leave.

Godgifu remained seated and held up her hand. "Please, sit back down, Detective. There was something else I didn't tell you yesterday. I so was shaken by the news of Bosco's death, I wasn't thinking straight." Her face softened. "You understand?"

Race sat down. "Go on."

"Last Saturday, I took my daughter to sell Girl Scout cookies in the neighborhood. We left right after dinner, around five; I wanted to get home before dark. The first house we stopped at was Bosco's. His gate was open. As I told you yesterday, there was a car with Nevada plates parked on the side of the garage. If I recall correctly, it was dark gray, maybe black, a four-door sedan. I don't know much about cars, so I can't tell you what make it was."

She stopped talking and eyed the cookies.

"Go on," Race said.

She picked up another cookie and tossed it down. She looked across at Race. "I was planning to see Bosco that evening, so I thought it would be fun to see his expression when my daughter and I were at the door. We rang the bell. But it wasn't Bosco who answered. It was a very frightening man." A shiver went through Godgifu's body. "He scared both of us."

"What was so frightening about him?"

"He had a burn scar on the left side of his face, near his eye," she pointed to the spot on her own face, "and the left eye itself was damaged. A milky-white color, very dull...," Godgifu's entire body shook again, "heinous, hideous. My daughter grabbed my hand so hard it hurt and she hid behind me. This guy had a mean, angry expression to go with that scary eye. He was well over six feet tall—taller than my husband—very broad and muscular. Bigger than Bosco. When he asked me what I wanted, he spoke with a heavy Irish brogue. My daughter peered from behind my dress and peeped that she was selling Girl Scout cookies. He smiled down at us, which in some ways was even more frightening than when he was scowling. He said he'd love to buy some. He pulled out a fifty and handed it to Thomasina, my daughter. She asked what kind of cookies he wanted and he said any type would be okay. He laughed with malevolent intent and told us he was visiting his cousin, to just to deliver the cookies to him when they arrived."

Race gave her a hard look. "It's hard to believe you would have forgotten something like that yesterday."

Godgifu glared at Race and crossed her arms over her chest. "Well, I did. And there was something else. The whole time we were talking to the Irishman, there was some sort of noise coming from the house, like an electric drill or saw."

"An electric drill?" Campos asked. "Like the kind you use around the house?"

She paused for a second and shook her head. "It seemed higher pitched…like a dentist's drill." She paused again and smiled. "Funny, the reason I think I associated the sound of the drill with the dentist, is that the Irishman was wearing latex gloves, like a dentist would wear."

Race and Campos looked at each other.

"He was wearing gloves. Seems odd you didn't mention that earlier," Campos said.

Godgifu shot him a hard look. "With that scary eye he had, it was hard to remember anything else."

"Fair enough," Race said. "Is there anything else you remember?"

She shook her head, still glaring at Campos.

Race stood back up. "Sorry for the way the interview started, Mrs. Godgifu. I do want to thank you for your cooperation. We'll let you get on with your day."

"Just a minute," Campos said. "Mrs. Godgifu, was your husband aware you were having an affair with Bosco?"

She shrugged. "I don't think so. But you have to understand, my husband is a Buddhist, he's a little more accepting."

"You don't think he would have a problem with what you and Mr. Bosco were doing?"

"I don't really know, and I don't want to find out." She stood up and laughed sarcastically. "Leo might even have been relieved that he didn't have to *service* me." She took a step toward the door. "Now, I have things to do."

Campos stood and he and Race followed Godgifu to the foyer. She opened the door and when Campos looked away, she gave Race a quick wink. "I hope I've been helpful."

Race felt a shiver go down his spine and gave her a shy nod. The officers left and as they walked across the foot bridge, Race kept his head down, shuffling his feet. "Pulling out the handcuffs like that," he muttered. "I don't know if that was the right thing to do."

Campos patted Race on the shoulder. "Don't be so hard on yourself, sport. You really got Godgifu talking. I'd say that was a genius move on your part."

The compliment coming from an experienced cop sent Race's spirits sky-high. Campos kept his hand on Race's shoulder, and everything seemed perfect. If he only could have had just one moment like this with his father. "I probably just caught a lucky break this time," he said.

Campos continued to smile at Race. "Give yourself some credit. I think that was more than luck."

Race nodded, thinking Campos could be right. "Did you notice how Godgifu kept referring to the deceased as 'Bosco'?"

Campos shook his head.

"She never used his first name."

Campos laughed. "I guess their relationship was one of convenience."

Race nodded. "And Godgifu told us Bosco looked at her like she was a piece of meat. I think it might have been the other way around."

Campos chuckled. "Maybe not initially, Race. But it sure seems that's the way it turned out."

"If Bosco was pursuing her, why were all the calls made from Godgifu's phone to his?"

"Those calls were made after Bosco hooked her. I'd be willing to bet she did put up a little fight."

"You really think so? Bosco didn't seem to have any problem finding younger, more attractive women."

Campos laughed. "Some guys, it's all about the pursuit. Once they land their catch, they put their rod right back in the water."

"That seems like a mixed metaphor, buddy."

Campos looked at Race impishly. "Aren't mixed metaphors a type of Girl Scout cookie?"

Race laughed. "I still think Godgifu was pursuing Bosco."

Campos stopped and turned to Race. "Tell me, what does that have to do with who murdered Bosco?"

"I've been thinking…maybe Godgifu got possessive. She became tired of sharing. Money and sex are strong motives for murder. It's not hard to imagine her beating Bosco to death," Race grimaced. "Did you see the way she looked at that poor maid? If looks could kill."

"Fortunately, they can't. But I see your point. What's with the story about the one-eyed Irishman? I bet she's throwing us a red herring."

Race shrugged. "Seems too weird to make up. I bet—" Helena's voice came through his earbud and Race held up his finger. "Just a second, Marcel. Helena has information she wants to send to my VR contacts." Race brought his wrist up to his face and said, "Helena, send the info to Officer Marcel Campos also, while you're at it."

Race's VR contacts turned orange, then the image of a driver's license photo appeared in his vision. The photos were of a hardened Irishman with a white, damaged eye surrounded by scar tissue. The name on the license was Olcas O'Suil.

Campos whistled. "Looks just like how Godgifu described him."

"Now I can understand how a murderer could answer the door at the crime scene," Race said.

Campos gave him a questioning look.

"Look at him," Race said. "He probably gets a kick out of scaring kids with that dead eye."

Campos nodded. "Godgifu wasn't throwing us a red herring after all."

Race shot Campos a wry smile. "No. She was serving up a white whale."

Chapter 29

There was no traffic on the neighborhood street, so Race and Campos walked downhill in the middle of the road and turned into Bosco's drive.

When they reached their cars, Race reached out to shake hands with Campos. "I appreciate the help. My partner's asked me to spend the rest of the day going through the crime scene."

Campos gave him a pat on the shoulder. "I'd like to have a look inside."

"If I knew you were coming," Race said with a laugh, "I would have tidied up the place."

Campos chuckled and gestured for Race to follow him to the front door.

Race reached into his pocket to remove the key for the house when his OmniPhone buzzed. There was an incoming call from La Joya of Melrose jewelry store.

"Detective, you won't believe what just happened." Mr. Raffles said with breathless excitement when Race picked up the call. "A big bodybuilder type just came in to have a Vacheron Constantin appraised. A skeleton watch." His voice dropped to a whisper. "Like the one you're looking for!"

Race's jaw dropped. "No shit. Is he there with you now?"

Raffles continued to speak in a whisper. "I told him the appraisal would take about an hour. He said he'd wait next door at the pizza place. You can catch him if you hurry down."

"We're on our way. Stall him if you need to." Race cut the connection.

"Couldn't help but overhear," Campos said. "You told Raffles that 'we're' on our way. I guess that means you'd like my help?"

Race hesitated. He didn't mean it that way, but Campos had been very helpful. And Race had never arrested a murder suspect before. "You wouldn't mind?"

"Hell no!" Campos broke out with a big smile. "This is the most excitement I've had in months." He patted his service pistol. "And if this is that O'Suil character, you'll need backup."

It felt good to have someone to help with the case. Race knew the police force was strapped for money, but still couldn't grasp how they could send him out with so little training. This took learning on the job to a new level—a level he didn't feel comfortable with. At least Campos took the initiative to jump in and help. He might as well take advantage of his experience. "What do you suggest, Marcel?"

Campos seemed to have a plan in mind and answered immediately. "When we get to the jewelers, park in front of the beauty salon, then walk over to the store. My car spells police. I'll park across the street at the high-rise and meet you at the entrance to the store. We don't want to scare this guy off before we can nab him." Campos paused before stepping into his cruiser. "Oh, and thanks for including me."

They jumped into their cars, Race following Campos. When they reached the main cross-street, Campos turned on his flashing lights and sirens and peeled off down the road toward Sunset Boulevard. Race placed a blue flashing light on the roof of his car and was about to pull out of the neighborhood and follow Campos when a semi pulling a slate gray trailer with at least twenty-six wheels came up the hill and blocked the exit. Race hit his steering wheel in frustration. He snapped his anxiety bracelet, worried that he'd miss the action at the jewelers, as the truck driver grinded gears and the vehicle struggled to inch up the incline. When the truck passed, Race weaved through the line of cars trailing the truck, then raced down the road as cars pulled to the side to let him pass. With his Nav-Drive off, he felt the exhilaration of the sports engine under the hood as the car topped one hundred miles per hour on the winding road. Heart pounding, he caught up to Campos about a half mile before Sunset. They sped through intersections, passed vehicles pulled over to the side, and were back in Hollywood within a few minutes. When they were within a couple blocks of the jewelers, Campos turned off his sirens and slowed to join traffic. Race removed the flashing light from his car and followed behind the patrol car.

Race pulled into the shopping center, found a parking spot in front of the cleaners, and waited in front of La Joya for Campos to join him from across the street. As he stood outside the entrance to the jewelers, an impossibly tall, hulking man—resembling more a grizzly bear reared up on its hind legs than a man—exited the pizza parlor, ducking as he passed through the door. His neck was thicker than both Race's thighs put together, and he filled out his blazer with slabs of muscle. He walked like a typical bodybuilder; arms too beefy to hang loosely at his sides, thighs so thick he waddled. The giant looked down and nodded as he walked past Race and entered the store.

A jolt of fear coursed through Race's body. He reached down and snapped his anxiety band, which did absolutely nothing other than cause his wrist to burn.

Campos scurried across the street. He'd gone through a metamorphosis. His face was deadly serious, his pupils widened, his nostrils flared. His body seemed to crackle with adrenaline, setting Race's neurons ablaze.

"You look like you just saw a ghost, buddy," Campos said to Race when he reached the sidewalk.

Race felt his breathing quicken. He tried to remain calm. "I think I just saw our man. Raffles said the guy who brought the watch in was a giant. He wasn't kidding."

"Is it O'Suil?"

Race shook his head. "Somebody else. The biggest man I've ever seen."

Campos took a step toward Race and looked him straight in the eye, unblinking. "Here's what we do. Go in the store and talk to one of the clerks like you're a customer. I'll clue the guard in on what we're doing. He can alert his colleagues in the monitoring office and have the doors lock if our man tries to make a run for it."

Race said he understood.

Race entered and the door chimed. He walked over to Philippe, pretending to be interested in diamond engagement rings. He glanced around. The giant was across the room talking to the manager. Raffles held a watch in his hands, nestled in a blue velvet cloth and craned his head to talk to his client, eyes reaching only to the giant's sequoia-like chest. Although the big man wore a sport coat and tie and smiled benignly, Race was nervous with a primal fear. He instinctively knew the behemoth could pick him up and crush him without blinking an eye.

The door chimed and Campos entered the store. Campos spoke quietly to the security guard, then headed to where Mr. Bodybuilder was standing in rapt conversation and stopped about five feet away.

"Nicko, what brings you to my part of town?" Campos said.

The giant turned. "Marcel, hi." He stuttered. "I…just came in to pick up my watch." The giant's voice was deep and bone-rattling.

Campos waved Race over. "Nick Painter. This is Detective Griffin. We'd like to speak to you privately about that watch."

Painter turned pale and beads of perspiration appeared on his brow. He pulled a handkerchief out of his coat pocket and dabbed at the sweat. The goliath's eyes darted between the two officers and he fidgeted with his sausage-like fingers. "What's wrong, Marcel? I'd just like to get my watch back. I'm pretty busy."

"*Tranquilo*," Campos spoke quietly and slowly. "Nothing to worry about. Detective Griffin just has a few questions to ask you about that watch. You answer them correctly, and you can be on your way."

The giant's eyes took in both officers, then he glanced at the door.

Campos moved his hand to his service belt, but before he could pull out his ElectroLaser, the giant moved forward with remarkable speed. More concrete slab than hand, he hit the officers with such force that Race was propelled backwards at least five feet. He hit the side of one of the cases and fell to the ground in a heap. Campos lie across the store, limp beside a tipped display case filled with scattered timepieces.

Painter lumbered to the door and pushed. It was locked. Race stumbled to his feet and pulled out his ElectroLaser.

The giant stepped back a couple paces, put his shoulder down, and rushed the glass door. The shatterproof glass was true to its name and didn't shatter. Instead, the entire door exploded off the frame and the hinges flew into the parking lot. The giant lost his balance and landed on the sidewalk atop the door.

While Painter scrambled to get up, Race sprinted over to the opening where the door once was. He pointed his stun gun at the giant. A red dot appeared on the man's back and Race pulled the trigger. With a sound of distant lightening, two bolts of blue light shot out from his gun and onto the man's back. The gun made a rapid clicking sound. Painter's body went limp. He screamed and moaned so loudly Race was afraid the man was dying. While the gun was still clicking and Painter's body paralyzed, Race moved forward and pulled out his set of metal handcuffs. He bent down and tried to place a cuff around the immobilized man's wrist. Painter's wrist was thicker than Race's thigh and the cuff didn't even go halfway around.

The gun stopped clicking. The giant stopped moaning and began moving his arms.

Painter rolled on his back and sat up. "Don't shoot me with that thing again," he said with a tone of fear.

Campos came up from behind Race and placed zip tie handcuffs on Painter's wrists, the ends barely coming together. The two officers helped the giant to his feet.

Campos rubbed his neck and appeared to be in pain. "You're not carrying are you, Nick?" He said.

Painter nodded, a look of defeat in his eyes. "I have a concealed weapons permit."

Race reached inside the giant's sport coat and pulled a Glock out of the shoulder holster. He handed it to Campos.

Painter was shaking as he looked up at them. "Look, I'm sorry I tried to run. Let me tell you the truth. This is all a mistake. What am I being charged with?"

"You're being charged with grand theft," Race said.

"And assaulting a police officer," Campos added, rubbing his neck.

Painter looked down at the ground, shook his head, and sighed. His chest moved spasmodically and he sniffled, trying to stifle a sneeze. His head went back once, twice, then he let out a gale-force sneeze. There was a popping sound and the zip tie handcuffs snapped and flew into the parking lot. Race reached down, picked his ElectroLaser up from the ground, and aimed the red dot at Painter's chest.

Painter raised his hands over his head and shook. "Don't shoot me with that thing again."

A smile creased Campos' face. "Let's put Mr. Painter in my patrol car, then we can process the scene." The officer sent a signal for his car's Nav-Drive to retrieve itself.

Race kept the red dot centered on Painter's chest and looked around. All the doors in the strip center were open. A small crowd had gathered and formed a semi-circle around them.

"You can all leave now," Campos said, shooing them away. "Show's over."

One by one, people left as Campos's patrol car pulled up to the curb. Campos helped the giant into the back of the car, then closed the door, locking him inside.

"You know that guy?" Race asked Campos.

"That's Nicolas 'Demento' Painter. Used to wrestle under the name of Captain Demento. Now he's an honest, hardworking security consultant."

Race slid the ElectroLaser back in his jacket and shuddered, the adrenaline rush subsiding. "I thought he was going to kill us."

Campos let out a short laugh. "He could have if he wanted to. I imagine he was just frightened and wanted to flee."

Raffles, Philippe, and two other jewelry store staff milled around wide-eyed, gazing at the destroyed entrance that looked like it had been plowed into by a charging rhino. Race suggested to the manager that they go to the back to talk. Campos said he'd keep an eye on Painter.

Stunned and walking like a zombie, Raffles wrapped the watch in the velvet cloth and led Race to the back of the store. After they took seats in the office, he handed the cloth to Race.

When Race pulled out the watch and looked down at the piece, a strange feeling came over him, similar to when he had been hypnotized in therapy. He became mesmerized by the chronograph. It indeed was a platinum Vacheron Constantin timepiece, with a rectangular face surrounded by over a hundred sparkling diamonds. The inside was transparent, revealing hundreds of moving parts flowing in perfect synchronization; wheels, springs, levers, jewel-toothed cogs, and other nameless parts. He couldn't take his eyes off the timepiece.

"You might be interested in the following," Raffles said, looking at his monitor. "Vacheron Constantin maintains a database, a registry of the owners of their watches. I took the liberty and contacted the company. Using the timepiece's serial number, they told me this watch was purchased by Mr. Donny Bosco in Geneva, Switzerland, five years ago."

Race didn't say anything and continued to stare mindlessly at the chronograph, watching the intricate movements of countless miniature gem-toothed gears moving another.

"It's a custom design," Raffles said, consulting the screen. "A true work of art. The parts are made of a platinum-rhodium alloy—rhodium by the way is the most expensive of all the precious metals, and extremely difficult to work with. The case is platinum, the band is alligator with a platinum-rhodium clasp. The crystal is quite unique. It's not glass, but rather a diamond composite material, almost shatterproof. And it wasn't cheap. Mr. Bosco paid the equivalent of 510,000 SDR in Swiss Francs."

Race snapped out of his trance and let out a whistle. "510,000 SDR. ¡*Puta madre*!"

Chapter 30

Campos helped Race handle the chain of custody for the watch, then told him to use his patrol car to bring Painter in to be booked. Campos said he'd handle the crime scene. Before Race stepped into the squad car, Campos leaned over and whispered to him, "Good job, Detective. You may have solved your first case."

Race didn't think it was going to be that easy. Something in his gut told him that the one-eyed Irishman was Bosco's killer, not Painter.

At the police station, Race took Painter in the front entrance and the desk clerk booked his suspect. Race then escorted him upstairs to the squad room.

Beane, who had been alerted by Helena, sat at a desk in a far corner.

"Detective Griffin," the captain said, "let's take this gentleman to the holding cell."

The captain opened a door marked Interrogation Room I. The room was narrow and windowless, the walls were padded. They led Painter to a metal table bolted to the floor. A one-way mirror took up most of one wall. Minicams were located in all four corners of the room and above the mirror.

Beane pointed to one of the three metal chairs in the room. "Take a seat," he told Painter.

Painter sat down, defeated and mumbled. "I need to call my lawyer."

Beane rolled his eyes and cursed under his breath. "Sure thing, Painter. Whatever you want."

Beane locked the door, then he and Race went to one of the DataPorts while they waited for Painter's lawyer to show. Helena's avatar hovered above the table.

"Helena informed me about your recent interview with Mrs. Godgifu," Beane said to Race and shook his hand. "Looks like you might have solved your first case. The man she described fits a man named Olcas O'Suil to a tee."

Race gave him a smile. "Now all we have to do is pick him up."

Race thought it over. He didn't think Painter killed Bosco, but believed O'Suil certainly did. Either way, he'd solved the crime.

"Helena, could you brief us on what you were able to pull up on this O'Suil character?" Beane said.

"Ireland does not have their entire fingerprint registry online," Helena said. "I contacted the General Registry Office in Dublin. The office was closing, but I was able to convince one of the clerks to stay after hours. She emailed O'Suil's prints to me."

"Good job," Beane said. "By the way, how did you get a government employee to stay after hours? The clerks here cut you off mid-sentence when it's time for them to go home."

Helena gave them a sly look and spoke with an Italian accent. "I made her an offer she could not refuse."

"Are you in the mafia?" Beane said with a laugh.

"Tell us what you did," Race said. "We'd never break *omertà*."

"I hacked into the Pope's calendar," Helena said. "I scheduled a half-hour private audience with His Holiness and the Irish lass."

Both Race and Beane cracked up laughing.

"I didn't think your programming allowed you to break laws," Beane said.

"It might be frowned upon, but it is not illegal to make an appointment with the Pope."

Beane wiped the laughter tears from his eyes. "Do we have a fingerprint match?"

"I used my proprietary algorithms to match O'Suil's prints to those previously marked unknown from the Bosco house. In one of the guest bathrooms upstairs, there was a match with O'Suil. I asked the crime lab here to verify my finding. For now, we can assume that Olcas O'Suil was at Bosco's house."

"And during the time frame Bosco was killed," Race said.

"That may be Painter's get out of jail free card," Beane added.

"We still have him for stealing Bosco's watch."

Beane nodded. "Painter has a clean record. If the crime wasn't premeditated, I bet his lawyer could plead him to probation and community service."

"That watch is valued at over a half-million SDR," Race said.

Beane whistled. "That changes things, doesn't it?"

The wall monitor came alive, and the visage of the evil-eyed Irishman appeared. "Here are a few photos of Person of Interest Olcas O'Suil," Helena said.

Race's eyes were immediately drawn to the scarred and dead white eye of the Irishman; it had the look of a rolled back shark's eye as it readies to eat its prey. Discolored scarred tissue surrounded the eye. A cold smirk played on his lips.

"It is what we know about the POI," Helena said. "He is originally from Ireland, born somewhere on the Bog of Allen, in the central part of the country. His father worked for a state owned company called *Bord na Móna*. He was probably born at home. His family lived in a peat house."

Race interrupted. "A *what* house?"

"A peat house." Helena spoke as if reading an article. "Peat is an accumulation of partly decomposed vegetation and is usually found in wet, boggy areas. It can be cut into square or rectangular bricks. The house is built dug down into the ground, it has earthen walls, peat bricks form the roof of the abode. Similar to the sod houses in Iceland or on the old American prairie." A photo of a peat house appeared on the monitor replacing O'Suil's leering mug.

"Sounds like a gruesome way to live," Race said.

"Beats living inside a computer chip," Helena said with a laugh. "There is no official birth certificate for O'Suil. A midwife probably handled the delivery and never recorded the event, not uncommon in the Irish bog area. The first time O'Suil pops up in the official records was when he was six. He was brought to a local emergency room for third degree burns on his face. Apparently, O'Suil's parents were fighting. The lad's mother was boiling potatoes and threw the pot of scalding water at her husband. She missed and hit the kid."

Both Race and Beane cringed.

"O'Suil underwent both skin and corneal transplants in Dublin. When he was sent home, his parents didn't follow through with the recommended post-op care. That is how he ended up with the keloids—or scar tissue—that you see on his face, and the permanent scarring of the cornea. He is completely blind in the left eye. The distinctive milky-white appearance of his eye is what Bosco's neighbor noted in her witness interview."

"I can understand why Godgifu's daughter was so afraid when they came to the door," Race said.

Beane nodded. "You'd think O'Suil would at least wear sunglasses in public."

"From the smirk on his face in the photo," Race said, "I'd say he likes scaring people."

Helena projected a different photo of O'Suil on the monitor, this one from when he was a teenager in Ireland. He had the hardened face and insolent sneer even back then.

"O'Suil spent his early years in and out of juvenile detention," Helena said. "Petty crimes like drug peddling and shoplifting. He also became involved in the Irish separatist movement and was a low-level soldier. He peddled drugs to help support the movement and provided muscle to help shake down local merchants. He disappeared from Ireland after being accused of raping a run-away girl who turned out to be the daughter of a prominent member of the Brazilian government. He turned up later in Boston, and was soon working for a man named Freddy Freeman. Freeman, at the time, was running a strip club in Boston for the Irish mafia. Now, he is the general manager of the Puce Palomino, the high-end strip club in Las Vegas. He brought O'Suil with him to Nevada."

"How about this?" Race said. "O'Suil was casing Bosco, finds out he's loaded, follows him home, and kills him in a robbery."

Beane shook his head. "If that were the case, why didn't he steal the watch? That thing's worth a fortune."

"Maybe he was after something much more valuable," Race said. "Ask yourself: why did Bosco *drive* to Las Vegas? Especially now, with the wildfires. Why didn't he take the bullet train?"

Beane made a "huh" noise and rubbed his chin. "I hadn't thought of that angle. But now that you mention it, it does seem suspicious. You're thinking Bosco was transporting something valuable back from Las Vegas?"

"That is a good point, Detective Griffin," Helena said. "I had not considered that, either."

Race felt a surge of pride rush through his veins, especially after the screw-ups earlier in the day.

"I finished analyzing the fingerprints of the man you have in the holding cell," Helena said. "Painter's fingerprints match those found on the nightstand in Bosco's master bedroom."

"Thank you, Helena," Beane said. "Things just keep getting worse for Mr. Painter."

Race tried to put all the information together. They were only on day three, and investigation was going well, maybe too well. They now had two prime suspects: O'Suil and Painter. They were both at the scene of the crime. Now the job was to figure out which one of them actually killed Bosco.

Race turned to Beane. "Captain, do you think Painter killed Bosco?"

"Probably not, Race. But I'd like to interview the giant before coming to conclusions. But my money's on the Irishman." He looked to Helena. "Put out an APB for O'Suil."

"I did that hours ago," she said, then gave him a coy smile, "But thanks for asking."

Race's OmniPhone rang. When he looked down to check his phone, the call was from Klaas Bruin. "I should take this. I'll just be a second." Race answered and listened to the voice coming through his earbud.

"Race, sorry I didn't call you back right away. I got tied up. How can I help you?"

Race turned toward the hologram. Helena looked back at him with a Delphic visage and the slightest smile on her lips. *Helena must have put in the call for me. Can she mimic my voice?*

The voice on the other end continued. "You mentioned you wanted to talk to me sometime today. I'm in West Hollywood and can meet you in the Golden Triangle. There's a great Indian buffet there. How about a late lunch? It's on me, buddy."

Race put his call on hold and asked Beane if he should wait for Painter's lawyer to arrive.

Beane shook his head. "Go ahead and meet with Bruin—you might learn something of value." Race stood up. "Take your time," Beane said. "We'll interview the Incredible Hulk when you get back. His lawyer can cool his jets."

"I'll see you in twenty minutes," Race told Bruin. "And save some food for me."

Chapter 31

Klaas Bruin had told Race to meet him at an Indian buffet restaurant a block off Santa Monica Boulevard near Rodeo Drive. Race pulled up to the restaurant and found there was no street parking. He pulled his car into the valet area and an attendant came running up to open his door.

Race placed his LOPD identification on the dash. "Don't move the car," he said. "I'm on police business."

He walked inside and was inundated by the aroma of cumin, coriander, and other Indian spices he couldn't identify. He was suddenly famished. He scanned the room and found the nattily dressed Bruin eating alone on the other side. It was hard to miss him dressed in his usual black and silk—black silk blazer, black fitted shirt, a floral silk tie on a black background, black linen-silk slacks, and black Italian dress shoes. And Bruin's hallmark, hanging from his blazer pocket like a melting clock from a Dalí painting, a cosmic latte colored pocket scarf embroidered with a bright crimson rose.

Race walked up to the table. Bruin, fork in hand, was digging into his plate piled high with goat vindaloo and naan bread.

"Couldn't wait to hit the buffet?" Race said.

Bruin looked up in mid-chew, a somewhat startled look on his face. He gazed at Race a moment, then broke into a big smile.

"Long time no see, buddy. I didn't recognize you at first with the short hair and the sport coat." He stood up, pulled Race to him, and kissed him on both cheeks. Then he gave Race a bear hug.

"You must be getting a lot of Russian clients," Race said.

"*Da*. They're my best customers." Bruin gestured to one of the empty chairs. "So, now you're working homicide. When did that happen?" Bruin seemed genuinely interested.

"This is my first week, really only my third day. I'm enjoying the change of scenery. Let me get a plate of food, and I'll join you in a flash-drive."

When Race returned, Bruin smiled and said, "Race, would you mind not recording this conversation on your police Omni? I don't want Helena overhearing what I'm about to tell you."

Race gave Bruin a quizzical look.

"It's for your own protection," Bruin said. "Ask the waiter to hold it for you, they do it all the time."

As Race undid the strap and took off his OmniPhone, he looked at Bruin through slitted eyes and tried to make sense of what was going on. Bruin knowing about Helena wasn't surprising—Race knew he'd always been one step ahead of the cops. He started wondering about what else Bruin knew and why the need for secrecy. Then he questioned if Helena eavesdropped on everything. He realized that might be helpful at times, but didn't really want her to monitor all his conversations. There would be things he wanted to keep private, so he decided he'd have to take the Omni off and leave it somewhere else at times.

Bruin flagged down a passing waiter. Race handed over his garish orange Omni. Bruin handed the waiter a twenty without saying a word.

When the waiter was out of earshot, Bruin said, "I pegged you for being undercover. I wouldn't have guessed LOPD though."

"Why's that, K?"

"The cocaine you were selling, almost always pharmaceutical grade. The only way to get that kind of *polvo* is right off the boats. I thought you were working for Customs. But the LOPD! Someone in the department must have a contact in Customs...or the coast guard...maybe even in South America itself."

Race nodded while sopping up curry sauce with a wedge of naan. Bruin was amazingly close to the truth, but Race wasn't about to tell him so. Or give him any specifics. "That was the first thing. What's the second?"

"You were very open about selling drugs, not worried about being arrested. Most people are a little more discrete. I figured you were trying to attract the big suppliers, make the big bust. You never did find them, did you?"

Race shook his head. "After seven years, I was burned out. No closer to finding Mr. Big than when I started."

"You know who the biggest supplier of *polvo* is in South California, even Vegas, you just can't admit it. I'm not going to say anymore. Maybe you really don't know. The less you know, the safer you are."

Race shrugged and continued eating. He wasn't sure what he meant about him knowing who the big fish is, and decided it was better to let that go since he was out of Vice anyway.

"You wanted to talk about Donny Bosco's murder?" Bruin said.

Race kept his head down and ate, trying not to show his surprise that Helena could imitate his voice, at least well enough to fool Bruin. What was amazing was that he'd only talked to Helena a couple times. And she'd picked up his voice that quickly.

Race finished his plate and looked over to Bruin. "It's probably no surprise to you that we found a number of your fingerprints in Bosco's home. We also discovered an impressive stash of drugs, which you must have supplied him.

Race thought about what Campos told him earlier, about being a poker player, and decided it might be a good time for a bluff. He looked at Bruin and put on his most serious face and said, "And, we have evidence placing you at the victim's house during the time frame when he was killed."

A look of concern crossed Bruin's face. He sat forward and grabbed Race's arm in his paw-like hand. "You don't think I killed Donny? Do you? He was one of my best customers. That would be like killing the goose who laid the golden egg."

"Why don't you tell me what you were doing at Bosco's house last weekend?"

Bruin sat back and caught his breath. "Last week, I got a call from Donny. He was in Vegas. He told me his stash was running low. He had plans to go sailing over the weekend, he needed to meet me before he left. Donny was big into *travka*, *polvo*, X's, meth, you name it. He went through enormous quantities, and he always wanted the best."

"I can see Bosco buying cocaine and meth from you," Race said. "But *travka*. You can buy marijuana legally from the smoke shops."

"As I said, Donny wanted the best. I have suppliers up in the Sierra Mountains who sell me their private stock. He was willing to pay extra for that. The only thing I didn't supply him with was *pizda*. Donny was able to find that on his own."

Race laughed. "No kidding. He was even getting that from the lady next door."

Bruin let out a short laugh. "That heifer! Donny really did live large." Bruin caught Race's eyes. He gave a slight shake of his head, a sad look descended over his face. "I think you would have liked him, Race. Hell, just about everyone liked Donny."

They both went back to the buffet.

While they were refilling their plates, Race said, "By the way, the bear hug, using terms like *travka, pizda…*"

"I have lots of Russian clients. They like to party and throw money around like there's no tomorrow."

They returned to the table and dug back in.

"We know you went to Bosco's house on Saturday," Race said. "What happened when you were there?"

"I swung by his house right before noon. I called him in the morning to see if he'd be home. I didn't get any answer, not too unusual for Donny, probably getting laid. I figured I'd swing by and drop the merchandise off. When I got to his house, there was a car parked in the driveway with Nevada plates. He spends a lot of time in Vegas, so I didn't think twice about that."

Race said between bites, "The car with Nevada plates. Can you describe it?"

"Sorry, I didn't really pay attention. It was dark, black maybe, four door, not very fancy. Kinda boxy shaped."

Race nodded. That matched what Godgifu had told him, so now he knew the car was there at least since noon.

"Go on. You were in the driveway."

"I went to the front door and rang the bell. It sounded like someone was in the house, but no one answered. I figured it must be some workers, or the house cleaners—they often won't answer the door. I've dropped drugs off for Donny before. He usually keeps the patio door leading to his office unlocked. I went around back, the gate was unlocked, climbed the stairs and let myself into his office. The house seemed really creepy. I got a weird feeling like…something wasn't right. I put his stash in a desk drawer, and got out of there as fast as I could. Was Donny dead already?"

That was a good question, Race thought. What if Bosco was already dead? Blowflies can sense a dead body from miles away. Perhaps Bruin was smelling the same odors. Although he couldn't put his finger on it, he knew something was wrong.

Race realized Bruin was waiting for his reply, and said, "We don't know. I couldn't tell you even if we did. Did you go anywhere else besides the office?"

"No. I had a lot of deliveries to make. It was the weekend, busy time for me. And I wanted to get out of his house as fast as possible. I had a bad feeling. It made my skin crawl."

"Besides selling him drugs, did you know Bosco personally? Did you have any business dealings with him?"

Bruin shook his head. "Donny was in a much higher social strata than I am. I didn't have the money to invest in his businesses. I never really knew him very well. He did invite me to a couple of his private parties over the years, probably three or four times."

Race nodded, remembering that Billings-Li had mentioned Bosco's wild parties.

"What were the parties like?"

Bruin frowned as if he had bitten into a lemon. "It was the same thing every time, bizarre for a man with his sterling reputation. I've been to these types of parties before. They're thrown by entertainers, sports figures, not a serious businessman. He'd hire porn starlets and lyscees and have them swimming around in his pool naked. In addition to trays of food, there were trays of drugs scattered around the house. Most of his guests seemed uncomfortable and wouldn't stay long. But he did have a few guys, and a few gals, who seemed to like the drugs and women. They'd pluck a girl or two out of the pool, and off they'd go upstairs where the guest bedrooms are located. Personally, I'm afraid of those types of women. Who knows what they could be harboring?"

"Tell me about the friends Bosco had at these parties."

"I wouldn't say those people were his friends. I don't think a guy like Donny had real friends. He seemed to be sizing everyone up—men and women—to see what they could give him. You might want to find out exactly where he was getting all that money. I've found that the people who are the most profligate with money are those who are spending other people's kale."

"I'm not sure what profligate means, but we're looking into where Bosco was getting his kale."

"Do you have any solid leads? I see you've arrested Nick Painter."

Race grabbed Bruin's arm. "How the hell do you know that?"

"A friend at the jewelers told me. I didn't realize it was you who arrested him."

Race thought it over for a moment. The information would be on the TV news later that day, so he didn't think it mattered that Bruin already knew.

"Painter was trying to sell a very high priced...what did they call it... chronograph, what we common people would call a watch. It belonged to Bosco and was missing from his house."

Bruin took hold of Race's arm. "Nick's done some work for me. Sometimes clients are slow paying for merchandise. Nick pays them a visit and they start paying on time. I know he's huge, but he abhors violence. Because of his size, people are intimidated. He's never had to get physical. I can't see Nick killing Bosco, it would be bad for his business."

Race pulled his arm away from Bruin. "You may be right. We're waiting for his lawyer to show up before we take his statement."

"With all the money Bosco threw around, I bet he was ripping his investors off." Bruin finished his meal. "You know those rich old farts: you can screw their wives and they don't bat an eye, screw with their money and they're ruthless."

"We're looking into Bosco's finances."

"How much time has LOPD given you to work this case?"

"You know about that? Until the other day, I wasn't aware that murder investigations were limited in time, based on how rich or famous someone was. One of the first lessons I've learned is that as far as LOPD is concerned, the lives of the rich, powerful, or beautiful are worth more than the rest of us. But to answer your question, we were given two weeks."

"You'll need to find the real killer by then. If you don't, the DA will pin the murder on Painter. They're more concerned about closing cases than finding the real murderers."

"You're pretty cynical, K."

"That's because I've seen the dark underbelly of the law. I won't name names, but I supply some of the biggest politicians here. They tell me things candidly. A drug dealer is like a bartender or a priest, that way. The DA's under pressure to close cases, and on the cheap. You better bust your ass to find Donny's killer. Nick's fate is in your hands." Bruin sopped up the remaining curry with his naan. "Well, old buddy. Time to get back to work."

Race stood up and gave the much taller Bruin a bear hug, minus the cheek kissing, and said, "*Dasvidaniya*."

Chapter 32

Race climbed the stairs and entered the squad room. Across the room, Beane was talking to an impeccably dressed man. Race thought it was probably Painter's attorney and walked right over.

"Detective Griffin," Beane said, "this is Mr. Peter Luzhin, Painter's attorney."

They shook hands.

Race had expected Painter's lawyer to be some slick, greasy shark. Luzhin, on the other hand, was dressed in warm colors, had a self-effacing look, kind eyes, and a friendly handshake: the kind of person one would trust and believe—a person you couldn't imagine representing a guilty party.

"I've explained to Mr. Luzhin that we're charging his client with grand theft," Beane told Race. "That we apprehended his client in possession of a very valuable watch."

The attorney had a dejected look on his face. "My client is willing to admit he stole the watch—he wants to be honest. I know you guys are homicide detectives, and the watch in question belonged to Mr. Donny Bosco. Seeing as how Mr. Bosco was murdered a few days ago, are we looking at more serious charges?"

Race was about to answer, but Beane held up his hand to him and told the attorney, "That, we don't know at this time. Let's talk to your client and see what he has to say."

They walked to the holding cell and when Race opened the door, Painter looked up expectantly. He was seated on the hard metal chair; because of his size, it looked like something from a grammar school classroom. Painter sat silently—it seemed like the air was being let out of his muscles—he looked smaller and less intimidating than he did a few hours previously at the jewelers. Painter dabbed at his face. The collar of his shirt was blotched where sweat seeped through. Painter's shirt, and even the armpits of his sport coat, were saturated. He looked like a trapped animal—a very large and dangerous trapped animal.

Luzhin pulled a chair around and sat next to his client. Beane sat across the table. Race ended up standing alongside the captain. Beane took the OmniPhone off his wrist and placed it on the table, telling Helena to record the interview.

Race said, "Mr. Painter, I understand you're ready to tell us how you came by this watch." Race held up a plastic baggie containing the timepiece and showed it to both Painter and his attorney. "As you know, it belonged to Mr. Donny Bosco, of Beverly Glen."

Painter nodded as he looked at the watch. He seemed less nervous now; the presence of his lawyer seemed to have calmed him down. "Yes, I took it from Donny's house on Saturday."

Race set the timepiece down and leaned towards Painter, placing his elbows on the table. "When on Saturday did you go to Mr. Bosco's house? And how did you come into possession of this watch?"

Painter sighed, he seemed resigned to his fate. "Donny called me earlier in the week, said he was in Vegas and would be home by the weekend. Asked if I could come by, he was running out of steroids. And he had a bit of security work for me."

"Steroids?" Race asked.

"Yeah. I don't know if you ever saw Donny, but he was ripped."

Race remembered seeing Bosco's body on the autopsy table, and that Painter was right, Bosco was covered in slabs of muscle.

"When he first moved here, he was scrawny," Painter continued. "And shy—especially around women. He used to hang around the gyms in Venice. We got to talking and he hired me as his trainer, asking if I'd supply him with steroids, which I did: Fenajet, Deca, veterinary steroids they give to cattle. Within two years, he'd put on over a hundred pounds of muscle. He also had plastic surgery. He ended up looking like a magazine model or a movie star, and it really boosted his confidence."

Race nodded to the giant. "You said he needed security work. He say what type?"

"I've done work for him before. He comes back from Vegas with merchandise, it must be valuable because he's willing to buy protection."

"Do you know what kind of merchandise he was carrying?"

"He never said and I never asked. Sometimes he'd carry a metal briefcase, which I assumed contained diamonds, or other precious gems. Other times a couple over-sized suitcases, probably stuffed with cash. He'd have me and a couple other guys to go with him down to the docks to drop them off. He'd pay us each a couple thousand for a few hours' work."

"What docks are we talking about?"

"Long Beach. Marina del Rey."

"Okay," Race said. "Go on."

"I got to Donny's house around six, Saturday evening. I knew Donny usually spent the afternoon with a cute, dark-headed woman. I see her at the gym a lot, can't miss her, she's a knockout, does a lot of spinning classes."

"You pulled right in?" Race asked. "Wasn't the gate closed?"

Painter shook his head. "I think he usually kept it open when he was home. At least I've never seen it closed."

Race thought it silly, why have a gate if you weren't going to use it? He nodded for Painter to go on.

Painter cleared his throat. "I figured when Donny didn't answer the door, he was probably in bed with the Polish goddess. I've been to his house quite a few times, did security work, like a bouncer, when he had his private parties. I tried the front door handle, it was unlocked. I decided to wait in his study and watch TV. When I walked in, something seemed weird, different. I'm not usually afraid, but I sure felt uneasy. Frightened. Like being in a horror movie, I was drawn onward. I walked into the living room and Donny's tuxedo coat was hanging on the stool by the bar. The bad feeling seemed to come from the master bedroom. I almost knew what I was going to find, but I wasn't emotionally prepared for what I saw."

Painter paused, his eyes started to tear, and his lawyer handed him a tissue. Painter dried his eyes while the lawyer placed his hand on the giant's shoulder. Painter took a deep breath before continuing.

"Donny was lying flat on his bed, face down, completely naked. Blood was splattered on the wall and sheets. I didn't know if he was dead or not, but when I touched his skin it was obvious. He was ice cold. His skin was mottled, purple and red and black. I've never seen someone dead before, except at a funeral, but I knew he was dead. My stomach turned. I ran to the bathroom and hurled."

Painter took a few deep breaths; it looked like he was going to throw up again.

"Donny was a good friend." He sniffled and tears ran down his cheeks. His lawyer rubbed his back.

Race looked on. It was hard to imagine a big man like that crying, but he also had trouble imagining that Painter could be putting on a show—he really did look shaken up.

The moment passed, and Painter wiped his eyes.

"After my stomach settled, I wiped my face, drank a glass of water, and went back into the bedroom. It didn't seem right that Donny was lying exposed like that. I was about to call the police, but first I took the sheet from the bed and went to cover him up—at least he'd have a modicum of dignity when the cops arrived. As I was pulling the sheet over his body, I bumped into his left arm which was out to the side and I noticed the watch." Painter glanced at the watch sitting on the table and shook his head. "I'd seen him wearing that thing and I really liked it. Then I heard a noise. Footsteps. They seemed to be coming from upstairs. Maybe it was just my imagination, but I panicked. I thought the killer could still be in the house. I was never so afraid in my life. Without thinking, I unclasped the precious timepiece, grabbed it, and ran out the front door. I jumped into my car and pulled out as fast as I could without looking back."

Painter's body was shaking, his face pale and sweaty, as if he relived the scene.

Race gave him a few minutes to settle back down. "Why didn't you call 911?"

"I was having a panic attack—I've had them before. When it passed, I thought things through. If I called and reported the murder and was found with the watch..."

Race nodded. He could understand the complications Painter would have run into if that happened. As it was, he was in the same situation right now. Actually worse. "You said you've done security work at Bosco's parties?"

"Y'know, the combination of drugs, alcohol, and naked women," Painter shrugged his bowling ball-sized shoulders, "can create a volatile situation. Donny would have me and a couple of my buddies from the gym attend the party in case someone stepped out of line."

Race couldn't help but ask, "I'm curious, Mr. Painter, just how big are you?"

Painter looked puzzled for a second. “I’m about six-ten and weigh just under four-fifty. I compete in World’s Strongest Man contests. Perhaps you’ve seen me on the holo?”

Race shook his head. “I’ll have to check that out. Besides working these parties for Mr. Bosco, did you ever do any other jobs for him?”

“At times he’d have me come along with him to his meetings with what he called ‘clients.’ He’d meet them in pretty dangerous parts of town, like the Long Beach docks or in warehouses. A lot of these clients were tough, mysterious looking Russians. We never had any problems, but he didn’t want to go alone.”

“Do you know what Mr. Bosco was doing at these meetings?”

“He told me he was investing money, or picking up merchandise. He’d trade one suitcase or briefcase for another. He didn’t stick around long. Beyond that, I don’t know and I never asked.”

“Do you provide security or protection for anyone else besides Mr. Bosco?”

Painter nodded. “I do freelance work and have more business than I can handle. A rich guy needs a bodyguard for a day or two. A woman has a boyfriend who gets too possessive.”

“You work for some of the high-end Licensed Sexual Companions?”

Painter looked at his attorney and they whispered back and forth for a second before he answered the question. “In LA, it’s hard to tell the difference between a lyscee and a gold-digger.” He leaned forward and put his forearms, bigger than Race’s thigh, on the table. “The difference, as far as I can tell, is the sexual companion tells you the price up front, the gold-digger tells you the price after. You get the same service, but when the bill comes after the meal, it’s a lot higher.”

Beane laughed. “That’s amusing, but you didn’t answer the detective’s question.”

Painter gave Beane a slight nod. “I’ve worked for both.”

“That’s all the questions I have right now,” Race said.

“You don’t plan to charge my client with murder, do you?” the lawyer asked.

Beane grimaced. “We’ll be charging him with grand larceny, and he’s going to be spending the night. We’ll let you know if there’s any other charges. Your client will have a hearing scheduled…well, you know the procedure.”

Race looked on as Painter's lawyer tried to console him. Although Painter was big, scary big, he had a gentle-giant quality about him. Race wished there was something that could tell whether Painter was telling the truth or not, because somehow he didn't think the giant killed Bosco.

Race paused at the door and turned back. "Mr. Painter, there is one more question I'd like to ask. Can you tell me what Mr. Bosco's corpse, or body, looked like? Try to visualize the scene in your mind and tell me what you see."

Painter looked off into the distance. He shut his eyes and spoke as if in a trance. "Donny is lying face down. His body is white and shiny, like one of those white whales washed up on the beach."

"A narwhal or a beluga?"

Painter shook his head, as if his concentration was broken. "I don't know what either of those things are." His eyes became unfocused again. "Now that I look closer, I can see the bottom part of Donny's body was black and blue."

"That's good, what else do you see?"

"Well, his body was really stiff. When I took the watch off Donny's wrist I could hardly move his arm."

"Okay. Anything else?"

"There's black, clotted blood in his hair. That's about it." Painter refocused his eyes and looked back at Race. "Does that help?"

"It might, Mr. Painter," Race said with a nod. "It might."

Beane stood and nodded for Race to leave the interrogation room. "We'll give you a bit of time with your client," Beane said to Painter's attorney.

When they left the room, Beane said, "How about a coffee?"

They went to the coffee machine and Beane poured two cups and handed one to his partner.

Race sipped his coffee and yawned. "What do you think, Captain? You believe his story?"

Beane shrugged. "I doubt we have Bosco's killer." He put his hand on Race's shoulder. "Listen, it's late, go home and get a good night's sleep. Helena will analyze the interview and we can get her thoughts on the matter tomorrow. And don't forget to dictate the reports on what you've done today."

Race stopped in his tracks. "I've been so busy, I completely forgot about that."

Beane gave him a little laugh. "When I was on active duty, before Helena, I'd spend at least two to three hours doing paperwork for every hour out in the field. Now you can dictate those reports to Helena on your ride home."

Race tossed his coffee back. "Sounds like a plan, Captain."

Chapter 33

Race left the precinct, undecided about what to do next. It really was time to knock off for the day; he started work before sunrise and had been working non-stop since then. However, he was too wired to go home—to an empty home, at that. If Painter was the killer, the Bosco case was closed, his job done; he could rest and go to sleep. But it just didn't add up.

It didn't make sense that Painter would kill one of his best friends. Or if not friends, the man who paid him well for his services. He wondered if Painter and Bosco got into a fight over Brigit Kojacy; perhaps he flew into a steroid rage and killed Bosco blind with passion. Kojacy certainly had the looks men have been known to kill for. Although Painter said he knew the Polish bombshell in passing, he could be lying to cover his tracks. He decided he needed to check into the relationship between the two of them.

It was obvious to everyone that Painter was taking steroids. Tons of steroids. Wasn't it possible that the drugs killed the giant's sex drive? Could even get it up? Did Painter see Kojacy as sexually attractive at all, in which case killing Bosco to possess her wouldn't make sense. He'd need to do research on how steroids affect men's sex drive…and violence. That thought was countered by acknowledging that Painter didn't seem like a violent man, just the opposite. If Painter was prone to fly into a steroid rage, if that even existed, wouldn't Painter have gone Incredible Hulk on them back at the jewelry store. Painter easily could have overpowered him on the way back to the precinct, yet he sat quietly and allowed himself to be booked. If the giant did have a violent streak, what would it take to set it off?

Then the thought struck him: Painter's statement could be the thing that tied Bosco to the slain Russian courier. According to Painter, Bosco had frequent dealings with the less than savory crowd. The Russian courier may have passed his merchandise on to Bosco and told his killers that fact before he was assassinated. Then they came calling on Bosco. Perhaps

Bosco finally got in over his head, or double-crossed someone. That still didn't explain how Dr. Sing, the physiatrist, was involved, that was going to require a second look.

If the giant man was telling the truth, that he stumbled upon the crime scene, and was too frightened to report the murder, then the real murderer was still running free.

Although the rest of his team wasn't buying it, Race couldn't shake the belief that Bosco's murder was related to those of the Russian courier and Dr. Sing. If the three killings were related, then it was even more unlikely the giant killed Bosco. That put the ball squarely in O'Suil's court.

He tried to think of what he could do to see if Painter's story held water and decided a good place to start would be to talk to one of the medical examiners, see if Painter's description of the murder scene was realistic.

He jumped into his car and placed a call to the morgue. A secretary put him on hold. When she came back, she told him that Dr. Tulp was finishing his last case of the day and Race could see the doctor if he hurried over. Race programmed his Nav-Drive, paid the toll to take the High-Speed lane, and sped down the freeway at one hundred-fifty miles an hour. In minutes, his red coupe pulled into the morgue's parking lot.

He entered the empty lobby and announced himself to the white-haired guard behind the desk.

"Speak up, son," the guard yelled. "My hearing aid's gone out."

Mine hasn't,

Race leaned forward and yelled in the man's hairy ear. "I'm here to see Dr. Tulp."

The guard nodded. "He's expecting you in his office. Need any help finding it?"

Race didn't want the old man to get up, fearing the guard would keel over before they made it halfway. "No thanks. I've been back there before."

The guard pushed the buzzer unlocking the doors. Race found his way to the medical wing. Down the dimly-lit hall, light bled from an office about halfway down. He walked over and peered into the room. Dr. Tulp's turban-clad head was bent over a stack of papers. When Race announced himself, Tulp looked up and gave him a smile.

He waved Race in. "Have a seat, Detective. I understand you have questions about the Bosco case."

"Yes I do, Doctor. Thank you for seeing me on such short notice."

"Think nothing of it." Tulp tidied the papers he'd been reviewing and placed them in his outbox. "What would you like to know, young man?"

Race told the doctor about the suspect they had in custody and the description they were given of Bosco's corpse.

Tulp gave him a nod. "First, the description you were given of the dead body is realistic."

"That's what I was hoping for."

Tulp wagged a finger at him. "You shouldn't *hope* for anything. Strive to rid yourself of preconceived notions. 'Realization of the Truth', that should be your guide, follow it wherever it may lead."

"Good advice," Race said. "What's the second thing?"

"The description can help in pinning down a time of death."

"How so?"

"Important information can be gleaned from your suspect's observations, if he was telling the truth."

"Doctor—"

"Ahem." Tulp cut him off. He held his hand up and looked sternly at Race.

Race decided the best course with Dr. Tulp would be to speak when spoken to.

"The first is the color of the skin, which we call the lividity, the purple-black discoloration that occurs in the dependent parts of the body. It starts within a half-hour or so of death. From the large amount of discoloration your suspect saw, Mr. Bosco would had been dead at least four hours. Another point that's helpful in finding time of death is the rigidity of the corpse, the rigor mortis. Mr. Bosco's body was found indoors, but the patio doors were open—the nighttime temperatures last weekend were in the sixties. Your suspect describes the arms as being stiff, in a state of rigor. From this information, we can infer that deceased died between ten to twenty hours before the suspect came upon the body."

Race mentally reviewed the time-line. Bosco attended the Getty Ball Friday night and went home with Dr. Singh. That meant he was alive until the wee hours of Saturday morning.

Tulp appeared to have finished speaking. "The suspect found the body around six Saturday evening," Race said. "So, Bosco died no later than eight that morning?"

Tulp nodded. "Although that's a ball park figure, it's a good place to start."

Race scratched his head. If Bosco died early Saturday morning, who did Billings-Li see picking up the newspaper? Was the old lady confused? She seemed sharp. Was it possible the killer picked up the paper on his way out? Stranger things have probably happened.

"Doctor Singh left the deceased—"

"Oh, such a shame." Tulp had a worried look on his face. "She didn't come in to work today, as could be expected. How is she doing?"

Race gave a small shrug. "I don't know. I was thinking of tracking her down after I leave."

That last comment came out of nowhere. He hadn't been planning to see her, but now that he said it, it seemed like a good idea.

"Doctor Singh left Mr. Bosco's place in the early dawn hours of Saturday morning. So he was killed sometime shortly after she left?"

Tulp's turbaned head nodded up and down. "That is consistent with the autopsy findings. Are you close to wrapping up the case?"

"We have the suspect I mentioned in custody, but we're still looking at a few other leads."

"As you should." Tulp folded his hands over his chest. "Avoid the temptation to become too attached to anything."

Race stood up, he'd admired Tulp's calm demeanor and apparent inner harmony, something he was always striving for. He extended his hand to the doctor. "I really enjoyed talking to you, Dr. Tulp. Would you mind if I stopped by sometime and chatted?"

Tulp took his hand and nodded.

Race could make out the trace of a smile through the doctor's beard.

"It would be my pleasure," Tulp said.

Race walked out of the medical wing and stood in the hallway, indecisive. He knew he should go home and get some sleep, but he still wasn't tired. He interviewed just about everyone related to the case, except for Dr. Singh. Beela said she'd taken the doctor's statement the day before, but it was done under such traumatic circumstances, and according to his partner, the doctor fell asleep before the interview was over. He hoped by now she would remember some bits of information that would be helpful. Race found the administrative wing of the building, stuck his head in Dutch Rolstoel's office, and asked if he knew how to get in touch with Dr. Singh.

Dutch had a stack of papers in his hands. He put them down and waved Race in. "Haven't seen the doctor today. I told her to take as much time as she needs off." He raised his wrist to his face. "Let me try her Omni."

Dutch transferred his OmniPhone to speaker mode and dialed Jennifer's number. There was no answer. "I'd bet anything she's at the gym." He gave Race Jennifer's home address and that of the gym. "Tell her to call me if she needs anything," he said as Race left the office.

Chapter 34

Race programmed his car to take him to Dr. Singh's address in Marina del Rey, then sat back and did research for the case. Fifteen minutes later, he pulled into the alley behind Jennifer's bungalow and went around front to ring the bell. When there was no answer, he peered through a window. The place was dark. He rang again, waited a moment, then decided it was time to go home. He descended the two steps from the porch to the walkway and headed back to the alley. Reaching the corner of the house, an elderly Asian woman, wearing a Dodgers cap and feeding a cat, called his attention. Race explained why he was there and the woman told him that Dr. Singh left less than an hour ago, heading to the gym on the beach in Venice.

Race didn't engage the Nav-Drive but drove the car himself, north on Speed Way. After a few blocks, he turned on Washington Boulevard and into the public parking lot along the beach. He pressed a button on the dash and the driver's side door swung open. As he slid out and was giving the car instructions to park itself, a trio of bikini-clad rollerbladers stopped and whistled their admiration of his sports car. All curvy and tanned, the women oozed sexuality and Race was at a loss for words. He felt his face blush, but did his best to smile and give them a small wave. The girls turned away and giggled as they skated off. Race chided himself for being so shy and snapped his anxiety bracelet, then headed toward the gym.

The promenade was filled with people jogging, running, biking, skateboarding, rollerblading, or just out for a stroll. Race walked north, dodging urban campers who fought the pigeons for scraps of food and bikers who didn't seem to realize that there was a paved bike and running path just steps away.

After almost getting run over by a jogger, Race stopped and looked out along the beach; his breath was taken away. The sun was perched just above the horizon, the soot from the fires creating vivid streaks of color—

orange, copper, crimson—a sunset unlike any he'd ever seen. As far as he could see, tens of thousands of tents dotted the area, reminding him of the NASCAR racetrack at Fontana on race week: the only things missing were the luxury motorhomes, bonfires, and someone singing Kumbaya. He'd been to Venice Beach many times, usually there were a handful of tents out on the sand housing the chronically homeless. But the mountain fires wiped out everything in its path: homes, ranches, even entire towns. People by the tens of thousands retreated from the flames and ended up here, refugees in their own country.

Race headed north along the promenade, moving along at the same pace as the crowds, until he reached the Muscle Beach gym. The weight pen was raised waist high above the level of the walkway and surrounded by a sturdy chain-link fence topped with a padded rail. Inside were lines of benches—some flat, some inclined—racks of weights, pulleys, dumbbells, squat racks, calf raise machines, and lots of other equipment Race wasn't able to identify. A handful of people—men and woman—exercised, oblivious to the on looking crowd.

Race peered through the fence trying to see if he could find Doctor Singh. On one of the weight benches facing toward him, a woman lay flat on her back, her gloved hands and taped wrists gripping an Olympic barbell with a forty-five pound plate and a couple smaller ones on each side. A man, whose muscles seemed like they were about to explode out of his skin, stood behind the bench with his fingers near the bar, and yelling encouragement. The woman's entire body fought to push the bar up off her chest—the sinews of her arms and legs taut as she slowly fought gravity and straightened her elbows. The lift done, the behemoth spotting her grabbed the bar and helped place it on the rack.

The struggle over, the woman sat up and took a deep breath as she unwound the cloth tape from around her wrists.

It was Dr. Singh.

Race put his face against the chain-links and yelled. "Dr. Singh."

The doctor looked in his direction, puzzlement on her face.

Race waved to her. "Doctor Singh! It's Detective Griffin. We met yesterday."

A flash of recognition, then a pained look washed across her eyes. Her lifting companion bent down and said something to her. The doctor shook her head, stood up, and walked the few feet to the fence. Mr. Muscle accompanied her.

Race felt his pulse quicken as the doctor approached. She wore a light-blue sports bra—cut low enough to accentuate the swells of her breasts—and black spandex workout shorts just covering the beginnings of her thighs. The setting sun glistened off her skin, which was covered in a light sheen of sweat. She had well-defined muscles and flat, six-pack abs.

"Detective." She looked down at him, breathing heavily. "This doesn't seem like a coincidence."

Race studied her face. She seemed heavyhearted, still in a state of shock. "I dropped by your house. Wanted to see how you were doing."

"That's kind of you." She wiped the sweat off her forehead with the back of her weightlifting gloves. "Mrs. Ng must have told you I'd be here."

Race nodded. He hesitated, having second thoughts about whether it was too soon after losing her boyfriend to be interviewing the doctor. Somewhere in the back of his mind he remembered reading that one should wait forty-eight or seventy-two hours before re-interviewing a victim of a crime. Since the department only allotted two weeks to work the case, he decided it wouldn't hurt to interview the doctor, he could always back off if she was still too emotionally fragile.

He craned his head up and caught the doctor's eyes. "I also have a few questions."

The rippling giant smiled down at Race. "This guy looks quite appealing." He turned to Jennifer. "Aren't you going to introduce us?"

Jennifer poked her workout companion in the ribs and laughed. "Where's my manners?" She draped her arms over the top of the padded fence and looked down at Race. "I'm sorry, Detective. What was your name again?"

"Detective Griffin. Call me Race."

She nodded. "Judge Minos, this is Detective Race."

She'd confused his name. Race chalked that up to the emotional anguish she must be going through and didn't feel now was the time to correct her.

The judge reached over the fence and shook Race's hand. It was like shaking hands with a boulder. "Nice to meet you, Detective."

Jennifer told the judge she'd get in touch with him. He gave her a peck on the cheek, then turned and left, his massive thighs rubbed against each other causing him to waddle like a duck, as he went to the dumbbell rack.

Race looked up at Jennifer, his eyes just about at the level of her thighs. "Dr. Singh. I'd like—"

She scowled down at him. "Having you look up at my hoo-haw makes me uncomfortable. Come around and I'll meet you at the entrance. You can look down my top like a normal guy."

Race felt his face flush and turned away. His eyes had been almost directly at the level of her "hoo-haw," and he'd been enjoying the scenery. He smiled as he thought about the view up top, which probably wasn't bad either. He walked around the perimeter of the gym to the gate, feeling smaller and frailer than normal among the bodybuilders mulling around—a Chihuahua amongst Great Danes.

Jennifer was waiting for him, gym bag slung over her shoulder, when Race reached the gym entrance. She led him a few paces away to where permanent stands had been set up for physique exhibitions. From her bag, she pulled a short-sleeve sweat shirt and cut-off sweat pants, putting them on before sitting on the concrete bleachers. She took a protein shake out of her bag and began drinking, asking Race to give her a minute to catch her breath.

Race sat facing the doctor, studying her. She didn't appear to have on makeup, but really didn't need any; her cheeks and skin had a healthy-looking pink glow, moist from her recent exertion. Her eyes were a mixture of green and hazel with flecks of gold—in spite of her obvious physical strength, they revealed vulnerability. She had a cute upturned nose, defined cheekbones, pouty lips, and a soft jaw line. And a fantastic figure.

"The guy you were working out with…uh…" Race stammered.

Jennifer smiled, but didn't look his way. "You want to know if he's gay and attracted to you?"

Race nodded.

"He tells people he first meets that they're 'appealing.' The joke is that he's a Federal Appeals judge."

Race chuckled. "That's funny."

Jennifer didn't laugh. "Not if you've heard it dozens of times." She caught her breath. "Well, Detective Race, to what do I owe the pleasure?"

Race gazed at the doctor, thinking she really did have quite a figure, even under the cut-off sweats.

He must have been looking too long without saying anything, because Jennifer said, "You wanted to ask me something?"

Race decided to take the interview slowly. "I really didn't get a chance to offer you my condolences the other day. How are you doing?"

"Thanks for your kindness, Detective. I'm better." She gave him a thin smile. "I've been cooped up in my house all day. It feels good to get outside and get the juices flowing." Jennifer looked past Race toward the ocean. The crimson color of the setting sun caused the doctor's eyes to sparkle like diamonds and lit her red hair up as if it were ablaze.

Race waited for her to look back at him, which she didn't. "You mind if I ask you a few questions about...Mr. Bosco's murder?"

She continued to look off to the west but nodded.

"Do you recall what time you left Mr. Bosco's home last Saturday?"

She frowned. "We'd been drinking...quite a bit the night before. I was foggy-headed when I left." She nodded to herself. "It was just starting to get light. But with the raging mountain fires, the pinkish color coming over the mountains could have been from the flames."

"We have a suspect in custody. A man by the name of Nicolas Painter—"

Jennifer looked startled and grabbed Race's arm. Her grip was like a vise and Race tried not to wince.

"Wait a second," Jennifer said. "Painter? Big, giant guy?"

"You know him?"

She released his arm and pointed to the concrete area surrounded by the bleachers. "Competes in World's Strongest Man contests right here."

"That's him. He told us he'd met Mr. Bosco at a gym in Venice." Race gestured with his beak-like nose at the fenced-in weight area. "Did they meet here?"

Jennifer shook her head. "They worked out at Gold's."

"Are you a member there as well?"

Jennifer smiled and waved as the muscular judge left the gym, then turned her attention back to Race. "I'm just a member here. It's close to my house and I can walk or run over." She closed her eyes and inhaled deeply. "It's not as well-equipped as some others, but I like working out al fresco—the ocean breeze, the salt air, the energy—you can't beat it." She looked directly at Race. "What does Nicko have to do with this case?"

Her green eyes locked on his and were enchanting. He knew he shouldn't stare back, but he was melting in her gaze. It was hard not to think about her sexually and he felt himself stirring. He reminded himself that he was working a case and needed information from Dr. Singh to help solve it.

And he needed to get a grip.

The doctor's eyes followed his hand as he reached down and snapped his wrist band. The look on her face changed, telling Race that she knew all about him. That she knew what had been going through his mind.

He snapped the band again, the sharp pain helped him to focus. He had to make a decision how much to confide in her. Yesterday, the major warned the detectives to be careful releasing information to Dr. Singh. But if he doled out a little information—information that would soon be public anyway—he might get her to open up, tell him something that might help solve the case.

"We caught Mr. Painter trying to get a watch appraised that belonged to Mr. Bosco," Race said. "He told us he went by the mansion to run an errand for Mr. Bosco. When he went into the house, he found Mr. Bosco's dead body on the bed and took the watch. Said it was an impulsive act."

Jennifer nodded. "I've seen the watch, it's beautiful. And quite mesmerizing. I can see someone taking it without thinking."

Race thought back to the hypnotic effect the watch had on him and had to agree with the doctor.

Jennifer let out a short laugh. "What is it with men and watches? A guy complains when a girl spends a couple hundred SDR on a pair of shoes, but they don't hesitate to spend tens of thousands on a watch.'"

"In this case, hundreds of thousands."

Jennifer whistled. "No kidding? It's worth that much? You don't think Nicko killed Donny for the watch?"

"We're not sure. Do you know if Painter does steroids?"

Jennifer leaned back on the bleacher and held her sides, laughing.

Race felt chagrined and tried to save face. "I'm sure he uses steroids, Doctor. I wanted to know if you have any personal knowledge of his use."

"His mother's an endocrinologist, I've met her a few times at conferences. She had him on HGH—human growth hormone—when he was growing up, hoping he'd be a professional basketball player. Now she supplies him with pharmaceutical-grade anabolic steroids for his competitions." Jennifer paused for a second. "You don't think..."

"Is it possible Painter suffers from 'roid rage?"

Jennifer hesitated and looked east at the fires raging in the mountains. She nodded a few times and smiled thinly. "It's possible. To get as big as he is...he'd have to be juicing big time. High doses of steroids can lead to psychosis and aggressive behavior."

"Psychosis?" Race said. "Like schizophrenia?"

"Not schizophrenia, per se. But it can cause paranoia. Steroid-induced psychosis is more often confused with bipolar mania."

"Could heavy use lead one to commit murder?"

Jennifer nodded. She arched her brows and had a look in her eyes that Race couldn't read. "Some people think heavy use of steroids can cause steroid-induced aggression, or 'roid rage. A person in that condition could snap," Race jumped when she snapped her fingers for emphasis, "and commit murder."

Race averted his gaze and leaned back on the bench. He'd need to research more about steroid rage, but what Dr. Singh told him seemed to ring a bell. He stifled a yawn and turned back to the doctor, who was looking over his shoulder toward the weight area. Men with impossibly big muscles were working out. Now that just about every drug was legal, everyone seemed to be on steroids, or something else to alter their performance. Nobody seemed happy with the bodies they were born with.

He felt enough time had been wasted and that he needed to get back to his reason for meeting with Dr. Singh.

"Would you mind telling me how you came to meet Mr. Bosco?"

"I told that whole story to your partner yesterday."

"You fell asleep before you got to that part."

Jennifer eyed him suspiciously. "I don't see how Donny and I met is any of your business."

Race paused. Perhaps she was right, the poor woman was grieving over the loss of her loved one. But then again, it didn't hurt to ask.

Race said slowly, "You may not know this, but Mr. Bosco appears to have been killed as part of a botched robbery. We're trying to piece together his last few weeks, and you spent quite a bit of time with him. You might be able to tell us something we can use to catch the killer."

"If that's the case." Jennifer dropped her head, her eyes seemed to glass over. She spoke slowly, as if in a trance. "How we met is a long story. Let's go somewhere we can have a beer."

Race was about to look at his Omni to check the time, then the image of his empty condo flashed through his mind. He had nothing waiting for him at home, except his cactus, and how often did that need watering? He was bone-tired, but it wasn't often that he got to go out drinking with such a beautiful woman.

Race gave Jennifer a nod. "That sounds great." He hesitated. "By the way, Race is my nickname. It's short for Horace Griffin."

Jennifer grimaced. "I'm bad with names." She stood up and grabbed her gym bag. "Follow me then," she turned and shot him a playful smile from over her shoulder, "Horace."

Chapter 35

The sun was about to set, casting everything in eerie shadows, as Jennifer led the way along the promenade. She strode with a purpose, chuckling as Race hustled to keep up with her long legs while she passed the crowds strolling along with bovine indifference.

Usually, she loved the vitality of Venice Beach, feeding off the energy, something her father referred to as *vigñana*. Tonight, although the boardwalk was teeming, the vibe was different. People displaced by the fires far outnumbered the casual tourists. The fire refugees were easy to spot: they moved aimlessly, had vacant looks on their faces, their eyes glazed—extras from a zombie movie.

Jennifer looked over her shoulder to talk to the detective. Race had fallen behind and she cut her pace to let him catch up. When he came abreast of her, she said, "Besides Painter, do you have any other leads?"

Race paused a second to catch his breath. "I can't tell you any specifics until the case is resolved."

She looked at him askance. That was a strange statement. Homicide always works closely with the MEs. Now they can't discuss specifics?

They can't be afraid I could be compromised as a witness should the case go to trial, can they?

Jennifer was so distracted by the detective's comment that she nearly missed the restaurant's street. She turned abruptly, bumping into Race and knocking him into a vacant-eyed fire refugee. Race apologized to the man, who mumbled something back with a glassy-eyed stare.

After about fifty yards, Jennifer stopped at a restaurant on the pedestrian-only street. The place had white and tan stucco walls. A green, white, and red awning covered the front door, which was flanked by artificial Tiki lamps. The windows were almost completely hidden by green vine-like shrubs and hanging baskets of flowering bougainvillea.

The smell of grilled fish and the sound of laughter poured out. A sign on the sidewalk and a neon sign taking up one half of the building announced: Playa de Jaime.

Jennifer felt the hunger pains start, as they always did, when she caught the aroma of fish tacos. She smiled down at Race. "I love this place. C'mon."

Inside the lobby, the maitre'd, dressed all in black, asked if they would like a table for two.

Jennifer waved him off. "We'll find one by the bar." She led the way through an archway into the barroom. Race followed close behind.

The bar area was partially open air and the salt air mixed with the smell of Mexican food. The atmosphere was young and noisy. A handful of customers sat drinking at the horseshoe-shaped bar. Mounted above their heads were wafer-thin Mega-Def monitors—so close together they appeared to be touching—each tuned to live sports.

Jennifer scanned the area looking for an empty high-top table, most were taken by groups eating fish tacos and drinking beer, their eyes riveted on the overhead monitors. She spotted an open table in the far corner, against the windows that fronted onto the sidewalk. Hanging her gym bag over one of the upholstered stools, she leaned toward Race and raised her voice to be heard above the background din. "The fish tacos here are the best. They do it the right way: *huachinango a la parilla*. And they make their own flour tortillas and salsa." She licked her lips. "Their salsa's killer."

Jennifer stood up and waved to one of the servers.

The blond-haired man, wearing a Hawaiian shirt and surf pants, smiled broadly when he spotted her. He finished with the table he was waiting on and hustled over, giving her a hug. "Where you been, Doc? We've missed you on the courts."

Jennifer looked down at his high-top basketball shoes. "Looks like you're ready to play."

He laughed.

"I've been swamped at work," she said. "By the time I get home, all I do is collapse in bed."

"*Qué lástima*," he said. "You having the usual?" Jennifer nodded. He turned to Race. "And what about you, sir?"

Race laughed. "I'll have the usual, too."

The waiter chuckled. "I like you, *güey*." He gave Race a fist bump. "I'll put the order in, then I'll be right back with drinks."

After he left, Jennifer waved to a gray-haired man working behind the bar. "I'll be right back," she told Race. "I've gotta say 'hi' to the manager." Jennifer wove her way through the tables on her way to the bar.

Race snapped his anxiety bracelet repeatedly, tapped his foot, and scanned the room. On the few areas of the walls not covered by television monitors were photos of poorly-clad, barefoot fishermen standing before primitive fishing boats, holding up their catch: red snapper. The tricolor Mexican flag hung above the archway leading to what Race assumed was the kitchen.

Jennifer returned just as the waiter came back with a sweaty metal bucket full of Pacifico beers and hung it on the side of their table. He placed a basket of tortilla chips and an assortment of salsas on the table. "Everything's made fresh here," he explained to Race.

Jennifer pulled three bottles out of the ice and handed one to the waiter. "Hold on," she said as he was turning to leave. "Have one with us."

They all cracked open a beer and clinked bottles.

"*¡Salud!*" Jennifer said.

They each took long draws.

The waiter wiped foam from his mouth. "I'd better get back to my tables. I'll try to stop by when your food's ready." He turned, taking the bottle with him.

Jennifer sat back, sipping her beer. She randomly picked one of the televisions and watched the action—a cricket match, a sport she didn't understand—between two teams she didn't recognize. She wanted to tell the detective about her relationship with Donny, but didn't know where to begin. Or how much to tell him—he was a cop, after all. And a man. She stole a quick glance at him. He was short, thin, angular, dressed fastidiously, his hands were delicate and nicely manicured—she figured he was probably gay. She closed her eyes, vegging out.

Out of the corner of his eye, Race watched the doctor. She seemed to be caught in an emotional current, strong and deep. He knew he had to wait, be patient. He could see that she was steeling herself for the story she was about to tell. His heart went out to her, and he wondered if finding Bosco's killer would in any way reduce her hurt.

Jennifer put her beer down, but kept her hands protectively wrapped around the cold bottle as if it were a precious stone. She looked at Race with a sad smile, then seemed to gaze into some unseen world. She spoke quietly, and Race had to lean forward to hear. Her cadence was slow and lilting, like a Gregorian chant.

"I met Donny only about three weeks ago," she said. "I mean three weeks before he was killed." Her eyes seemed to fill, but no tears ran over the quivering edges. "It seemed like I had known him for years."

Jennifer tilted her bottle back and took a slow sip.

Race did the same, letting Jennifer tell her story at her own pace.

Jennifer gazed at the brown beer bottle. "The tale of how Donny and I met actually begins in British Columbia."

Race raised his eyebrows. "You met in Canada, eh?"

Jennifer looked over to him and shook her head. "A little over a month ago, ten of the medical examiners from our office flew to Vancouver for a four-day continuing education seminar, and to squeeze in a couple afternoons salmon fishing and glacier skiing. On the last day of the program, they assisted a world-renowned forensic pathologist from France as he performed a number of autopsies. One was a man from Laos who'd died under mysterious circumstances on a cargo ship coming from Southeast Asia. When the pathologist opened the chest cavity, a giant cyst, or tubercle, burst open. Although everyone wore standard paper masks, they all became infected with treatment-resistant TB."

"Sounds like something out of a Tolstoy novel," Race said.

Jennifer squinted her eyes and scrunched her nose, lost in thought for a moment. "You're probably thinking of Turgenev's *Fathers and Sons*. Ironically, the treatment for resistant TB nowadays is right out of Thomas Mann's *The Magic Mountain*: isolation at high altitudes, which is where my colleagues are right now."

"What does tuberculosis have to do with meeting Mr. Bosco?"

Jennifer pointed her beer bottle at him. "I was getting to that. We're now critically shorthanded: two doctors trying to do the work of twelve. Dutch Rolstoel's the morgue administrator. You've met him; he's the guy in the wheelchair. Anyway, Dutch came up with the idea that the medical staff should get out in public, attend functions where we could meet influential people, let them know about the importance of our work, and make our case for better funding. He pressured Doctor Tulp and me to attend black-tie charity events, political meetings, the opera, things of that sort. I hate going to those stuffy events," Jennifer shrugged and gave Race a helpless look, "but what are you going to do? One day, Dutch talked me into attending a ritzy charity fundraiser for the L'Orange Opera Company. I didn't have a decent evening gown, so I picked one out at a consignment shop in West Hollywood."

Jennifer smiled as she relived that afternoon in her mind. How, when she tried the gown on and looked in the full-length mirror, it was as if the tectonic plates under her feet shifted. She wasn't an over-worked pathologist hacking open dead bodies all day long. She was Cinderella. And she was going to the ball.

Race smiled, he could tell Jennifer was enjoying thinking about the gown. "What did you end up buying?"

That cinches it, Jennifer thought, this detective's definitely gay.

"Why buy a gown when you can only wear it once or twice," she said. "I rented one. After the fundraiser, I brought it back, and traded it in for something practical."

Race laughed.

"I wore a black, silk chiffon gown with sequins, if you really want to know," Jennifer said. "By an haute couture designer I never heard of."

"I bet it looked great on you," Race said.

Jennifer smiled and decided not to respond to the detective's comment. "The Opera hall was packed with people I recognized from the holos—Hollywood actors, famous directors, athletes, local politicians. It was exciting. Dutch knew a few people, made the introductions. When people found out what I do for a living, they'd ask me what I thought about such and such a case they'd seen on one of the holovision crime shows."

"I bet that happens a lot," Race said.

"Goddesses, yes!" Jennifer let out a groan. "A lot of people came over and introduced themselves, no doubt intrigued by the unusual couple Dutch and I made."

"Beauty and the Beast."

Jennifer gave him a mischievous smile. "I don't know if that was a compliment or an insult." She let out a little laugh. "Where was I?"

"You were with Beauty at the Opera fundraiser."

Jennifer laughed and looked at Race carefully for the first time. *That guy's pretty funny, for a dick.* "Then I saw him. Donny. He was talking to a group of county commissioners." She sighed. "He had an air of elegance. Of confidence. People listened, raptly, as he spoke. I know this may sound silly, but he reminded me of a Greek god."

Race thought back to the autopsy the day before. He could see how Bosco in life would resemble a classical god like Apollo or Zeus.

"I asked Dutch if he knew who he was," Jennifer said. "Dutch wasn't sure and asked a local politician standing nearby. We were told the man's name was Donny Bosco and he was one of the hosts of the fund-raiser."

Jennifer took a pull on her beer. The memories of that night came flooding back. When she looked back Donny's way, she saw him looking over the crowd and their eyes met. A flash of heat coursed through her body. When he gave her a roguish smile, she could almost feel her knees weaken. They made eye contact and time stood still. It was as if she were in a movie, when the camera zooms in, and they were the only ones in the room. Then a couple came up to her to introduce themselves and she was distracted for a second. She smiled as she looked back to where Donny had been standing, but he'd vanished. She was crestfallen. Her smile wilted with the feeling of disappointment. As she turned to tell Dutch she was going to get a drink, there he stood. Donny. Right in front of her. Up close, he was much bigger than she'd expected, broad and muscular. He had an easy smile on his lips. His eyes sparkled. He had an intense look that made her feel as if she was the only person in the room who mattered. In fact, the only person in the room, period.

Jennifer had been quiet for so long that Race jumped when she began talking again.

"He introduced himself," Jennifer told Race. "I was speechless." She arched an eyebrow Race's way. "That's unusual for me. Dutch butted in and told Donny we were essentially there to beg for money. Donny took that in stride and told us he'd be happy to help. Next thing I know, he's introducing us to the mayor, the chairman of the County Commission, the County Finance chief, all of whom seemed to be his confidants. He made sure to steer the conversation to our money problems, and Dutch and I did our little dog and pony show."

"Sounds like he was an excellent fundraiser," Race said.

Jennifer nodded. "After a while, the lights dimmed and brightened a few times. I was drinking champagne and was a little tipsy. I said something to Donny like: 'I can see how the Opera needs money, they're cutting off your electricity.' When he actually laughed at my bad joke, he had me hooked."

Race laughed along with Jennifer.

"He explained that Opera was putting on a short performance and it was about to begin, we should head into the *theatre*—he used the French pronunciation."

Jennifer sighed as she remembered how he offered her his arm. Women turned and looked, some with envy. A possessive feeling came over her—that he was hers—even though they just met minutes before. They sat with Dutch in the handicapped section, listening to a half-hour program of arias from famous operas. When it was over, Donny asked Dutch if he could "steal her away" for a minute. They found a quiet corner in the lobby where he said he was "enchanted" by her and would like to get to know her better. She gave Donny her OmniPhone number, which he entered in his mini-tablet Omni.

"After the program, Donny said he had to work early the next day and bid farewell. Since it was late, Dutch and I decided to leave, too."

"Before your carriage turned into a pumpkin."

Jennifer laughed. "Well, I did meet my Prince Charming."

The waiter came with their order and gave Jennifer a wink. "Told you I'd be back." In the middle of the table, he placed a sizzling platter covered by an entire grilled red snapper with parallel charred marks on each side where the fish sat on the grill, and a ceramic container containing freshly-made flour tortillas.

As he turned to leave, Jennifer grabbed his arm. "You know what, bring the marijuana menu, also." Jennifer finished her beer and opened two more, passing one to Race.

Race grabbed the beer, took a sip, then followed Jennifer's lead as she pulled meat off the fish, placed it on a warm tortilla, added a dab of the salsa, and folded it over. Jennifer moaned when she took the first bite. She closed her eyes to enjoy the food, but what happened after the Opera fundraiser flashed through her mind.

The next morning after the Opera event when she arrived to work, there on the front desk was a hand-painted porcelain vase filled with dozens of red roses. The desk clerk said they were for her. A note attached to the bouquet read: "These roses are but a meager attempt to match your beauty. Thank you for making my evening special. DB."

That day went by like a blur. When she finished the last case and changed back to her street clothes, she checked her messages. Donny had called twice.

"I made plans to meet Donny on Sunday," Jennifer told Race. "He said he had a boat in Marina del Rey, and we could go sailing."

Race mumbled, his mouth filled with taco. "Could you tell me about Mr. Bosco's boat? We weren't aware he owned one."

"It was called the *Medes*."

"Like the…alcoholic drink?"

Jennifer spelled the name. "Like the ancient Iranian people. The Medes. His sailboat was small compared to the yachts docked near it. I'd call it an old school boat, made of seasoned wood instead of those synthetic materials. You could tell it had spent time out in the deep ocean, as it was weather-stained."

Race took a swig from his beer. "Thanks. Back to you and Mr. Bosco. What happened next?"

"Sunday morning, I met Donny at the marina. Overnight, the Santa Ana winds kicked up, the mountains were in a state of conflagration. The seas were rough and choppy. The coast guard had issued a small craft warning. The plan had been to cruise to Catalina, hike the trails, and have lunch. But Donny said rough seas make him queasy. We drove to Santa Monica instead and had a leisurely brunch at one of those fancy hotels overlooking the beach."

Jennifer smiled thinking about that evening. A band played out on the veranda. They drank mimosas and listened to Latin fusion jazz until dusk. Then, they walked over to the Santa Monica pier. Donny bought cotton candy, and they rode the Ferris wheel while the sun went down. Although things with Donny seemed perfect, she had felt that things were moving too fast. She was getting overwhelmed—didn't quite know how to handle so much attention from someone so fabulous. They'd just met. And she'd been burned before.

Jennifer frowned, her brows wrinkled. "When he dropped me off at home, Donny told me he was going to be in Las Vegas on business the coming week."

Race nodded, thinking: Las Vegas, that's where O'Suil is from. "Did Mr. Bosco tell you what his business plans were?"

Jennifer shook her head. "Something about looking at a few parcels of land his company was interested in buying."

Race nodded. "Sorry to interrupt."

"We made plans to attend another charity event together, this time a formal ball the next Saturday, benefiting the Pediatric Burn Center at Mount Sinai Hospital."

A ball meant dancing, and she wasn't much of a dancer. All week long, Aída and Carlos gave her lessons between cases. They danced around the dead bodies in the examination room, the "*danse macabre*," they'd called it.

"I *rented* another gown. These events were getting expensive."

Race gave her a sympathetic nod.

"Donny picked me up in his Bentley and we rode in style to the Beverly Wilshire Hotel. The grand ballroom was decorated like a scene out of the movie Casablanca. Donny told me that attending fancy events like this was really part of his job. He ran a company that invested rich people's money and this was the best way to reach his target customers and gain their trust."

And a great way to take advantage of people when they let their guard down, Race thought.

"While we dined, hospital personnel gave presentations about the important work they did at the burn center. I made a mental note to mention this to Dutch—we could sponsor a charity event and present slides of our most gruesome cases while people dined on finger food and steak tartare! We'd probably make a fortune."

Race grimaced. "I like your gallows humor."

"After dinner, a full orchestra played Viennese waltzes and couples headed to the dance floor. Donny was talking to the people at our table and I could tell he had no intention of asking me to dance. So I stood up, gave him my arm, asked our table companions to excuse us, and led him to the dance floor.

"Even the mighty Achilles had a weak spot—Donny was a God-awful dancer. I led him around through the waltz steps, trying to keep from getting stepped on. An older man, who must have recognized the predicament, came to the rescue. He made a formal bow to Donny and asked if he could have the next dance. Donny obliged, looking grateful. The gentleman was a surgeon at Mount Sinai and an accomplished ballroom dancer. I danced with him, and several other men, until the orchestra stopped playing. When I made my way back to the table, Donny was engaged in a discussion with a group of men.

"Donny introduced me to a couple US Congressmen. I told them I was a medical examiner and the conversation turned to the grim situation my colleagues were facing. Although no one seemed to have a solution for our funding problems, I was able to get the congressmen interested in increased screening and quarantine for TB."

"Is it that much of a problem here?"

"Amongst the homeless, yes. And in the Mississippi Delta, treatment-resistant TB is endemic. There's times I'm convinced those loveable, microscopic balls of fat will be the downfall of human civilization. We'll go back to the Stone Age." Jennifer sipped at her beer she was holding. "And it'll be a disaster—there won't be anywhere to buy *cerveza*."

"Putting it that way would drive a person to drink."

They shared a laugh.

Jennifer took a long swig on her beer and gazed at one of the monitors, but her mind was elsewhere.

When the evening was over and they left the hotel, Donny asked if she wanted to go back to his place. Jennifer told him she was very tired after long hours on her feet. In reality, she wasn't sure what her intentions were. Donny seemed just too good to be true, and she didn't want to get her heart broken. Donny said he understood and asked for a rain-check. He engaged the Nav-Drive, they crawled into the backseat, and made out like teenagers as his land-yacht sailed back to Marina del Rey.

"When we returned to my house, Donny told me he was going to be in Las Vegas again on business. He invited me to join him at the Getty Center for yet another gala. And you know all about that night."

Jennifer choked up and wiped her eyes with the napkin.

Race studied her: in her vulnerable state, she seemed smaller, fragile. He felt his eyes tearing up as well and was at a loss for words. Although he empathized with her, he also felt a sexual stirring. He grabbed his beer and took a sip, feeling guilty.

Then he remembered what Painter told him a few hours ago, about Bosco having dealings with possible Russia underworld figures. He thought it wouldn't hurt to ask.

"I know Detective White asked you this yesterday, but did Mr. Bosco act strangely or differently that night at the Getty?"

Jennifer wiped her face and thought about that a second. She hadn't wanted to say anything the day before about Donny's behavior, and the unusual behavior of Senator Schwarzenegger, but this was the second time she'd been asked that question, maybe they knew, or suspected, something.

She nodded. "Now that you mention it, Donny did seem nervous."

Jennifer went on to tell Race about the two senators and the man they introduced as a Russian inspector, and the fact that the Russian's name was eerily similar to a Russian detective she'd meet a few hours prior to the ball. How the Russian seemed to badger Donny at the ball.

Jennifer's eyes welled up again and she fell silent, thinking that Donny might have been murdered in some complicated Russian intrigue.

Race mulled over everything that he'd learned that the day as he sipped his beer. Two senators and a Russian inspector. A one-eyed Irish thug. The world's strongest man. A Polish-American beauty. The streaker-neighbor Bosco had been having an affair with. Her North Korean diplomat husband. The murdered Russian courier and the physiatrist. He ran his hands through his hair. How did all these pieces fit together?

Chapter 36

Jennifer dried her eyes and waved their waiter over. "Another round of fish tacos, *caballero*." As the waiter turned to leave, she grabbed his arm. "And bring us an order of Yosemite Redbud." She gave Race a brave smile and raised her beer bottle. "Finish your beer, Detective. Chop-chop."

"Another beer?" Race said.

Jennifer gave him a scolding look. "My boyfriend just died. I think I'm entitled to drown my sorrows."

Race raised his beer and tossed it back. He understood why she'd be drinking after losing her boyfriend, especially after the way she found out Bosco died. It made sense, she had a lot of sorrows to drown.

Jennifer pulled two chilled beers from the bucket and handed one to Race. She cracked hers open and took a pull. "I spilled my guts, now I need to drown my sorrows and forget," she hiccupped, "or remember."

That's an unusual thing to say, Race thought as he drank his beer. "I don't follow you," he said. "Most people drink to forget." He wasn't sure how much of himself to divulge to the doctor. But the alcohol dulled his inhibitions and loosened his tongue. "At least I do." Race breathed a sigh of relief when the doctor didn't seem to catch that statement.

"Memory is a traitor," Jennifer said. "Those you want to brush aside cling like lichen on a wave-battered rock. Those we want to forget fade away like…" Jennifer struggled for words, thinking about the roses Donny sent her right before he died.

"Like a woman's beauty," Race interjected, which he immediately regretted.

Jennifer shot him a hurt look. "I was going to say like a rose bloom."

"That's a better analogy," Race said, trying to save face.

"My childhood, before high school…it's a blur. I even have trouble remembering parts of my adult life."

"I'd think drinking would make it harder to remember."

"Alcohol didn't cause the memory losses from when I was a kid. As far as I know, I didn't drink back then." She caught his eye. "You remember the Daly City earthquake? The one that hit San Francisco about twenty years ago?"

Race nodded. "Of course."

"Well, I grew up there—"

"I thought you grew up in Palo Alto."

Jennifer shot Race an icy stare. "What the hell! You've been checking up on me?"

"I *am* a detective."

"And *I'm* not a suspect." She crossed her arms over her chest. "I'd expect some privacy."

The doctor's frigid stare gave him a chill, his heart began thumping, and he couldn't take a deep breath. Race snapped his wrist band, then knocked back the rest of his beer. He felt a tad calmer.

"The only information I gathered on you is readily available," he said. "I noticed that you have opted for the highest level of redaction that the Digital Privacy Law provides."

"I don't want anyone, with a few clicks of a mouse, to find out what brand of cereal I eat…or that I buy the cheap champagne."

Race laughed. "You'd be surprised, most people don't seem to care about their privacy. But there was nothing about you being born in San Francisco."

Jennifer uncrossed her arms and sat back, eyeing her beer. She realized the detective was right and he wouldn't be doing his job if he didn't do a bit of background research on both the victims and the witnesses.

She looked back at him and gave him a thin smile. "After the quake, cyberterrorists breached the county's firewalls and corrupted their data. My identity was stolen so many times," she laughed, "all of a sudden, there were over one-hundred Jennifer Singhs living in Nigeria alone."

"Why did they pick on you?" Race shrugged. "What was so special about your identity?"

"It wasn't just my identity. Cybergangs stole identities of lots of young white boys and girls from the Bay Area and sold them in developing countries."

"I imagine that created all sorts of problems."

"Tell me about it." Jennifer laughed. "It was so bad, the county offered re-chipping to people affected by the security breach. After the police brought a Nigerian girl to our doorstep whose microchip said she was me, my parents took me in to get rechipped. A new name. A new identity. It was as if I was born again. That's why you didn't find out that I was from San Francisco. It was after the quake when we moved to Palo Alto."

"What does that have to do with memory problems?"

"Maybe nothing." Jennifer clucked her tongue. "Maybe everything." She paused, and relived that terrifying day. "Our house sat right on the fault line. The quake hit during summer break when I was just about to turn ten. What happened? It's just flashes. Like bits of a movie.

"There was the sound of a giant explosion. Things flew through the air. I was flying in the air. The walls and ceiling cracked, everything covered in white ash. People screaming. Sheer panic. Our house was severed in two and collapsed. I woke up, buried under debris. I didn't know it at the time, but it was the next day. Almost twenty-four hours. My head pounded.

"Somehow, I dug myself out. One side of our house was three feet higher than the other. My head, my clothes, caked with dried blood. I wandered the streets for hours, in a daze. Everyone was in a daze. Worse than those fire refugee zombies on the promenade. Emergency vehicles, heavy equipment were everywhere. News helicopters buzzing overhead. Fires. Fires everywhere. I didn't even recognize my parents. It's as if the earthquake shook my memory banks clear. I'd suffered a fractured skull and a severe concussion."

"That's what caused your memory to short circuit?"

"Good way to put it, Race. It's like my brain sometimes shorts out. I just have vague and contradictory memories from before the quake. It's called retrograde amnesia."

"I wouldn't mind a bit of that for myself," Race said. "My childhood was no bed of roses."

Jennifer arched an eyebrow, nodding for him to go on. She wanted to bury the memories of the quake.

"Both my parents suffered from schizophrenia. The paranoid type." Race spoke slowly, tying not to slur his speech—the long day and the beers were having their effect. “I’ve had problems. Nervous. Emotional. You could say since childhood. I’m not ashamed to admit it. We—my brother and I—growing up, it was really crazy, chaotic. Our parents drank and fought all the time. And they were big, like sumo wrestlers. I was always nervous as a kid. That’s why I’m so small, at least according to the doctors.”

Jennifer leaned forward towards Race. “You have a brother?”

“Yep. He suffers from schizophrenia. I don’t know if the childhood stress made him susceptible—”

Jennifer shook her head. “Stress doesn’t cause schizophrenia. He inherited it. Where are your parents now?”

Race looked away. “They died when I was a teenager.”

Jennifer sighed. “We have something in common. My parents died right after I graduated high school. They were on a missionary trip to Nepal.” She looked away. “Buried in a landslide.”

“Sorry to hear that. I’ve been meaning to ask you. You don’t look Indian. I mean your name…”

“My dad was Indian, Nepali really, but three generations removed. My mother…mainly Irish.”

One of the waiters dropped off a tray of moist, red-budded marijuana and rolling papers. Jennifer rolled a flaca, lit the joint, and shared it with the detective. Race sat back and took a deep toke.

Maybe it was the alcohol and marijuana. Maybe it was the doctor’s demeanor that impelled him, like being sucked into a gravitational vortex, to open up. Verbalize things he’d kept inside since he was a teenager. Tell her things he’d never told anyone before.

He spoke hesitantly, his voice shaky. “I feel responsible for my parents’ deaths.”

Jennifer let out a short laugh. “You didn’t kill them, did you?”

Race looked down. “In a way.”

Jennifer sat up, put on a serious face, and grabbed Race’s hand. “I was just kidding.” Race continued to look down. “What happened? Get if off your chest.”

“It’s pretty simple, really. But it’s riddled me with guilt.” Race took another hit of the flaca. “My parents got drunk and passed out in bed, like they did every night. I went to bed, woke up coughing, and went to see what was wrong. One of them must have had a lit cigarette in bed and it started their room on fire. Smoke poured out from under their bedroom door. My brother and I shared a room. I ran back, woke him, and we hustled outside. I never woke my parents." His eyes watered. "I could have saved their lives."

Jennifer gave Race a look she'd perfected working in the morgue, the look that said: it's not your fault. "They were already dead from smoke inhalation by the time you noticed the fire."

Race looked into Jennifer's eyes. She seemed so sure of herself that he felt the guilt melting away. "Really?"

Jennifer nodded. "You can take that to the bank. Most people die of inhalation long before the flames burn their bodies." She pointed an index finger at him to emphasize the point. "And, I can guarantee you that's what happened in your parents' case."

Race blew out a long breath, downed the beer in front of him, and grabbed a fresh one. "This calls for a celebration." He cracked the top and drained half the bottle in one swill. "I'd been carrying that guilt around for years."

"Glad I could help." Jennifer sensed that Race needed to talk the issue over more. "You were mentioning your brother. Tell me about him, Race."

Race? He tried not to show his surprise. *Now she's calling me Race? Maybe she's getting comfortable with me. Who knows where that might lead?*

"He has treatment resistant schizophrenia," Race said. "I take medication similar to his. You know what's amazing? With all the advances in..." He struggled to find the word.

"Psychopharmacology," Jennifer said.

"Right," Race said. "The most effective medication for schizophrenia is still a medication that was synthesized back in the late 1950s."

"Clozapine?"

Race nodded. "You know what's ironic?"

Jennifer shrugged.

"The company that discovered the medication is best known for manufacturing a powder to make chocolate milk."

Jennifer smiled. She was enjoying the buzz. And enjoying listening to Race.

"I know I'm not supposed to be drinking on medication," Race said. "But I grew up in an alcoholic family."

Jennifer was peeved. Why was it that everyone who had more than the occasional drink was labeled an alcoholic?

"It's not uncommon for people with schizophrenia to drink," she said, "that doesn't necessarily mean your parents were alcoholics."

"Regardless of what you want to call it," Race said. "I've been around drinking all my life. It seems everyone is drinking, at least here in California."

"Kind of like the Russians and vodka," Jennifer said, languidly.

Race nodded in agreement. He was high and waxed philosophical. "Maybe we've lost a sense of purpose after the Financial Tsunami. And with the Nav-Drive, you can't even use the excuse that you can't drink because you have to drive home."

"Were your parents on Clozapine?"

Race laughed. "Yeah, but they hardly ever took it. Instead, they drank constantly. My childhood, it was a mess. *Loco*. My mother had this belief, this delusional belief, that men's bodies were filled with the devil."

Jennifer was about to ask what he meant when the waiter returned. He set up another sizzling platter of red snapper, accompanied by homemade tortillas and all the fixings.

Race groaned. "I don't know if I can eat another round of tacos." He looked at Jennifer. "I had lunch at an Indian buffet."

Jennifer rubbed her hands. "More for me, then."

The waiter laughed as he looked at the jam-packed table. "Anything else?"

Jennifer looked over the bounty. "More salsa."

The waiter cleared the empty platter. "I'll be back in a *pico*."

As they waited, Jennifer took a toke of the flaca. She grabbed a fresh Pacifico and sat back, sipping an ice-cold beer while gazing at the Clippers game on screen above the bar without really seeing it.

"I'd think you'd drink to forget about all the dead bodies you see every day," Race said, breaking Jennifer's concentration.

"Drinking is an occupational hazard among medical examiners," Jennifer said. "But not in the way you'd think."

"How so?"

"The dead bodies, you get inured to them. It's the grieving loved ones…that you never really get used to." She continued to look at the television monitor, but her eyes became glassy. "The worst is parents. Breaking the news of the loss of a child," Jennifer shook her head, "that's always gut-wrenching." She grabbed her beer. "That'll drive anybody to drink."

The waiter returned with two types of salsa: one a green tomatillo sauce, the other a burnt-red *chile ancho* sauce. Jennifer and Race teased chunks of meat off the fish and rolled their own tacos, washing them down with icy-cold beer.

"What do you do when you're not solving crimes?" Jennifer said to Race as she wiped her mouth.

Race averted his eyes and blushed.

"What's wrong?" Jennifer smiled, strangely enjoying the detective's inquietude. "Sorry if I embarrassed you."

"That's okay." Race took a toke of the flaca and set it down. "I've done a bit of acting."

"Acting?" Jennifer arched her eyebrows. "I didn't peg you as an actor."

Race's face blushed further. "I'm not that good. I have trouble getting in character." He gave Jennifer a lopsided grin. "I specialize in Richard the Third."

"I love that play," Jennifer said and held up her food. "My kingdom for a fish taco."

Race laughed. "I've played Richard the Third twice. The first time at USC. Then last year in a community theater production in Mission Viejo."

"Let me know when you're going to perform again. I'd love to attend." Jennifer looked the plate over, the fish carcass was bare. She picked up the joint and finished it off.

Jennifer studied Race. *So he was a Shakespearean actor?*

She shivered. For a second, she thought about seducing him, then thought it was too bad that he was such a shrimp. And a cop. But he did remind her of someone, an old-time actor. "You kind of remind me of this actor, but I can't remember his name."

Race chuckled and said without hesitation. "Al Pacino?"

Jennifer chuckled along with Race. "I guess I'm not the first one to say that?"

Jennifer squirmed in her chair. Nature called and she excused herself to go to the bathroom.

Race's eyes were like a hawk and moved in perfect time with the sway in the doctor's hips as he watched her make her way to the back. The restrooms were on the other side of the building, through the dining room. When Jennifer disappeared from sight, he sat back in his chair, nursed his beer, and looked through the windows. Outside, couples ambled past the restaurant, many arm in arm. They all looked so carefree, so sure of where they were going. It made Race question where he was going—approaching thirty, and still single and alone. Then he wondered if he'd used the excuse that he needed Doctor Singh's opinion on Painter's testimony in order to go out with her. He had to admit to himself that he probably was just such a cad. He also realized he needed to remember the doctor just lost her boyfriend. Bad luck piled on bad luck—not only did she lose her boyfriend, but to find out about it the way she did. He knew there was no way he could make a move on her.

Hell, who am I kidding? She is light years out of my league.

His thoughts meandered back to the case. He wondered how Dr. Singh would feel about her ex-boyfriend if she knew the real Bosco, if he told her what he'd found out about him today. The successful and respected businessman, this pillar of society was, in fact, a serious drug addict, money launderer, and Ponzi scheme operator. Not an esteemed philanthropist, but a notorious philanderer. A person who used his considerable charm to take advantage of everyone he came in contact with. A man whose good looks was based on plastic surgery and anabolic steroids. It wouldn't be fair to tell her that Bosco's whole life, at least his recent life, had been a sham—even his sexual prowess was an act brought about by huge doses of sexual enhancement drugs. His renowned philanthropic work was just a means to seduce the wives of rich men and gain access to their money. Race decided he wasn't going to tell her that—maybe he wasn't such a cad after all.

Jennifer left the bathroom and turned down the hallway to head back to her table. She came to an abrupt stop, almost bumping into a pair of beefy men blocking her path.

"Excuse me," she said as she moved to the side to let them pass.

Neither of the men budged. "We would like to talk to you outside," one of the men said with a strong Russian accent.

She looked them up and down. They had dark Slavic looks and could have been twins, except the man doing the talking had a Russian Orthodox cross tattoo on his neck. Both were a head taller than her. They were dressed in black, from black tee shirts, which barely hid their chiseled upper torsos, down to their commando-style pants and military boots. They were both bald and had deadly serious looks on their faces.

"Please move out of the way," Jennifer said, becoming angry.

The tattooed man reached out toward her.

Jennifer stepped back a pace and pushed his hand to the side. "I'm warning you, back off," she spat at them.

They both smiled.

"We need to talk to you," the tattooed man said.

"I have nothing to say to you two."

From behind the Russians, a male voice said haltingly, "What's going on here? I need to use the bathroom."

The Russians both turned their heads. The previously silent Russian said, "Bathroom broken. Go outside."

The man waiting for the bathroom gave them a strange look, then turned on his heel.

Their attention focused elsewhere, Jennifer tried to squeeze between the Russians. They closed the gap between themselves and she bumped into their bodies, which were as solid as stone walls.

"This is your last warning," Jennifer said. "Step aside."

The Russians looked at her with amusement on their faces. The tattooed man's hand shot forward and he grabbed Jennifer's arm in a vise-like grip.

She gritted her teeth and looked up at him. She could easily pivot, smash him in the throat with the heel of her hand, and crush his trachea. But that seemed to be a bit of overkill for the situation. And even if she did that, she didn't know what the other Russian might do. She decided to bide her time and relaxed her muscles, making herself firm, yet flexible as bamboo.

"Come outside. We have a friend who would like to have a little chat with you," the tattooed Russian said.

Just then, a voice boomed out from behind the Russians. "Hold it right there."

Jennifer caught sight of a uniformed cop standing a few feet away, legs firmly planted on the floor, right hand near his pistol.

"Keep your hands where I can see them," he ordered.

The Russian without the tattoo turned his hands palm up toward the officer. "Everything okay, Mr. Policeman," he said.

The other Russian hesitated, then scowled and his shoulders slumped. He released Jennifer's arm, and raised his hands chest high toward the officer. "We were just seeing about hiring this lyscee."

Jennifer felt her blood boil. She gritted her teeth until they were about to shatter. Now that he'd called her a prostitute, she wished she had crushed both of his testicles as well as his trachea.

The officer seemed to relax. "Is that true?" he asked.

Jennifer pushed her way past the Russians. "I'm not a lyscee," she said in anger. "Those guys wouldn't let me through the hallway."

"We were only discussing prices," the tattooed Russian said, his voice smooth as silk.

The officer looked at Jennifer. "Does anyone want to press charges?"

"I do," Jennifer said with her hands on her hips. "For false imprisonment."

The officer seemed to hesitate.

"We weren't putting her in prison," the non-tattooed Russian said. "She was telling us how much she charge for to do two men."

"Get out of here," the officer said. "Next time, you guys are going to spend the night in jail."

The Russians nodded and disappeared out the front door.

"Why didn't you arrest those guys?" Jennifer yelled at the cop.

"Settle down, ma'am" the officer said quietly. "You don't want to get arrested yourself."

She took a few deep breaths. "Okay. Why did you let those thugs go?"

He smiled at her sadly. "You're obviously intoxicated. Your speech is slurred and you're unsteady on your feet."

"I've only had…" Jennifer struggled to remember how many beers she drank. "Not too many."

"And your eyes are red. You've been smoking reefer. If this case went to trial, your testimony would be thrown out."

"But you saw them boxing me into that hallway."

"The only thing I saw was the backs of their shoulders and them talking to you."

"Then what were you doing here in the first place?"

"A guy flagged me down on the sidewalk. Said there might be trouble."

Jennifer took time to process what happened. The officer was probably right, there really wasn't a case. She decided to save face. "Thanks for your help, Officer."

"Sergeant Webb." He handed her his card. "I'm sorry I couldn't arrest those two. But at least I got them out of your hair."

Jennifer nodded sadly and returned to the table, her nerves on edge. She picked up her beer and threw it back.

Race had a look of concern on his face. "I couldn't see the restrooms from here. Where were you so long?"

She patted Race on the back, then sat down. "I had a run-in with a couple of Russian brutes."

"You sure they were Russian?" Race asked.

"I speak a few words of Russian, not enough to recognize regional accents. But they seemed to be speaking with a Russian accent."

Race was intrigued and wondered if they could be the killers they were looking for. "What did they look like?" When Jennifer described the two men, Race sat up. "They could be the guys that murdered the Russian courier and Dr. Sing."

Jennifer felt embarrassed, the alcohol might be affecting her more than she was willing to admit. "Shit. I didn't think of that. I should have told that to the cop who helped me out."

Race gave her his best sympathetic look. "But then again, there's any number of Russians wandering around L'Orange that look just like that."

Jennifer nodded. Southern California was teeming with Russians, and these guys could have been just another group of bodyguards out trying to find women for their billionaire boss.

The waiter returned and placed two shot glasses of tequila, a plate of sliced lemons and limes, and coarse salt on the table. "Compliments of the owner," he told them.

Jennifer didn't want to drink anymore, she felt that she'd reached her limit for the night, but she wanted to stay on good terms with the management. And her nerves were still shaken from the run-in with the Russians. She held the tequila up, about to toss it back, when something about the clear liquid reminded her of Donny and she felt her eyes watering up. She tossed the drink back and sucked on a lime wedge, trying to hide her watery eyes.

"How do you like working Homicide?" she asked, trying to distract herself from the thought that she'd never see Donny again.

Race laughed. "Today was my first day on my own, and things didn't go well. I tried to arrest someone when I should have been using persuasion. The very first person I was interviewing today, I was so anxious and flustered I could hardly get a coherent word out."

Jennifer smiled sympathetically. "When I saw an autopsy the first time, just as the doctor made that incision, I threw up."

"That makes me feel better. Fortunately, I ran across an older cop who pretty much babysat me all day and explained how things are done. And not done."

"I noticed that you're a detective grade level seven. That's very high level, so how come—"

Race finished her sentence because he was used to the question. "So how come a grade seven detective knows nothing about investigation?"

Jennifer nodded tentatively.

Race smiled. "Most people don't understand how undercover work operates. One thing, I never made an arrest or took part in interrogations. Think about it for a second. If I did, my cover would have been completely blown. When I had an arrest that needed to be made, I'd pass the information along to my boss, and he'd get that over to the patrol division who'd do the pickup. From there, the investigating detectives in the appropriate department handled the interrogations. I'd interface with them, anonymously, behind a two-way mirror. Today's the first time I ever arrested anyone, or did interviews."

"In medicine, there's a saying that goes: see one, do one, teach one. The idea is that you can watch somebody else do a procedure as many times as you want, but until you actually do one yourself—"

"You'll never be good at it," Race finished the statement.

"Exactly." The waiter came by and asked if they needed anything else. Race was surprised when Jennifer told him to bring another round of tequila shots.

"Tell me," Jennifer asked Race when the waiter left, "how did you end up a cop?"

Race laughed. "It's a long story, but it doesn't start so far away as your story did. Mine starts in Long Beach. I don't know if you'd be interested in hearing…"

"My evening plans were to lie in bed and fall asleep doing the New York Times crossword puzzle."

The waiter returned with the drinks.

Race hesitated and saw the doctor eyeing him, waiting with her shot glass raised. He was on his fourth beer, this would be the second shot of tequila, and he had to report to work first thing in the morning. But he couldn't let her show him up in drinking. He looked at Jennifer through slitted eyes and wondered if she was trying to get him so drunk he'd blab something he shouldn't about the case. He dismissed the idea. Even though she was one of the last people to see Bosco alive, Billings-Li insisted she saw the victim Saturday morning, after Jennifer left the house.

They both downed the fiery liquid, then sucked on a lime wedge.

Jennifer sipped her beer and studied her drinking companion. He was rather small for a policeman, and too young looking to even be out of college, much less a high-level detective. She pegged him as an accountant type—he'd be too shy and timid to be a used car salesman. He even dressed drab like an accountant, which, now that she thought about it, seemed to be the same brown clothes he was wearing the day before at the morgue. She was intrigued at how his face was so angular and hawk-like, how his narrow, pointy nose resembled a beak, and his eyes even seemed to move like a bird of prey, scanning the area for lurking danger.

Race looked out into the distance, his eyes slightly unfocused, as he thought about his years on the police force.

Chapter 37

"My journey began my junior year at Long Beach State," Race said. "I was studying sociology, anthropology, psychology, anything with an 'ology. I was taking all sorts of classes, hoping my career would magically appear. One day, I attended a job fair on campus. All the booths had signs that they were looking for motivated, hard-working individuals. I jokingly asked a recruiter where a person would go if they were unmotivated and not hard-working. They pointed me to the L'Orange County employment booth."

Jennifer laughed. "Seems an appropriate referral."

"I stopped by LOPD's booth, lured by the free pen and a key chain. As I picked up the bait, the recruiters expressed interest in me. I never really thought about being a cop—I'm short, small...and really not that aggressive. I'm not afraid to admit that I'm kind of timid and gun-shy. But, I got to thinking that being a police officer wouldn't be so bad. I wouldn't have to worry about being pushed around, I could carry a gun, show my badge, wear a uniform, and people would respect me. The police force had other plans for me. I spent the last seven years in Vice, where I didn't carry a gun or a badge, I didn't wear a uniform, and I didn't get any respect... quite ironic I guess."

"You never know where life's currents are going to take you," Jennifer said. "I planned on practicing psychiatry, but look where I ended up."

"I wanted to work Homicide," Race said, "but there weren't any openings at the time. I spent the first three months of my police career receiving extra training at the academy, specializing in undercover work. The Vice commander picked me to infiltrate one of the local high schools and work my way up the ladder to crack the crack suppliers at the school. Before I started Vice, I could never figure out why, if alcohol, marijuana, steroids, and just about everything else is legal, why was the department worried about illegal cocaine use in the high schools? After all, those kids could buy Coke-Point Five legally as soon as they turned twenty-one. What's your take on the use of cocaine?"

"Coke-Point Five has about the same amount of cocaine as the coca leaves that the Incas have been chewing for over five thousand years. And it has about the same amount of active cocaine that used to be in a number of very popular soft drinks at the turn of the twentieth century."

"I was referring to illegal cocaine. People die using that stuff, don't they?"

Jennifer shrugged. "Alcohol, cigarettes, pain pills—they're legal, yet our morgue handles over two hundred deaths from each of them a month. We see one or two deaths over the same time period from cocaine. So if we were going to outlaw anything—and I'm not suggesting we should—those are the real dangers."

"Pain pills?"

"Pain pills." Jennifer nodded. "Pain pills combined with nerve pills and alcohol are one of the leading causes of death in Southern California."

"I didn't know that," Race said.

Jennifer leaned in close and looked around to make sure nobody could overhear her. "You want to know why cocaine is still illegal?"

Race leaned in and nodded eagerly.

Jennifer took a drink of beer. "Because LOPD's making too much money off it being illegal."

Race felt shocked. It took him almost seven years working Vice to figure that out for himself. "You're right," Race said. "Too many people in government are making too much money from *polvo*. Legalization would cause the police force to lose a lucrative source of income."

Jennifer laughed. "Everybody has a scam these days."

"What's yours?"

Jennifer thought that over a second, then frowned. "You know what? I guess I'm one of the few that doesn't have one."

"The morgue probably pays you enough to live on."

Jennifer laughed. "I wish."

"Try working for LOPD. Working for them is like being a waiter. They pay you so little you have to find ways to supplement your salary."

"How did you survive in Vice?"

"I became an expert in the forfeiture laws. I brought in so much money to the department that they moved me up the ladder fast and gave me a ton of bonuses."

"It seems to me that you guys abuse those forfeiture laws," Jennifer said.

"We just use the laws as written."

Jennifer gave him a look of disagreement. "You were saying, they assigned you to the high school beat."

"I was right out of college, and there I was, right back in high school."

Jennifer shivered. "I'd like to forget high school."

"You're not the only one." The corners of Race's mouth turned up. "They had me enroll as a junior transfer student at Hollywood High School. Physically, I looked the part of a high school student. Problem was, I didn't have any parents and was living on my own, which is unusual for a high school student. So they assigned me a fictional uncle: an older undercover cop."

"How'd that work out?"

"I gave up my studio apartment and moved in with my new mentor. He'd been working the unlicensed prostitution and the street crack trades. By the time I'd moved in with him, he'd become jaded. He was locking up the low-level hustlers and prostitutes, but was never able to make any headway with the root of the problem—the sex slaves being brought in from Mexico and Central America. Little did I know that I'd eventually become jaded, just like him."

"That's how I've been feeling at work lately. We've been so overwhelmed, it's been hard to treat the corpses with the respect they deserve."

"I guess we all change over time." Race sipped his beer. "Anyway, in lieu of stopping illegal prostitution, my fictional uncle dated them. He shook down the dealers for drugs. He drank beer for breakfast, scotch for lunch, tequila for dinner, and cheap wine for a midnight snack. He smoked crack to stay awake, and opium to fall asleep. He was a great role model." Race scoffed. "I was young and naïve. And still idealistic."

"You're too young to lose your idealism."

Race looked away and took a sip of his beer. It was warm and had gone slightly flat. He pushed it to the side and grabbed another out of the sweating bucket.

Race caught out of his peripheral vision a deeply tanned man, dressed in board shorts and a Hawaiian shirt wave over to Jennifer. The doctor didn't seem to notice the man until he was at the table throwing his arms around her in a very intimate manner. Jennifer seemed to cringe just a little and didn't put her arms around the newcomer.

"Jennifer," the man said with a beaming smile. "Haven't seen you in ages."

Jennifer acted rather frigidly to him. "We've been inundated at work."

The man glanced at Race, looked him up and down, and had a weakly hidden look of disdain. "Is this the new boyfriend I've heard you've been seeing?"

Jennifer let out a little laugh, like how could anybody think she'd be dating him. "This is the restaurant's owner, Jaime Pescado," she said to Race. "And this is Detective Horace Griffin."

"A police detective?" Jaime said. He looked at all the empty beer bottles on the table. "Are you on a case?"

Race gave him a nod. His head was spinning from the alcohol and he struggled to speak clearly. "That's right."

Jaime leaned across the table and thrust out his hand. His Hawaiian shirt came open, revealing his hairy chest. "Nice to meet you." He turned back to Jennifer and leaned very close to her. Race strained and barely heard what he said. "The dinner invitation's still open." Jennifer shrugged. "Give me a chance."

Jennifer shook her head. "You had your chance and you blew it."

Race felt his blood rush to the surface. He knew he and Jennifer weren't an item. He knew she was out of his league. He knew technically she was a suspect. But he couldn't control the jealousy coursing through his veins.

And Race assumed the owner didn't know that Jennifer's boyfriend, Bosco, had just been killed.

"C'mon," Jaime said to Jennifer. "I don't know why you were so upset."

"You were flirting with another woman right under my nose."

Jaime raised his hands as if in surrender. "She was an old friend of mine."

Jennifer laughed dismissively. "Old friend? She was barely out of her teens."

Jaime took Jennifer's hand and stared into her eyes with an intense look. "Let's have dinner and talk it through."

"Not now." Her eyes caught Race's and she whispered to Jaime. "Let me work some things through."

Jaime smiled and gave Jennifer a peck on the cheek. "I'll give you a call." He turned to Race and gave him a big smile, as if the matter was settled in his favor. "Enjoy your dinner." Then he left and began talking to the group at the next table.

"An old boyfriend?" Race asked.

Jennifer didn't make eye contact. She let out a deep breath. "None of your business," she finally said.

True, Race thought as he slowly sipped his beer. Just because he was a detective it didn't give him the right to pry into every facet of a person's life. And did he really want to know about all the men Jennifer dated over the years? That would just make him uncomfortable, and he couldn't figure out why he was already having possessive feelings about the doctor. She'd never given him the least bit of reason to believe she was interested in him.

He looked down at his beer bottle, thinking he needed to slow down, but he had such a good buzz going that he wasn't nervous being around such a beautiful woman. He looked her up and down. Although she was beautiful, she was formidable, solidly built under a soft exterior. He knew the marijuana was affecting him, because she began to look dangerous. He held back a chuckle as he thought that if they got in a fight, she could probably kick his ass.

Jennifer turned her attention to the television behind the bar. The Clippers game had less than a minute to go and the score was tied. In her peripheral vision, she could see the detective eyeing her. Let him look, she thought. She could never be interested in a pipsqueak like him. But she was impressed, in a way, because the little guy was deeper and more complex than she initially thought. He seemed passionate about a great deal of things, and yet had a certain innocence and vulnerability that would be appealing to certain women. Women with more maternal instincts than she had.

The game ended, a basket at the buzzing giving the Clippers the victory. A waitress, dressed in a Hawaiian shirt and surf pants, came to their table and dropped off an order of redbud. "Compliments of the owner," she said as she cleared away the plates, then lit the candle sitting on the table.

Jennifer rolled a flaca, lit up, took a puff, and passed it to Race.

When Race reached over, he caught Jennifer's eyes. Light from the flickering candle highlighted the golden flecks in her green eyes and he felt himself melting inside. Her hair, messy as it was, only made her look more attractive.

Jennifer saw him looking at her. She tilted her head, but kept his gaze. In the dim candlelight, the detective's angular features softened. His chocolate-colored eyes glowed and no longer seemed piercing. His face took on a gravitas, as if he were an accomplished actor, not an inexperienced cop.

Without taking her eyes from him, she said, "So, you're no longer idealistic, Race." Jennifer could tell her voice was slurred. She spoke carefully. "What happened?"

Race clinched his jaw. He snapped his anxiety bracelet and took a puff from flaca. He exhaled, saying through a cloud of smoke, "A girl."

Jennifer chuckled. "You're blaming a woman?"

"What's so amusing? Women blame everything on men."

"That's because men are to blame for everything. What did this poor woman do to scar you?"

"It wasn't anything she did." Race shook his head sadly. "It was something I did."

Jennifer sat back and sipped on her beer. She looked at Race through half-lidded eyes. "This I've gotta hear."

Chapter 38

"Her name was Aset," Race said.

He watched as Jennifer scrunched her nose in thought.

"Aset?" she said. "Was she Egyptian?"

"Good guess," Race said. "Her family was originally from Lebanon."

Jennifer looked on as Race's face seemed to soften and his eyes took on a far-away look.

"I was working undercover at USC," he said. "To blend in with the other students, I took a full load of classes. One fateful day, I met Aset in a Shakespeare acting class."

"I'm a big fan of the bard," Jennifer said.

"I wasn't before I took the class, but I am now," Race said.

"Sorry to interrupt. You were talking about Aset."

Race put his arms on the table and smiled. "She was like an angel. A dark-skinned angel. She had dark hair straight down to her shoulders, caramel-colored skin and creamy-brown eyes. She was my height, maybe a little shorter. She had a very small, delicate body, like a precious bird.

"Sounds like a carbon copy of you."

Race looked at himself in the reflection off his beer bottle and nodded. "I never would have had the nerve to go up and introduce myself to her, but through a quirk of fate, we were assigned to be partners, to act out a scene from Hamlet. I was to be the Danish Prince, she was to be Ophelia."

"I hope you didn't send her to a nunnery."

"Funny," Race said. "One thing led to another, and we began seeing each other outside of class. Since I was technically on duty, I was unsure whether I should get emotionally involved with a student. I took things slow, which seemed to impress her and she made the first move. Eventually, we became a couple and toward the end of the semester, she invited me to her parents' house for dinner. Her father, Reza, was a Lebanese refugee and owned a chain of Greek restaurants."

"You're speaking about her father in the past tense," Jennifer said. "I take it he's no longer alive."

Race tightened his jaw and nodded. "Aset's father supported not only his family, but an extended family back in Lebanon and relatives in Columbia. On top of that, he felt personally responsible for all his employees, over a thousand of them. Although his business grossed millions a year, his expenses were even greater. He'd fallen seriously behind on his taxes and the interest and penalties kept mounting. He was afraid he was going to lose his entire business, letting down all the people who depended on him."

"Sounds like he was under a lot of pressure."

Race nodded. "Reza's parents treated me like one of their own. Since my parents are dead, and the only family I have is a brother, and he suffers from schizophrenia, I enjoyed being part of a warm, happy family for the first time in my life."

"I can sympathize," Jennifer said with a sigh. "I'm in the same boat."

"One day, after eating Sunday dinner at their home, Reza's father asked me to join him in his study. He said he knew I was making good money—I drove an exotic sports car, had my own place by that time—and that I was a drug dealer. I didn't deny it, but my expression must have given me away. As we smoked an opium-filled hookah, Reza laid out his financial problems to me and made me a proposal, which I wish I'd rejected out of hand. His brother lived in Columbia and, through contacts, could purchase cocaine directly from the source in the mountains.

"The problem was that they had no way of selling the drugs in the United States. His family was in the restaurant business and didn't have a distribution network for cocaine. Reza's proposal was simple: he would fly down to meet his brother outside Cali, purchase a hundred pounds of pure cocaine, and fly it back here. He asked if I would be able to move such a quantity and what they could expect to make. I agreed to help and told him he could expect to make a two million SDR profit. Reza wanted to go ahead with the deal, saying that would just about pay off the IRS.

"He chartered a private jet from a shady company out of Van Nuys. I flew down to Columbia with him and a suitcase full of cash. I stayed with the plane. Reza, his brother, and a team of armed guards drove into the mountains to exchange the cash for two bundles of cocaine. I flew back with the merchandise. Reza flew back commercially—I didn't want him in the jet when we landed in case something went wrong. If I were arrested, I could always duck the charges, being an undercover vice cop. But he'd spend decades in prison.

"Everything went smoothly. I landed at the Santa Monica airport, where, at the end of the runway, a police cruiser was waiting. We off-loaded the cargo before heading to the terminal and going through Customs. In less than two months, I was able to sell the entire amount and passed the profits to Reza. One thing I failed to calculate was with surge in supply, the street price of *polvo* would drop. When I handed over the profits, it was less than one million SDR. Of course Reza wanted, no needed, to do it again—he was so fixated on completely paying off the IRS. So we planned another trip to Cali.

"Two days before we were scheduled to go, Reza received a call that his sister-in-law had a stroke and was hospitalized over there. She wasn't expected to live. Reza lost his head and panicked. He left immediately, forgetting to notify me about the change in plans. Off he flew with another suitcase of cash. He made it to the hospital and was able to see his relative just before she passed away. After the funeral, he and his brother picked up one hundred-fifty pounds of cocaine. And Reza flew back to LA. What he forgot to do was arrange to have me pick up the cocaine before the plane made it to the hanger. When he reached the terminal, the customs inspector saw that the plane just came in from Cali. And with Reza sweating and stammering, he brought in the drug-sniffing dogs and searched the plane. It didn't take long. They found the stash in a false compartment in the hold, and Reza was arrested.

"He was able to get out of jail on bail, but he was a broken man, blaming himself for being so stupid and greedy. He told me he was worth more dead than alive. I wish I'd understood what he was trying to tell me, because that night he died when his car went over the guardrail on the Pacific Coast Highway just north of Malibu. With his death, his IRS debts went away and his wife collected on a nice insurance policy, allowing the family to take over the restaurants debt-free."

Race fell silent, his eyes seemed to water.

"It looks like that hit you hard," Jennifer said.

"It did." Race took a deep breath and put on a brave smile. "Reza's death hit me really hard. I felt I was personally responsible. He was just trying to support his family, run his businesses, and I got him into something way over his head. I felt so guilty and ashamed. And every time I saw Aset, it just made the feeling worse. She was a constant reminder of my role in her father's suicide." Race finished his beer in one large gulp. "And I didn't have the courage to tell her the truth about my involvement in her father's death. We grew apart and stopped seeing each other.

"I took a hard look at myself and didn't like what I saw. I was corrupting and damaging many more lives than just that of poor Reza. I was the Big Pescado. Ironic, I spent those seven years trying to discover myself, in a sense. I had to get out of Vice. I couldn't just ask for a transfer because my bosses were making too much money off my little enterprise. I told my lieutenant that if he promised to transfer me to Homicide, I'd set up a meeting between him and my contact in Columbia—Reza's brother. The department was so happy to have a steady supply that they agreed. Not only did they transfer me, but gave me a raise and upgraded me to detective level seven. One week later and here I am, working my first homicide case." Race swayed on his seat and caught himself from falling by grabbing the edge of the table. "And I'm really drunk."

Jennifer finished her beer and set it down. "I've got a buzz too." She reached out and touched his hand. "I'm impressed that you had the *cajones* to leave. Brave thing to do." She looked in the bucket, all the beers were gone. "C'mon, let's blow this place."

Race pulled out his wallet. "Can we split the bill?"

Jennifer nodded and waved to their waiter, gesturing that they were ready for the bill.

The blond haired man came over and said, "The meal's on the house."

Jennifer sighed. She didn't want to be beholden to Jaime, but money was tight. "Thanks," she said, and handed him a twenty.

"See you on the basketball courts sometime soon?" the waiter asked.

Jennifer stood up and patted him on the back. "I hope, pal." She thought about the mess at the morgue. "I hope so."

Chapter 39

The sun was down and a cool wind blew from off the ocean, pushing the sooty air inland and revealing a star-lit sky. Thousands of people milled about the promenade. Bright lights from the storefronts added to those of the street lights, making the area look like daytime. Jennifer felt chilled, grabbed a hooded sweatshirt from her gym bag, and pulled it on. Race shivered and tightened his blazer around himself, walking on the lee side of Jennifer, drafting like a NASCAR driver while trying to stay warm.

They both walked unsteadily as they wove their way about the crowd, occasionally bumping into an oncoming pedestrian.

I've got to stop drinking like this, Jennifer thought. It's going to ruin my health.

What kind of impression am I making on the doctor? Race wondered. It won't be a good one if I get sick.

"Where'd you say you parked, Detective?" Jennifer said, her voice slurred.

Race looked up at Jennifer. *Detective? Why so formal all of a sudden? What happened? She'd been calling me Race back at the restaurant.*

He knew his speech was going to be slurred as well, so he spoke slower, fighting to enunciate. "My car's in the Washington Boulevard lot. At the end of the boardwalk." Race looked around for a bathroom. "Those drinks have gone right through me. I need to make a pit stop."

Jennifer waved him on. "There's restrooms up ahead."

They passed the Muscle Beach gym, dark and empty, then Jennifer turned right, heading toward the ocean. Just before the tree line ended, a beige brick building with outdoor shower heads and a dozen or so public toilets sat adjacent to the lit basketball courts.

"I'll wait for you at the courts," Jennifer told Race.

Race took off for the restrooms and Jennifer headed to the courts. She had trouble walking a straight line. The palm trees seemed to be spinning around as if in a clothes drier. She took deep breaths to try to control a wave of nausea.

On the courts, a game of three-on-four was taking place. One of the players shot, the ball careened off the rim, and came rolling her way. She moved to pick it up, stumbling over her own feet as she scooped up the ball.

"Doc," the man who'd ran over to retrieve the ball said. "How about some four-on-four? We've got an odd number of players."

Jennifer bounce-passed the ball back to him. "I just finished dinner and I'm walking someone back to his car. Maybe I'll come back later." She felt as if she were on a ship tossed about by the waves—there was no way she'd be able to play later.

"We'll be out here all night," the man said, and ran back to the court.

Race staggered back, his face pasty and damp. "I need to sit down for a minute. I'm not feeling well."

Jennifer wasn't feeling all that well herself. "Let's sit on the beach wall. The ocean breeze might help."

She led Race to a stone wall about thigh-high, which separated the tree line from the sandy beach. They swung their legs over the irregular rock wall and sat looking out at the dark ocean. Jennifer breathed in deeply. The cool breeze off the ocean blew her hair around and helped sober her up. The salty, fishy smell opened her sinuses making breathing less of a chore. Above, the sky sparkled with stars.

Race let out a soft moan and Jennifer peered over. The detective was shivering, his head was down, buried between his hands.

"Breathe slow and deep," Jennifer told him. "Look out to the horizon." She searched her gym bag to see if she had anything to help keep the detective warm—the bag was empty except for a couple towels. She handed one to Race, which he used to wipe his face. The other she draped over his shoulders. Although she didn't want to do it, knowing how he'd probably interpret the gesture, she squeezed next to him and put her arm over his shoulder, hoping her body heat would be of help.

Despite feeling sick and battling rising bile, Race became aroused by her feminine presence. Beneath the soft layer of skin, the doctor's body was hard and solid, and didn't give as he snuggled closer. He rested his head against her sinewy shoulder; she didn't move away. The heat of her body took some of the chill off and he no longer felt as if he were freezing. He looked up, the stars seemed to spin around his head and became streaks of light. He needed to talk, to keep his mind off the waves of nausea surging up his throat.

"What do you think of the Big Bang?" he asked.

Jennifer rolled her eyes and pushed Race away. "That's about the lamest come-on line I've ever heard."

"I meant…well," Race stammered. "I was just looking up at the stars and then got to thinking."

"Right." She gave him a harsh look. "I know what you were thinking."

Race laughed to himself. Now that she mentioned it, he couldn't deny she'd aroused primal urges—wouldn't any red-blooded man react the same pressed against her body. "Your assistant told me you'd dated an astronomer. And on my way over here, I saw that you've written a couple articles on cosmology."

Jennifer was impressed the detective didn't say cosmetology. But his spying on her pissed her off and she felt her anger rise.

"Why are you spying on me? Is there something wrong with you?"

Race turned his palms up. "I already told you, I'm a detective."

Jennifer jumped up and put her hands on her hips. "I'm not a suspect. Am I?"

She waited for Race to answer. He didn't make eye contact with her.

"I'm entitled to my privacy," she yelled at him.

"I'm sorry," Race blurted out. The waves of nausea were no longer controllable and he bolted up. "I'm going to be sick." He rushed back to the restrooms and disappeared into one of the stalls.

Jennifer sighed and sat down. She could kill that little shrimp. Griffin told her he was just gathering information to find Donny's killer. But she wouldn't be surprised if he was eying her as a suspect all along. Isn't that what all cops do? The first person they suspect is the person closest to the deceased.

She took a few deep breaths and calmed down. She realized he never said she was a suspect, perhaps he was right to do research into someone he was about to talk to. She really couldn't blame him for finding out what he could about everyone involved in the case. At the morgue, sometimes the smallest, seemingly least significant clue can lead to the answer. And now that those photos from the Getty ball were printed in the LA Times, her privacy was shot, at least for the time being.

Race emerged from the stall, wiping his face with Jennifer's gym towel. His color seemed to have returned and he sat back down on the wall.

"Sorry about flying off the handle a minute ago," Jennifer said.

He gave her a sad smile. "I didn't take it personally. It's just that I was reviewing information on you in the public domain, which is standard procedure by the way, and buried amongst all the times you've been cited in the forensic pathology literature, were two articles you wrote relating to astronomy." He shrugged. "They just seemed to stick out."

"Astronomy's a hobby of mine."

"And I noticed you have an observatory on the roof of your house."

Jennifer laughed. "I inherited that from the previous owner."

Jennifer remained seated, but kept space between herself and the detective. She looked up at the dark sky. Thousands of stars twinkled like diamonds. It was a great night for astrophotography—her telescope was probably active right now. The nausea and vertigo seemed to have passed; she felt a warm, pleasant buzz. And her anger at Race had dissipated.

"Were you serious earlier?" she asked him. "About my thoughts on the Big Bang?"

Race nodded and waited.

"I don't really buy the current theory," Jennifer said. "It doesn't make sense. The entire mass of the universe compacted into an infinitesimal point, then exploding and expanding outward, forming the galaxies as we see them today." She turned and looked at Race. "That's the theory, more or less, right?"

He gave her a nod. "But if I understood your articles, you're not buying that?"

"It doesn't make sense." Her didactic juices began to flow. "Look at it this way: if the entire mass of the galaxy was compacted down to one point, why would it explode? If we accept Einstein's theory of general relativity, which I do, how could there even have been an explosion? The gravity produced from that giant universe-sized black hole would have been so strong that nothing could have escaped. The escape velocity would have been billions of times the speed of light."

Race nodded. "What do you think happened?"

Jennifer looked over and smiled. Race had the towel wrapped tightly around his shivering shoulders. She scuttled next to him and put her arm around his shoulders, pulling him close.

Race's teeth chattered, his body shook, and his nose was red

"I think the universe expands and contracts," Jennifer said. "At the end of the last contraction, during the Big Crunch, most of the mass of the universe was present in a small number of super-massive black holes, each the mass of tens of billions of galaxies. As the universe became smaller and smaller, these mega-black holes circled around each other, spiraling in, faster and faster, conserving angular momentum. One fateful moment, two of these bodies collided head-on, producing an explosion so powerful that if every person on Earth, all seven plus billion of us, exploded a nuclear bomb every second since the beginning of time, over fifteen billion years ago, it wouldn't even come close to what was released in the Big Bang."

"That's hard to envision." Race scratched his head. "But how could the universe expand? Wouldn't gravitation from that compacted universe be too high to allow anything to escape?"

"The usual explanation is that spacetime was expanding rapidly in the early history of the universe, the Inflationary Universe Theory. Here's what I think is the solution to the problem. The speed of light is the maximum speed anything can reach in our common experience—but the compacted universe wasn't a common condition. The gravitational spacetime curvature would have been immense. Look at any wave phenomenon, as the medium the wave moves in becomes denser, the wave moves faster. Think about the sound wave. Sound moves faster in water then in air, it moves even faster in iron. Light is a wave, the medium it moves in is gravitational spacetime. The gravitational spacetime at the moment of the Big Bang would have been higher than it is now by more than a trillion-trillion, and the speed of light, the speed limit so to speak, would have been proportionally higher as well. That is what allowed the matter in the early universe to expand. And it also explains the relative homogeneity of the universe. The theory that the speed of light increases as the temperature increases seems silly, because temperature is nothing more than the measure of random motion of particles, so there doesn't seem to be any connection between the two, since they are both just measures of speed of motion. That seems to be a classic tautology—"

"Something that defines itself?" Race said.

"I'm impressed." Jennifer nudged Race. "Pretty big word for a detective to know."

"You'd be surprised what I know." Race snuggled in closer. "So what you're saying is that the theory that light travels faster when temperatures are high is just repeating the same thing twice, which in this case doesn't make it true. Your theory, it could explain what happens inside the black holes we see today, like the one in the center of our galaxy. If you're correct, it would mean that inside black holes, time and motion haven't come to a standstill, even though we cannot observe it directly, things are still happening inside."

"No shit, Sherlock." Jennifer chuckled. "Since we now have fairly good evidence that the universe is a closed system and will contract someday, we are essentially living inside a black hole, at least to a hypothetical outside observer, and things haven't come to a standstill here."

Race chuckled. "Except on Capitol Hill."

Jennifer laughed. "That's the biggest black hole in the known universe."

"So you think our universe will one day contract?"

Jennifer nodded. "Are you familiar with Torcido-Luz geometry?"

Race shook his head.

"According to the theory of the Chilean mathematicians Torcido and Luz, the universe is at least nine times smaller in volume than had been thought at the beginning of the century. Hence the critical density of the universe, Omega, is well over one, making it a certainty that our universe will end in a Big Crunch."

Jennifer stretched out her arms and yawned. Then she squirmed and stood up. "I need a bathroom break, and I'm not gonna use those public toilets. I don't live too far from here." She gestured to Race. "Follow me."

Chapter 40

Jennifer was enjoying Race's company and didn't want the evening to end so soon. The detective was more knowledgeable than the typical cop who just wanted to get in her pants. And there was something about him, a vulnerability that, even though she didn't have strong maternal instincts, elicited nurturing feelings in her.

"Why don't you walk me home?" she said. "I live a few blocks away. You can use my bathroom before you head out." She let out a short laugh. "It's slightly cleaner than the facilities on the beach."

Race agreed.

They walked side by side along the promenade. Jennifer kept an arms distance from Race. Just before they reached Washington Boulevard, Jennifer stopped at a stand-alone coffee bar called Café Expresso.

"How are you doing, sweetie," the rotund woman behind the counter said.

Jennifer ordered a double espresso, Race ordered the same. Sipping her coffee, she led Race along the beach until they reached a footpath perpendicular to the ocean, then turned inland, leaving behind the three-story glass-and-steel houses fronting the ocean. They crossed the one-lane road called Speed Way, and walked down the pedestrian path made of square concrete blocks bordered by grass. The houses on either side were wood shingled, single-story bungalows, brightly-painted in primary colors. Each was fronted with a three-foot-high picket fence. Most had flowering bushes in their postage stamp-sized front yards and potted plants on the front porch.

Jennifer reached her one story bungalow, painted bright green with white accents, and opened the gate. She led Race up the two steps to the covered porch where two white wicker chairs and potted flowering plants sat. At the stained wood front door with its leaded glass inserts, she reached into her gym bag for her keys. A neighborhood cat crouched in one of her shrubs, ready to pounce on any unsuspecting bird that strayed into its range.

She was enjoying the buzz, and thought it might be a good idea to have another drink or two and smoke one last flaca before bed. She decided to invite Race in for a drink, show him she wasn't angry at him for trying to hit on her, even though he denied trying to do so.

Jennifer turned toward Race and smiled. "Home sweet home. Why don't you come in and use the bathroom? I'll open a bottle of champagne and we can have a drink before you have to hit the road."

Race nodded. He'd been at it all day, but no one was waiting for him back at his place. And it was hard to pass up the opportunity to spend more time with the doctor. *Who knows where things might lead.*

Jennifer found her keys and unlocked the door's deadbolt. She peered in and let out a loud gasp. "¡Hijo de puta!"

She jumped back so quickly that she bumped into Race, sending them both sprawling. They landed in the bushes where the cat was crouching. The terrified animal went scurrying after letting out a bloodcurdling screech. Race bore the brunt of the fall, landing on his back. Jennifer landed on top of him, knocking the wind out of him.

Jennifer rolled off him and got to her knees.

"What's wrong?" Race wheezed in pain

"¡Puta madre! My house has been broken into. It's in shambles."

Jennifer scrambled to her feet, then reached down and helped Race up. He grabbed his stomach, trying to catch his breath.

Jennifer jumped onto the porch, pried the door open, and peered inside. Race moved behind her and craned his neck to see over her shoulder. The house had indeed been ransacked. Furniture was overturned, drawers were pulled out and the contents scattered on the floor.

"We'd better not go in," Race whispered. "Someone could still be inside."

Jennifer snapped at him. "Are you a *pizda*? I'm not going to let someone steal my shit. Follow me."

Race hesitated. "I don't have a pistol." He pulled out his ElectroLaser—a device similar to a pistol, but with an orange barrel, generating a laser-induced plasma channel through which a powerful electric current was sent. "Just this."

"Grab your stun gun then and follow me."

Jennifer crept into her house. Race called the burglary in to Helena, then followed.

They tiptoed through the dark living room, dodging the mess that was strewn on the floor.

Jennifer led the way down the dimly-lit hallway to the back of the house. She stopped suddenly a few feet from the entrance to the kitchen. She held up her hand. Listened intently.

A faint sound came from the kitchen. A person breathing. The sinister smell of sweat and fear came from the room. An unfamiliar shadow was cast on the wall. A motionless man. Lurking.

Jennifer pointed two fingers toward the kitchen. She looked back to make sure Race had his stun gun ready. She took one more little step. A shadow emanated from the kitchen. A man's shadow. Skulking.

She steeled her muscles. Then pounced.

Chapter 41

Head down, Jennifer flew across the room.

Her shoulder crashed into solid flesh. The intruder's ribcage. The man let out a painful groan. Air was knocked out of his lungs. She drove him backwards, smashing him into the refrigerator and causing it to teeter precariously. The man's head whiplashed into the metal appliance with a thud. His muscles went limp, his legs crumpled, his body began to slide to the floor.

Jennifer swung around behind him, wrapped her arms around his neck in a sleeper hold, and held him up.

"You son of a bitch," she hissed between gritted teeth.

The man came to and flailed about, grabbing onto Jennifer's arm. She squeezed his neck harder and pressed a thumb into the soft tissue under the man's jaw, searching for the pressure point to paralyze him with pain.

Suddenly, there was a flash of lightning and the crackle of thunder. Jennifer was jolted with electricity. Unbelievably intense, searing pain racked her body. Her muscles went into spasm and wouldn't respond. Helpless, paralyzed, she collapsed on top of the intruder.

The interloper's head hit the floor with the sound of a watermelon being cracked open. His nose and forehead turned into a geyser of blood. A puddle of urine grew on the floor.

Jennifer lay still, muscles not responding, groaning in unbelievable pain. The man beneath her was limp, unmoving; probably knocked unconscious from the fall.

Something—the size of a grizzly—sprang from the shadowy corner of the kitchen. Flashing lights from a police cruiser appeared through the kitchen window and Jennifer caught a glimpse of the shape as it flew across the room. It was an impossibly large man, dressed in black, an evil snarl on his lips.

"Freeze," Race screamed.

The man thrust his arm out, hitting Race in the chest, sending him flying backwards down the hallway. He hit the doorway leading to the living room and skidded to a stop. The ElectroLaser flew from Race's hand, hit the wall, and exploded into pieces, breaking the connection with Jennifer's back. The pain and spasms stopped.

Once again able to control her muscles, Jennifer rolled over and caught sight of the bear-sized man as he sprinted towards the back door. She reached out to grab his ankle. His calf was so thick her arm was thrown to the side. However, his foot slipped out from under him in the puddle of urine. He reached forward to catch his balance, but hit his head on the granite counter. He let out a moan and fell to the ground. The floor shook. He didn't move.

The flashing lights grew close. Tires screeched to a halt in the alleyway. A car door swung open. Blinding light played around the room.

An authoritative voice boomed out. "Police. Hands up."

A uniformed police officer appeared in the doorway, flashlight in one hand, pistol in the other. He swung the light around the room.

Race stumbled into the kitchen and raised his hands over his head, yelling, "I'm a police officer." He pointed to the floor. "That's the thief."

The officer shined his light on the black-clad man lying on the floor at his feet. "Keep your hands where I can see them," he yelled.

The giant man shook his head, rose to his knees, and looked up. The policeman's flashlight glinted off his sunglasses. Skin around his left eye was covered in scars from an old burn. He began to raise his hands, palms out. A sneer formed on his lips. The officer backed up a step, but when the man's hands were chest high, he thrust them out and grabbed hold of the policeman's wrist. Two shots rang out, the gun firing toward the ceiling. Plaster rained down.

The two men struggled, covered in white powder. The man in black slammed the heel of his hand into the officer's jaw, whipping his head backwards. Then, he smashed the officer's wrist against the kitchen cabinet. The officer went limp. The gun flew out of his hand and skidded towards Jennifer. She sprung forward, landing in the urine, as she reached for the weapon. As her fingers curled around the pistol, the man in black grabbed her wrist and squeezed. It felt as if her arm was about to snap, but she refused to let go of the gun. She looked at the man, his contorted face inches from hers. She used the back of her free hand to ram into the man's trachea. He raised a shoulder and deflected the blow.

Coming from Jennifer's side was the sound of a spray bottle. The scar-faced man looked up. Race, blood dripping from his scalp, held a canister of paralyzing spray inches from the man's nose. First with a quizzical look, then peaceful, the man's grip weakened, and his hand fell from Jennifer's wrist. His head slumped forward, and he collapsed to the ground, landing right next to her.

Race stood above him, his hand trembling, as he continued to empty the canister at the now unconscious man on the floor.

Jennifer got her wits about her, jumped to her feet, and pulled the canister from Race's hand. He looked at her, shaky, in a state of shock.

Another set of flashing lights pulled into the alley and another uniformed cop wearing a police sergeant's badge ran into the room, flashlight on, pistol drawn.

Jennifer pointed at the two motionless men on the floor. "These are the guys that broke in my house."

The officer flipped on the lights. It was Sergeant Webb. Jennifer squinted, temporarily blinded. The other police officer sat up, rubbing his jaw which was bent at an abnormal angle. The back door was shattered, hanging on a hinge. The floor was covered in broken glass.

"You okay?" Webb asked the other cop.

The other officer nodded.

Webb spoke into the communicator attached to his epaulette. "Dispatch. Adam One Hundred. Requesting two ambulances. Code Three."

Feet crunching on the glass, he stepped into the room and took the pistol from Jennifer, then gave her a hand up. "You okay?"

Jennifer nodded.

"Didn't think we'd meet again so soon."

Jennifer looked down at the two men lying on the floor, both unconscious. She knelt by the larger of the two, the one clad in black. He looked like one of the Russians she'd run into earlier at the restaurant. "Help me roll this guy on his back," she said to Sergeant Webb. He knelt down beside her and together they rolled the unconscious man over and Jennifer got a look at his face. It wasn't the Russian. This was an even bigger guy, if that was possible—almost as big as Nick Painter. He wore sunglasses and had old burn scars around his left eye.

Jennifer checked his pulse and respirations. His heart was racing, but he wasn't breathing, and his skin was ashen. He was in respiratory arrest.

Jennifer pulled the Narcan syringe—an opiate antidote—from the canister.

"Hold on," Webb said. "Let me get this guy cuffed first." He pulled out a set of cuffs big enough to go around an elephant's leg, and snapped one over each wrist of the sleeping giant, cuffing his wrists in front. He nodded to Jennifer.

Jennifer pulled up the man's sleeve. His arm was thick and hard like a tree trunk and bulged with veins. She held down the antecubital vein with one hand and uncapped the syringe with her teeth.

"That's Olcas O'Suil," Race said, looking over Jennifer's shoulder. "You know, he's the guy who killed your boyfriend."

Jennifer inserted the needle in the man's vein and pulled back to make sure there was blood flow. "I swore an oath to save lives," she said with the cap between her teeth. She pressed the plunger, injecting the opiate antidote intravenously. She recapped the needle and looked over her shoulder at Race. "I'm not going to be jury, judge, and executioner."

Race shrugged. "I hope you know what you're doing, Doctor."

Within seconds, the man took a deep, shuddering breath and groaned. He took a couple shallow breaths, then began coughing.

"Help me get this guy into a sitting position," Jennifer said to Webb.

Together, they got O'Suil sitting up. He wobbled and swayed, still groggy.

Jennifer looked over at the other man, now beginning to stir from where he lay face down in a puddle of blood and urine.

Jennifer gestured at O'Suil. "Keep an eye on this one," she told the sergeant. "Let me check this other guy." She nodded to Race. "Give me a hand."

In the distance, a pair of sirens blared out.

Jennifer and Race moved to the other man who was dressed in Bermuda shorts and a Hawaiian shirt. His feet were bare and his huaraches were scattered next to him. Under his head was a growing puddle of blood. Race handcuffed the man's hands behind his back, then Jennifer turned him over. She took a good look and froze.

Even with his face covered in blood and his nose pushed to one side, she recognized him. "Dr. Polynesia?"

Race looked over at her. "You know this man?"

Jennifer nodded. "He's a neighbor." She moved herself to get in his field of vision. "What are you doing here?"

Polynesia's eyes were glazed. He mumbled something unintelligible.

"Give me a hand," Jennifer told Race. They helped the doctor to his feet. "Be careful," she said. "The floor's covered in broken glass." Jennifer asked Race to help carry the doctor to the breakfast nook where they sat him in one of the chairs.

While Race removed the handcuffs, Jennifer bent over and peered down at her neighbor. He had an oozing gash on his forehead, but she knew he'd be okay, the bone is pretty thick there. The nose, on the other hand, was a mess. It was bent to one side and gushed blood. She pulled a handful of ice out of the freezer, wrapped a kitchen towel around the cubes, and handed the cold compress to Race, telling him to hold it over her neighbor's nose. She looked at Polynesia again. He seemed more alert and gave her a weak smile.

More flashing lights pulled up behind her house, doors swung open, and two teams of EMTs piled into the kitchen. Even though the room ran the width of the bungalow, it wasn't large enough for ten people, and Jennifer and Race were cornered in the breakfast nook.

One team of EMTs began tending to Dr. Polynesia, the other to the injured officer.

The emergency handled for the moment, Jennifer took stock. Her clothes were soaking wet and smelled rotten. She looked down: her sweatshirt was covered in vomit, sweat pants drenched in urine, and both were stuck to her skin.

Despite all she'd drank at the restaurant, she didn't feel the least bit drunk.

She pushed her way through the mass of people crowding her kitchen and went down the hallway to the master bedroom. She slammed the door closed, turned on the light, and sighed. Everything was scattered on the floor. Even her precious mattress was pushed off the bed and crammed into one corner. Jennifer tried, but couldn't calm down; not only was she burning with anger, she was now starting to become afraid. First, Donny was killed. Now, her house was broken into. There had to be a connection, she just didn't know what it was. She seethed inside, her orderly life was coming apart.

She shed her wet clothes and took a cold shower. Mad as hell, she rummaged around on the floor to find something to wear. She put on clean sweats, then glimpsed herself in the mirror. She looked pale. Her hair was matted to her head, so she pulled on a baseball hat.

When she returned to the kitchen, the officer with the broken jaw was being escorted to the ambulance by one of the EMT teams. The other team tended to Dr. Polynesia. Race was explaining to Webb what had happened. Webb kept his pistol aimed at O'Suil, who appeared groggy and was still seated on the floor.

Jennifer walked over to her neighbor. The bleeding had stopped. He had an IV in one arm.

She stood in front of him. "Doctor Polynesia?"

One of the EMTs looked up from his ministrations. "You know this guy?"

She nodded. "He's a veterinarian. Lives a couple doors down." She addressed her neighbor. "What were you doing in my kitchen, Grey?"

The seated man's speech was hesitant. "Last thing I remember, I was walking down the alley to the beach. I saw men, two I think, running out of your backdoor. Sprinting past me. They were Russians. Dressed in black. The door was open. Broken. I didn't have my Omni, so I ran in to see if you were okay." He stopped and rubbed his head. "The last thing I remember is walking through the shattered door."

"He's suffering from post-concussion amnesia," Jennifer said to the medic. "That's why he can't remember what happened after."

Mrs. Ng poked her head in the door and asked if everything was okay and offered to make tea.

"Everything's okay," Jennifer said. "You can go back to bed, dear."

Ng shook her head and made her way to the stove and began to brew a pot of green tea.

Jennifer asked the medic if he'd move the icepack from Polynesia's face for a moment. She took a good look. His nose was bent flat against his cheek. She placed her thumb on one side of his nostril, her index and middle fingers on the other. "Quick," she said rapidly to the veterinarian, "what's the correct dosage of Valium for a sixty-nine pound Chihuahua?"

As a puzzled look crossed his face, Jennifer jerked her hand to the side. Polynesia's nose made a crunching sound and he let out a howl.

Race's knees bent, his face turned green, and it looked like he was going to lose his lunch.

Jennifer inspected her work and smiled thinly. The nose was swollen, but seemed to be back in place. She nodded to the EMTs and told them to continue icing it down. She turned to Race, noticing that blood continued to ooze down the back of his neck. Jennifer gestured for him to come and have a seat next to the veterinarian. She borrowed the EMTs medical bag and used a flashlight to look at Race's scalp. There was a clean laceration in the back of his head, about three inches long. Usually, she would have done it herself, but she'd been drinking and wasn't sure how steady her hands were. So she supervised while one of the medics sutured and dressed Race's laceration. The EMTs then strapped Polynesia down to a stretcher and wheeled him to their ambulance.

Flashing lights on, the two ambulances took off.

That part of the excitement over, Jennifer sat down next to Race.

Webb kept his pistol aimed at O'Suil's chest and came over to join them. He gave Jennifer a nod. "After I left the Playa de Jaime, I got to thinking that I've seen you around the neighborhood."

Jennifer gave him a thin smile, then looked down at the handcuffed man sitting on the floor. O'Suil looked back at her through his dark sunglasses, like a rattlesnake about to strike, and gave her a streetwise smile.

"Dr. Singh," he said. His voice was deep and he spoke with a thick Irish brogue. "Pleasure to meet 'ya, lass."

Jennifer was taken aback that this brute knew her name and seemed so brazenly confident.

"Let's get up, sir," Webb told O'Suil. He turned to Race. "Give him a hand, won't you, Detective."

Race went to put his arm under the man's arm, but O'Suil brushed him aside.

"I can stand on my own," O'Suil said with a sneer.

Webb ushered the Irishman to take a seat on one of the kitchen chairs. The seat groaned and seemed to give under the man's weight. Jennifer looked him over. He had the unmistakable look of a steroid juicer and easily weighed three-fifty, most of that was muscle.

Race walked up to him and got in his face and said with a tone of contempt, "Let's see what's under those sunglasses, Mr. O'Suil." Race reached to remove the glasses.

O'Suil jerked his cuffed hands up and brushed Race's hand aside as if it were an irksome mosquito. Then leaned toward Race and slowly removed his glasses himself.

Jennifer was startled. There, surrounded by swirls of scar tissue, his left eye was milky white. Dead.

His other eye, however, was active, alert—intelligent, in a cunning sort of way.

"So you know my name, Detective," O'Suil said, smiling. "You wouldn't be so cocky if it weren't for these handcuffs and that officer there."

Race dropped his gaze, admitting to himself that O'Suil was right. He'd be nervous if he was alone with this murderer. He looked his suspect over. The guy was huge, not as tall as Painter, but at least as thick. Another in a long line of steroid abusers.

O'Suil laughed. "Don't worry, Detective. I won't hurt you." He paused and looked at Jennifer. "And I didn't kill her boyfriend."

"Good luck convincing a jury of that," Race said.

Jennifer looked at Race. "You're sure this is the man who killed Donny?"

Race thought her question over for a second. O'Suil was going to find out soon enough that he was the main suspect in Bosco's murder. Might as well put the screws to him right away.

"That's right, Doc. He's going away for a long, long time."

O'Suil laughed again. "You don't scare me. It just as easily could have been her." O'Suil gestured at Jennifer. "She was the last person to see Bosco alive."

Race got up into O'Suil's face. "You piece of shit," he yelled.

Webb moved between the two men and pushed Race back. "Now, you two. Let's act civilized. Leave the name calling to the lawyers."

Jennifer was steaming and she clenched her fist to her sides. First, this brute broke into her house and all but destroyed it. Then, he had the audacity to accuse her of murdering her boyfriend. Her Donny.

She pointed a finger at O'Suil. "You better hope they send you away for a long time. Otherwise, you're going to have to answer to me."

"You're a pretty feisty cailín." His good eye looked her up and down, while the other remained fixed and dead. "You a natural redhead?"

Jennifer went to slap O'Suil in the face. Webb grabbed her arm. "Let's all play nice here."

O'Suil continued to smile. He gazed deep at Jennifer with his good eye. "I'm sure we're going to meet again, Doctor. And under much nicer circumstances, at least for me."

Webb moved Jennifer away from O'Suil and raised a hand. "Let's all settle down." He took out his scanner and ran it over O'Suil's left forearm. He looked at the device and frowned. He ran it over the other forearm, checked the device and shook it. He tried scanning both forearms again. He arched an eyebrow and put the scanner back in his service belt. "No microchip." He turned to Race. "I take it you two know each other?"

O'Suil spat on the floor. "Never met the man in my life."

"Although we haven't met," Race said, "allow me to introduce Olcas O'Suil. He was at Donny Bosco's murder scene last week. I'm bringing him in on First Degree Murder charges."

"And don't forget Breaking and Entering," Jennifer said.

"You invited me in," O'Suil said to her.

Jennifer shot him a hard look. "That doesn't even deserve a response."

Webb turned to Jennifer. "What happened here?"

Jennifer was still angry and glared at O'Suil.

"I know you're upset," Webb said, "but just give me the simple facts, ma'am."

Jennifer explained what happened.

Webb turned to Race and gestured to O'Suil. "You want to borrow my squad car to take this one in?"

Race froze and knew his eyes dilated, his timidity again exposed. Even handcuffed and separated by the barrier in a squad car, his skin still crawled thinking about being alone with this man. There was something about him, something that shook him right to the core. He stole a glance at O'Suil. Physically, he was reminded of his father, with his sumo wrestler-type body. But he couldn't let his primal fears control his behavior.

"I'd love to take this…man in." There, he said it. He wasn't going to be controlled by fear.

Mrs. Ng came over and placed cups of steaming green tea on the table in front of Jennifer and Race, and handed one to Webb.

"What about me?" O'Suil said. "I'd like a spot of tea."

"Go suck it," Ng said, then turned and began cleaning out the refrigerator. Both Jennifer and Race sipped their tea, and remained silent, letting the adrenaline rush subside, while they watched as Ng threw away a trashcan full of old take-out food.

Webb said, "When you're ready, he's all yours, Detective. I'll walk the suspect out to the car with you."

Race finished off the tea and stood up. "Let me use the restroom first."

"The guest bathroom is down the hall, second door on the right," Jennifer said.

Race went into the room, the lights came on, and he used the toilet. When he turned to wash his hands, he saw himself in the mirror. His face was blotchy. His hair a mess, matted down with clotted blood. His eyes were bloodshot and he smelled like vomit. He splashed cold water over his face, then grabbed a washcloth, which had L'Orange County Morgue written on it, and dabbed at the clots in his hair. He looked back at himself, then broke out into a big smile and fist-pumped the air.

His first day on his own as a homicide detective and he'd solved what was probably going to be one of L'Orange County's biggest murder cases of the year. A commendation was probably heading his way. Maybe a raise. It felt so much better than working Vice. There, he spent months, or years, building cases on guys who were just supplying the demand for cocaine. Now, in less than a week, he'd taken a dangerous man, a killer, off the streets.

He knew there were still a lot of unanswered questions. How was Bosco's murder related to those of the Russian courier and Dr. Sing? According to the statement of Dr. Singh's neighbor, O'Suil and the two Russians must be working together, was there someone even higher up behind them? Those, and plenty of other questions, would probably be answered when O'Suil's Russian partners were apprehended; they could get them to testify against each other. He looked forward to learning from Captain Beane and Beela, experienced interrogators, as they pried the information out of them. And he wouldn't be surprised to find that effective interrogation would be more fruitful than the torture O'Suil and his band of thugs practiced.

Race felt great and thought: I was made for Homicide.

He returned to the kitchen brimming with confidence. He gave Jennifer a smile and thanked her for her help.

"I had a great time this evening, Detective," Jennifer said. "My house was broken into. I was electroshocked. I almost killed my neighbor." She laughed. "We'll have to do this again sometime."

Race laughed, then gestured for O'Suil to stand. "Let's get going."

Webb pointed his gun at O'Suil and gestured to the back door. "I'll be back and process the crime scene," he told Jennifer. "And I'll call a friend of mine who can fix that door of yours."

O'Suil stood up and made a feint at Race, who flinched. O'Suil laughed and pointed his cuffed hands at Race. Then he turned, gave a slight bow in Jennifer's direction. "I'm sure we're going to see each other again."

Jennifer snarled at him and said, "Go to hell!"

Chapter 42

Jennifer's head was spinning and she felt chilled, the adrenaline rush subsiding.

Ng finished cleaning, grabbed a tea, and sat down at the table with Jennifer. "Strange thing for a one-eyed man to say."

"What was that?" Jennifer asked.

"That he'd *see* you later."

Jennifer's anger dissipated and she shared a laugh with Ng.

"What was all that excitement about anyway?" Ng said.

Jennifer explained that the police believed that O'Suil was the man who killed her boyfriend, Donny Bosco.

Ng put her hands one of Jennifer's forearms. "What do you believe, daughter?"

Jennifer thought that over a second. "They seem to have the right guy. What I don't know is why he did it."

Jennifer sipped at her green tea while numerous other questions ran through her mind. Was O'Suil working with the two Russians she'd run into at the restaurant earlier? She assumed they were the same guys Dr. Polynesia saw fleeing her bungalow. And was O'Suil and the Russians working for someone higher up? Perhaps they were working for one of those Russians, Porphyria, or whatever they called themselves, that she ran into the night of the Getty ball. And the lecherous Senator Schwarzenegger, what, if anything did he have to do with Donny's death? As much as she despised the senator, she found it hard to believe he'd be involved in such a despicable crime. She imagined the answers to those questions would be answered in the next few days. But she did feel a sense of closure knowing that at least one of Donny's killers was behind bars.

"What a psychopath that Irishman is," Ng said, breaking Jennifer out of her reverie.

Jennifer grimaced. "Growing up like that, with a face deformed and unfinished, I suppose he's determined to prove a villain."

"That doesn't justify what he's done," Ng said.

"No…," Jennifer thought about what Ng said, "but you have to admit, he was dealt a weak hand."

Ng pounded the table. "They should take him out back and shoot him like the dog he is."

"Mrs. Ng!" Jennifer was shocked and was sure her face showed it. She'd never heard Ng advocate violence.

Ng said, "What's the point of locking him up in prison for life and wasting the taxpayer's money?"

Jennifer made a note to herself not to tell Mrs. Ng that she'd saved O'Suil's life a few minutes ago. She wondered, if she didn't take the Hippocratic Oath so seriously, if she could have stood by and let him die of respiratory distress.

"You may have a point there, Mrs. Ng. Your solution might be the most humane for all parties involved."

"At least that man's no longer on the loose." She looked at Jennifer with a deadly serious expression. "I bet he was here to kill you, too."

Jennifer hadn't considered that, but Mrs. Ng could be right. Whatever O'Suil was looking for in her house, presumably he hadn't found it, which could explain why he was lying in wait for her. She considered herself fortunate that she'd invited Detective Griffin back to her place for a nightcap. As ineffectual as he appears, he probably did help save her life. Otherwise, who knows what might have happened?

"Thank the goddesses the Irishman's behind bars," Jennifer said.

Jennifer and Ng sat silently while Webb went around the house taking fingerprints and photo-documenting the damage. Jennifer had just about dozed off when Webb joined the two women at the table. Ng went to the stove and poured the officer a cup of tea, then excused herself and headed home.

"Quite a night," Webb said.

Jennifer nodded and struggled to keep her eyes open.

Webb's face became serious. "I wouldn't recommend you barge into your house after it's been broken into."

"I can handle myself," Jennifer said. "While I worked as an Emergency Room physician at Camp Pendleton, the Marine Corps Close Combat Fighting Forces taught me their version of Krav Maga. And Mrs. Ng and I practice Wing Chun."

Webb frowned at her. "You don't think that Irishman knows those same moves? And I can assure you those two Russians you ran into at the restaurant are experts in hand to hand combat."

Jennifer shrugged. "I have the element of surprise. Men always underestimate women."

"Let's not forget those guys outweigh you. What do you weigh, Doctor?"

Jennifer smiled and remained mum.

Webb laughed. "I forgot: never ask a woman her weight. Regardless, those guys outweigh you at least two to one. And they're ruthless."

"I'm willing to concede they have the weight and muscle advantage," Jennifer said. "But not the ruthlessness advantage. You mess with my body, or my stuff, and you haven't seen ferocious."

Webb nodded. "I can imagine. My wife can be quite the hell cat." Webb put his hand on Jennifer's shoulder. "Do me a favor. Next time, wait outside and call the cops. That's what you pay us for."

Jennifer nodded, but wasn't willing to concede the point. Her eyelids drooped and she didn't have the energy to fight to keep them open.

"Why don't you catch a couple winks," Webb said. "I'll wait here until the locksmith arrives. Since that door opens to the alley, I'd suggest a bank vault-level door with a biometric lock. It's more expensive than a wooden door and a deadbolt, but well worth the investment."

"Whatever you think, Sergeant." Jennifer yawned. "And thanks for everything."

"In the morning, make an itemized list of anything that's been stolen. You can call me Friday and give it to me."

Jennifer stood up, shook the officer's hand, and shuffled down the hallway to her bedroom. It had been one of the most eventful days in her life; she helped catch Donny's killer. How could anything top that?

◇◇◇◇◇◇◇

Race programmed the Nav-Drive to take them to the Marina del Rey police precinct where he planned to book O'Suil into jail. The squad car made it out of the alleyway, then north up the equally narrow one-way road called Speed Way, finally turning onto Washington Boulevard, heading east.

Race looked into the cruiser's rearview mirror; O'Suil was staring back at him. Race was glad to have the metal mesh barrier between him and the musclebound Irishman.

Race couldn't believe his luck. Bosco's murderer just about fell into his lap. The case was sure to be on all the morning's news programs and he'd probably get a few seconds of face-time. After he booked O'Suil, he needed to go home, try to catch a few hours of sleep, then wear his best outfit to work in the morning.

O'Suil seemed to have read his mind. "This case isn't over yet, mate."

Race looked back and saw O'Suil smiling at him. He couldn't help but smile back, thinking about how he'd feel watching the jail doors slam shut behind the Irishman.

"Keep smiling, mate," O'Suil said. "You're barking up the wrong tree."

Race knew the Irishman was trying to goad him, but he couldn't resist saying, "You won't look so smug when a judge sentences you to life in prison without parole."

"It will never come to that. I've got friends in very high places."

"I don't care if the President's your wife and the Pope's your father. Nobody's going to get you out of a murder charge."

O'Suil laughed. "I'm talking about more powerful people than them."

Race decided not to bother talking to O'Suil, knowing he was just being baited.

"Pussy got your tongue, Detective?" O'Suil said in his thick brogue. "Don't tell me you're afraid of me."

Race looked back. In truth, he was afraid of O'Suil, despite the handcuffs and the metal barrier. But he didn't want to admit it aloud.

Race couldn't help but saying, "Why don't you just admit you killed Bosco, and save us all a lot of trouble?"

O'Suil leaped forward and pounded his fists against the barrier. It sounded like a bomb went off and the barrier bent inward a couple inches. Race jumped.

O'Suil sat back in his seat, laughing to himself. "You just wait, mate. You just wait."

The squad car passed the marina on the right, then began to slow to enter the traffic circle at Lincoln Boulevard. Race sat back and began to relax. Looming ahead in the moonlight was the residential/commercial complex called Playa del Vista, a single building taking up thousands of acres, housing tens of thousands of residents, and most importantly, home of the Marina del Rey police precinct.

The squad car pulled up to the traffic circle and waited for traffic to clear. Out of the corner of his eye, Race saw a pair of headlights speeding around the traffic circle from his left. The headlights didn't continue around the curve, instead they bore right down on his car. He saw O'Suil smirk and his head disappear below the seat and his feet brace themselves against the driver's side rear door. The Nav-Drive's collision avoidance alarm screamed. Race reached to disengage the system and take evasive action, but in the blink of an eye, the headlights were on him, blinding and big as dinner plates.

His police car was T-boned by the speeding vehicle. There was a loud crash. The sound of metal on metal. The windshield and side windows exploded, sending granular pieces glass flying. The driver's side door collapsed. The impact rammed Race against the center console. He was pinned between the savagely bent door and the car's computer. The front bags deployed. The side bag partially filled, air seeping out of a gash in the fabric.

The impact caused his car to careen and spin in circles. The tires squealed. The car slid sideways and a light post rushed toward Race's face. They were about to have another high speed collision.

He heard O'Suil let out a wicked laugh.

The squad car hit the concrete light post broadside, the driver-side door crumpling further. Race's head was jerked to the side. First one way. Then rebounding the other. His head whiplashed into the door post of the car. His head exploded in white light.

Then everything went black.

The sound of smashing glass jarred Race awake.

As he pried his eyes open a crack, thousands of small pieces of glass fell from his face, so he quickly closed them again. He reached up to rub his throbbing head and winced as shooting pain coursed up his arm, into his shoulder.

A pair of hands grabbed the lapels of his blazer, pulling him against the center console computer, the edge digging into his ribs, causing excruciating pain. He looked toward the passenger's side window. O'Suil's face was poking into the car, his broad shoulders preventing him from reaching in farther, as he tried to drag Race out of the mangled vehicle.

"I'm going to break your neck, you little weasel," O'Suil yelled.

Race fumbled around in his sport coat, looking for something to defend himself with. His ElectroLaser was laying broken on Dr. Singh's floor. His paralyzing canister was empty, also back at the doctor's bungalow. A shotgun was clipped to the console against his legs, but with the inflated airbags and O'Suil pulling him sideways, he couldn't get close to reaching it. He knew if O'Suil somehow pulled him out of the car, he could kiss his ass goodbye. Luckily, the four-point seatbelts were still engaged—the only thing saving him from having his neck broken.

A series of sirens rent the air, coming from multiple directions.

O'Suil's hand were ripped off Race's jacket. Two brutally large Russians dressed in black commando outfits strained to pull the Irishman away from the car.

"Let's get out of here," one said with a thick Slavic accent.

"Hand me your gun," O'Suil yelled back at him. "I want to take this effin' maggot out."

The Russian yelled back at him, "You kill a cop, we'll have the entire state on our asses."

The sirens were getting very loud and Race could make out the flashing lights reflecting off the windows of nearby buildings.

O'Suil leaned down and looked inside the car. He caught Race's eye with his one good one, the dead white one staring blindly ahead. He gave Race a snarl of a smile. Then he turned, gave one of the Russian's a harsh push on the shoulder, and walked out of Race's sight. Race heard the sound of three car doors slam, then tires peeling rubber.

A four door black sedan sped past Race's cruiser, passing an emergency vehicle heading his way. In the flashing lights of the vehicle's flashers, he caught the license plate of O'Suil's getaway car. Nevada plates. He read the numbers and repeated them over and over as the black sedan disappeared from sight.

Race grit his teeth and swore: I'm gonna get that one-eyed Irish son of a bitch.

Fin

Glossary

Así – Like so (Spanish)

Bahl'shoe yeh spasiba – Thank you very much (Russian)

Blya! – Curse word, similar to dropping the F-bomb (Russian)

Bratva – Russian brotherhood, or Mafia

Cabrón – Son of a bitch (Spanish)

Cailín – girl (Gaelic)

Cajones – balls (Spainish)

Cariña – Darling (Spanish)

Cervezas – beers (Spanish)

C'est la vie – that's life (French)

Culo – ass (Spanish)

Da – Yes (Russian)

Dasvidaniya – Good bye (Russian)

Dharma – Hindu concept, similar to "right living"

¡Dios mio! – Oh my God! (Spanish)

Dirndl – traditional Bavarian dress (German)

¿Dormiste con tu chavo? – Did you sleep (have sex with) with your boyfriend (Spanish)

El jefe – the boss (Spanish)

Encantado – Delighted (to meet you) (Spanish)

Entendido – Understood (Spanish)

Eres un verdadero caballero – You are a true gentleman (Spanish) Note: Jennifer misuses the phrase and should say *"Usted es"* in place of *"Eres"*, but being a *gringa*, she misses the subtleties of the Spanish language.

Estrella – Star (Spanish)

Federal'naya sluzhba bezopasnosti – Russian FSB, equivalent to the FBI

Flaca – Thin marijuana cigarette

Fräulein – women (German) St. Pauli girl being one of the author's favorite examples.

Gringa – Feminine form of *gringo*; refers to a female English speaking foreigner, especially American. The term is often used in a disparaging sense, but is not derogatory. (Spanish)

Güey – Dude (Spanish)

¡*Hijo de puta!* – see Puta Madre (Spanish)

Hukam – Sikh religious concept similar to God's commandment

Itadakimasu – Enjoy your meal (Japanese)

Konnichiwa – Hello (Japanese)

Lederhosen – German leather breeches (German)

Lyscee – Licensed Sexual Companion

Mafiya – Russian Mafia

Mayah daragaya – My darling (Russian)

Mierda – shit (Spanish)

No me digas, chica – Don't tell me, girl (Spanish)

Nyet – No (Russian)

O mój boże! – Oh my God! (Polish)

Opa – Grandfather (German)

Pip pip – along with wanker and cheerio, the author's three favorite British expressions

Primos – cousins (Spanish)

Proust – cheers (Dutch)

¡Puta madre! – Spanish curse word, similar to dropping the F-bomb

Qué lástima – What a pity (Spanish)

¡Que metiche eres! – How nosey you are! (Spanish)

¿Qué pasa? – What's happening? (Spanish)

Quinceañera – Latina girl's 15th birthday party (Spanish)

¡Salud! – Cheers (Spanish)

Tranquilo – Calm down (Spanish)

Travka – Slang word for marijuana (also Russian word for grass)

Triaga una jarra of agua de sandía – Bring a pitcher of watermelon water (Spanglish)

Ty krasotka – You are so beautiful (Russian)

Ya, vayate – Get out of here already (Spanish)

Michael McLarnon

is a retired forensic psychiatrist and emergency room physician.
He is married, has two sons, a Siamese cat, a pond full of koi,
and a Miniature Dachshund named Zoë.

Like the main character in the book,
he is tall, an expert crossword puzzle solver, and can't surf.
He lives in Jackson, Georgia.

L'Orange Fire is his first novel,
and the first book of the L'Orange series.

If you enjoyed this book,
please leave a review at:

amazon.com
goodreads.com

Follow me at:
lorangefire.com

Coming April 28, 2015

The conclusion to the L'Orange Fire story

L'Orange Fire

Book Two
